Martina Cole is the No. 1 bestselling author of eleven hugely successful novels. Her most recent novel, *The Graft,* was No. 1 on the *Sunday Times* hardback bestseller list for eleven weeks, as well as a *Sunday Times* No. 1 bestseller in paperback, and *The Know* was selected by Channel 4's *Richard & Judy* as one of the Top Ten Best Reads of 2003. *Maura's Game* and *Faceless* both shot straight to No. 1 on the *Sunday Times* bestseller lists and total sales of Martina's novels now exceed four million copies. *Dangerous Lady* and *The Jump* have gone on to become hugely popular TV drama series and several of her other novels are in production for TV. Martina Cole has a son and daughter, and she lives in Essex.

Praise for Martina Cole's bestsellers:

'Martina Cole pulls no punches, writes as she sees it, refuses to patronise or condescend to either her characters or fans . . . And meanwhile sells more books than almost any other crime writer in the country' *Independent on Sunday*

'Distinctive and powerfully written fiction' *The Times*

'Intensely readable' *Guardian*

'Martina Cole again explores the shady criminal under-world, a setting she is fast making her own' *Sunday Express*

'The stuff of legend . . . It's vicious, nasty and utterly compelling' *Mirror*

'Set to be another winner' *Woman's Weekly*

Broken

Martina Cole

headline

First published in 2000
by HEADLINE BOOK PUBLISHING

First published in paperback in 2001
by HEADLINE BOOK PUBLISHING

This special promotional hardback edition published in 2006
by HEADLINE BOOK PUBLISHING

1

ISBN 0 7553 3120 6

Printed and bound in Great Britain by
Mackays of Chatham plc, Chatham, Kent

Headline's policy is to use papers that are natural, renewable and
recyclable products and made from wood grown in sustainable
forests. The logging and manufacturing processes are expected to
conform to the environmental regulations of the country of origin.

HEADLINE BOOK PUBLISHING
A division of Hodder Headline
338 Euston Road
London NW1 3BH

www.headline.co.uk
www.hodderheadline.com

For Peter P.

In memory of Junior
Arnold Govia

Dux femina facti:
The leader of the enterprise a woman.

—Virgil

Prologue

1992

Melanie Harvey walked sedately along Bayler Street in Grantley.

She had been born in the small Essex town, and she was now at college there. She felt this gave her an air of sophistication, being educated, and she was enjoying it, something her teachers would never have believed. But she loved the place, it was her home and it was where she wanted to work and raise her children. Especially since the new order had arrived. Grantley was growing, going up in the world and she wanted desperately to be a small part of it. Gradually the green belt was becoming flats and housing estates – private, of course. The older properties were being knocked down or renovated to make way for the commuters who liked being forty minutes from Fenchurch Street in a place that still felt countrified enough to justify bringing up children there; they would pay through the nose for a small three-bedroomed house. She jogged the same route every morning and was amazed at how fast the places were being built. Obviously they were not meant to last any reasonable amount of time.

Workmen were whistling at her, but she ignored them. At seventeen years old with a DD-cup she was used to dirty old men as she thought of the workers who catcalled from afar. She ignored them as she ignored everyone. Melanie was quite arrogant in her own youthful way.

Dressed in a small top, shorts and Reebok bumpers, with her dark hair swept back and encased in a ponytail, she allowed her eyes to scan the old buildings nearby that were being knocked down.

As she glanced over, she saw a bulldozer begin trundling towards the last of the units to remain intact. The bright sunlight was blocked by cloud for a few seconds and so it was easier for her to see her surroundings.

That was when she saw the movement on the roof of the building. It was only a small movement but it caught her eye. She stared up. The sun was blinding her again and her eyes were watering. But she had seen something moving, she was sure of it.

Then, as she once more heard the dull drone of the bulldozer, the sun disappeared behind cloud again and she saw a small blond head. It was just a glimpse, but it was enough for her. She registered the fact that it could only be a child. An adult would have been easy to make out, whereas the low parapet at the top of the building would hide a child, more or less.

Then she saw it again.

Realising that the man in the bulldozer was about to start demolishing the unit, she ran on to the site. The men laughed at her as she tore across the uneven ground, her white bumpers kicking up dirt and brick-dust, heavy breasts hammering against her ribcage with each heartbeat. She was trying to attract the attention of the man in the bulldozer. She certainly had that. He was watching her with a mixture of appreciation and fear.

She was nearly in his path now. He began to brake. As he halted in front of her she was still trying to draw his attention to something above his head.

The site manager, Desmond Rawlings, ran over to her, his face angry and his language even angrier.

'What the fuck you think you're doing?'

Melanie was out of breath, still pointing up at the roof of the building. 'There's someone or something up there.'

He automatically looked up and saw nothing. 'Is this some kind of game, love?'

Melanie shook her head. 'There is definitely someone up on that roof, mate. Go and look for yourself.'

The driver of the bulldozer was climbing out of his cab now. 'What's going on, Des?'

He shrugged, heavy body sweating under the jumper he had put on because it was cold that morning and the donkey jacket he wore with 'Site Manager' written on the back.

'Fuck knows. This bird reckons there's someone up there.' He pointed once more to the roof of the building. Now all the men were looking up.

'I can't see nothing.'

'Well there *is* something there. I saw it myself.'

But Melanie's voice was not so assured now as she realised that she couldn't see anything either from this vantage point.

'I was on the street when I saw a little blond head up there. You'd better check, just to be on the safe side.'

Des sighed heavily. He had everyone on his back. The contractors were useless; everything was going wrong, he was weeks behind his schedule. None of the drawings matched and the steel was late as usual. Now, on top of everything else, he had some silly bird telling him there was a kid in the building he was about to knock down.

They were surrounded by men and Des knew they were all enjoying the light relief. Melanie was growing confused. Suppose it had just been a trick of the light?

'I'm sure I saw something . . .'

A small man with green eyes in a dark-tanned face volunteered: 'I'll go up and look, Des. Keep the young lady happy, eh?'

He nodded and sighed. What he wouldn't give for a few hours in the bookie's, a wad of cash in one hand and a bottle of beer in the other. The green-eyed man disappeared into the skeleton of the building. Des had a quick shufti at the girl's breasts before meeting her cynical eyes.

'Had your look, you old perve?'

The other men laughed and tried not to do the same thing.

The noise died down then as they all turned to stare at the roof of the building. Melanie was nervous, wondering if she had actually seen anything and hoping she had because otherwise this lot were not going to be very happy.

She consoled herself with the fact that, whatever happened, she had done the right thing.

Regina Carlton pulled herself out of bed with difficulty. She pushed the sleeping man beside her. He grunted and turned over, emitting a loud fart in the process.

Regina pursed her lips and sighed. 'Where the fuck did I find him?'

The words went unanswered as she glanced wearily around the chaotic room. Clothes were strewn everywhere; the place was ripe with the smell of dirty laundry and unwashed crockery. She lit a B&H and pulled the smoke deep into her lungs. The nicotine rushed straight to her brain and she sighed happily.

Scratching her sagging stomach, she wandered from the room and down the hallway to the kitchen. After putting on the kettle, she searched through the debris on the table until she found a bottle of pills. She opened the canister and popped two blue ones with a sip of water then lit herself another cigarette from the butt of the previous one. The kettle boiled and she made herself coffee, sniffing the milk suspiciously before abandoning it and settling for black.

Walking back into the hall, she opened her kids' bedroom door.

Michaela, aged five, was still asleep, her golden hair spread over the dirty pillowcase. Hannah, ten months, was lying awake in her cot, a soaking nappy filling the room with the smell of ammonia and making her mother's eyes water.

She looked towards the bed that should have held Jamie, two, and frowned. Walking back into the lounge area, she scanned the small room then went back into the kitchen, even looking under the table.

'I'll slaughter that little fucker!' Her voice held anger rather than fear.

She walked back into the lounge and, pulling back a smoke-stained net curtain, scanned the area in front of her block of flats.

No Jamie.

Coffee finished and feeling the first buzz from the Driminal she had taken earlier, Regina went back into her bedroom and pulled on a pair of jeans and a Bart Simpson sweatshirt. Dragging her hair back into a ponytail, she surveyed herself in the mirror of her dressing table.

Her eyes were dark hollows, her cheekbones lost in a face that was puffy from too much of everything, from booze to drugs to sex. Meanwhile her body was thin but sagging, from her breasts to the skin at the top of her arms.

She was twenty-five years old.

Regina went to the bed and shook the man awake.

'Fuck off, will ya? I'm trying to sleep.'

She looked down at him and felt nothing. Not even annoyance. Lighting up another cigarette, she went in to the girls and woke Michaela up by slapping her behind through the quilt cover.

'Sort Hannah out and make a cuppa, love.'

Michaela sat up immediately.

'You seen Jamie?'

The child shook her head.

Regina went out of the flat and down the four flights of stairs to the street. An old lady on the second floor ignored her as she stamped past, a thunderous look of annoyance on her face.

'You seen my Jamie?' she asked the old bitch in a rasping voice. After fifteen minutes even Regina was getting worried. Her little boy was missing. With everything else she had on her plate, that was the last thing she needed: the police looking too closely into the chaos of her everyday life.

'Fuck him, the little bugger! Like his father, always causing aggravation.'

She went back into the flat to begin clearing it of anything dodgy before she felt comfortable enough to phone the Old Bill.

But before that she phoned her social worker. Regina knew she was going to need all the help she could get.

PC Black and WPC Hart arrived within fifteen minutes of the call. As they entered the flat they both grimaced as the smell of urine and stale sweat hit the back of their throats.

Regina smiled sourly at them, ready for a fight.

They looked around the shabby abode and decided

to stand rather than take a seat.

'Hello, love, I'm WPC Joanna Hart and this is my colleague, Richard Black. Now, we understand your little boy is missing?' the female constable began.

'I *rang* you, didn't I?' Regina's voice held contempt but also an underlying fear that Hart was quick to pick up on.

'Look, love, we're not the enemy, OK? If your boy's missing then the sooner we get the preliminaries over with the better, eh?'

Regina relaxed visibly. 'He's a wanderer. As young as he is, he's streetwise. Let's face it, he'd need to be with me as his mother, wouldn't he? I've been everywhere he might be and I can't locate him. He is definitely gone.'

WPC Hart felt a surge of compassion for the woman before her, one she had dealt with on several other occasions, seeing her drunk, drugged and aggressive.

'I might not be mother of the year but they're my kids, right? I care about them,' Regina continued.

PC Richard Black snorted and shook his head sadly. 'Yeah, it looks like it.'

Regina was across the room in a split second and WPC Hart put herself smartly between the two antagonists.

'Look, Richard, you have a nose round the neighbours. I'll deal with Miss Carlton, OK?' Her firm tone of voice was a command and, turning slowly, her colleague left the room.

'Fucking wanker! Judge me, will he? Who the fuck

does he think he is?' Regina took quick puffs on her cigarette, barely inhaling. The WPC smiled.

'You want to try working with him.' Her voice was low, conspiratorial. Desperate to establish some kind of rapport.

'Oh, fuck off, lady. You ain't playing your mind games with me. I know you and your sort. I know what you think and how you think. So cut the fucking crap and find my boy.' Regina was scared, and it showed.

Hart was saved from having to answer by a loud voice coming into the room from the cluttered hallway.

'Hello, love. It's me – Bobby.'

The voice was high-pitched and effeminate. A tall man walked into the room. He had dyed brown hair, worn rather long and with two-inch roots showing, and blue eyes in a friendly open face. He held his arms wide and Regina walked straight into them and broke down. WPC Hart watched them for a while, glad to see someone who could maybe help the situation.

'Are you a relative?'

Regina faced her and sniffed. 'He's better than a relative, love. He's me social worker.'

The man held out a limp hand. 'Robert Bateman, darlin'. Social worker to the stars.'

WPC Hart sighed heavily. This was all she needed.

PC Black came back into the flat and said loudly, 'A little boy, answering to the name Jamie, has been found on a building site on the other side of town. Blond, blue-eyed, fit and well.'

Regina visibly relaxed. 'That sounds like him. That

sounds like my boy.' Her voice held relief though her face betrayed nothing.

'How did he get there?' WPC Hart's voice was suspicious.

Black shrugged. 'How should I know? They're taking him to the hospital for a once-over.'

'Oh, Bobby, run me over there, will you?' Regina asked.

The social worker smiled widely. 'Of course I will, dear. What about the other two?'

Michaela was standing in the doorway with a changed and sweeter-smelling Hannah in her arms.

'They'll be all right. Me bloke's asleep in the bedroom, he'll watch them.'

Robert rolled his expressive blue eyes at the ceiling. 'Do the kids actually know him, dear, or is he a transient?'

Regina closed her own eyes a moment. 'They know him well enough. Now can we go, please?' Her tone of voice brooked no argument.

Five minutes later they were gone.

Michaela was spooning Weetabix into Hannah's mouth when the man walked out of the bedroom, naked and with a half-erection from the need to urinate.

He looked at the two children in the untidy kitchen and said acidly, 'What the fuck you staring at?'

Michaela tossed back her thick golden hair and answered him in the same fashion. 'I could ask you the same bloody thing, mate.'

10

PC Black walked into Grantley Hospital with an air of righteous authority. He made his way through the A&E department and up five flights of stairs to the children's ward. WPC Hart was sitting outside an office there, drinking coffee. She smiled as he approached.

'What's happening then?'

'I have two witnesses who put Miss Regina Carlton and her son at the site at six-thirty this morning. One is a woman, a cleaner for Kortone Separates. She parks there and gets a lift to work with a friend. Another is a man who walks that route every morning for his paper. It seems she dumped the kid there.'

Joanna Hart frowned. 'Why would she bother getting in touch, then?'

Black shrugged. 'Perhaps she thought he'd be dead by then. They were about to demolish the building where he was found.'

'Oh my God! We'd better get in touch with plainclothes.'

'Already done it. They'll be here shortly. Let's see the slag get out of this one.'

He sounded pleased and Joanna was reminded of why she didn't always like him very much. He saw the look and shrugged.

'Attempted murder, ain't it?'

'Depends on whether she did it in her right mind. You can't convict her without all the facts.'

PC Black shook his head pityingly.

'You just don't see it, do you? She is so chemically enhanced she's in danger of being named as the first genetically modified human being in history. Yet you still try and defend her. All the times we've been to her drum for fighting, drinking and general arseholiness, and you can still find it in your bleeding heart to give her the benefit of the doubt?' His incredulous laughter was loud in the confines of the corridor.

'She has three kids, for Christ's sake, and this morning one of them was nearly buried under rubble and killed. How can you defend that? She needs locking up, mate. If it was left to me I'd throw away the fucking key.'

'I am sure you would, dear.' Robert Bateman appeared in the corridor behind them, his voice surprisingly firm. 'She also comes from a much worse background than her children's, believe me, and is trying to get herself together. Whatever Regina may be, she loves her kids in her own way.'

PC Black shook his head once more.

'Preach to the converted. As far as I'm concerned, she's a piece of scum. Those kids would be better off out of it. She's on the bash, she's an habitual drug user and she leaves them in situations that are down-right dangerous. Her flat stinks . . .'

'You can't lock people up just for having a dirty flat.' Joanna's voice was high-pitched with annoyance.

'. . . her flat stinks and her kids walk around like rag bags. Every time we go there they're either in bed or just got out of it. Their lives are a nightmare, poor little sods.'

Robert Bateman sighed heavily. 'You're on your soapbox early this morning. Get out the wrong side of the bed, did we?'

Heels clicked down the corridor and they all turned towards Detective Inspector Kate Burrows who smiled lazily at them.

'So what's the score?'

She closed her eyes tightly as the three of them all began to talk at once. Holding up her arms for them to pipe down, she insisted, 'For Christ's sake, one at a bloody time, eh?'

As they all stared at her in annoyance, Kate sighed. What had started out as a bad day was slowly but surely getting worse.

BOOK ONE

He healeth those that are broken in heart:
and giveth medicine to heal their sickness.

147:1 *Prayer Book*, 1662

But God bless the child that's got his own.

—Billie Holiday
('God Bless the Child', 1941), 1915–59

Chapter One

Patrick Kelly looked around him and sighed again. He hated it when people did this to him, though Kelly being who he was, people did not often let him down without so much as a phone call. He saw all the other diners taking surreptitious looks at him as he sat alone, with only a mineral water and a resigned expression on his face.

He was such a good-looking man, although he didn't realise it. His dark hair was well cut and conditioned, with just enough grey to make him look interesting, his deep-set blue eyes and excellent bone structure made both women and men take a second look. He had the build to match his looks; taller than average, he wore his clothes well. He was always immaculately turned out and he had the air of a man who knew what he wanted and would get it whatever it took.

Standing up abruptly, he walked from the busy room and made his way out to the foyer then through to the bar. He looked cross. Consequently no one approached him for a good while. Eventually he summoned a waiter and ordered a large Scotch, then taking out his mobile he punched in a number.

Two women sitting nearby watched the handsome man as he barked into an answering machine somewhere. 'Patrick Kelly here. You, Micky, have fucking blown it.'

The waiter placed his Scotch before him together with a bucket of ice.

'Bring me a ham sandwich and a newspaper,' barked Patrick.

The boy nodded and backed away.

One of the women, a petite redhead with toning table and fake tan written all over her body, called huskily, 'How can you get a ham sandwich in here? We couldn't.'

Patrick Kelly didn't even glance at her as he answered abruptly, 'Easy, darlin'. I own the fucking drum.'

The woman raised her eyebrows at her friend in a shocked manner and they resumed their conversation, while both keeping a beady eye on Patrick Kelly.

Patrick, for his part, had forgotten they even existed. As he wolfed down his sandwich he wished his Kate was with him. She calmed him, and today he needed calming. Though he wondered if even she could relax him after the morning he'd had.

The redhead tried one last time to get his attention. 'Do you eat here every day?' Her voice was coquettish, friendly, with a hint of promise. He stared at her blankly for long moments before rolling his eyes at the ceiling and then abruptly leaving the restaurant.

The redhead shrugged at her friend's shocked expression.

'Well, it was worth a try.'

They both laughed together to cover her embarrassment.

Regina looked into Kate Burrows's face and shook her head slowly.

'I wouldn't do that. I admit I might be a bit slapdash with them now and again, but I would never, ever hurt my kids. Least of all my Jamie.'

'Two people put you there early this morning.'

'They can say what they like, I was in bed at home with me bloke.'

Kate Burrows stared hard at the girl. 'This is the same bloke you met two nights ago in a local pub?' She held up a hand so she could continue uninterrupted. 'His name's Milo something or other – your words, not mine. And he was with you till this morning. You jacked up together late last night, and were out of it until then.'

Regina nodded. 'That's about the strength of it, yeah.'

Kate looked at the effeminate man sitting beside his client and raised her eyebrows slightly. 'And *you* are the social worker?'

Robert Bateman smiled faintly. 'I am. And I believe her, Miss Burrows.'

'Let's take a break and have a cup of tea, eh?'

Kate walked from the small interview room followed

by Bateman. He accompanied her to the canteen and didn't speak until they were seated.

'I know how it looks, but she didn't do anything to that child. She wouldn't.'

He watched Kate's reaction and grinned.

'She gives them Valium sometimes to make them sleep so she can go out working. Now, to me and you that's awful, shocking, but to her way of thinking she's putting them safely to sleep so they don't wake up and go wandering off somewhere or start a fire. As she sees it, she is still sort of taking care of them, see?'

Kate shook her head. 'No, actually, I don't. On top of everything else she gives them prescription drugs to take – is that what you're telling me?'

The man nodded. 'But, you see, Miss Burrows, you're looking at all this from a normal person's point of view whereas Regina is not normal. She is an habitual drug user. Her life is chaos. Complete and utter chaos. She stumbles from one major disaster to the next. But – and this is the big but – she loves those kids. Her eldest, Michaela, actually looks after her mother. Keeps the other two in hand and tries in her own sweet little way to be a help. To make her mother's life that bit easier. They love her. Whatever we think about the situation, we have to think first of those kids.'

Kate smiled. 'My own thoughts entirely, and the sooner they're away from her the better.'

The social worker closed his eyes and sighed heavily. 'Away from her means in care. Split them up and they'll be unhappy. Don't judge everyone by your own standards, Miss Burrows. It never works, you know.'

He looked deep into her eyes, his gaze penetrating. She glanced away.

'I'm sorry, Mr Bateman. I appreciate you're trying to help your client but frankly I think that away from her is about as good as it's going to get for those children.'

He pushed his hair away from his face in a surprisingly female gesture.

'Regina's mother was a university lecturer in Ethics.' He nodded at her surprise.

'She also systematically abused her two children by burning them, humiliating them and starving them. When Regina was nine she was found in a large detached house with a quarter-of-an-acre garden. She was suffering from malnutrition and her younger brother had been dead for five days. Their mother had left them to go on a trip to Finland of all places. There was no food in the house, nothing. But the children were too frightened to use the phone and get help. They were found by accident. A neighbour had come by to drop off some gardening catalogues of all things.

'That memory is what Regina lives with every day of her life. Now I'm telling you, Miss Burrows, she would not harm her kids intentionally. She can't cope with the day-to-day running of her life – being a normal person is beyond her – but I tell you again, she would never hurt a hair of those kids' heads. Believe me, I *know*.'

Pushing his chair back gently, he walked from the canteen.

Kate watched him go. He looked burdened down. It was in his walk, his eyes, his whole demeanour. But, unexpectedly, she found herself liking Regina Carlton's social worker.

Patrick Kelly sat in the back of his Rolls-Royce and listened to Willy Gabney, his driver and confidant, expounding on the advantages of having a girlfriend. As usual. Willy had been seeing a woman for a few weeks now and was happier than Patrick had ever known him. He looked almost handsome nowadays which for a man as ugly as Willy had to be a miracle.

Patrick let him prattle on; it saved having to answer any questions. He lay back against the leather upholstery and sighed. He wanted to get home and inside Kate as soon as possible. He smiled at the thought.

Just then, his mobile rang. 'Kelly here.'

He listened for a few seconds then, turning off the phone, yelled at Willy to turn round and drive back towards the West End. His face was like thunder.

Willy saw immediately that he had had bad news. 'Everything all right, Pat?' Silly question.

Kelly shook his head. 'No, Willy. Everything ain't all right.'

Estelle Peterson was not young though she looked it. Long black hair, dyed and conditioned to within an inch of its life, actually made her look quite innocent instead of hardening her features. It was a look the other women were jealous of though none of them envied her her large nose, squinty eyes set too close together and child's rosebud mouth.

She was also very short-sighted so that she habitually peered at people, making her seem interested in what they were saying – which she never was, unless it was a pimp or a customer.

Today, though, she looked frightened. She sat in the empty lap-dancing club, hands shaking as she sipped at a very large brandy. Her mascara had run into her eyes, giving her a clown-like appearance.

Tommy Broughton was staring at her as if he had never seen her before. She shuddered again, looking frail and haunted.

'I want to go, Tommy. I ain't getting involved with Old Bill.'

He topped up her glass and nodded. 'Kelly will be here soon. We'll take our lead from him, OK?' He tried to sound reassuring, but it was obvious to both of them that he was more frightened than she was.

'Can't you cover him up at least?'

Tommy sighed. 'As I said, it's best not to touch anything until Kelly gets here.'

Estelle started to cry again and he walked towards the phone.

'I'll ring him. See how long he'll be. OK?'

Estelle nodded, her eyes firmly fixed on the glass in her hand.

Regina looked terrible and Kate guessed that she

would usually have had a little something to lift her by now, had she not been under arrest in the police station.

'Are you a registered addict, Regina? If so, I can get a medic to give you something to bring you up a bit.'

Regina stared at her blankly a moment before speaking.

'Listen to me, Burrows. I don't care if my own mother put me by that building site this morning – I wasn't there.'

'Then how did your son get out of the house and over to the other side of town? How did he climb up inside a building that was falling apart and which had no real staircases? He had to have been lifted bodily from floor to floor. So, if you didn't take him, Regina, who did? Now you say that even at two he's streetwise – but not *that* streetwise, surely?'

Regina began pulling at her hair, physically tearing at it in terror and distress. 'I don't fucking know! Someone must have taken him . . . I don't fucking know!'

She was crying now, a painful animal sound, repeating over and over, 'I don't know! I don't know!'

Kate Burrows stared down at the girl and unexpectedly her heart went out to her.

'Were you higher than usual last night? Could you have done this and not realised what you were doing? Was there anyone else at your place other than the man you'd picked up at the pub? Does anyone else have a key? Can you give me one reason not to believe you knowingly took that child and left him in a dangerous situation which could easily have led to his death but for the keen sight of a young girl?'

Regina looked up at her tormentor and shook her head. 'I don't know what happened. I swear to God, I really don't know how he got there.'

Kate looked into the haunted face. The eyes were pleading for understanding. The girl's whole body language screamed out, trying to make Kate believe what she was saying. Her hands, nails bitten to the quick, were trembling visibly as she attempted to light a cigarette.

And for a few seconds, Kate Burrows was inclined to give her the benefit of the doubt. But only for a few seconds. She had encountered liars of Olympic standards over the years. Had heard what she considered every story in the book.

This girl's story didn't add up at all, which was why Kate couldn't understand why she had not even tried to change it over the last four hours. Most people changed their story over and over. Others came well prepared and changed their story as and when a hole appeared in it. Regina just kept repeating hers over and over, different words but never deviating from the main point.

As far as she was concerned her kids had been in bed asleep. She had no idea how her son had managed to get to the building site. She was so out of it, she could not have walked across town, let alone carried her two-year-old son. She was also strung out, weirded out and tired.

Kate was wondering how she herself was going to

get on with interviewing the boyfriend. She needed caffeine and nicotine soon. Her head was thumping, her eyes were aching and all she wanted was to wrap this case up and get home.

But it wasn't going to be that easy. She had a feeling that Regina was going to stick with her story, as implausible as it was, and that this was going to be one hell of a long day.

Patrick Kelly walked into his night club, Girlie Girls, at just after one in the afternoon, his face set into a mask of anger. Manager Tommy Broughton was sitting at the bar nursing a large brandy. At this hour the whole place looked rundown. No club ever stood up to the harsh light of day.

Tommy nodded at Patrick, his face ashen, teeth tightly clamped. Patrick walked through to the small back bar and stared down incredulously at the battered body of his old mate Micky Duggan. One hand over his mouth, he shook his head sadly.

Micky had been savagely beaten to death. His mutilated body would not have looked out of place at the scene of a train wreck or some other terrible accident. But lying in a pool of his own blood, face stuck to the plush carpet, he looked wrong. All wrong. His neck had been snapped, one savage twist of bone and muscle by a strong man the only explanation.

But why?

Everyone liked Duggan. He was a crack, a laugh. Hard enough when he had to be but basically a nice person. His main fault had lain in his natural talent for aggravation. With a drink in him he got lairy.

'Fuck me, Pat, he looks rough!' Willy Gabney's voice was high with shock. 'Do you reckon he's dead?'

Patrick took a deep breath and said through gritted teeth, 'Unless he's thinking of walking around with his face looking at his arse, I'd say he is dead, Willy, yes.'

His driver was offended and it showed. 'I was only asking, Pat.'

Patrick sighed heavily. Willy was loyal to a fault but about as intelligent as a gnat, and at times like this – especially at times like this – it could be wearing.

'Do you reckon he was murdered?'

Patrick did not even bother answering that one. Instead he sighed heavily again and walked back to Broughton and Estelle.

Regina's boyfriend was a scruffy, ignorant young man called Milo Bangor. As Kate looked at him she marvelled at the way people somehow always lived up to their names.

He looked suitably weird but then, as she knew very well, he was frightened. Terrified, in fact. It showed in the way his hands shook and his voice trembled whenever he answered her questions.

As she watched him making another match-thin roll-up she knew he had been in prison and that he was under the firm impression he might be going back there.

'So, Milo, I guess you know what I want to ask you about?'

He looked at her directly for the first time and smiled nervously, displaying brown crooked teeth.

'Do I need a brief, lady?'

Kate grinned. 'You tell me, Milo, you're obviously the expert.'

He sat silently for a few seconds. He was actually thinking. Kate was impressed. She would have laid money that actual real-life thinking was beyond him.

'I never touched no fucking kid,' he said finally. 'And if that cunt has, and thinks she can lay it at my door, you can tell her from me I'll break her fucking back.'

Kate raised one perfectly plucked eyebrow. 'In those exact words, or shall I soften the blow a bit?'

Now he was talking he couldn't seem to stop.

'She treats them kids like slaves, man. I mean, she shouldn't even be allowed to have a dog, let alone those poor little bastards.'

'You sound like an expert on childcare. Now, can you tell me all your movements from yesterday lunchtime, please?'

Milo started laughing then. A low, scornful sound. 'I can't even remember getting up half the time. I mean, please!'

His arrogant yet frightened voice irritated her and she said loudly, 'Well, you'd better remember, boy. In fact, you can have a good bloody think while I get you a brief, OK? Suddenly I think there's a very good chance you'll need one.'

28

Kate stood up and was pleased to see a sober expression on Milo's face.

'I never touched no fucking kid, lady. You better believe that.'

She smiled again. 'I think you'd better convince me of it, don't you? After all, you were there, you were out of it, you are a prime suspect. I mean, for all I know, you and Regina worked a flanker. Did it together. I don't know, do I? But someone does. Someone was there, someone saw what happened, someone did the deed . . . and, Milo, I intend to find out just who the hell it was. Got that?'

Her hard voice penetrated his fogged brain and he looked very young suddenly and vulnerable and Kate felt a surge of reluctant pity for him. For Regina. For all the wasted lives she saw on a daily basis.

She ended the tape and quietly left the room.

Patrick Kelly sipped at his brandy. He knew he was in shock which didn't help dispel the trickle of fear that was slowly creeping over him. A man he had known all his life was lying dead in the club they'd owned together – a club where he had a feeling a serious amount of ducking and diving had occurred over the last few months without his knowledge. Otherwise why else would someone waste Micky?

He stared at Broughton. 'All right then, what's the scam? What has been going on?'

Tommy Broughton shrugged. 'I don't know, Pat. I take oath on that.'

Patrick finished his brandy in one gulp. 'Don't fuck

me about. Not today. I really ain't in the mood.'

Broughton shrugged. 'You know what he was like, Pat. One minute he was all over you like a rash, the next he wanted to fight ya.' He held out his arms in supplication. 'Micky had more rows in here the last few weeks than fucking Adolf Hitler on a bad trip. Christ, his nickname was Wanker – that says it all, don't it?'

Patrick stared at Broughton. What he'd said was true enough. Micky had argued with everyone. Rumour had it he'd argued bitterly with his mother, brothers, wife, girlfriends – even with the lap dancers and he had trumped most of them.

That was how Micky was made, unreliable in many respects. But, Christ, everyone who knew him respected his foibles. They were part and parcel of Micky. He wound everyone up, but if you were in a tight corner, he was the man to go to. He would move heaven and earth for a mate. Even a mate he had cunted into the ground a few days before.

None of this made sense to Patrick.

'How about the dancers?' he asked. 'Any jealous boyfriends about?'

Broughton shook his head. 'Not that I know of. Most of them are sorts, Pat. You know the score. A few nice ones, a few slags. The usual. Nothing much for Micky to get his knickers in a twist about, though. You know he hated silicone tits and there's enough of the stuff here to keep Bill Gates in microchips until the next century. There was a bit of hag with the bloke dancers, but that's only to be expected. Micky hated them, especially the straight ones – I think a bit of jealousy was at work there. Some of them are right good-looking boys and we take more on the hen nights lately.'

'No faces been round? No one you noticed 'specially?'

Broughton thought for a few seconds. 'Only Jamie O'Loughlin. But they was mates of a sort. He was in the other night. Bought a bird, shagged it up in the office. The usual.'

Patrick's eyes widened. 'Shagged it up in the office? You mean, *my* office?'

Broughton looked shamefaced. 'Well, Pat, be fair. I wasn't in a position to argue the toss with Micky, was I?'

'What a fucking liberty! Good job he's brown bread. If he wasn't, I might have the urge to do the deed myself.'

Broughton, desperate to change the subject, said: 'Hang on a minute, Pat. I tell you who *was* in the other week, and he and Micky had a row – a loud one out the back – Leroy Holdings. You know, the coon with the white convertible? Drug dealer, tall . . .'

Patrick sighed heavily. 'I know who you mean. What did they row about?'

Broughton held out his arms again. 'I dunno, Pat. I can't tell you that one, mate.'

Patrick shook his head slowly. 'You are a fucking right good front man, you are. How much wedge are you collaring off of me? You're supposed to be my eyes and ears in this place. Helen fucking Keller could have done a better job! I'll tell you what, how about you tell me what you *do* actually know? That way we can cut the conversation by about nine hours and Micky can be moved before rigor mortis sets in, eh?'

Broughton looked offended. His bald head was shiny with sweat, his powerful body rigid with suppressed anger.

'No need to be fucking funny, Pat. I did me best. Wanker – I mean Micky – wasn't the easiest of people to work with.'

Patrick calmed down a little at his words.

'I know. But I mean, be fair, who needs this on a Wednesday afternoon? My own mate and business partner topped in the bogs and I am having dinner this very night with an Old Bill. Remember Kate, my old woman, the love of my fucking life? Cheer her right up, this will, especially as I'm supposed to have got rid of all my dodgy dealings. Good job we ain't married or I'd be in the divorce courts within the week.'

Estelle was listening to all this with half an ear. Patrick suddenly remembered her and turned to where she was, sitting at the bar with a bottle of brandy and a pack of Marlboro Lights.

'Comfortable, are we? Can I get you a sandwich or something?'

Willy, sensing Pat was about to blow, stepped in.

'We'd better get Old Bill in, Pat. Any longer and we'll have even more explaining to do. Just report it and go home. They can get in touch later and you can act all shocked like. That way you're out of it all, eh?'

Patrick nodded. 'Well, I wasn't going to pop round Soho Central meself, Willy.' He took a wad of money from his pocket and gave it to Estelle. 'Take this, piss off and keep your trap shut, OK?'

The girl nodded and slid from the stool. As she reached the door he called out to her, 'If I hear you have preached one word I will personally cut your tongue out. OK?'

Estelle nodded again and left the building.

'Where's Micky living now?'

Broughton relaxed at Pat's change of tone.

'I don't know, to be honest. Round here some-where. I think he still keeps Marianne on the go.'

'That's all we need. She'll be straight round for her compensation. Mouthy mare she is. So we can't dump him at home and let someone else do the dirty then?'

Broughton shook his head. 'You get off, Pat, I'll deal with it from here, OK?'

'That's fucking big of you, Mr Broughton. Am I being dismissed by any chance?'

Willy took his arm gently. 'Leave it out, Pat, he's doing his best.'

'That's right, Willy, you cheer me right up.'

As he walked from the club Willy raised his eyes at the ceiling and Broughton nodded sadly. Patrick Kelly was strung out – and with Kelly that meant he wanted answers, and quick. Broughton wasn't sure what answers he was willing to give. He would play it by ear for a while.

Since the death of his daughter Mandy, Patrick had changed. He seemed harder outside, but there was

now an inner core of softness to him that in their
world spelled certain death. Maybe not physically, but
definitely businesswise. Word on the street was that he
was finished, over the hill, and that was just from the
kinder of his peers.

Whoever had killed Micky Duggan was after the
crown and Broughton hoped they had a head big
enough to wear the bastard if and when they finally
got it.

Patrick went home, devastated. Micky could be a
handful, true, making more than a few enemies in the
course of any average day, but it was part and parcel of
him and his life. Someone had once said Micky could
start a fight in an empty pub. But why kill him like
that? Whoever it was had either hidden in the club or
else Micky had let them in. Maybe even arranged to
meet them there.

From what Broughton had said he had left Micky
locking up alone the night before. Estelle said she'd
come in for a quick fix from him and had found him
there in the late morning. The place had been open all
night. How they weren't robbed Patrick didn't know.
Anyone could have walked in. Even the alarm was off.

The fact Micky had still been dealing was annoying.
All of that ducking and diving was supposed to be a
thing of the past. How could they front a respectable
club when one of the partners was still banging out
skag to prostitutes?

Micky never did have any class, that was part of his
rather dubious charm. For charming he could be
when the fancy took him. Now he was dead, and

there would be an investigation, and Kate would know Patrick was still holding the reins in Soho even though he had led her to believe he no longer had any interests.

He was so annoyed he could happily have strangled Micky Duggan himself.

The phone rang and he ignored it. He already knew what the caller was going to tell him and he wasn't ready to do his big surprised act just yet. He had to sort out what he was going to say to Kate. Because she was going to launch him into outer space when she heard about this.

Willy came into the room with a pot of coffee and an uneasy smile.

'That was Kate on the blower,' he said. 'I told her you were on another call. She's cancelling dinner this evening. Has to work. Sounds like a terrible case, Pat, child abuse of all things. Life's a right bastard really, ain't it, for some people?'

Patrick nodded, relieved to be putting off the inevitable until later. He cared what Kate thought of him; her opinion really mattered. He could not bear the thought of seeing her face as she realised they had, in effect, been living a lie for the last few years.

Why did he have to get a capture now, when everything was going so well and they had even talked of marriage? It was so unfair.

He poured himself some coffee and looked around his beautiful drawing room. Kate's picture now sat beside that of his dead wife Renée on the mantelpiece of the Louis XV fireplace. Her presence was everywhere in the house. Her perfume lingered in the bathroom. Her clothes hung beside his in the closet. Her make-up and creams thrilled him every time he saw them on the dressing table. He loved her with an ache. After losing Mandy and Renée, the two people closest to him, he knew about love. About making the most of it as and when it happened.

So many people never learned to do that.

And he had jeopardised it all for the sake of a few measly grand a night. Money he didn't really need but couldn't resist earning. It was his nature.

As he sipped his coffee, Patrick knew that Kate's late night was only postponing the fireworks that would erupt at some point within the next twenty-four hours.

Kate was going to court to ask for another twenty-four hours in which to question Regina and Milo.

Her heart was aching. The Carlton children were now under a care order and were to go to a foster family for the night. They were all distressed without their mother as Robert Bateman had predicted, trying to make her feel guilty and succeeding only too well.

But Kate pushed that thought to the back of her mind. She needed to know what exactly had gone on, and she needed to know fast.

Chapter Two

Patrick opened his eyes and stared at the ceiling, feeling apprehension wash over him. Turning, he pulled a sleeping Kate into his arms. She nestled into his body and he looked down at her face. Kate was everything to him. He adored her. Just looking at her lying beside him gave him a feeling of immense peace.

She slipped one slender arm across his body and nestled against him, and he instinctively pulled her even closer. He glanced at his watch. Nearly six-thirty. In a few minutes Kate would stir. That was another thing he loved about her. Most of the women before Kate wouldn't even contemplate getting out of bed before ten. They had been aimless, depending on men like him to keep them. Using their bodies as opposed to their brains to get what they wanted.

His respect for her was boundless, and he depended now on the respect she had for him in return. But how long would that last when she found out about yesterday's fiasco? The cold feeling around his heart returned. Kate expected everyone to be like her. What you saw was exactly what you got. Upfront, straight and honest. That was his Kate.

The alarm went off, clamouring in the quiet of their bedroom. She opened her eyes while he turned it off, lay back against the pillows and smiled at him. Then, closing her eyes again, she stretched dreamily.

Patrick watched her, enjoying the morning ritual. Willy would bring in a tray of coffee in ten minutes. By then Kate would have showered and washed her hair.

He was amazed at how well they fitted together. Life-long early risers, Kate and he both enjoyed this part of the day together. Reading the papers for ten minutes and chatting over the headlines was a great start for them both. He was even willing to have the *Mail* delivered so she could peruse the women's pages, exclaiming over the facelift trials, the alternative medicines and sundry other crap he would know nothing about but for her.

Every bit of it was a joy to him now.

The phone rang on Kate's side of the bed; it was her work line, especially put in for her use when she had come to live with him three years ago. For the first time ever he was glad to hear its shrill ringing this early.

Kate answered it, stifling a yawn. 'Burrows here.'

He watched the changing expressions on her face and saw how her eyes dilated at what was obviously distressing news. She replaced the receiver and leaped from the bed.

'What's up, Kate?'

'One of my suspects tried to commit suicide this morning. Bit clean through her own wrist. I'll have Dave Golding's balls for this. I told him to have her watched. I must get along to the hospital, see what I can salvage.' She disappeared into the shower.

Patrick toyed with the idea of jumping in with her, felt the usual stirring in his groin. Then Willy knocked on the door, and the coffee and papers were there, and Kate was dressing quickly. Kissing him and leaving.

As she walked to the door she half turned. 'You OK, Pat?'

He nodded. ''Course I am. You?'

She grinned. 'Never better. Speak to you later.'

Then she was gone, leaving him feeling bereft. He loved her so much, so very very much. But he knew that he was living on borrowed time.

Regina had been given six stitches in her wrist. Kate gazed down at her and wondered at a life that could at once be so complicated and yet so ineffectual. In repose, Regina's face showed a prettiness it lost when she was animated. The sour look was gone; the lines that anguish had imprinted there were smoothed out. She looked what she was: an attractive young woman with good bone structure and thick auburn hair that would probably have been glossy on another woman. One with self-respect, one who still cared about herself.

Kate took Regina's hand in hers and held it gently. The warm pressure was returned and the gesture made Kate think of her own daughter, Lizzy, when she had overdosed. Unlike Regina, her mother had been there for her; her granny had too. Regina, it appeared, had no one to depend on. To share things with. All she had was three children, a council flat and drugs. A lethal combination. Loneliness was the worst kind of unhappiness, something Kate herself knew only too well.

She saw the girl's eyes open. 'You're OK, Regina,' she said softly. 'Try and sleep.'

Regina was still half drugged. She nodded and said in a hoarse voice, 'I never hurt my baby . . . not my baby. The only person I've ever hurt is myself.'

Kate didn't answer her. She didn't know what to say.

Outside the hospital Kate lit a cigarette and sat on a bench while she gathered her thoughts together.

She remembered coming to this same hospital when Patrick's daughter Mandy had been attacked. Kate could still see her lying in the hospital bed after what they had hoped would be a life-saving operation. Her head had been opened up to relieve the pressure on her swollen brain. Mandy Kelly had taken a beating that had been as vicious as it had been random.

Kate would never have dreamed that night, as she waited in the hospital, that Mandy's father – a local hard man and local businessman to boot – would not only garner her respect, but also her love. Patrick's helplessness at his daughter's plight had struck a chord inside her. She had seen him vulnerable and frightened, as she guessed no one else ever had. Not even his wife Renée, or his daughter Mandy, who had died at the hands of the Grantley Ripper.

George Markham came into her mind then, his face. His little smile.

She had been on CID ten years then and she had learned so much since then that, these days, she could make sense of Patrick Kelly and his life. He was bad, she knew that. But he lived by a different set of rules and Kate had to admit that, against her better judgement, those rules worked for him. In fact, her boss Ratchet was in league with him.

But no matter what she had found out about him – she had known he was a villain from the off – his personality and his innate sense of right and wrong, however twisted it seemed to her, had drawn them together. She had forgiven him so much, had chosen to believe in him and in the fact that he had changed for her.

He had given up his various nefarious businesses. He had become legit for her. That was all the proof she needed to fall even deeper into his life and allow the natural love inside her to encompass them both.

For a man like Patrick to turn his back on his whole way of life spoke volumes.

Finally she had a man she could love and respect properly. And God Himself knew, she loved him with every ounce of her being.

Patrick sat in the conservatory listening to Willy in amazement.

'It seems, Pat, that Micky was dabbling with Joey Partridge and Jacky Gunner.'

'Who told you this?'

Willy shrugged. 'I hear a few beats off the street still, Pat. I ain't bleeding dead.'

'So it would seem. What business was he in with them, then? Christ knows, he was into enough of them.'

Willy grinned. 'The oldest profession. Be fair, Pat, it was always Wanker's forte, weren't it?'

Pat felt a sickening lurch in his stomach. 'Not European birds? Not that?'

Willy nodded.

'How did you come by this information?'

'A little bird told me.'

Patrick laughed at Willy's smug expression. 'Lived up to his name, didn't he? All this hag. I mean, the chances are Partridge or Gunner's done him then?'

Willy shrugged. 'Someone done him, Pat, and let's face it, Micky could be a ponce when the fancy took him. Even I've felt like cracking him one before now.'

'Everyone in recorded history has felt like giving Micky a dig before now. So where are they running the birds from?'

'Paddington as usual. They have a couple of flats there and other places all over the smoke and the South East. Right ropey some of them birds are, and all. Dosed up to the eyebrows a lot of them and that's not counting the HIV-positive ones. Micky offers them the earth, see. They pay up to a grand to get out of their country, he sorts it for them and then takes their passports and papers and tells them they have to work off the excess money they owe. It's a doddle really. He was earning off them all over the place. If they got a bit lairy like, they'd get a right fucking hiding to sort them out. I always said Wanker was a scummy bastard.'

Patrick sighed. 'So if he's out of the game, who'll be sorting it from now on?'

'Well, Partridge and Gunner will be looking for someone else to bring in, won't they? I reckon they'll want to see you.'

'Unless I see them first, eh?' Patrick said thoughtfully. 'Get the car ready, Willy. Me and you are going on a pussy hunt.'

Willy left the room and Patrick felt a hand tighten around his heart. Kate would have his balls and nail them to the dining-room wall if she got wind of any of this.

He knew that everyone thought he was off his trolley to take up with an Old Bill, even if she had found the murderer of his daughter. The daughter he worshipped, adored, who had been his whole life. He knew that people thought he was soft, losing it, that Mandy's death had left him lacking the natural aggression he needed to be a hard man. He was aware of all that, but over the last couple of years he and Kate had proved themselves to be a good partnership.

The only bugbear was, Kate really thought he was straight now. He had been in every kind of business under the sun, anything from massage parlours to debt collecting. She thought he had given it all up. She thought he was straight now.

He closed his eyes in distress. The moment she heard about this latest piece of skulduggery she was going to go ballistic – and who could blame her? He knew he was a lying toe-rag.

The day she had moved in with him he had promised her that he would be straighter than a Catholic nun having a vision. He had not kept his side of the bargain. In fact, he had never had any intention of keeping his side of the bargain. Not for a good while anyway.

Like the man crying in the courtroom, he wasn't sorry for what he had done, he was sorry he had been caught. Even he admitted there was a big difference between the two.

Harris Jenkins was a small man with large teeth and thick lips. His job was unhealthy but he loved it. Emptying bins was his life. He said he could tell what type of person lived in a house simply by the rubbish they threw out. And with his eagle eyes he readily saw things he could take away and sell on. A walking car boot sale, was Harris. A true believer that one man's crap was another man's treasure.

At the moment he was sorting through a pile of rubbish left by the bins at a small block of flats for old people. They threw out some great stuff. As he picked through the cardboard boxes he smiled happily. Let his colleagues wait. He needed to sift through this stuff carefully. Some of it was crockery and that could be worth a few quid.

Meanwhile Denny Gardener and John Piles were sitting in the bin van talking. They were used to Harris and his treasure-seeking. In fact, they welcomed it as an excuse for a break.

'Here, Denny, how do you make an Essex girl's eyes light up? Shine a torch in her ear!'

Both men cracked up with laughter.

Denny carried on rolling himself a cigarette. He placed a bit of skunk in it and John automatically opened the window.

'You get caught smoking that and you will be well up Shit Street.'

Denny shrugged. 'Who cares? What kind of job is this anyway? They call me a champion shit-shifter down the pub.'

'It's a job, son, remember that.'

Denny didn't answer. In the side window he watched a woman hurrying down the street, a small boy beside her. Then, lighting up, he took a deep drag.

'Fucking boring job and a boring life. That's me.'

They both laughed.

John grinned. 'Don't knock boring, boy. The sun's out and life is sweet enough if you think about it.'

Jason Harper was sitting in his brand new BMW looking through his Filofax. He had fucked up two meetings in an hour. He knew he should be more organised but it was hard. The glare of the sun was blinding him through the windscreen and he slipped on his Ray-Bans. A bin van was parked in front of him; it had been there for about five minutes. He watched as a woman with a small child walked across the road. She was nothing spectacular, and he only glanced out of habit. She was tallish with blonde hair but a very average face.

It was only when she stopped and glanced up and down the road that he looked again. Then, in pure disbelief, he saw her pick up the small child and tip him quickly into the crusher. For a few seconds Jason wondered if he was going mad. As he saw the woman striding off alone he catapulted himself from the driver's seat.

Harris heard the commotion just as he was carefully looking over a china fruit bowl. It was a good one or he would eat his binman's gloves.

A resounding shout made him fumble with the bowl and nearly drop it. Striding out of the alley he was amazed to be confronted by his two workmates and a bloke in a suit trying to climb into the back of the crusher.

'What the fucking hell are you lot doing?' He thought they had all gone mad. Carefully placing the bowl on the grass verge, he walked over to the men. 'What's going on, Den?'

'Christ knows, Harris. Do us a favour – go in the flats and phone Old Bill and an ambulance, will you? We have a kid in here somewhere.'

'A what?' Then he heard a faint cry and it spurred him into action. Running back to the flats he trod on the fruit bowl. The sound and feel of the fragile object crunching under his feet lent added speed.

His stars in the *Sun* had said he would receive a surprise today and they were right!

Jason was in shock and Kate realised that. She took him by the elbow and sat him down on the kerb. He put his head in his hands.

'I can't believe it,' he mumbled. 'What woman would do something like that to a child? I mean, suppose I hadn't been there? They would have crushed the poor little sod.'

He started crying and Kate put an understanding arm around his shoulders. He could smell Joy perfume and cigarettes, and in some strange way, was comforted by it.

'But you *were* there, Jason, and you saved his life,' she said gently. 'Without you he would have been crushed and so I think you should pat yourself on the back.'

He hastily wiped away his tears, suddenly aware of all the bystanders watching him. One of the residents of the street had phoned the local paper and Jason saw a scruffy young man with a beard taking a photo of him.

'You are a hero,' Kate said kindly. 'Now let's get you into the ambulance so they can have a look at you, eh? I think you're in shock, love.'

Jason's eyes were dark brown and Kate smiled into them. He tried to smile back but couldn't. She helped him get up and walked him slowly to the ambulance.

Then she turned to PC Black and sighed.

'This is weird. Two cases like this in three days – what on earth is going on?'

'Beats me, Guv,' he shrugged. 'Weird's the word all right.'

All Kate could think about was the child's frightened eyes. If Jason hadn't been parked there it would have been a murder case. She hoped they found out who the child was soon. Bless his heart, he was well dressed and fed, they knew that much. A woman with long blonde hair, tallish . . . but that could have been because she was wearing heels. None of the men had looked hard enough. Which meant she wasn't all that special. One thing they were all sure about was the fact that she'd been in a hurry. But she would have been, wouldn't she? If she was dumping a child in a crusher she would have been as quick as she ruddy well could.

Kate looked at Jason's BMW and realised why the woman had not spotted him. The reflected glare of the sun on the windscreen made the inside of the car look dark and empty. So she had obviously thought herself unobserved.

Whoever she was, she had meant to kill the little lad. The knowledge left Kate feeling deeply depressed.

Caroline Anderson walked unsteadily into her small terraced house. She was still half drunk from the night before. Going straight to the bathroom, she had a long satisfying wee. As the strong-odoured water came out of her body she felt herself relaxing. She hated that smell. It was the smell of men. Strange men. It was bitter and acrid. The smell of her own degradation and the complete fuck-up her daily life had become.

After wiping herself, she ran a bath. She poured in half a bottle of Ralgex and watched the bubbles mounting, smiling in anticipation. A good scrub and she would let the kids out.

Stripping off, she stepped into the steaming water and lay back. She glanced at her watch. She was later than ever today. She had had an overnighter – and Christ, she had worked for the money! Three blokes and enough 'toys' to set up an Ann Summers shop.

She was sore everywhere.

Closing her eyes, she let the hot water do its work.

Kate watched as the little boy wolfed down another hot dog. He was obviously starving. A good-looking, golden-skinned Anglo-Caribbean child, he was bright and alert, with a fabulous smile. He seemed happy enough in the canteen with everyone making a big fuss of him. His big brown eyes were merry, and he had a sturdy little body. He was obviously well cared for, too, in his expensive clothes. A real little designer babe. But what was his name?

The child was no more than eighteen months old, though large for his age. The doctor had said he was in perfect health and none the worse for his ordeal. But he was a quiet child and would not or could not answer any questions. Kate found herself smiling at him again. He beamed across at her and shoved another large bite of hot dog into his mouth.

'Quiet, ain't he?'

Kate nodded at Black's observation. 'But someone knows who he is. Has Social Services arrived yet?'

'Nope. Handsome little lad, though.'

'Probably another poor little git with a waster for a mother,' Kate said quietly. 'I don't know. Why do people go through all the hag of childbearing and then not bother to care for the poor little fuckers?'

The little boy sipped at his orange juice and Kate felt tears prick her eyes. He looked so helpless, so vulnerable. So bloody *small*. She swallowed down her anger and her pity.

It was all she could do.

Caroline was sleepy; the heat of the water and the night's exertions had tired her out. She pulled herself reluctantly from the bath and wrapped a big towel around her body as she walked through to her lounge. It was as always pristine.

Lighting a Rothman's, she pulled on it deeply and absent-mindedly straightened a cushion that was already perfectly aligned. Opening her handbag, she pulled out £300 in twenties and another £150 in tens. She had the money for that coffee-table she fancied and for Christian's new trainers.

Caroline felt a glow inside. The night before had been worth it, after all. Something to put out of her head, like all the other nights she had so conveniently forgotten.

Yawning, she walked through to the kids' bedroom. After pulling back the big bolt on the door, she pushed it open, smiling in readiness. But it was empty. The small, designer-decorated room was completely empty!

Caroline felt her heart stop in her chest. Rushing inside, she pulled back the covers on the beds and even looked under them. Her eyes were darting around the room, expecting at any minute to see her children standing in front of her.

The plate of sandwiches she had left was still on the night table. The bottle of orange was still there too. So they had not had their breakfast or anything.

Then she tore from the room and searched the house from top to bottom, panic mounting in her breast. Finally she collapsed on the sofa. Picking up her mobile, she dialled a number and waited for it to be answered.

As soon as the connection was made she screamed into the phone: 'How dare you take my children, you rotten bastard?'

Her face drained of colour as she listened to Jiggsy Gaston explaining that he was currently in Liverpool with his sister and had not been anywhere near the kids. He sounded alarmed.

Realising that this was even more serious than she'd thought, Caroline broke the connection and phoned the police. Her heart was beating so loudly she could hear a crashing in her ears.

Where the hell were her two little boys? Where were Christian and Ivor?

Patrick walked into a small spieler in Custom House.

It was practically empty except for two elderly men and a young woman who worked behind the bar. The girl was Lesley Partridge and as Patrick walked towards her she smiled to see him.

'Hello, Pat. Long time no see.'

He grinned at her. 'You look well, Les. Is the old man about?'

She shook her head. 'Dad's on the missing list again, I ain't seen him for three days. You know what he's like.'

'Joey's a lad all right. Give me a Beck's, love.'

She opened the bottle of beer and placed it on the counter with a glass.

'Me dad makes me sick, Pat. Still chasing strange at his age. But that's him all over. I expect he's still shagging some sort and will emerge eventually. He always does.'

Willy came into the small room and nodded at the two older men as he made his way to the bar. Lesley automatically poured him a Britvic orange.

'Hello, Willy. Me mum was asking after you the other day. How's things?'

He shrugged. 'OK, love. Kicking, as they say nowadays.'

She laughed. 'I'll see if I can track me dad down on his bent mobile, eh?'

Patrick nodded and she walked from the bar, her large behind swaying suggestively.

'He's gone walkabout, Willy.'

'He will, won't he, Pat? He don't want no one seeing him for a while. Wouldn't surprise me if he was abroad like. Tenerife or Marbella would be my guess.'

They drank peacefully for a few moments until the girl returned to the bar, shaking her head.

'Can't get him, he ain't answering.'

Patrick swallowed down the last of his beer. 'When you do hear from him, tell him I need a word, will you?'

She nodded and cleared away. As they walked out into the light and air, one of the old lags stopped them.

'Listen, Pat. I don't know what's going down but some foreigners were looking for Joey a couple of days ago. They were likely lads and all. No please or thank you. One of them was Frankie Oberzaki – and that is one dangerous cunt. He wasn't looking too thrilled either.'

Patrick nodded solemnly. 'You think Joey might have had a capture?'

The man shrugged theatrically. 'Who knows? But he's been ducking and diving a lot recently. Had a tear-up in Epping Country Club a week ago. Honestly, it's like he's going through a second childhood, the dozy twat. He was rowing with Dickey Dalton – the younger that is. Slapped him all over the place. Even the bouncers gave it a wide one. I mean, no one wants to be caught up in all that, do they?'

Patrick looked at him in amazement. 'He had a tear-up with a little nonce like Dalton, at his age? Has he finally fell out of his shopping trolley?'

The man sighed. 'It's the okey doke, ain't it? More

goes up his hooter than on a dental association outing. Makes him paranoid. He's rowing with everyone, and let's face it, Pat, Mr Amenable he never was. One awkward ponce is Partridge.'

'Well, thanks for the SP.'

The man shook hands with them and walked to his brand new Merc. They both watched him pull away.

'That was a touch, Pat. He's normally very tight-lipped, old Tom Ellis. Must have been well annoyed with Partridge to spill that little lot.'

'He owes me a favour. His boy's doing life for murder. I gave him an easy set in Durham. Single cell, et cetera.'

Willy nodded. 'Least he can do then really. Where to next?'

'To be honest, Willy, I don't have a clue,' Patrick sighed.

Christian ran into his mother's arms and Kate was pleased to see there was a genuine closeness there. She was dreading the woman's next question.

'Where's Ivor?'

Caroline's pretty face was expectant and Kate sat her down gently before explaining how Christian had been found, and that he was alone.

'You're telling me that my son was thrown into a bin van and my other son's still on the missing list?'

Kate could hear the rising hysteria in the woman's voice.

'So where the fuck is Ivor then? Who's got my Ivor?'

Kate shook her head sadly. 'We don't know. Until we heard from you, how were we to know that two children were missing? Also, three witnesses gave a description of a woman who could be you at the scene. So we have a dilemma on our hands. Do you understand what I'm telling you?'

Caroline looked as if she had been punched in the solar plexus.

'How come you didn't notice you'd mislaid your children until nearly lunchtime today? Most kids are up and about by eight. And how come you don't have any idea who could have taken them from under your nose? In short, if you tell us the truth about what happened, maybe, just maybe, we can try and locate Ivor for you. But without you telling us the full story, we can't help you at all. A three-year-old child is wandering around out there somewhere and it's imperative we find him before he harms himself. So, Caroline, let's start at the beginning, shall we?'

The other woman looked into Kate's eyes and felt the tears welling.

'You think a nutter has him, don't you?' Fear was all she felt and tasted. 'Where is he? Where's my little Ivor?' she said frantically.

'I was hoping you could answer that,' Kate told her. 'Listen, Caroline, you were placed there at the scene. We're going to ask you to take part in an identity parade some time today. I suggest you get a solicitor and take advice.'

Caroline's eyes were terrified, giant orbs in a white

face. 'You think *I* have something to do with all this, don't you?'

Kate shrugged. 'An ID parade could clear you, remember that. But as we have three witnesses who gave a description that sounded remarkably like you, we cannot rule you out of our investigation just yet. I feel, though, that there are a lot of unanswered questions here and only you can provide us with the necessary answers.'

Caroline's face changed. 'My boys are my life, whatever anyone might think. I admit I do a few things wrong but I love them boys and I do what I do for *them*. You must believe me.'

'I deal in facts. Plain and simple facts. The only ones I have now are that your children were taken from under your roof, one child was dumped in a bin van, the other is still missing. We need to find him. Fast.'

As Kate watched the changing expressions on the girl's face she wasn't sure whether the mother was behind the children's disappearance or not.

Suddenly, Caroline leaped from her seat and roared at the top of her voice: 'Where is my little boy? You're the police. Fucking go and find him!'

As she began screaming uncontrollably Kate bundled up the small boy who stood as if turned to stone by his mother's shrieks and hustled him from the room. She called a medic, watched as the girl was sedated, and then when she was under a modicum of control, Kate started to question her properly. At the back of her mind she was always aware that somewhere a three-year-old child was either dead, dying or being held captive.

Time was running out for Ivor Anderson. If it hadn't done so already.

Patrick looked around his office in Canning Town in sheer disbelief. The place had been well and truly trashed. All his papers were strewn across the room; his account books had been ripped apart. Even the photographs of his dead wife Renée and daughter Mandy had been destroyed, and this upset him more than anything.

Willy stared at the scene open-mouthed. 'Blimey, Pat, someone was after something.'

'You know what, Willy? You always state the fucking obvious. Sometimes it really gets on my tits.'

'I was only saying . . .'

'Yeah, well, don't in future. But I tell you one thing: whoever did this is on a fucking death wish. I will find out who is responsible and kill them.'

'Could it have been kids?'

Patrick shook his head. 'This is too professional for kids. My guess is they were after me holding books. Even the floorboards have been prised up. Luckily I keep them separate. What we need to know now is why someone wants them. I own the businesses so why are the books of any interest to an outside party?'

'Well, maybe whoever did this is after a slice of the pie themselves.'

'Precisely. Now we have to guess who that could be and rout the fuckers. Put the fear of Christ up them.'

Willy wiped one large hand across his face. 'My

guess is either Partridge or Gunner.'

Patrick's voice was a sarcastic growl as he answered, 'Fuck-all gets past you, eh, Willy? Magnus Magnusson been on the blower yet for *Mastermind*?'

Willy was hurt and it showed. 'No point getting all bolshie with me, Pat. I'm on your side.'

As he spoke he picked up Renée's photo and tried to smooth it out with his big clumsy hands. 'Whoever did this will get a right-hander off me just for this little fiasco,' he mumbled. 'This is getting bleeding personal.'

Patrick saw that the big man was visibly upset and put an arm round his shoulders.

'I'm sorry, Willy, but all this is getting to me now. I have someone after me and I don't even know who for sure. I can guess, I can fight, I can hurt . . . but I still have to find out for definite who I'm dealing with and, more importantly, why.'

'My poke is on Gunner, Pat. I've never liked him, the ponce.'

'Well, whoever it is had better have some heavy weapons because they're going to need them. A joke's a joke, as my old mum used to say. But this is turning into a fucking pantomime.'

There was raw anger in Patrick's voice. Then the phone rang and they both realised it was the only thing in the room that had not been destroyed.

He picked it up. 'What?'

A woman came on the line. A quietly spoken woman.

'Mr Kelly?'

'The same.'

'You have two minutes to vacate the Portakabin. It is going to blow.'

He stared at the mouthpiece for ten seconds in incredulous silence before looking at Willy and saying loudly, 'This place is going to blow up in two minutes. Some sort just told me they were blowing up my fucking drum! Can you believe the nerve of that—'

Willy took him roughly by the arm. 'In that case, Pat, let's get out of here, eh?'

As they hurried outside Patrick stared around him at the yard he had had for over thirty years.

'This has got to be a wind-up.'

Willy pushed him into the car and backed it out on to the road. Then, parking as far away from the yard as he could, they sat and watched.

The yard blew all right.

Patrick could still hear the ringing in his ears when the fire brigade and police arrived, but by that time he and Willy were driving sedately along the A13, Patrick muttering over and over: 'Unbelievable. Fucking unbelievable.'

Willy kept quiet.

Chapter Three

Leroy Holdings was tired out. He had been up for two days speeding and knew he should go to bed but he had a meet with another dealer about broadening their horizons around the capital. Drug dealing and prostitution were more lucrative than he could ever have dreamed. Thank God for women and pharmaceuticals – that was his mantra these days.

As he looked around his state-of-the-art kitchen he smiled contentedly. He had come a long way from Manchester. He liked living in Docklands. There was an anonymity about the place that appealed to him, but his girlfriend Letitia had left the place in a mess and that irked him.

Lately she couldn't be bothered to do anything. Pregnancy was not doing her much good. In fact, since she had found out about the baby she had done practically nothing. That included the bedroom department as well.

When he heard the door open he shouted: 'Hey, Letitia, I'm in here.' His voice was loud and aggressive. He was going to bawl her out, he had decided. He might not have been home for a while but, hell, it was her job to see that the place was kept in good condition.

As he looked across the Thames he felt his usual stir of pride at living in a Docklands loft. Coming from a council estate in Manchester, he appreciated this turn in his fortunes more than the average dealer. Not for him a cage in a local authority flat where everyone came calling at all hours of the day and night. He didn't need to do that himself any more and certainly didn't live on top of the business. He had invested his money in property and cars, the latter being his first love.

When he went to friends' houses and saw the bars on their doors and windows he felt stifled. It was like being banged up again. No, he liked his smart new life, it suited him fine.

He strolled from the kitchen area into the large lounge. It was then he saw the two men with shot-guns standing on his immaculate white shag-pile carpet.

'Hello, son.'

The man's voice was friendly. Friendly enough for Leroy to think all he was getting was a warning of some kind.

When the guns went off he was so shocked that the look of utter incomprehension was still on his face when Letitia found him there twenty-five minutes later.

Stingo Plessey was old. Very old in comparison with the other men who lived on the caravan site with him. As he walked carefully across the rubbish tip he was whistling. The smells of rotten food and stinking garbage meant nothing to him. He was used to it. Today he was keeping his eye out for stuff he could clean up and sell on. Anything, in fact, that caught his eye.

Seeing a child's brand new trainer he grinned, showing greying false teeth. Picking it up, he saw it was a Nike. Now if he could find the other one he would be set. A good clean and he had at least a fiver in his pocket. A nice bottle of sherry or fine ruby port. He rubbed his hands together in glee.

As he pushed the rubbish about with his thick yew walking stick he saw the other trainer. Only this one was bloodied and stained. He swallowed down fiery bile as he realised that inside the small trainer there was still what looked like a foot.

Glancing around the rubbish tip he saw the other sifters looking through the trash with the seagulls and the gypsies. He tried to call out but couldn't. His throat had seized up, his whole body stiff with revulsion and fear.

As the police turned up in three large minibuses Stingo realised he had just found what they were looking for. Digging his stick into the rubbish, he marked the spot and started to wave his hands in the air to let people know he had found something important.

No one took any notice.

The wind picked up and flapped newspapers and soiled nappies in its wake. It picked up the smell of the trash and forced it into noses and mouths. Stingo felt the prick of tears in his eyes as he started calling out with all his might. To end your days on a rubbish tip seemed a terrible fate.

It never occurred to him that that was exactly what he had to look forward to himself.

'Sweet Jesus. Have they found his head?' DC Golding was subdued even by his standards. 'Well, what *have* they got then?'

He listened for a few seconds before replacing the receiver. Then he made his way to the interview room with a heavy heart. This was going to put everyone on a downer. The death of a kid was every Old Bill's worst nightmare.

He slipped into the interview room and listened to Kate's interrogation, making sure he wasn't interrupting it at a crucial point.

Caroline had her solicitor with her, a woman called Angela Puttain. She was an experienced brief and Golding felt glad that at least the woman had some kind of support with her when she was told the bad news. He was actually sorry for her now, even though he still suspected that she was the culprit.

Caroline was crying as she gave her statement.

'I know what I did was wrong, Miss Burrows, but I was at the end of my tether. Their dad had jogged on. He only gives me money when he remembers. I started escort work last year and it sort of went on to prostitution. I never *meant* to go on the game, it just sort of happened. I don't have a sitter for the kids because I never wanted anyone to know what I was doing. People are streetwise where I live and they would have sussed it out quick smart. So I locked the kids in their room with some food and drink and that was that really. They were safe enough. I locked the house up after me and they were always asleep in bed when I left. They didn't even know I was gone half the time.' Her voice was low, full of pain and shame.

'Did you ever give them Valium to make them sleep?' Kate asked.

Caroline was scandalised at the thought of giving her children drugs. 'Never! What makes you ask that?'

Kate shook her head. She wondered if this was the new thing with some young mums. Knock the kids out, then if there was a fire or whatever they could sleep peacefully right through it.

Golding took his chance to tap her on the shoulder and ask if he could have a word. As Kate followed him to her office she felt depressed. It was as if all the effluent of the world was parading about as regular people. She wondered what went through the minds of women like Caroline Anderson. If she was earning good wedge – and Kate had never met a tom yet who wasn't – then she could easily have used a babysitting service.

'What've you got for me?' she asked the detective tiredly.

Golding looked her in the eye. 'We have a small pair of trainers from the dump. One still has a foot in it.'

Kate ran her hands through her hair in despair.

'It's murder, then? I was hoping we were wasting our time looking over the dump.'

'I had a feeling we'd find something there,' he told her. 'I think she did it. I think her and that Regina are a pair of murdering bitches.'

'If I were you I'd keep that particular gem of wisdom to yourself. Innocent until proven guilty in this station, mate. Now is there anything else I should know before I go back in to her?'

Golding shook his head. 'It was a Nike trainer. I'll keep you posted as to what else turns up. Do you want me to get you some coffee sent in?'

She nodded. 'Any calls for me?'

He shook his head again. 'Not a dicky bird.'

Kate watched him as he left the office. David Golding was a strange man. A good officer, he got the job done but he didn't really mix with the others. In fact, Kate could never remember him talking about anything personal ever.

He was a good-looking man in a boyish, intellectual way. He had the large blue eyes of an innocent that seemed to take in everything at once, and sandy-coloured hair and eyebrows which made him look amiable. However, after even a brief conversation, people were in no doubt as to his strong opinions and his rather aggressive personality.

Golding despised burglars and petty thieves and he hated sex offenders, but he seemed to have an affinity with what he regarded as career criminals – bank robbers, big-time hoods. He was a prime candidate for the Serious Crimes Squad; they were also renowned for their ability to like – even admire – the people they were going to bang up.

Kate dismissed Golding from her mind. She normally would have had a message from Pat by now. He hadn't been right for the last few days – he had seemed very edgy somehow. But she couldn't think about that at the moment. She had too much else to worry about. This was murder, and she was starting to get a bad feeling about it all. For starters, why would two women decide overnight to try and murder their own children, and in such strange ways? People battered kids, they lost their temper with them, some people even tortured or harmed them. But to her knowledge nobody just upped and dumped them on building sites or in bin vans. Not while they were still alive, anyway.

Nothing shocked her any more, or so she had thought until today. She had honestly believed she was past shocking. But something here was all wrong, and she didn't know what it was. Something was bugging her – really bugging her, but maybe it was just the circumstances. She thought of Christian and his little smiling face. Had his brother been dumped in a bin van too? Had he been alive when it had happened?

It was almost too awful to contemplate, the terrible fear young Ivor must have experienced. Kate became hot and clammy at the thought of it. Christ knows what the child must have felt, having it actually happen to him.

She shooed Golding from the room and sat alone, smoking a cigarette for a few moments. She needed to pull herself together and quick. She had some serious work ahead of her.

As she walked from the office her phone rang, but she ignored it. It would be Chief Inspector Ratchet for an update and at this moment in time she wasn't ready to share anything with anyone. Not until she had sorted it out in her own mind.

A picture of her daughter Lizzy in a white dress at her third birthday party came into her mind. Kate pushed it away. This case was emotive enough as it was without making it any harder on herself by starting to judge the women involved.

As she had said to Golding, innocent until proven guilty.

Patrick heard the door shut and took a deep breath. Kate came into the drawing room like a gale-force wind. She kissed him hard on the mouth.

'I needed that, Pat. What a bloody day.'

She looked tired and as she sat down on the sofa he went to her and removed her shoes. He rubbed her feet and she groaned with pleasure.

'That is *so* good. I only have a couple of hours, for a shower and a quick change and then I've got to go back. A little boy was found at the dump – I expect you heard on the radio?'

He nodded sadly. 'Any idea who did it?'

'No – although it does seem as if the mother had something to do with it. She reckons she left her kids alone in their room – locked in, of course – while she did a moonlight as a prostitute. But whoever she works for must be pretty scary because she won't say how she gets her contacts. Came home before lunchtime and they were gone. We had one kid by then. He'd been dumped by a woman fitting the mother's description in a bin van. Looks like the dead child met the same fate. We've found his feet and torso so far.'

Patrick looked into her deep brown eyes. 'Come to bed with me,' he said softly.

Kate stretched out on the sofa and stared back into his eyes. She felt the pull of him. Ten minutes later they were in the shower, her legs wrapped around his waist while she had the climax of the century. As he came inside her she scraped her nails gently up his back, knowing it would drive him wild. When he collapsed against the side of the shower she started to laugh and he joined in.

'Put me down before you drop me.'

He looked into her face, the face he adored. 'I love you, Kate. Remember that, whatever happens.'

'I love you too, Pat. Are you all right?'

He placed her gently on her feet. Her face was so serious it reminded him of the night they'd first met, when his daughter had been attacked and raped by George Markham, the serial killer. Even to this day they didn't discuss the case. It was taboo between them.

Kate loved Pat but loathed his lifestyle. Now she was going to find out a whole lot more about it and Patrick was frightened of the consequences. Terrified, in fact, because she would walk out on him – he knew that as well as he knew his own name. He should be the one to tell her, but he couldn't. He could not bear to see the bitter disappointment in her eyes.

Leila Cadman was pretty, very pretty, and Kate had always liked her. Since she had come to Grantley as the new forensic pathologist the two women had become firm friends. Today Kate could see the strain of tiredness under Leila's eyes as she outlined her findings.

'It's a young male, about two years old. Been there maybe a week. I can be more accurate after some tests. He's Caucasian, well-nourished . . .'

'Hang on a minute, did you say white?'

Leila nodded.

'Not mixed race?'

'No way.'

Leila could see the confusion on Kate's face.

'And you think the body has been there about a week?'

'I can't say for certain the body parts were on the dump itself for that time, but the injuries on the limbs we have recovered were, in my opinion, caused at least seven days ago. As I said, I will know more after further tests.'

'Jesus Christ, we're looking for a little boy of mixed race. If this child is white, then who is he and why has no one reported him missing?'

Leila looked sad. 'Sign of the times.'

Kate nodded unhappily. 'So it would seem.'

★ ★ ★

Chief Inspector Ratchet was seething with anger. His eyes were darting around his office, taking in all the trappings of success. Would they be enough to get him out of the large and rather deep hole he seemed to have dug himself into? He didn't hold out too much hope. Even his award for bravery seemed to be mocking him.

Ratchet sighed and sipped at his coffee. It was lukewarm and a skin had formed on the top. He felt it adhere to his lip and grimaced at the disgusting feel of it.

Kate came through the door as he was wiping his face. She smiled at him and he motioned for her to take a chair. As she seated herself he decided she really was a good-looking woman. Her hair looked different; it was glossy and thick, longer lately than she had worn it before, and her eyes, though worried, were clear and bright. The deep red lipstick she wore looked sexy on her. All in all, he thought she looked well. The perfect advertisement for a good sex-life. He had a strong suspicion that was what put the spring in her step and the wiggle in her arse.

Feminism never was Ratchet's strong point.

He knew Patrick Kelly well and had been amazed when he had not heard any gossip concerning him and nubile young women since the start of the relationship with Kate. Patrick had been the slag extraordinaire of their mutual lodge, a byword among the other Masons in the getting of young crumpet and keeping of it. But since taking up with Kate he

71

had turned over a new leaf and against his will Ratchet was impressed by the woman before him. She was keeping Kelly on the straight and narrow. Sexually anyway. If only the same could be said for his business dealings.

'How's it going, Kate?'

'Frankly, sir, it's a mess. We have a dead child who is apparently unknown. I have one of the team liaising with other nicks, to see if the body was brought here from another part of the country and dumped. We have another little boy still missing, though his brother was found. I have two perps, both of whom are the mothers and both of whom were placed at the scene yet each one denies any involvement whatsoever. One, I might add, tried to top herself. And on top of all that we're no nearer a solution than we were when we started. Psychologists are trying to talk to the kids but it's basically a waste of time. Both are too young and any good brief would argue that anything we got was put in the child's mouth to further our own agenda.'

Ratchet nodded, but Kate was amazed to see he wasn't really listening.

'Look – I have to talk to you about something else – something personal,' he announced awkwardly.

She raised one eyebrow and then frowned. 'What is it?'

Ratchet twiddled with some pencils before saying carefully, 'Can I get you a coffee, dear?'

Patrick was in Old Compton Street. He slipped

straight through a sex shop and out into a back office, his face plainly registering disgust. A small woman in her sixties was sitting behind a wide mahogany desk there and she grinned at his obvious discomfiture.

Her thick guttural accent grated on his ears but he liked Maya, she was OK. A grafter, she always made sure that whatever job she undertook earned her and her partners money. She was trustworthy, honest by the laws of villainy, and hard. The three main attributes Patrick looked for in his business associates.

Today, though, he had the hump and Maya knew this. It was not hard to understand why either so she made allowances.

'Sit down,' she told him. 'Relax and we'll talk.'

He sat opposite her, and his dark countenance and steely eyes warned her that he was still a force to be reckoned with, and for only the second time in her life she felt real fear.

Maya Baker had come up the hard way. From turning tricks in her early teens she had gradually established a network of porn outlets and gentlemen's clubs. These exclusive little enclaves catered mainly for S&M and spanking, a pastime she found many rich older men rather liked. She made a fortune, adhered to strict rules and was feared by colleagues and workers alike. Maya's Achilles heel was her love of money. Real money. It was this that had led Patrick Kelly to come looking for her.

'You've heard about Leroy, I take it?' she began.

Patrick nodded.

'I take the blame,' Maya admitted. 'I had to remove

him, he was getting to be a pain in the arse. I didn't know you wanted to talk to him or I would have left it a few days. Now, can I help in any way?'

Patrick was impressed despite himself. She had held her hand up, apologised and offered friendship, all in three sentences. Most men he knew would have spent ages beating round the bush before getting to the point. He also admired the way she didn't try to apologise for what she had done, only for the timing. It had happened, was over, and now they must try to repair the damage.

'Do you know anything about Duggan?'

'Enough. Women – Eastern European mainly – plus a few local brasses.' She grinned. 'He was third-rate, Patrick, you knew that deep down.'

'Have you any idea why he was topped and whether Leroy had anything to do with it?'

Maya clasped her heavily jewelled hands tightly together.

'Of course I know. I know everything that happens in Soho. Leroy was planning to branch out. He was putting new girls out and about. Not the usual brasses, Pat, more the Awayday type. You know what I mean: come up from the suburbs for the evening, do a bit of collar then go home again. None of them wanted to embrace the life full-time. Leroy was doing quite well by all accounts but he trod on a few toes. Yours and Duggan's for a start. A couple of the lap dancers were moonlighting for him. Duggan got annoyed, they fell out. That really is the crux of it. But the little black shit wouldn't have had the guts to kill Duggan.'

'So what made you remove Leroy then?'

Maya shrugged and lit a small cigar. 'That's private business, but I will tell you anyway. He was selling skag to a few of my girls. I warned him on more than one occasion and then he poached a couple. I had a word. He fucked me off so I had him wasted. Simple economics, Pat, nothing personal.'

He smiled and wiped his forehead in a comical gesture.

'That's all right then.'

She grinned. 'He was shit on our shoes. Better we finish him now before he became too rich and protected.'

He nodded. 'Who do you think wasted Micky, then?'

'Please, Pat, where do you want me to start? He had more enemies than me and you put together. He courted trouble. It was bound to happen. Plus he was a cokehead and that always causes trouble in business. With his temperament coke was the last thing he needed, don't you think?'

'Heard anything on the pipeline, anything at all?'

'Only speculation. I'll keep my ear to the ground and if I hear anything interesting you'll be the first to know, OK?'

Patrick rubbed his eyes. 'I suppose that will have to do for the time being,' he said tiredly.

Maya reached across the desk and took his hand.

'Micky was an accident waiting to happen. Remember that in all your other business dealings. No matter how good the scam, first look at the perpetrators and decide whether you actually want to be with these people. It's what I do and it's stood me in good stead. Take a hard look at all your workforce on a regular basis, and decide whether they are working *for* you – or against you.'

Pat liked Maya but her constant preaching gave him the hump at times.

'Good advice.' He forced a smile on to his face.

She smiled back. 'You know it makes sense.'

Caroline was in a small holding cell. Her make-up was gone, her skin was blotchy and her heart was rising and falling inside her chest so erratically she wondered if she was going to have a seizure.

She thought of Ivor, and tried to push the horrific images out of her mind. She saw him dead, disfigured, still smiling at her. And closed her eyes once more.

The cell door opened and she was given a thick white mug of tea and a sandwich, which she wolfed down hungrily. The cheap margarine made her grimace. She took a long noisy sip of scalding tea to compensate.

The sergeant watched her. So this was a concerned mother? He wondered what the world was coming to. When his youngest daughter had had mumps he'd not been able to sleep properly for a week through worry. This woman had mislaid a child, possibly killed it, and she was noshing away like it was a family picnic.

But that was what you were dealing with these days. Scum. None of them married. None of them with a man. He saw them every day of his working life and it depressed him. The whole fabric of society was broken and no one seemed to give a fuck.

He slammed and locked the cell door loudly, reminding Caroline of exactly where she was and how much shit she was in.

It certainly made him feel better.

Patrick walked into his house and ordered coffee, the newspaper and a sandwich from his housekeeper. As he settled himself in the conservatory and waited he looked out impatiently over his perfectly manicured lawns. This house got on his nerves at times; it was like a library, too quiet.

He picked up his messages and scanned them. Nothing he could be bothered with right now. Food and sustenance first then his thinking cap on. He was going to have to go into overdrive soon and start getting some answers.

He picked up a pad and started to make a list of people he was going to see. Something was niggling at him but he couldn't put his finger on it.

Sitting in his leather wing chair, Pat thought about Kate. She was going to go ballistic, but he was sure he could talk her down eventually. He only hoped he had the guts to explain everything to her before someone else told her. Kate was so good, so honest, that at times it grieved him.

In the past, he had always felt that people like her were mugs, to be taken advantage of. Now, though, her goodness was the basis for his love and admiration. Kate would never bat away from home, he was as sure of that as he was of his own name.

She was decent.

She had swallowed what had happened with his daughter.

She had known that he had tried to arrange the murder of George Markham. But she had understood his anger, his feelings of fear and loathing because he had not been able to protect his only child. She had seen first-hand how the death of his beloved Mandy had affected him. He had needed to relieve his feelings of inadequacy and hurt, and he had done it in the only way he knew how. He had made sure that George Markham would pay.

However, by a cruel twist of fate, Markham had died at the hands of a prostitute. A fitting end for him.

But Patrick would have had him murdered, and would have slept better at nights knowing he'd done it. He had paid a serious amount of money to see that man dead; it was money he would never have regretted, and even though Markham died a vicious death, an agonising death, Patrick still felt deep inside that he had lost out.

He would do it all over again. Kate knew that; and he thought she could accept it.

But that was the other thing he loved about her: she could see two sides to everything, and unlike most people could admit when she was wrong. If only he shared those attributes, life would have been a lot easier over the years.

He took some deep breaths and concentrated his

mind on what he was doing. The list was growing longer, but held out little hope. It occurred to him then that he was clutching at straws. What he needed was one good kick and he was on his way. If he could tell Kate what was going down before she heard the official version, he would be halfway home. But just the simple fact he owned the lap-dancing club was going to cause him aggravation of the highest calibre.

He wished now he had confided in her about it sooner. She wouldn't have liked it but it was legal and above board, and she might have accepted it. Now it looked as if he'd been trying to get one over on her. That was what would cause the real hag.

The coffee had given him indigestion and he rubbed at his chest. This was all he needed on top of everything else. He glanced at the clock and saw it was getting late. Normally Kate had rung by now. A prickle of fear touched the back of his neck and he shivered. He shrugged off the feeling by reminding himself that she was working on a difficult case that was also very emotive, so he could not expect the usual banter and chatter two or three times a day. But that icy hand still seemed to be gripping his heart.

Hoping to lose himself in the news, he opened the paper. There was an article on the Internet and it depressed him. He had already been offered an in on over six different porn sites. Kate came into his mind again and he sighed. There was real money to be made on the net and he knew that if he got in now, he would coin in a fortune at some point. But for Kate, always Kate, sitting on his shoulder whispering reproaches in his ear.

He smiled. She was a good woman, none better, and since being with her he had not had a moment's inclination to stray, which was strange in as much as Patrick Kelly could have anyone he wanted. Most women he dealt with were there for the taking by the highest bidder. And therein lay the crux of his problem: he didn't want to buy sex, not even with presents and trips abroad as opposed to good hard cash. He wanted sex with someone he loved. Someone he cared about. Though he knew that most men of his acquaintance would have had him committed if he'd said that out loud.

But he would miss Kate so much if she weren't there. He could talk to her about anything. A little voice inside was saying: *Yeah, except your lap-dancing club and the other businesses she knows nothing about.* He forced the voice from his mind and concentrated on the newspaper article.

When the phone rang at last, it wasn't Kate. It was more trouble.

Taking a deep breath, Pat listened to a high-pitched female voice telling him that four of the hostesses had not turned in and that the others were all handing in their notice. Patrick slammed down the phone and quelled an urge to throw it through the glass window of the conservatory and into the pool. Instead he went up to his bedroom and had a long hot shower. It occurred to him then that he was waiting for something to happen. It was an oppressive feeling, bearing down on him all the time.

As he stepped from the shower he felt the stab of indigestion again. This time it was a slow burn. He went to the bedside cabinet and ate a couple of Remagels, chewing them furiously to try and counteract the pain in his chest. Then he picked up the phone and dialled Kate's extension. A recorded message came on and he replaced the receiver. He dialled her mobile and was once more greeted by voicemail.

He was getting annoyed now, and paranoid. Was she avoiding him? But he knew that was silly. He was getting things out of proportion.

Opening the wardrobe, he pulled out a dressing gown. Without knowing why, he opened Kate's side of the wardrobe and then he knew what was bothering him so much. Just seeing her clothes there had quietened his racing heart. For one awful moment, he thought she might have left him. It had been in the back of his mind all day. He had half expected to see empty closets.

When he heard the front door slam he felt faint with relief, listening with joy to the sound of her heels on the stairs. As she burst through the bedroom door he was smiling widely, so pleased to see her he felt his whole body would burst.

Then she stopped dead and stared at him coldly.

'You have some explaining to do, Patrick Kelly, and believe me when I say it had better be fucking good!'

Chapter Four

Kate's eyes were hard. Patrick had made a fool of her and she was not going to forgive him.

'Listen, Kate . . .'

She shook her head angrily. 'No, *you* bloody listen. I had to sit there like a right lemon while Ratchet told me in no uncertain terms that I was compromised by the man I lived with. He told me about your bloody lap-dancing club . . . he told me *everything*. I have broken bread apparently, in this very house, with a man who has recently been murdered – murdered in the club *you* owned with him. A club run for scum, by scum. So you had better have a good excuse, Pat, a damn good excuse. I also understand that you're a suspect in the murder enquiry, though no one has actually come out with that gem yet. But I know they would have to have you bang to rights before attempting that one. You'd better get all your Masonic friends around you like a cloak, boy. They want you bad. Even Ratchet was expecting me to enlighten him about you and what you're up to nowadays.' She looked demented. Even her hair bristled with fury. He had never wanted her more than at this moment.

'Do you know something, I could cheerfully murder you right now,' she burst out. 'I have a dead child and the possible attempted murder of other children to contend with and now I find that I have been sharing a bed with a lying, scheming bastard. You *promised* me, Pat, you *swore* that your days of ducking and diving were over. I must have been bloody mad to have ever believed one word that came out of your mouth. You said that the sex game was over, remember? Over and done with. Now I find out you're involved with murderers and whores as usual . . .'

'The lap-dancing club is perfectly legal,' he said lamely.

She nodded furiously. 'Oh, I'm aware of that. Don't try and tell *me* the law, arsehole. I *know* the bloody law, boy. But it is *morally* wrong and you know it. You know I constantly have to deal with the fallout of what people like you do in their *legal* businesses. I've got a prostitute in a cell in Grantley nick, thanks to people like you. After Mandy, and that murdering bastard Markham's taste for porn and easy sex, I thought you might have finally learned something about the so-called legal business of whoring, but no. Money's at the root of everything with you, isn't it? Bloody money.'

She paused and took a painful breath. Then: 'Try the girls out first, did you? I understand that was Duggan's forte. A bit of strange, as you call it. Too strange to sit in on business dinners – you had me for that, I assume. Nice to have someone who didn't look like a grandchild sitting beside you, eh?'

He winced at the vitriol in her words.

'Once more you have made a blasted fool of me, Pat. I had to forgive and forget, even when you were going to murder George Markham. I actually understood where you were coming from and I went against every belief I had ever held to hang on to you, to keep you in my life. Well, I have finally had enough of it, of all you believe in and all you seem to think you can do without even considering how it affects me. You've blown it, boy. Better dust off the phone book, but then again maybe not. They'll all be too old for you by now, eh?'

'Don't, Kate. Don't say things you will regret.'

She looked into his face, and shaking her head slowly she said quietly, 'I don't need you, Pat, not like you think I do. I've learned so much from you over the last few years, and do you know what the main thing is? Cover your own arse. And that, Patrick, is exactly what I intend to do.'

She pushed past him and started pulling clothes from drawers, piling them on the bed.

He watched her in distress. 'Please, Kate, listen to me. I never thought you'd need to know.'

She faced him, her anger mounting as she looked at his handsome face.

'You never thought, period. Good *old* Kate, eh? The filth, the *Old* Bill. Mrs Respectable hanging on your arm. Maybe you thought I was a bit of added protection, eh?'

He grabbed her hand and dragged her round to face him, his own anger surfacing then.

'I didn't tell you because I knew you would act this way. I knew you hated what I did. But if I don't do it, someone else will.'

Kate laughed nastily and shook her head mockingly, a gesture she knew would infuriate him.

'Remember when that girl died in your scummy, shitty massage parlour? Remember what you said then? You felt responsible for her. You couldn't protect Mandy, and you couldn't protect her. I bet you don't even remember her name now, do you? Be honest with me. What the fuck was her name, eh?'

She could see the confusion on his face and pushed him away from her.

'I thought so. Crocodile tears then, and crocodile tears now. You really are a piece of work, Kelly. But then, I expect you know that.'

She pulled a couple of suits from the wardrobe and, bundling everything in her arms, she stalked from the room. Patrick followed her, nonplussed, unable to talk because he knew she was really going to explode at some point and what she needed now was a cooling-off period. He followed her down the stairs and into the hallway. She dragged the front door open and stormed across the drive, knickers and bras dropping on to the gravel at regular intervals.

As she opened the car door and threw her clothes inside she shouted over her shoulder: 'By the way, Pat, her name was Gillian Enderby. A pretty girl, a drug addict. Remember her now?' Slamming the car door, she wheel-spinned off the drive and was gone.

He stood watching her, bereft, angry and chastened. Gillian Enderby's mother came back to mind then: her hatred of him and subsequent attack. Sighing heavily, he walked back into the house.

Willy had a large Scotch waiting in the den and Patrick took it without a word.

'I had a feeling she might have the hump, Pat. It'll pass, she's a sensible girl.'

Kate drove back to the station at speed. Her temper was so acute she could taste it. It was a metallic taste, reminiscent of sucking a penny when she was a child. That Patrick could have been a part of all that without telling her spoke volumes. Now Duggan was dead, and Pat was going to be questioned at some point. In fact, Ratchet had insinuated that *he had to have been involved*. Those were his words exactly. Off the record, of course. Ratchet would never actually admit to his own name unless it was on a sworn affidavit, and Kate had her doubts about that even.

Sweet Jesus, she was so upset that she could have hurt Pat physically. How could you live with, sleep and talk with a man, and yet know absolutely nothing about him? She saw now that all his talk of turning over a new leaf was just that – talk, plain and simple. He had bought into Girlie Girls almost immediately, it seemed. But it had been a strip club first, a few hostesses and a late drinking licence.

The metallic taste was back and she opened a pack of Juicy Fruit chewing gum she kept in the ashtray of her car. As she chewed, the sweet taste brought tears to her eyes, but she knew they hadn't been far away. All afternoon she had felt like crying. She let them flow now, needing the release.

Her mobile rang and she looked at it. Patrick's number flashed up. She ignored it, driving faster.

He was old news now. She had to accept that fact and get on with what she was doing. Concentrate on finding out what had happened to the children. Put him on the backburner.

He had humiliated her in front of her boss and for that she would never forgive him. When Ratchet had explained that if and when Patrick was interviewed, the chances were she would be too, Kate had felt an animal strength surge into her body that had frightened her. The urge to swing back her arm and fell her sanctimonious boss to the floor with one punch had been almost overpowering. He knew that she was well aware of his close personal friendship and even business dealings with Patrick Kelly.

Between them she was pushed to her limit.

Well, Ratchet she must live with, he was her superior, but Patrick Kelly was her lover and as such was dispensable.

She *would* make sure of that.

DC Golding listened to the phone message three times. He was smiling with glee. Wait until he put this one round the canteen! Wait until Kate Burrows found out that he had listened to her voicemail.

No, damn it. As soon as he opened his mouth she

would know where the rumour came from. But he would store it up for future reference. Ratchet was interested in all her doings and would be kept up to date. For a price, of course. It would do that uppity bitch good to be knocked down a peg or two, and Golding was just the man to do it.

As he lit a cigarette Kate's voice reached him from behind.

'Comfortable, are we? Can I get you anything? Coffee? Tea? Or how about a verbal warning?'

He jumped up fast, nearly unbalancing a pile of papers on her desk.

'Sorry, ma'am. I was just taking five minutes off . . .'

'That's what the canteen is for. Remember that in future.'

She held the door open for him and he walked sheepishly from the room. She had needed an outlet for her anger and Golding, being the two-faced rat he was, had given it to her. The thought pleased her and she smiled. Her first real smile for hours.

She listened to Patrick's message twice before deleting it. If he loved her so much, he should have thought long and hard before taking on Girlie Girls. Even the name of the club made her cringe. She wondered how often he had visited the place. It just did not bear thinking about.

What she needed now was work, and plenty of it. And that was exactly what she had. She only wished it was a common or garden murder instead of a child's. She had enough heartache as it was.

As she turned on her computer she sighed. She would have laid money that Patrick was above board with her, but she should have learned her lesson from her ex-husband Dan. Men could not be faithful, honest or true. It just wasn't in their natures.

But she would miss Patrick Kelly. Christ Himself knew, she would miss him.

Willy followed as Patrick walked into his solicitor's office. Kate was gone and Willy had a feeling that she was not coming back, whatever he'd said to his boss. He had warned Pat as much when he'd started up Girlie Girls, and Pat being Pat had told him to keep out of it. Unlike Renée, Pat's late wife, Kate wouldn't stand for crooked business dealings. How could she, when she spent her whole working life trying to put them to rights? He could not for the life of him see how Patrick Kelly had believed he would get away with it all.

Willy nodded to himself sagely. Yes, Pat was a mug and no mistake. If Willy himself had been lucky enough to get someone like Kate he would never have ballsed it up for money, especially money he didn't need.

As Patrick outlined his current problems to his solicitor, James Spalding, Willy's thoughts started to wander and he had difficulty keeping his mind on what was being said. It was only when he heard Patrick say that he had been with Kate the night Duggan died that he was brought sharply back to the present.

Because he knew that his boss had just lied.

Patrick Kelly had been in negotiation with a known face about distributing certain videos of the more exotic nature. In fact, they were so hot they were burning the hands of the two blokes who wanted to get rid of them. Another worry for Patrick was that one of the men was Lucas Browning. Someone Pat didn't like much and had no intention of working with. It was a lucrative offer, but Patrick had shied off – and Kate had been foremost in his mind when he had declined to get involved.

Willy understood that he would not be asked to alibi his mate, because he wasn't exactly an upstanding member of the community himself. Whereas Kate was beyond reproach. But how she would react to being used like this was debatable. Especially after the shock of the clubs. Patrick Kelly was digging himself in deeper and deeper.

Willy wondered if the man was having a mid-life crisis. He had read about them in *Woman's Own* the last time he was at the doctor's. They sounded serious. Worse than a woman's change, by all accounts. Or so the article had said.

Whatever was wrong with Pat, Willy wished he would sort it out so they could all get back to normal. When *he* was more on the ball than his boss, times were definitely dangerous.

Even Willy Gabney knew that much.

Kate looked at the photograph of the dead child's shoe and felt an urge to cry. There were no local children missing of the same age and size. But how on earth could a small child be dead and no one have reported them missing? What on earth could lie behind all this?

The mother had to be missing her child, or was she dead too? That seemed the most likely explanation. But if so, where the hell was her body? And how had the child and the woman not been reported missing?

That was easier to explain, Kate conceded with a sigh. So many people remained anonymous nowadays. A true sign of the times. You only had to read the papers – people dead for weeks before the neighbours noticed a rancid smell. But they were usually old people who had always kept themselves to themselves. How could you do that with a toddler?

Small children were hard work. They needed food, nappies and trips to the park on a regular basis. But that was for normal people and Kate knew that they were soon going to be the minority. Or at least that's how it seemed to her. Some of the characters she dealt with would blow the average person's mind. Scummy types, people who saw their own children as nothing. Who used and abused them without a second's thought.

Look at Caroline and Regina.

Both mothers, both unable to distinguish between right and wrong. Though in fairness to Caroline she at least seemed to do what she did for her kids' sake. Regina seemed to see hers merely as things that just happened to be there, something she had done. She had produced three good-looking and completely uncared-for kids and no one, including Social Services, seemed to think this was in any way abnormal, or that the way such families lived was totally and utterly wrong. That kids were entitled to be treated well, fed well and loved well. That they had the right to be educated from birth to become regular people.

Kate frequently visited homes where the sons and daughters were already parents, yet still at school. Dirty, filthy people who reproduced at an alarming rate then dumped their kids on the streets to get them out of their hair. Three- and four-year-olds playing out all day and into the night. No one checking on them, no one worried they might be taken away.

She wiped a hand across her face and sighed. This was just her anger, manifesting itself against other people instead of against Patrick. It was he who was making her feel like this. Making her feel that all her efforts were futile. She had to pull herself together. But she was hurting so much, it was a physical pain.

Who did the tiny trainer belong to? What was his sad little story, and would she ever be able to piece it together so that at least, for once in his short life, someone cared enough to find out what had happened to him?

Lucas Browning was not the usual sort of pimp. In fact he was as unlike a pimp as anyone could imagine. For a start he was grotesquely fat, so big he had trouble walking and breathing and spent most of his time in his flat in Hoxton ensconced in a large armchair. He slept there, he ate there, he even had sex there – not an easy feat by anyone's standards.

But he scared the girls easily.

He obtained them from an ad in the local papers, recruiting for escort services and promising big gains financially. They came running. Then he talked them through what he expected from them, and gave them a large drink of whatever took their fancy. This he laced with Valium or sometimes Norval, depending on how he felt.

Two friends would then give them the business while Lucas watched, and while he videoed it. Most of the girls were from nice homes, at school or college, looking for a bit of escort work to tide them over.

He dragged them deep into a pit of despair and then used them. Threatened them with exposure, with violence, and worst of all – with a repeat performance. Once they saw the video, he had them and he knew it. He also had their address, their phone number; he even knew what school they went to and what their siblings' names were. He came over like a big fat puppy at first, and they warmed to him. He was such a nice man. They confided in him. Told him their little wants and dreams. And Lucas let them believe their dreams were within their grasp.

At first, that is.

After a year or two he let the clubs or the pimps have them. They were too jaded now for his clientèle who liked them young and fresh. Liked them when they were still nervous, still new to it.

All in all Lucas had a good little earner without even getting out of his chair. This appealed to his lazy nature. And once they had done the delights for him, with his disgusting body, they would do it for *anyone*. It was all about breaking down taboos, breaking down spirits, and Lucas was an undisputed master of that.

Such was the mind of Lucas Browning.

Now he had a little problem and was wondering how to solve it without getting into too much trouble.

A plump young girl with thick red hair and fat thighs was sitting opposite him, smiling. But he wasn't seeing her, he was seeing Micky Duggan. A dead Micky Duggan.

'Has Kelly been into the club, do you know?'

Clarissa Shelly shook her head. 'Not that I know of, but they ain't going to tell me, are they?' She lit a cigarette and he saw that her fingers were stained with nicotine. 'Can I go now, please?'

'No, you can't fucking go yet.'

She sat back in her chair and smoked nervously, taking little puffs and inhaling loudly.

'When was the last time you schlepped Duggan?'

'A week ago, ten days. I don't remember.'

He could see her mind wandering, knew she was terrified and toyed with the idea of making her do something disgusting just for the hell of it. She still looked fresh enough to appeal to him, but Lucas was a worried man. He would have an easier time trying to raise the *Titanic* at this moment.

'Try and get round Broughton, see what you can get out of him.'

She nodded.

'Keep me posted.'

She was grateful that the meeting was over. She had been let into the flat by one of Browning's henchmen and they always made her nervous.

As she stood up Lucas grinned at her.

'You're a good girl, Clarissa. I've heard nice things about you.'

She smiled in relief. 'Thank you, Mr Browning.'

He smiled again, this time showing his black broken teeth. 'You're welcome.'

He watched her make her escape as fast as possible and grinned again. She had taken to the life and didn't even realise it yet. But she would, and when she did it would destroy her. Whores were born, not made. He had proved that over and over again.

Ratchet looked at Kate and nodded to her to brief him.

'We have witnesses that put both mothers at the scenes,' she said. 'They have both had ID parades and were both picked out. We have to charge them. Regina Carlton is unfit to be questioned any more. She was taken to Rampton after her suicide attempt. The second mother is still proclaiming her innocence and is still missing one child. On top of all this, we've been searching for two days and can come up with nothing. We also have the body, minus head and arms, of a child who seems to have been born and raised with no one knowing anything about him. We have tried all over the country and cannot find a DNA match for him. If it wasn't so sad it would be laughable.'

Ratchet felt a spark of pity for her. She was a good policewoman, was Kate Burrows, none better. If anyone could piece all this together it was she.

'What extras do you need?' he asked.

'Only manpower really. The national press are going to start screaming for a result soon, you know they are. We need to get on top of this and now.'

He nodded agreement.

'They want me to bring in someone else, Kate, but you must have expected this. Kelly's position is delicate at the moment. If the press were to get wind of it . . .' He left the statement hanging in the air for maximum effect.

Kate sighed heavily. She *had* been expecting this, only not quite so quickly.

'Fuck Patrick Kelly.'

'I'll leave that to you, Kate.'

'Well, sir, you and I both have something in common then, eh? Because Pat will use anyone and anything to get himself out of this mess and if he has to fuck one of us to do it he will.'

She was pleased to see the man before her go pale.

'You knew him long before I did. I mean, you are a close personal friend of his, aren't you?' A hint of malice lay beneath the apparently artless question. Kate was enjoying herself. The last thing she had expected to do today, under the circumstances.

Her eyes travelled towards the window and she felt her heart sink as she saw the carrion that passed for the media converging once more outside the police station. She knew that Ratchet was also aware of them. This time she avoided eye contact with her boss.

Marianne Bigby was pretty in a vacuous way. From her dyed hair, carefully permed and styled, to the nose and boob jobs, she was every inch the woman a bad man might consider as a life partner.

As she let Patrick Kelly into her home she was talking. Marianne never stopped talking; it was her biggest failing. Because when she talked she moaned. She also talked fast. Fast and Furious was her nickname.

'It took you long enough to get your arse round here, Kelly. I want me bleeding compensation, I do, and it had better be good, too. No pennies and halfpennies, thank you very much. And I'll tell you something else: that ponce left me in debt up to me eyebrows. I knew he was going to get himself murdered, the stupid fucker! I told him over and over, "You'll get murdered, you will, if you ain't careful . . ."'

Patrick and Willy were on auto-pilot. Patrick knew her well enough not to listen until she started crying, a trick Micky Duggan had taught him. Eventually the tears started and he took the opportunity to talk to her.

'Come on, Mal, I wouldn't see you without a couple of quid, girl. You know that.'

She sniffed loudly. 'If he was here now, Pat, I'd kill the ponce myself. Imagine him getting topped like that. I mean, the embarrassment for me! Not like he

went down to Old Bill or got himself shot. Oh no, he
had to get bashed up, him. Useless ponce he was . . .
But that was him all over, no *thought* for anyone else.
I mean, where's the prestige in that, eh? But I warned
him about Broughton. I fucking warned him when
the ponce came round here, all testosterone and
baseball bats. I saw him off that time. On me own as
usual because that cunt Micky was strumping something in the club.' She pointed one long red nail in
Patrick's face.

'I blame you for it all. Letting him run that club –
him, who couldn't run a bloody race without fourteen
guide dogs and a police escort! Thanks to you he was
dragged into gambling dens and the like. You know
what a fucker he was for the horses and that. Like a
kid in a candy store he was with all that dough.
Money coming out of his arse and betting like there
was no tomorrow. Him who couldn't win a fucking
argument.'

'Not with you anyway, girl. He couldn't get a
fucking word in!' Willy's voice seemed to shut her up
for a second.

She went over to him and, wagging her head with
each word, she said shrilly, 'I am the grieving bleeding
widow, thank you very much.'

By now, Patrick had had enough. 'Sit down and
shut up for two minutes, Mal. You are getting comp
so put a fucking sock in it.'

'The kids are in private school. I have the house,
this flat, me car . . .'

'It will all be taken care of,' he said wearily. 'Now

why did Broughton come round here with baseball bats?'

Marianne shook her head as if she didn't understand what he was asking her. 'Don't you know?'

Patrick took a deep breath and said as evenly as he could, 'No, Mal, I don't know. That's why I am asking you.'

For the first time she fell quiet. Finally she said, 'He was after Micky over the money you took from the club.'

Patrick screwed up his eyes. 'What are you on about? It's my money – it's my club.'

She stared into his face, the lines of strain round her eyes etched into her fake tan.

'Not the takings, Pat. The five hundred grand the Russian bloke left there.'

Patrick felt as if he had been pole-axed.

'Five hundred grand, left in *my* club by a fucking Russian? Are you on drugs, Mal, or are you off your fucking skull? What Russian?'

'Mr Stravaneely or something. He has a right weird name, I don't know what it is. He does the mortgages and that for the big Russian drug dealers.'

Patrick felt his heart sink into his bowels.

'I thought you were in on it with him? That's the impression I got. They're using the club for transfers of money and as a front.' She was babbling now in fear. 'You must have known, Pat.'

'Fuck me, Pat. You're a dead man,' Willy commented. As if he didn't know.

'Is anyone else involved?' he pressed Marianne.

She shrugged. 'I only know about Broughton. But you know what he's like – probably has half of Silvertown in it with him. Couldn't piss on his own, him.' She could see the fear on Kelly's face and it was frightening her. If *he* was scared then there really was something to be scared of.

As he walked from her flat she called out shakily, 'Don't you forget my comp. I want it before you're trashed, thank you very much.'

'One thing I will give Mal, she knows how to get round a bloke, Pat. No wonder poor old Duggan was like he was, listening to that going all hours of the day and night.'

'We are well in the shit, Willy,' said Patrick hollowly.

Willy unlocked the door to the Rolls. 'That's one way of putting it, I suppose.'

'Where's the latest Russian hang-out?'

'Girlie Girls, from what she said, mate,' Willy told him, starting up the engine. 'Perhaps you should show your boat there at some point. Save all the hag of looking for them, like. Let them find you.'

'They'll find me when they want me.'

'Wise words. Good job you fell out with Kate. They would love to get their hands on her, Pat. They live by bent Old Bill. Any bent Home Office, in fact. I mean, they do everything now. Passports, guns, you name it. They call parts of Notting Hill "Moscow" these days.'

'Willy,' Patrick's voice was low. 'Why don't you shut the fuck up?'

They drove out of London in silence.

WPC Hart put a mug of coffee on Kate's desk.

'You look tired, ma'am.'

Kate stretched. 'I am. Anything I need to know?'

'You had a phone call earlier,' the girl informed her. 'Robert something or other. Social Services – about Regina Carlton. I said you would call him back tomorrow.'

Kate yawned. 'Thanks, pet. Get yourself off home.'

The WPC nodded and said gently, 'That's what you should be doing.'

The phone rang and Kate picked it up. 'Hello, Lizzy. How're things?'

There was joy in her voice to receive the call and, smiling goodbye, the constable left her alone.

Kate listened to all her daughter's doings in Australia. It was Lizzy's third visit there and Kate had a strong feeling she wasn't going to come back this time. She didn't mind. Australia fitted Lizzy like a glove and Kate knew that she was happy out there. In the sun, in the land of youth. She so wanted her daughter to be happy.

'How's Granny?'

Lizzy laughed. 'Loving it as usual. Going to the beach all day, then getting ready for a barbecue.'

'Sounds good. Any nice boys about?'

Lizzy quietened. 'A few, nothing spectacular.'

Since Kate had read her daughter's shocking diary entries all those years ago when she was a schoolgirl, any mention of boys, men or sex always left them both feeling uncomfortable. Kate was again reminded of how you could never fully know someone, not really. It seemed to be the story of her life.

She had thought she was lucky with her teenage daughter and then found out that Lizzy was on drugs and sleeping with anyone who had a joint, a pleasing face or a nice car to offer. Afterwards Lizzy had taken an overdose; Kate had picked up the pieces as best she could and they had all somehow got on with their lives.

Nearly losing her daughter had been a turning point for Kate. She had turned to Patrick Kelly.

Now she listened to Lizzy rabbiting on and thanked God her child was better again. But the sound of her voice, echoing down the phone line, made Kate feel lonelier than ever.

Her eyes strayed to the picture of the little Nike trainer. It was an image she knew she would never forget.

'I miss you, darling.'

'I miss you too, Mum. How's Patrick?'

'Oh, he's fine. You know Pat – nothing fazes him.'

Lizzy missed the sarcasm in her mother's voice. 'Give him my love. 'Bye.'

And she was gone.

Kate stared at the receiver for long moments, then replaced it gently. What she ought to do was get back to her own house and air the place. Lizzy would miss living at Pat's, that was for sure. Another reason for her to stay on in Australia. Kate chided herself for thinking such things about her own daughter but inwardly acknowledged they were true. Lizzy always looked after number one. It was something she had been taught by her father. Dan had been the same. Only interested in what he wanted, needed, cared about.

Kate sighed heavily. Why should Lizzy worry? She was young and the young had no real cares. Life seemed so long still, and they had no idea how quickly it passed by.

Kate sipped her lukewarm coffee, grateful for the rush of caffeine. She was missing Patrick so much it hurt.

She had been the same after Dan had gone. Dan the womaniser. Dan who thought he could get through life with a set of white teeth and a big cock. She knew how to pick them all right.

She could hear phones ringing, people talking, lives being lived. It all seemed separate from her. She had had everything she'd wanted stripped from her by a few choice words from Ratchet and she knew she could never take Pat on again.

No matter how much she might want to.

Chapter Five

'Forensically, we can put both mothers at the scene.'

Kate nodded, then commented, 'You could put them with the children at any time, surely, because they are in such close contact.'

'That's true, but I can only report what I've found and that's evidence to suggest that both mothers were at the scenes too.'

Kate wiped a hand across her face.

'Any good brief will shoot you down in flames,' she said. 'Was there anything at all from the sites that was found on the mothers' clothes or shoes?'

'Nothing too positive,' Leila told her. 'We have taken dirt samples from where they live to get comparisons. I bet they'll be near enough to rule them out.'

She stared at her friend. Kate looked terrible. 'You should think about getting help on this one, Kate.'

Kate took a long drag on her cigarette. 'Ratchet thinks so too. What he wants, though, is me out of the way. It'd make his life a lot easier.'

Leila sat down and said gently, 'You can choose someone yourself, Kate. Someone who has dealt with this type of crime before. Face it, they would be working *with* you, not against you. Choose the person yourself and you guarantee that. If Ratchet chooses, they'll row you out.'

Kate's eyes scanned the small office. 'It's a dump, Leila, but it's *my* dump. Ratchet is worried about my relationship with Patrick. He thinks shit will stick . . .'

Leila smiled, showing crooked white teeth. 'Which it will, love. But you'll weather it. You are one of the most able officers I know. Even Ratchet can't dispute that. You've put away a lot of bodies over the years, mate. That can't be forgotten by anyone. It's all there in black and white. Plus your relationship with Patrick has given you quite a bit of kudos. Old Bill love real villains, even you must have realised that. Pull in a good colleague, Kate. Get some help. Specialist help.'

'Perhaps you're right.'

Leila pinched Kate's cigarette and inhaled.

'I thought you'd given up?'

'Only in public. In private, I puff away like the Magic Dragon.'

Kate laughed. 'Fancy a drink later?'

Leila nodded. 'I thought you'd never ask.'

'I can't stop thinking about that little boy, Ivor. Where the hell could he be?'

Leila shrugged. 'He must be dead. It's been nearly four days now. Any more from the mother?'

'Not a dicky bird. Still insisting that she left them all

night and they were gone when she got home. The father was in Liverpool – he has a watertight alibi. No one else has a key to the place, the kids were locked in the room. In reality, what she's saying is unbelievable. But she has never deviated from it.'

Leila closed her eyes. 'Look, Kate, once her brief gets in the heavy mob, you won't get near her. They will have psychiatric reports – the works. You need someone *now*. Let me look through my files and see who I can find, eh? If she was placed at the scene, you'll have something to work with. Hopefully, the boy will turn up alive. Until then, I would give her the sympathy vote, and hope against hope that she can be brought to court with a bit more than you have now.'

Kate was tired, she was also worried and her face looked older than usual. She had to find the child and fast.

'I am going to interview Anderson again at five,' she said. 'All she seems to do is eat. And I mean eat. Christ knows what's going through her mind. But I have to charge her today and charge her I will, whatever her brief says. She is in her right mind, I would lay money on that. I think she is laughing at us.'

Leila grinned. 'Wouldn't be the first time. Certainly won't be the last.'

'That's true. A late drink then, eh?'

'Ring me on my mobile. In fact, why not come to the flat? I'll do a few sandwiches.'

'You've got me – I'll see you later. And please, do look through the files – see if you can come up with someone relatively normal for me to work with.'

Kate watched Leila's pert bottom wiggle out of her office, and she smiled her first real smile of the day. Leila was sexy and funny. She was also a good friend, and Kate badly needed one of those at this moment in time.

Ratchet is out to get me, she thought. Pat is on his way to a capture and I want to make sure I don't go down with him.

Well, she had a few cards up her sleeve yet. So they had both better watch out. Kate Burrows was angry and the sooner Kelly and Ratchet realised that, the better.

David Mentorn was a happy child. It was in his nature.

As he staggered across the parkland in his heavily soiled shoes, he was laughing. Jonathan Light, his friend and co-conspirator, was also giggling. Both blond, blue-eyed and of stocky build, the two boys could have been brothers. Today they were playing truant from school. At twelve, they thought they knew more than their parents and teachers and they hopped off now and again for an adventure.

David's mother was a lone parent, his father having disappeared a few years earlier. She worked in London and commuted there daily. Jonathan's mother, on the other hand, didn't work and was known to be here, there and everywhere all day. No one seemed to care what the boys got up to.

As they approached the fence leading to the gravel

pits they were still laughing. They knew they could make as much noise as they liked. The mud on their boots was heavy, and when Jonathan started walking like Frankenstein's monster, David rolled to the ground doubled up with mirth. It was an action he soon regretted.

As he rolled, he could see underneath the bushes. A black bag had been stuffed beneath them. This wasn't unusual in itself, but a small blue swollen hand was hanging out of it. David immediately stopped his rolling, and the laughter died in his chest.

Jonathan thought he was still joking and kicked him amiably. Then he watched as his friend rose on to his knees and started to crawl away.

'Look under the bloody hedge,' David said hoarsely. 'There's a person.'

Jonathan looked under the hedgerow and caught his breath. 'What are we going to do?'

David sat up and swallowed deeply. 'We'll have to tell someone.'

Jonathan nodded; all the while his brain was working overtime. 'We'll get in right trouble.'

David pulled himself to his feet. 'Tough, we have to tell. Let's get one of the workmen from the gravel pit. They'll know what to do.'

They slipped through the hole in the fence.

'The police will want to talk to us.'

Despite himself, Jonathan was beginning to get excited. The two lads were now part of something bigger than anything they could ever have imagined.

Kate saw Patrick out of the corner of her eye and felt the familiar pull of him. As he approached her car, she turned to face him. She knew what he wanted, and she was determined that he would not get it.

'Please, Kate. I just want a word.'

She ignored him. As she unlocked her car she said, 'Go away, Pat. Haven't you caused me enough grief?'

He took her arm roughly and walked her towards his BMW. Kate knew she was in full view of the police station and had no choice but to walk with him. Inside his car, she was fuming.

'How dare you do this to me!'

His eyes were pleading and she knew that she must not look at him. Or listen to him; if she did so, she would be lost. He had the knack of talking her round.

'I'm sorry, love, but I have to talk to you.' He was searching her face for any signs of softness.

'If you think a few choice words will change what's happened,' she said heatedly, 'then you are even more arrogant than I thought. You consistently lied to me—'

'I never lied, I just never told you everything. That's the difference.'

'The result is the same. You did things you knew would compromise me, Patrick. What happened to truth and trust and honesty? Now you're in the shit, and I am not going to get pulled in with you. You promised me a good life . . .'

Patrick was getting angry himself now. He found her more alluring now than he ever had before. He adored her and she knew it. The club meant nothing to him really. Its appeal was monetary and that was that.

'Listen, Kate, I need you more now than I've ever needed anyone. The love I have for you is immense. I care more about you than any other living being. When you're not there I miss you beside me in the morning, I miss reading the bloody papers and drinking coffee with you. I miss you in bed with me. I miss you so much it hurts, but I am not here to ask you to come back, love. I'm here to ask you a favour.'

She gasped at his bare-faced cheek. 'A *what*?'

He stared into her eyes. 'I need a favour, Kate.'

'You have a bloody brass neck, Patrick Kelly. After humiliating me in front of my boss, suppressing information you knew could put me in a very difficult situation, you then sit here and ask me for a fucking favour. Do I look that stupid?'

'Do you know something, Kate? You still talk like Old Bill, don't you,' Patrick said irritably. ' "Suppressing information". Why can't you say "I kept stumm", like normal people.'

Kate's eyes were hard now. 'Because, unlike your so-called normal people, I happen to have half a brain and I don't like to talk like a cheap-rate gangster. Forgive me, Patrick, present company excepted, of course.'

The barb hit home and she saw he was fuming.

'You lairy bitch. Have a pop at me – go on. I know you better than you know yourself. I know *everything* about you, woman. You can come the big "I Am"

111

with those little shitbags in that nick but don't you *dare* to use that tone with me, lady. I picked you up and brushed you down after that little mare Lizzy shagged half of Grantley and popped enough pills to get the whole town high. I never threw it in your face, mate. I listened to you going on about that fucking geek Dan, and I got shot of him for you, so don't you "gangster" me. When it suits you, I'm useful. I admit I am not kosher, not by your standards anyway, and if a few punters want to look at some tits what's the bloody problem? As long as I don't show them *yours* what's the big fucking deal?'

She stared into his face; it was still the face she loved. The face she wanted beside her. Even if he was a little greyer, a little more wrinkled. He was gorgeous and she would never get over the sheer sexuality of him. But he was not getting away with this.

'Don't talk to me like I'm one of your little gangster sluts, Patrick Kelly.'

He slapped her hand in annoyance. 'Will you stop calling me Patrick Kelly! You sound like me bleeding mother.'

'Don't you touch me like that. Always violence with you, isn't it? The hard man, the big bloke. Well, you don't impress me, Patrick Kelly. You don't impress me one bit. You lied, schemed and broke all the trust I thought we had. I wanted something you could never give me, and that was honesty. I am always honest with you, about everything, but then I don't need to duck and dive, do I? I don't do anything that would offend you or make you feel disgusted.'

He was sorry for her. He knew she was being truthful, he knew how much she was hurting. He loved her and to see her so hurt made him feel bad. But he had an agenda and he had to keep that in mind.

'I need you, Kate,' he told her steadily. 'I want to ask you to do something for me that I know will make you crazy. But I will ask it, darling, because you owe it to me. I would do it for you at the drop of a hat.'

Kate was quiet at the anxiety in his words. She could feel the underlying fear in him and she was hushed by it.

'I'm in shit so deep you would not believe it,' he went on. 'I've got myself into a situation that I cannot get out of without hurting some people very badly. I am telling you this because you wanted honesty and, by fuck, you'll get it this time. I need you to go against everything you believe in to help me, but I know you will, once I explain it all to you.'

He looked into her strained face, at the deep-set eyes, flashing with fear, at her straight nose, her high cheekbones, and he felt an urge to kiss her. But he knew that was not going to happen. He had blown it and it would take time to regain her trust. Time that he didn't have.

'My God, Pat, what have you done?' Her voice was low and it angered him. She thought he had killed Duggan. He realised that now and it hurt.

'I have done nothing except become a partner in a business. I swear to God, Kate, that is the truth. But I need you to do something for me.' He tried to take her hand and she shrugged him off. 'I want you to say I was with you the night Duggan died.'

She thought back to that night and realised he had been gone most of the evening, supposedly seeing a man about a golf course.

'Where were you, Patrick? Who were you with if you weren't with Duggan?'

He looked at the dashboard, avoiding her eyes. 'I can't tell you that.'

'Were you with a woman or a man?'

'I can't divulge that information, Kate. I am sorry.'

Her face screwed up in abject disbelief. 'You want me to lie for you, swear an affidavit for you and you won't even tell me where you were, or who you were with?'

He shrugged. 'Basically, yeah.'

She shook her head furiously. 'No chance, mate. I am sure you have plenty of cronies willing to lie for you – can't you get one of them to do it? Why must it be me, eh?'

'Because no one would doubt you, and I could be off the hook and out and about finding out who *did* kill Micky and why they want it to look like it was me. Another thing, before you carry on, I am on someone's wanted list now as well. So if they get their way you will be burying me, darling.'

They were both quiet and then he said softly, 'I have never asked you for anything, Kate, not once. I am asking you now as a friend. A friend who would do anything you asked. Anything.'

Before she could answer, Golding banged on the

window and said loudly, 'The boy's been found, ma'am. He's dead.'

Kate opened the car door and walked unsteadily towards the police station entrance. Why had all this to happen now? It was a question she knew she could never answer.

She turned and saw Patrick looking at her, and she was reminded of the first time she had seen him, frightened, angry and waiting for a daughter they had both known was not coming home. He had seemed vulnerable then, as he seemed now.

But what he was asking her to do was too much.

Far too much.

Ivor's mother was keening. It was a high-pitched wail, almost animal in its intensity, and other prisoners were complaining about the noise. Kate watched as a female social worker put her arms around Caroline's plump shoulders and tried to comfort her.

It was Ivor's little corpse, there was no mistake. It looked like suffocation as no marks had as yet been found on the body. No needle marks, bruises or cuts.

A picture came into Kate's mind of a little girl stabbed to death by her father, and she tried to blot it out. It had been one of her first cases and she had solved it in a few hours. The man, overcome with remorse, had confessed.

It had been a harrowing experience and Kate had gone home, grateful that her own daughter was OK. Yet, as Kelly had pointed out, Lizzy had not turned out as she had hoped. But Kate loved and accepted her, nonetheless. She could never imagine wanting to kill her. Yet it seemed parents saw their kids as something they owned, something they could use and abuse. Now she had to decide what course of action to take with Ivor's distressed and hysterical mother.

First thing was to let the duty doctor examine her and get his report. At least that would give Kate a breathing space as they tried to collate some evidence from the child's body. But as she walked along the holding cell corridor the woman's sobs were painful to her ears.

Terry Harwick was a fixer – a good one. In fact, he took a pride in his work that was uncommon in the criminal fraternity. He bragged that he could fix anything for anyone, at a price.

Terry was a large man with a bald head and protruding blue eyes. In prison, he had been classed as A grade. Dangerous to know. Inside he had created a network of people whom he trusted. People who helped him get the ins he needed to carry out his daily business.

Married to the delectable Tracey, a small woman with brown eyes, black permed hair and a large bust, he was a happy man. He drove a new BMW, owned a nice house in Manor Park and sent his kids to private school. His neighbours thought he was a financial adviser and that suited him.

When he saw Patrick Kelly walking up his drive, with his hard man Willy Gabney in tow, for a split second Terry felt fear. Then he shrugged it off. He was a sought-after man these days, so it was not unknown for dangerous villains to visit his home. But, normally, they rang first and arranged an appointment. It was this fact that was bothering him.

Putting on a smile, he thanked God that Tracey was getting her hair done, and opened his front door in a friendly manner. He took a deep breath before speaking, hoping his voice wasn't too wobbly.

'Hello, Pat. Long time no see.'

He ushered them into his large hallway. 'Come through and I'll get us a drink then we can talk properly.'

The fact that neither Patrick nor Willy answered him made him more nervous. He walked them through to his lounge, which overlooked the gardens that were landscaped and maintained to perfection. Patrick and Willy stared incredulously at what lay before them. A fountain, which was a bad copy of an Italian design, left even Willy, who normally loved bad taste, nonplussed. There was a dovecote, a large pool area, and lawns that were striped like a tennis court. The barbecue area was all red brick and black metalwork. The *pièce de résistance*, however, was a statue of Elvis in full regalia holding a microphone to his mouth.

'The wife loves the King . . .' Terry's voice was apologetic and Patrick looked at him as if he had never seen him before.

'Do you mean to tell me you let her put that in the middle of your garden – and didn't even attempt to argue with her? Have the neighbours complained?'

Patrick was having trouble keeping the laughter out of his voice.

Terry grinned sheepishly. 'You know my Tracey. If she wanted Idi Amin she'd have had him. She had the kitchen done in bright red; I told her it was a violent colour and she said not half as violent as she'd be if she didn't get her way. The house is her domain, Pat. What can I do?' He held out his arms. 'The kitchen's still red!'

Willy roared with laughter and it broke the ice. 'She's a girl, her. Even I'd be wary of young Tracey.'

It was a compliment and Terry smiled his thanks at Willy. Tracey was an acknowledged handful and Terry was proud of that fact.

'So what can I get you?'

Patrick shook his head. 'We're OK for the moment.'

'Well, please take a seat and we'll talk, eh?'

Patrick and Willy disappeared into a large white leather sofa. Pat felt something digging into his leg and held up a half-chewed toffee bar.

Terry took it from him, silently cursing his cleaner. 'Probably Tracey Junior's.' He put it in the bin and perched himself on the edge of his seat looking as if he was about to start a race.

'So what can I do you for?'

Pat smiled at the joke and then said seriously, 'I need to speak to a couple of Russians. Can you fix it?'

Terry's heart sank into his boots as he plastered a friendly smile on his face. 'Any ones in particular like, or just those involved in certain businesses?'

Pat looked him in the eye. 'I need to talk to Stravinski. Boris Stravinski, in case there's more than one.'

He saw Terry go pale, and sighed. He hoped Terry was more frightened of him than the Russian because he needed to talk to Boris and soon.

Terry shook his head softly, weighing up his words before speaking. 'He's a hard nut, Pat. No disrespect to you, but be wary of him. He's a bona fide nutter. Most of the Russians are.'

Patrick flapped a hand as if he didn't have a care in the world. 'There's a few in England too, in case you ain't noticed.'

Terry looked at the dark brown carpet on the floor and took a few seconds to think before he spoke again. This time his voice was quietly determined.

'It'll cost you, Pat. Big time. I ain't running risks for a poxy few quid. Not with Boris, anyway. He is a lunatic of the first water. And I mean head case. Have you heard about him?'

Patrick nodded, his blue eyes steely.

Terry Harwick felt as if he was caught between a rock and a hard place. He didn't want to refuse the man in front of him and he definitely didn't want to talk to Boris the Russian, as he was known. 'I will see what I can do, OK? No promises.'

Patrick stood up with difficulty; the chair was like a bucket seat in a low-slung sports car. 'I will give you enough, don't worry about payment. You fix me a meet and you get it quick, all right?'

Terry Harwick nodded. Boris was scary, 'treble

scary' as his kids might say. And now he'd been dragged into something he would rather be kept out of. Still, he was a fixer, and he was good at it.

Sally McIntyre looked out of her front-room window and watched as her neighbour, Kerry Alston, dragged her little girl along the street. Kerry was only seventeen and already had a four-year-old and a two-year-old. It looked like the two-year-old was being taken out now.

Sally shook her head in annoyance. It was scandalous the way that girl carried on. Her music was on all hours of the day and night, men coming and going. She was a right little slut and no mistake. And if you complained! The language! Eff this and eff that. Those two beautiful little girls already had a vocabulary like a sailor in port.

She saw Kerry disappear around the corner and toyed with the idea of phoning the police. Or even Social Services. Mind you, Kerry was so aggressive, people were chary of reporting her because when they did she slagged off everyone who came near her. The other week, when the police came about the noise, she stood on the balcony flashing her breasts at all and sundry as they walked past and screaming, 'Had your effing look eh?' It was scandalous. Shocking.

And where was the other little mite? The elder one with the long black hair and the big doe eyes. A stunningly beautiful child. End up just like her mother she would, left there with Kerry and the people who visited her flat. All on drugs, all drinking. The smell of cannabis was overpowering in the lobby.

Old Mrs Railton swore her arthritis was better from

breathing in the fumes. Sally had laughed at that along with everyone else. But it wasn't funny, not when it concerned those little girls.

An hour later, Sally heard a car door bang and looked out of her window again. It was Kerry getting out of an old Escort alone, and Sally felt relieved. She didn't have to do anything, and that suited her. She liked to keep herself to herself. It paid in this area to do just that. Keep out of everyone's business.

She went and made herself a cup of tea and as she sat down to watch *Morse* she sighed with happiness. She liked a good mystery and John Thaw was a bit of all right for his age.

A hammering on her front door pulled her from her seat. Through the glass panel she saw the outline of Kerry and she opened the door with trepidation.

'Can I help you, love?' She forced a friendly smile on to her face. Kerry was not above punching people who upset her.

'Have you seen my Mercedes?'

Sally shook her head. 'I saw you with her a while ago, love. I thought you was taking her to your mum's.'

Kerry's face screwed up with annoyance. 'What the fucking hell are you on about, you silly old bitch? I been shopping all afternoon.'

You've been shoplifting all afternoon, you mean, thought Sally.

'You trying to cause trouble, as usual? I left them both in the flat and I just got home. Mercedes is nowhere to be seen, so do you know where she is? I know you give them biscuits and that, and I also know you spend your life looking out the fucking window. So who did you see with Mercedes and when?'

Sally was frightened. 'I thought she was with you. I am sure it was you . . . dragging the poor little mite down the road—'

The punch, when it arrived, was painful.

When the police got there, Sally was battered and blue, and Kerry was looking for another fight. It was what she did whenever she was upset, and Kerry was upset. Very upset. Plus she loved fighting with Old Bill.

Chapter Six

Kate stared at the girl before her. She knew Kerry, everyone knew Kerry – she was a legend in her own lunchtime.

A big girl, overweight and with bad skin, Kerry was not what you would call pretty. She had learned at an early age that to get attention from boys, you allowed them liberties, and to get attention from everyone else you became a figure of fear. She swore all the time, issued veiled threats as an intrinsic part of her vocabulary and she was proud of herself. That was what made Kate really pity her.

Kerry thought she was clever – a somebody, someone to respect. She honestly didn't see anything wrong with her life at all. Now, as she stared back at Kate Burrows with a mixture of fear and anger, she looked almost feral.

'Calm down, Kerry. We only want to sort out what's happened here. Now, do you know where your youngest daughter is?'

Kerry's face was hard under the bright lights of the interview room.

'No, I fucking don't. I was looking for her when that cunt McIntyre started winding me up . . .'

Kate slammed a fist down on the table, making the other people in the room jump.

'I do not want any more of your language, OK? You have a child on the missing list – even *you* must see the sense in working with us on this one. I'm not having any us and them situations here – right? I want answers, girl, and I want them tonight. If Mercedes is wandering around on her own then I suggest you help us find her before she comes to harm.'

Kate glanced at the social worker in attendance and her eyes spoke volumes.

Bernie Kent took Kerry's hand. He said gently, 'Come on, love, we need to sort this out now. No more time-wasting.'

Kerry nodded almost imperceptibly.

'Let's start from the beginning,' Kate said quietly. 'Where were you today and when was the last time you saw Mercedes?'

Kerry wiped a grubby hand across her face. 'I was at Lakeside all day shopping.'

She saw the sceptical expression on the DI's face and frowned. 'I came home about eight this evening. I got a cab back, and the baby was gone. My other girl, Alisha, said that she fell asleep and when she woke up, Mercedes wasn't there.'

'Who was supposed to be looking after the children?'

Kerry licked her cracked lips and said almost inaudibly, 'No one. No one was looking after them, really. When I left, little Mary Parkes was there, but she had to get home by five. I meant to be back before then but I was caught up with something. She locked them in the flat and put the key under the mat as usual. That's how I got in.'

Kate sighed. 'So you left the kids all day with a young girl. How old was she?'

'Eleven. But she's a grown-up eleven, if you know what I mean.'

Kate knew she meant an early developer and probably sexually experienced, which did not mean she was grown up. Though the girl probably thought it did.

'We'll be bringing her in soon and getting a statement. Isn't her father Lenny Parkes, the armed robber?' Kate felt awful using fear like this but she had dealt with the Kerrys of this world long enough to know it was all that made them amenable. 'Did he know his daughter was at your flat when she should have been at school?'

Kerry's brief, a small balding man called Harry Dart, held up a hand. 'This has no bearing on the case at all.'

Kate smiled at him. 'I beg to differ. Mr Parkes is an extremely well-known face in these parts and he will not take lightly to the fact that we are knocking on his door about his beloved daughter. We need to know the score, for safety's sake.' Kate was using the man and she knew it, but what else could she do?

'I don't know whether he knew. I expect he didn't. But all the kids come round to me, everyone knows that.'

Kerry was justifying herself and Kate felt even more pity for her than before. She had Kerry on the hop and was going to keep her there.

'Is there anyone who might have taken Mercedes? A friend, relative – her father?'

Kerry laughed nastily. 'I don't know who her father is to be honest.' This was said with the customary bravado. 'I just want her back.' It was rather more heartfelt.

'But we have three witnesses who say they saw you walking down the road with her an hour before you reported her gone.'

'Then they were wrong. I was over Lakeside as I said.'

'Can anyone put you there? Did you see or talk to anyone you knew?'

Kerry shook her head. 'No. But I got a cab home . . .'

'Lakeside is a ten-minute drive home from your flat. You had ample time to get there and back in thirty minutes. Can you see where I'm coming from? Three people saw you with the child, Kerry. Now what is going on? They all know you, know who you are. Let's face it, round your flats you are the star, aren't you? You make sure of that. They recognised you all right, love. You had hours in which to get home, do what you had to do and get back over to Lakeside. Now, have you anything sensible to say?'

Kerry wiped her nose with the back of her hand. Then, jumping up like a maniac, she started laying into everyone she could get hold of. Including her social worker and her brief.

It was pandemonium.

And Kate was no nearer finding out where the child could be, and more importantly, who she was with.

Ten minutes later she went back into the room. This time Kerry was quieter and much more civilised.

'I swear on my kids' heads, I have no idea who took her or why everyone thinks it was me. I was drunk out of me brains, I admit that, but I was skanking over Lakeside. Thieving, for fuck's sake! You can do me for that, but not for harming me kids. I love them. Whatever anyone thinks of me and my life, I *love* them fucking kids! I would never hurt them. Never. And if anyone tries to say different, I'll batter their brains out and all!'

'Whose brains have you already battered out then?' Kate's voice was quiet.

Kerry's eyes filled with tears.

'You have twice been arrested for violence towards your children . . .'

Kerry interrupted, screaming, 'I smacked them, that's all. Everyone smacks their kids.'

'Once you *smacked* your eldest daughter around the head with a shoe. Am I right? She had to have five stitches.'

Kate saw the social worker close his eyes in distress.

'You were given Alisha back only five weeks ago. She had been staying with your mother, am I right again? You are under a supervision order yet you left two small defenceless children with an eleven-year-old girl while you went out thieving. Now you say your daughter was taken by a stranger and you know nothing about it! Am I getting all this correctly?'

Kerry was crying now, the real Kerry, an overweight girl whose hard front had disappeared in less than five minutes.

Getting up, Kate said gently, 'Talk to your brief and I'll be back in fifteen minutes, OK? See if we can make some sense of all this.'

Both the brief and the social worker looked at her unhappily. She was putting the ball in their court and they knew it.

Kate walked back to her office and lit a cigarette. Pulling on it deeply, she saw a note on her desk saying that she was to expect a call from Detective Inspector Jenny Bartlett. It was signed by Leila and Kate thanked her lucky stars for her friend's help.

It was procedure that if a case was difficult then officers could bring in someone regarded as an expert in that area. It was in no way regarded as a slur on the officer in charge. In fact, it was often recommended by the Home Office, especially if a case was going nowhere. But experts were most often called in for crimes of paedophilia or child death, when specialist help and advice would be needed.

Jenny was all right, and this was just her kind of case. She specialised in child abuse and abduction. Kate made a mental note to kiss Leila, the first chance she got.

She now had three local women, all of whom had apparently decided to kill their children overnight. All claimed they were innocent and all were known either to police, Social Services or both. Such things happened, Kate knew that. It was a part of everyday life. But to have three practically overnight on her patch was stretching things too far.

The witness statements were the strangest part of it all. Each woman had been observed with her child, though they were all adamant that they had been nowhere near them at the time. All admitted neglect, leaving the children alone, but not actual murder.

If they were telling the truth, where did that leave the police? And what about the body of the child on the rubbish tip?

Who was he and why wasn't anyone looking for him? *Someone* must know who he was. Surely *someone* must care?

Kate closed her eyes in consternation and tiredness. She was missing something, she knew she was. Eventually it would come to her, she knew, and then everything about this disturbing case would become clear.

At least she hoped so.

She deserved a break.

Boris Stravinski watched the screen with clinical detachment. He was scanning CCTV videos, trying to piece together some information.

The girl beside him stirred and he moved away from her slim body. She opened her eyes and smiled at him. She was very pretty and she knew it.

He stared down at her. 'Get dressed and fuck off. Sergei will give you your money.'

His harsh words made his accent lose its appeal and the girl got up without a word and started dressing. He ignored her as he scanned the screen.

At the door she turned to face him and said sheepishly, 'Will you want to see me again?'

He shook his head, his long thick hair making her jealous of its glossy beauty.

'You weren't worth the money, my dear.'

She left the room crushed and Boris felt a flicker of compassion which he fought down. When paying for sex, you got a fuck and that was it. He paid up, he fucked them. Why did he always hate them so much afterwards?

Or maybe it was himself he hated. He was an extremely good-looking man, he knew that much without being vain. Women adored him, and yet he still preferred to mix with whores. He pushed the troubling thoughts from his mind.

Whores were just there and when you were finished they went on their way. That was the big attraction for him.

Since losing his girlfriend Anna two years before, he had not bothered with regular women at all. Anna, the mother of his son, had been shot in Moscow while she shopped. He had lost three good men with her that day and it rankled still. But he missed her. He missed her and her humour and her tidy mind so very much. His son missed her too.

He recognised one of the faces on the video and paused the tape, smiling.

Then, getting up, he walked through to his shower

room and stood looking at himself in the mirror. He was a big man, in every way. Long thick black hair hung to his shoulders in glossy waves. He looked like a darker version of Richard Gere. Women, especially Englishwomen, were always pointing that out. He marvelled at the combination of beauty and power. Irresistible.

Yet beauty in a woman did not really affect him *per se*. He valued character, a sense of humour in a woman, a *brain*. He liked to talk with them, have fun with them, and then make love with them. At least, that was how he used to be. Before Anna died.

He stepped into the shower and turned on the water. As he washed he wondered where Kelly was and when he would learn what had happened to his money.

That was Boris's chief concern at the moment.

Everything else could wait.

Patrick had moved from home into a small flat in Ilford. It would not have been his first choice, but no one knew him there and that suited him. As soon as he had realised what was going down he had started covertly moving stuff to his car, taking just a few things that were important to him, ever conscious of being watched.

His brief was not a happy man, saying Patrick would soon be declared wanted in connection with murder. But Patrick knew something he didn't. And neither did the police.

Patrick knew who had killed Duggan and why. It

had to be the Russian after his money. If Kate came up trumps and lied for him, he was home and dry.

Willy was sitting watching football. Patrick poured them both a stiff drink.

'Fucking Manchester United give me the hump, Pat, they really do. Like a load of fucking shirt-lifters they are. Unbelievable.'

Pat didn't listen. Willy was a dyed-in-the-wool Millwall supporter and always would be. Greater teams, and they were legion, gave him the hump.

'Willy, as we are going to be stuck here together for a while, can we lay down some ground rules?'

The other man grinned. 'All right, Pat, I'll button me mutton, no danger.' He held his arms up in supplication. 'But look at them!'

'I know, they're all woofters. But can we let it go now, please?'

Willy was quiet while Pat sipped at his brandy.

'My cousin Laurie's fighting tonight, over in Rettenden. Fancy it, Pat? I mean, it's only local faces, no one important. He's in with a right chance, fighting a Yugoslavian bloke. Right hard nut to crack by all accounts.'

Pat shook his head. 'You go, take your bird. Have a night out. Just be careful.'

Willy grinned. 'Maureen likes a bit of a fight, bless her.'

'From what I've heard she could take the Yugoslavian on herself.'

'She's a right handful,' Willy agreed proudly. 'Makes Mike Tyson seem like a pussy cat. But she's got a heart of gold. Do anything for you, like.'

Pat nodded. He was not looking forward to meeting Maureen. He had heard enough about her to last him a lifetime. But something Willy had said struck a chord. Maureen would do anything for him, including lie for him. On oath if necessary. Which was more than Kate would do for him, Patrick thought bitterly. She *had* to change her mind. Christ, the club was *legal*. She had no call to punish him over it. But in his heart he knew it wasn't the legality or otherwise of the premises that had galled her. It was because it was a dump that she'd hated it.

If he was honest, he agreed with her about the clientele, the workforce, the whole ethos of the place. But it made money, good money. *Legal* money. And that had been his only reason for owning it. The women he employed certainly didn't attract him.

Now the club, and the man who'd run it for him, were the cause of all his current misfortunes. Even he could see that much. He had a mad Russian after him, his bird was gone and he was living in a fucking drum in *Ilford*.

Life certainly had a way of kicking you in the nuts, as his first wife Renée would point out at every available opportunity. God paid back debts without money was another gem of hers.

Still, he reasoned, once Terry Harwick had arranged a meet, he could get it all sorted out. Then he could concentrate on winning back Kate. Getting her back in the fold. Back home where she belonged.

Maureen was a tubby woman in her early forties. Much taken with tight clothes, she had four catalogues on the go at any given time and the same number of empty flats to have the stuff delivered to. She made a bare living selling the stuff on but it was enough for her. It certainly beat kiting, for which she had served a three-year sentence.

Back on the street, older, a little wiser and a lot more battered, she had set her sights on Willy Gabney and had got him as she knew she would. She liked Willy. He treated her well and cared for her in his own way. Her children were grown up now. She was a grandmother three times over. A fact that pleased her one minute and depressed her the next.

Her youngest boy Duane was still at home. Not the brightest bulb on the Christmas tree, he was nineteen now and working on a building site. He was off her hands and that suited Maureen. She could have a bit of a life of her own these days, and thanks to Willy Gabney that was exactly what she was doing.

When she saw him pull up outside her flat in Dagenham, she rushed out to meet him, tripping towards his car on impossibly high heels. She got into the BMW with difficulty and Willy laughed at the expanse of leg she was showing as she tried to get comfortable. She was well padded, old Maureen, and that was just what he liked. She was a proper handful and he wouldn't have her any different.

'Bleeding hell, Willy, it's like trying to sit on a skateboard!'

He grinned and they screeched away from the kerb.

Maureen hoped her neighbours could see her. Give them something to talk about.

'You look nice, love. Smashing.'

She preened herself. 'Got to make the effort. Where's the bundle taking place?'

'Over in Rettenden, a big barn on Solly Campbell's place. He always has a nice fight, him. Plenty of booze and a good atmosphere. Should be a top night. I'm having a monkey on me cousin. If I win I'll treat you, OK?'

She smiled happily.

Willy would treat her anyway. He always did. A couple of bar a week at least was pushed into her hot little hand. He was kind, was Willy. Kind and caring in his own way. His reputation as an enforcer was well earned, she knew, yet with women he was a diamond geezer. A real nice bloke. Ugly, she admitted, but she wasn't exactly Rita Hayworth herself so that evened it out. The days of a handsome boatrace giving her the eye were long gone and if she was honest she was glad.

At her time of life, she wanted a nice man with a few bob and no real complications. Willy Gabney didn't even have the usual baggage as he had never married or fathered any children that he knew of. He had seemed to share Pat Kelly's daughter with him if all he said was true. It was certainly the case that he and Kelly went back years.

All this was part of Willy's charm really. He was the big dependable man she had been looking for all her life. And if he wasn't exactly Rudolph Valentino she remembered the old adage: you don't look at the mantelpiece when you're stoking the fire.

All the way to Rettenden they laughed and joked. Maureen liked him more every time she saw him. Even Duane liked him, and that was a plus. He was normally funny about her *amours*, though she was honest enough to admit that there had been more than a few of them over the years. A few too many for Duane, anyway.

She shrugged the dark thoughts away. She had Willy now and that was enough for her. More than enough. Plus he wasn't bad in the kip, so all in all she had fallen rather pleasantly on her feet.

Long may it last.

Lenny Parkes was a small man with a big personality.

An habitual offender, he happily divided his time between home with his wife Trisha and their two children, Mary and Ian, or inside a top-security prison with his mates. All in all he was a contented con. Gutted if he got a capture, but with the frame of mind that allowed him to do long bird with a smile and a cheery wave.

Providing no one upset him, of course.

His only real hatred was the police. He saw them as the enemy, as taught to Lenny by his father and his father before him. Lenny's real pride and joy was his eleven-year-old daughter Mary, an ugly girl who wore too much make-up, and had a fat body and the eyes of a much older woman.

She was what he had made her, albeit without

realising it. Mary tried to be what she thought her father liked in his women: sluttish, fast-mouthed and sexually able, or so she thought. She dressed too old, picked up sassy soundbites from TV and tried to come across as a streetwise woman.

She was a deeply disturbed child who put on an act most of the time. She lied constantly, caused trouble for her friends, was a nightmare for her teachers and all in all was heartily disliked.

Her mother saw through her like a pane of glass and there was a long-established rivalry there from when Mary was a small child. Her father's absences made the girl vulnerable and when he wasn't about, her mother tried to make up for Lenny's spoiling of their daughter by giving her a harsh crash course in perspective. Trisha knew she was wasting her time, though.

Mary gravitated towards the dirt of society as her father did. She was comfortable with people no one else would want to be with. It was behaviour learned from a father who took her to slum pubs and working men's clubs and let her sit in with what she thought were real men. Just like her dad.

Consequently, Lenny thought Mary was great, while everyone else, including his cronies, secretly bemoaned the fact that she was a pain in the arse with her frequent interruptions of their conversation and thin veneer of sophistication which made her look far more whorish than either she or her besotted father realised.

Ian, two years older and a nice boy, was overlooked

in favour of Lenny's little girl.

As Trisha opened the front door to the police, Lenny and his precious baby were on the sofa, cosily watching *Alien* together.

When DI Kate Burrows walked into the front room Lenny closed his eyes in annoyance.

'If there have been any robberies today, Miss Burrows, I had nothing to do with them. I was at the hospital having blood tests for suspected diabetes.'

Kate smiled gently. 'I have come to speak to your daughter who I'm surprised to see is still up at this late hour.' It was a quarter to one in the morning.

Lenny's face darkened even as Mary's face paled.

Trisha Parkes was on to her daughter immediately. 'Have you been thieving again, you little mare?'

Mary, realising that she was in over her head, did her little girl lost look and hoped for the best. 'No, Mum, of course not! Bloody hell.' Her voice trembled and she tried to calm herself down.

'What's she supposed to have done?' Lenny's voice was harsh. He turned off the sound to the TV and stood up and looked at Kate and her retinue belligerently.

She stared back at the man before her, deliberately keeping him waiting before she answered. She saw the anger welling up inside him and smiled inwardly.

'Mary was babysitting at a flat today when she should have been at school. The flat belonged to Kerry Alston. I am sure you have heard of her.'

'What's this got to do with Mary then?' Trisha's voice was scared as if she knew what was coming. Shoplifters didn't get routed at one o'clock in the morning. This was serious.

'Kerry's youngest child is missing. It seems she left the children with Mary as usual so your daughter was the last person to see the kids. I have a responsible adult at the police station if neither of you wants to make the trek, but Mary's coming with us.'

Lenny screwed up his eyes in disbelief. 'You're bringing her in?'

'Got it in one, Lenny. This is serious. A child is missing and your daughter is a witness. We have to bring her in, take a statement and then see what develops from there.'

Even Mary picked up the seriousness of what was being said and the first cold fingers of fear touched the back of her neck. She started to whine, 'I never did nothing! I was only helping because Kerry is so wicked to them! *I* am the only person who helps them. She don't feed them properly or nothing.'

She looked at her shell-shocked father and said hysterically, 'She beats them up, Dad, and I have to go round and make sure they're OK.'

Lenny looked at his little daughter. Her make-up was smeared and her roots were coming through. Suddenly he saw her as the policewoman saw her. As others saw her. As her own mother saw her. And he felt a sickness inside him. What had Trisha said to him only that very morning? 'She'll be pushing a pram before her fourteenth birthday and we'll have you to thank for that one, Lenny.'

There had been another row over her at breakfast. As usual she didn't want to go to school. They'd had the whole gamut. Belly ache, feeling sick, etc. In the end she had slammed out of the house leaving the air blue and her mother fit to be tied. Lenny had found it amusing as usual. Now he saw that she was in trouble, real trouble, and she was scared. For the first time in ages Mary was acting like a child. The spoiled child he had created.

'Get your coat and wash your face. Now!' His voice was loud and Mary rushed from the room to do as she was told.

'Has anyone any idea where the child could be?' Mary's mother asked, obviously concerned.

Kate shook her head sadly. She liked Trisha who'd had a hard life and tried to make it as easy as she could for her kids though she knew she was fighting a losing battle. Especially with her daughter.

She also guessed that Lenny didn't know the half of it and that gave Kate the edge so far as Mary was concerned. She had already been warned that the girl was an habitual liar, willing to grass anyone and everyone to get the blame shifted from herself. At eleven she was also an accomplished shoplifter and a regular truant from the local school.

'How long has the little mite been missing?' Trisha's voice was sad.

'We aren't sure, Mrs Parkes. But we understand that the mother, Kerry, went out and left her children with your daughter all afternoon. What time did she get in tonight?'

Before Trisha could open her mouth Lenny butted in, 'You ask her when you get down the Bill shop, OK?'

Ten minutes later a chastened Mary was put in the police car with her mother. As Lenny walked to his car, Kate stopped him.

'I counted eight Special Brew cans in your lounge. Surely you aren't going to drive?'

He sighed heavily. 'Fuck you, *Ms Burrows*. Not content with hassling me, you start on my family. Is that official new Old Bill policy, eh?'

She looked deep into his eyes. 'Every second that passes is vital for the missing child. We have search parties out, we are combing the area with teams of officers. Now, that little girl is just two years old. Your daughter was the last person to see her and until we find out what happened, she might even be a suspect. Do you realise how serious this is, *Mr Parkes*? A two-year-old is missing and no one, including the mother, has any idea where she is. If the child turns up safe and well, I'll be happy. But if she doesn't, I'll want answers and I'll want them soon. Do you understand me?'

Lenny looked into her eyes and felt the first stirring of fear. Not for the missing Mercedes, but for his beloved daughter. All his wife's wise words came back to him as he phoned a cab to take him to the police station.

Kerry was silent in her holding cell. She had not even asked where Alisha was, assuming she had gone to her grandmother's house.

If Mary opened her mouth, she would kill the little bitch. But she trusted Mary enough to know that the girl wouldn't put herself in it. Kerry stared around the cell. She had read all the graffiti and drunk her tea. She had smoked her last cigarette.

As she lay on the bunk she sighed deeply. Fear was weighing down on her. If they searched the flat, and she had a feeling they had done that already, the shit could hit the fan at any moment. Then she would be in double trouble.

She wished she had a joint to calm her nerves. The Valium from the duty doctor had not been enough for an habitual user like herself. It barely took the edge off.

Lenny Parkes would break her neck and that was just for starters. But if Mary used her loaf and they didn't find the evidence, which she had hidden well, they might just scrape through this.

Maureen stormed back into her flat at 12.20 a.m. and she was fuming. Willy Gabney had only fucked off and left her in the middle of a bare knuckler in Rettenden, without a bleeding word!

She could not believe it!

She'd had him sussed as a gentleman and then he'd upped and left her in the middle of nowhere and expected her to get herself a lift home! She had had to blag a ride to the nearest station from a man with bad breath and an A-reg car!

If Willy Gabney had the front to ring her or come round here again she would smash his bleeding face in and tell him a few things as well. Who did he think he was!

She felt the sting of tears then. She had liked him. Really, really liked him. And he had treated her so well. She had thought she had fallen on her feet at last. But he turned out to be just like the rest of them.

A big, fat, untrustworthy ponce.

She made herself a strong drink and picked up the phone. Then she started calling all her friends and telling them what had befallen her. She needed sympathy, and she needed it now.

She was still on the phone when Patrick Kelly tried to get through at two-thirty in the morning. He'd guessed that something had happened to Willy, and his guess was confirmed. Someone had rung his mobile and told him Willy was being detained for a while but that he would be back soon with instructions for Mr Kelly.

But was he coming back dead or alive? And, more to the point, did his kidnappers know where Patrick was now?

He left the flat and got into his car. He wasn't sure where to go, something that had never happened to him before. Patrick Kelly always knew what to do. At least that was how it had been before all this. But the Russian was scaring him, seriously scaring him, and Patrick admitted that to himself.

He was driving along a road in the middle of the night with no real destination in mind. If it hadn't been for the fear inside him it would have been laughable. His world was upside down.

What was Kate's saying of old? *Show me the company you keep and I'll tell you what you are.* Never had a few words made so much sense to him, even though they were a bit late in sinking in.

He wished he could go to her, but even if she let him he would put her in danger. They had taken Willy and he was a hard nut to crack. If they could take him, they could take Kate. Patrick had better warn her and fast.

Fear was making him feel physically sick now. He finally admitted to himself he was in over his head.

Chapter Seven

It was just past 3 a.m. and Kate was tired out. Mary Parkes had given them nothing except denunciations of Kerry and what a bad mother she was and how Mary went round there to be the heroine of the hour. None of which rang remotely true. Mary was hiding something, and now the social worker had said enough was enough for the poor little girl and she was to be brought back at lunchtime the next day. Kate saw the smug expression on the eleven-year-old's fat face and suppressed an urge to slap it hard.

Questioning her had been a waste of time. Mary insisted she had left the kids in the flat asleep as usual. Due to her own age it was impossible to press her harder as the law still regarded her as a child. Pity her parents hadn't treated her like one, then she might not have been in the police station at all.

Kate had a strong feeling Mary Parkes would see the inside of a few more police stations before she was much older.

Still, she had spoken to Jenny Bartlett and faxed

through everything about the case so far. The DI was hoping to join them in a day or two. At least Kate knew now that real help was on the way. Specialist back-up. Somehow she felt sure all these cases were linked. There was a common denominator, something she was missing. There had to be.

As she sipped her lukewarm coffee she saw WPC Joanna Hart tearing down the open-plan outer offices towards her. She rose as the girl pushed open the glass door to Kate's office and said breathlessly, 'Has Mary Parkes gone home yet?'

Kate nodded.

'You'd better get her back then. Wait until you see what we found in Kerry's bedroom!'

Willy opened his eyes to hazy darkness. He closed them again quickly. He was still in shock. He knew that whoever had him now, had followed him and was annoyed with himself for not being more careful. Whenever he was driving Pat, Willy kept a look-out from force of habit. It was being with Maureen that had made him careless. Thinking of her alarmed him. Did they have her too? Was she OK? Did they have Pat as well?

He tried to calm himself down. This had been a professional kidnap which meant he would be treated well enough until such time as he had outgrown his use. And in the meantime he had better decide what he was going to do if the opportunity to run presented itself. He needed to see where he was, try and work out how many of them were about if he did a runner, and whether he could gain access to some kind of transport.

On another level, he wondered if his cousin had won the fight. Willy never could keep his mind on one thing for long. It was the way he was made.

Tommy Broughton opened his front door and saw Patrick Kelly standing before him with a face like thunder and the outline of a gun visible through his jacket.

'Hello, Tommy. On your own, are you?'

'Yeah. The old woman's away on holiday with the kids. What's wrong, Pat?'

Patrick walked into his house uninvited and grinned at him nastily.

'I was hoping you could tell me that, mate.'

Tommy's face paled. 'I don't know nothing, Pat, except the filth was at the club with a warrant for your arrest. I tried to get in touch but you weren't available so I assumed you had done a poodle. I was waiting till you contacted me.'

'Which I have, Tommy. Haven't I? Personally like.' He walked through to Tommy's lounge and sat down heavily.

'By the way, Harwick phoned and left a message for you,' Tommy told him. 'He's still trying, whatever that means.'

Patrick nodded.

'What's that all about then, Pat?'

He looked at the man before him and sighed.

'Wouldn't you like to know? Give you something to

talk about, would it?' Then, taking the gun out of his jacket, he pointed it at his former friend and colleague. 'You have exactly five minutes to tell me what is going on with Boris the Russian spider and Duggan and now me. Now think long and hard before you open your trap because I have guessed most of it, Tommy, and I want the whole truth, not the edited version. Are we both clear on that?'

Tommy nodded. He was in big trouble and he knew it. He had sent his wife and kids away for a holiday because he was scared, caught up in things that went right over his head. Now Patrick Kelly wanted answers and he had to give them. Either way he was a dead man.

Duggan had made it all sound so easy and so lucrative. Patrick had been the proverbial sleeping partner. He had known nothing of what was going on at the club. Now, though, he had woken up with a vengeance.

Tommy wondered briefly if Pat would kill him in his front room. His wife would go ballistic if he did. It had just been decorated.

Kate looked at the photographs and shook her head wonderingly. Kerry Alston must have been mad if she'd thought she could get away with this. She threw them on to her desk in disgust.

'Get her out of the cell and into an interview room – now. And get her social worker back, and her brief. She's going to need them.'

Kate had marvelled at a woman who could be so

calm and collected while her small child was missing. But after looking at the photographs she wondered if Kerry had known exactly where her child was all along.

She pressed her eyes with her hands, rubbing at them viciously. Every day her job seemed to teach her a little bit more about the human ability to destroy whatever was good and innocent. It depressed her, and made her more determined to stamp out all the badness she could. But she had a feeling she was fighting a losing battle.

Mary Parkes was sitting with her father on the settee at home. She was feeling jubilant. She had talked herself out of trouble once more. As her mother eyed them sideways Mary ignored her as if she was beneath her notice.

'Don't you think it's time she went to bed?'

Lenny looked at his wife in annoyance. 'The kid's had a stressful night, Trish. Give her a break.'

Trisha shook her head and sighed. When had she first realised that she didn't like her daughter? Was it only recently? She knew it was a long time since the resentment of her had set in, and that it had stemmed from Lenny's obsession with their younger child. Mary had always been a shrewd kid, out for the main chance. She was like her father in that way. But there was something else – something overtly sexual in her now and there had been for a while. Trisha had watched her with men. Mary liked them. Liked them too much.

Lenny had not understood the full significance of his daughter's being round at Kerry's flat when she should have been at school. He was unaware of their neighbour's filthy reputation. Lenny only knew the heavy villains. For herself, Trisha couldn't understand what made her daughter want to go round there in the first place. What was the attraction? Being able to smoke in peace? Have a drink? Mix with men? She had an idea it was all three.

It was all Lenny's fault. He'd treated Mary like his girlfriend instead of a daughter. And this was the result.

There was a violent knocking at the front door. No one moved. As the door was banged on again, Trisha said a silent prayer. She'd had a feeling all along there was more to this than met the eye and she was being proved right. It gave her no satisfaction at all.

She heard her husband swearing and carrying on as the police poured into the lounge for the second time that night. Saw Mary's eyes turn round as flying saucers as the policewoman said they had uncovered new evidence – photographs that needed to be explained. Noticed her husband's face darken as he realised there was definitely something fishy going on with his little Mary.

The girl started screaming. She kept it up all the way to the police station while safely ensconced in her daddy's arms.

Lenny was shown the photographs at 4.39 a.m. He had to be physically dragged off his daughter ten seconds later.

★ ★ ★

Kerry was terrified and it showed. Her face had lost its usual expression of bravado and she sat slumped in a chair facing Kate. The fire was gone from her eyes and her language was tame.

Kate found it hard to look at her without showing her distaste.

'Who took these photos, Kerry?'

She stared back silently.

'I will ask you again, for the benefit of the tape, who took the photographs, Kerry? The suspect, Kerry Alston, is shaking her head, refusing to answer my question.'

Kate glanced at the girl again, then turned off the tape before saying, 'You have a small child missing and half of Grantley is out searching for her. You are in possession of pornographic photographs of your children and other children so far unnamed, but we'll find them.' She looked steadily at the young woman. 'Mary Parkes is about to spill everything she knows. Her father will hear what she has to say. If I was you I'd be scared, Kerry, very scared. You are basically in shit so deep fifteen paddies with shovels couldn't get you out of it. Now my advice to you is to open your mouth and we'll get this over with, eh? Because as God is my witness I'll see you go away for this little lot and that is from the heart. You're scum, Kerry, and you and I both know it.'

Kerry's brief did not say a word at Kate's harangue. The photos had thrown him as much as they had the police. They were hardcore porn and for them this girl was going away, whatever she said or didn't say. Because she was in each photograph, too, smiling and laughing even though the children featured with her looked distressed and terrified.

'You have ten minutes to compose yourself before you give me a statement, OK? Then I am coming after you, lady, with everything I've got.'

Kate walked from the room. Her heart was pounding in her ears and she felt sick. As she entered her own office WPC Hart followed her.

'I have an ID on two of the kids in the photos already. They're little Ivor and his brother Christian.'

Kate closed her eyes in distress. 'Are you sure?'

Hart nodded sadly. 'You'll have to look at them properly, ma'am. We've got to track all these kids down.'

Kate looked into the girl's pretty green eyes and said with feeling, 'What the hell is going on with these people? When did this happen to the world? How could a woman do that to her own child, Jo? You tell me if you know because I can't for the life of me understand any of it.'

Joanna shrugged helplessly. 'I'm still brand new at all this, ma'am. But it seems life's getting stranger by the day hereabouts. I reckon the kid's dead, though, don't you?'

'Yeah, on the face of it I'd say she was,' Kate sighed. 'But what's really intriguing me most is, are these women in league with one another? Was this all planned in advance and they thought they could just get away with killing off their kids? Where's the logic behind it all?'

Joanna Hart shrugged again. 'I guess that's what you have to find out, ma'am.'

Tommy was crying and Patrick stood watching him, bemused. The weeping man was totally silent, reminding Patrick of his own little Mandy when he had told her that her mother had died.

Patrick hit him again, harder this time.

'You've tucked me up, ain't you, Tommy? I gave you seriously good wedge to do a job for me and your greed made you tuck me up.'

Patrick punched him in the head again, knocking him back to the floor. He looked down at his one-time friend and bellowed: 'Do I look like a cunt? Have I got "Cunt" written across my forehead by any chance? Only everyone seems to take me for one. I was wondering if I was missing something, like. Something everyone else seems to see as plain as fucking day. I must be a cunt because *everyone* is trying to fuck with me.'

His whole body bristled with suppressed violence and anger and Tommy knew that Pat was on the verge of killing him.

'I had to do it, Pat,' he blubbered. 'I had no choice. I ran the money through the club to clean it up for Stravinski, so it was all legal like. He provided the invoices, everything.'

'Fucking invoices? For my club!'

'He's dangerous, Pat – fucking hell, even Old Bill are wary of him. He covers his arse so well . . .'

'Dangerous? Did you say dangerous? I'll give you

fucking dangerous, you two-faced ponce!'

Patrick began the real beating then. Anger and hurt at what Tommy had done were overtaking him. He knew he should calm down and think rationally but he couldn't. The chances were that Willy was dead. He would be used as a warning. The thought of his friend of so many years being taken by Boris, an acknowledged nutter, was sending Patrick off his head.

'I trusted you and you gave them Willy Gabney, you bastard scumbag. After sending me and him running round after people like Leroy Holdings, who you knew were pennies and halfpennies. People who had nothing to do with any of this. You led me a right fucking dance. Set Willy up too, didn't you, eh? To cover your own arse. Well, when I've finished with you, boy, you'll wish you'd never heard of me *or* fucking Boris.'

He beat Tommy unconscious then. Afterwards, his arms and shoulders aching from exertion, he poured himself another drink. Then he went through all Tommy's address books. When he had what he wanted he picked up the phone and dialled a number.

'Tell Boris that Patrick Kelly wants to see him and soon,' he said when it was answered. 'You also tell him that if anything happens to Willy Gabney, I'll be after him personally.'

He slammed down the receiver then looked at the body of his one-time friend. Kicking Tommy hard in the ribs, he woke him up.

'Get up and get your jacket on. Me and you are going for a little ride.'

★ ★ ★

Caroline was aware that the photographs had her children in them but she was denying ever having met Kerry Alston let alone allowing her to interfere with her kids. She admitted to knowing Mary Parkes, and allowed that Mary was sometimes paid to take her kids out for an afternoon in the park.

There was a wariness in her answers that depressed Kate. There *was* collusion between them all, she was sure. But she could not prove it.

It was the longest night of her life and at 6.30 a.m. she admitted defeat and left the station. She turned on her personal mobile when she got into her car and saw seventeen missed calls. She deleted them without even listening to them. Patrick was as far from her mind as the moon. She had too much to think about as it was, without torturing herself with his lies.

As she drove back to her old home, she passed Mary Parkes's block of flats and felt a moment's pity for the girl's father. Mary was in the photos and she was there as a star, smiling into the camera as she performed outrageous acts on innocent little children. There was no way she was an unwilling participant. The men in the photos were unknown to them but not for long, Kate believed. She had a feeling that Lenny Parkes would know who they were soon enough. And when he knew, *she* would know – because she would have to arrest him after he had dealt with them.

Mary's mother had pushed her daughter away from her and told the social workers to take her with them after they'd shown her the photographs. Kate hadn't the heart to tell the mother then that Mary would be off to a secure unit as soon as they were finished with her. She was an accessory to a serious crime.

Kate sighed. Tomorrow, or rather today, she would have DI Jenny Bartlett to help her, a specialist in child abuse, murder and rape. These Grantley cases had to be linked. If Kate could just untangle the connection between them then they'd be halfway to solving them, she knew.

As she pulled into the driveway of her semi she smiled sadly. This was the last place she had expected to be returning to. But here she was, back where she'd started, and so very alone.

Inside, she walked through to the lounge and what she saw made her gasp with fright.

On her sofa, asleep and covered in blood, was Patrick Kelly.

Julie Manning walked her dog every morning at 6.15 precisely. He was a sausage dog and she loved him, a roly-poly little fellow with calm brown eyes and a sweet disposition.

They took the same route every day. Into the woods at Monnow Green and through to the lake by Grantley golf course. This part of the wood was dense and thick. Little Demon, as she called the dog, loved it here. He sniffed and peed to his heart's content.

As they came to a clearing used mainly by joggers and dog walkers, Julie saw a strange sight. Lying on the grass, her little shoes and socks neatly arranged beside her, was a small child. She was blue with cold and breathing heavily.

Taking off her own thick padded jacket Julie wrapped the child in it and started to run back to her house, all the time keeping her eyes peeled for another adult – hopefully one who could tell her what the hell this little girl was doing out here on a freezing morning, covered in dew and obviously either drugged or unconscious. She had read about children being dumped by their parents but had never thought she would come across something like it in her lifetime.

As she ran she realised that Little Demon was barking like mad. She ignored him and carried on running. The child in her arms didn't move. Julie hugged her tighter, willing her body heat to penetrate the frail cold limbs.

Patrick looked terrible and Kate stood motionless before him as he started to talk.

'I'm in trouble, Kate. I really need your help, love. I have nowhere else to turn.'

She took in his bloodstained clothes and his frightened expression. How much more could she take tonight?

'Look, Kate, it's all my own fault, I admit that,' he said to her. 'But I never dreamed anything like this would happen. It's to do with a Russian bloke called Boris. Apparently he was using my club as a front for money laundering, prostitution, you name it. I had no idea, I swear to you. Now I have to sort it all out, and

I will. But I need your help, love.'

She sat on a chair by the fireplace and said coldly, 'What do you want me to do?'

'I want you to look on the computer at work and see what you have on this geek Boris. Forewarned is forearmed so to speak.'

Kate held up her hand. 'Do you know something, Pat? You really are a piece of work. You expect me to jump each time you open your mouth. Did it ever occur to you that you are in this shit because of the way you live your life? That dealing with scum leaves you wide open to this type of thing? I despair of you, Pat, I really do.'

She watched him run his hands through his short dark hair and bite his lip – his way of keeping his temper under control.

'Listen, Kate, you knew where I was coming from. I never tried to hide anything from you.'

She interrupted him, sarcasm heavy in her voice. 'Oh, didn't you? I knew about Girlie Girls then, did I? *How* did I know about it? By telepathy, or was it written in six-foot letters on a fucking fence? You must be taking the piss, Patrick Kelly. You couldn't be honest if your life depended on it. It's not in your nature. Money, that's all you're interested in. Greedy, dirty money, eh? Girls and women debasing themselves for a few quid. Keeps the punters happy . . . is that what you're still telling yourself? Maybe George Markham would have liked your club, Pat,' she said cruelly. 'Sounds just his cup of tea, doesn't it?' "Tits and slags" I remember you describing Joey Barnard's club. Is that where you got the idea from?'

'Don't you bring my daughter's murderer into this, Kate! Mandy has nothing to do with any of this.'

Kate laughed nastily. 'Doesn't she? I seem to remember you re-evaluating all that you stood for not three years ago in this very room. But that was just an act, wasn't it? Where did I fit in, Pat? What was my attraction other than being a tame filth to hang on your arm?'

He stared at her for long moments.

'You really don't see it, do you, Pat? Shall I tell you something? I have child murder and paedophilia to deal with. I have mothers who have knowingly put their own children at risk with sick men and women. Photographs to prove it. Little girls and little boys of two and three having oral sex with punters. Now I wonder if they will end up in one of your so-called fucking clubs in years to come. People like you break down the fabric of society. Oh, you say it's a laugh. Men just want to let off steam and it doesn't mean anything. But it does, Pat. It means a young woman feels she is nothing more than a piece of meat to satisfy a stranger's lust. It means that men debase themselves with drink before going to make a public show of themselves before other so-called men. It means you coin in a fortune at the expense of vulnerable people. It means that Russians like this Boris, or whoever he bloody well is, want a big chunk of the fortune you are making.'

Her voice had risen to a screech of fury and frustration.

'You brought all this on yourself. Now you have a murder charge hanging over your head and you're on the run, in a policewoman's house, asking her to help you when you've disregarded her from the day you met her. I have nothing left for you, Pat, and after tonight there's even less than there was. So take your problems and your ignorant bloody ways and leave me alone.' Kate sat back heavily, feeling at the end of her tether. 'I have to deal with *victims*, *Patrick*, real *victims*, the aftermath of people like you saying, "Let the punters have what they want." Well, once you break down one taboo there're plenty more to go, and fucking little children seems to be next on the agenda for the pay-for-sex lobby. Give it another twenty years and you can open a lap-dancing fucking nursery! Because *that* is how society is going, thanks to people like you.'

He looked at her with tired eyes. 'I'll take that as a no then. About helping, I mean.'

He walked to the door and looked back at her. She could see how desperate he was and inside her a small spark of pity was fighting against the anger. But she knew she couldn't back down now. Patrick had gone too far this time.

'By the way, Kate, your mother rang the house. Give her a call, will you? She is missing you.'

'Where are you going, Pat?' Her voice was low now.

'Never you mind. I won't be bothering you again. I know where I ain't wanted.'

She heard his footsteps as he walked down the hallway and out through the kitchen. He was using the back door and the knowledge depressed her even more. Sneaking in and out. Running from people. What the hell kind of life was that for anyone?

She was better off out of it. She knew that inside, but it didn't make it hurt any the less.

Mary Parkes's father was sitting at home. Lenny was in shock. Seeing those photographs of his daughter had taken its toll. His face was grey with sickness and disgust.

His little Mary, eleven years old, doing those things with men and with little children . . . He felt the bile rise again in his throat, fought the sickness down, and took a deep slug of whisky.

Trisha gently took his hand. 'What are we going to do, Len?'

'Did you look at all the photos, Trish?'

She shook her head. 'No, love. I saw enough with the first couple, thank you very much.'

'Well, I did and I know one of the men. It was Kevin Blankley, the filthy cunt! My so-called mate.'

Trisha closed her eyes in distress. 'No. You must have been mistaken, Len . . .'

'You couldn't see his face, but you could see his tattoos as plain as day, love.'

'You'll have to tell Old Bill, Len. We can't let that go.'

'No Old Bill, I want that cunt meself. I want him and I want to see him beg me for fucking mercy for what he has done to my girl and to them babies.' Lenny's voice was breaking.

'Because they were babies, Trish.' He had to swallow down the tears lodged inside his chest though part of him wanted to give vent to his pain in a long scream. 'And that fucking little mare of ours was right in the thick of it all.' His voice broke again and he gulped at the whisky, coughing at its rawness on his throat.

He laughed bitterly. 'I thought you had a downer on her, Trish, I really did. According to Mary, everyone was jealous of her. Everyone was an arsehole. How could I not have seen what was going on under me bleeding nose? Last Sunday in the pub she was sitting on Kevin's fucking lap and I was smiling at them. They were laughing at me! Pair of bastards. I thought she was just a little girl, Trish . . .'

Trisha had heard enough. His self-pity hit a nerve in her and she felt the anger inside her boil over. Pulling him around to face her, she stared into the face she had loved once – many moons before, when they were young and life was fun and he was still a nice bloke. She looked around at their shabby council flat. Make do and bloody mend all her married life. Keeping it all together until he came home, the conquering hero, and she had to take a back seat again.

'She never was a kid, Lenny, you saw to that,' Trisha told him bitterly. 'Traipsing her round pubs with the scum of the fucking earth – what did you expect? She looks like a fucking whore. Plastered in make-up. Dressed like a woman, for Christ's sake. *Other* men take that on board even if you don't. And let's face it, Lenny, the men you mix with are all slags.

Womanisers. Whore chasers. You only have to look at the type of women in the pubs you frequent so fucking often. No decent girl would be seen in them. Yet you took Mary there from a baby. Everyone making a fuss of her, and her bright enough to learn early that if you say something clever you get the kudos. Well, she wasn't that clever and, as God is my witness, I knew something like this would happen one day. I knew it. Mary learned too much far too soon.'

She sipped at her own drink, trying to control the bitter hurt and resentment she had felt towards him for so long. 'My mother and my sister Kathy won't even be seen with her in public. They certainly don't let their kids mix with her no more. Now I wonder if anything happened, and with you being so fucking lairy, no one dared to say anything to us. Mary knew that you and your rep saved her from a hammering time and time again. She used you, Len, you're right about that. She learned to use people at an early age and she learned it from you. At your knee.'

'I don't ever want to clap eyes on her again, Trish.'

She snorted with suppressed mirth. 'We have to go to court yet, Lenny. This will be all over the estate by the weekend. You know you can't keep anything secret round here for long. We'll be made a fucking show of and people will talk behind our backs because, let's face it, they ain't going to say anything to our faces, are they? Not with you and your temper and your drinking and your fucking shitty ways!'

She stood up and said desperately, 'I loved it when you was banged up, Lenny. I had a life then. I could tell that little madam where to go and that boy of ours, your son, got a look in now and again. It's like Ian don't exist for you. What's the matter, Lenny, too masculine for you now he's a six-footer, eh?

'When you went away we had the perfect marriage. You courted me with letters and I visited you regularly and had a chat. Something we'd never have had while you were home because you always had people to see, things to do. Money to steal. You're a *tealeaf*, Lenny, not a real robber. You're nickels and dimes in comparison to the real villains. Just another nutter who strongs it. And Mary learned all that at your knee.

'Look at the way we live,' she burst out. 'And you called yourself an *armed robber*? If it wasn't for my job in the newsagent's we'd be hard pushed to pay the bleeding rent some weeks. You taught her about easy money, that's what happened to Mary. Because I can guarantee you they paid her for her slagging, Len. When I think of the trouble this is going to cause, I could cheerfully murder the pair of you!

'And when you're beating up Kevin, remember the times you took her round that pub to him. You gave our little girl to him and people like him without even realising it. You gave her a taste for the scum of the earth, Lenny. It's all she's comfortable with nowadays.'

Lenny was in shock. In all the years he had been with his wife he had never heard her say so much, or talk such sense.

He cried.

Trisha looked at him without compassion. She was

dead inside. Had been since she saw the first photograph.

'Be a man and kill Kevin, Lenny. Kill him. Make sure no other little mites have to endure what he wants from them. For once, Lenny, be a real fucking man! Go down for something worthwhile.'

He just nodded, didn't answer her. There was nothing left to say.

'And before you kill him, find out who else is involved. Let's nip this in the bloody bud. If nothing else, we can help pay back the debt that little whore has dropped in our laps. Those children were used and abused by evil men and women. And someone, somewhere has to pay for that.'

Chapter Eight

As Kate stepped into the shower her phone rang. Cursing, she answered it, naked and wet.

'Ma'am?' It was DC Golding's voice.

'What's happened?' Kate was ready for anything. Sleep had eluded her and she was already wide awake. Patrick Kelly had seen to that.

'Mercedes Alston has been found. She's in Grantley Hospital suffering from hypothermia. She'd been dumped in the woods by the golf course. Bless her little heart, ma'am, she'd taken off her shoes and socks as if getting ready for bed, and waited for someone to come.'

'But the golf course was searched earlier. How could they have missed her?' The anger was back in Kate's voice again and Golding was wary now.

'You'll have to ask the search teams that, but the dogs missed her as well don't forget. Unless she wandered there from somewhere else.'

Kate banged the phone down and went back into the shower.

It rang again.

'Hello, Kate, Ratchet here. You are to be interviewed today in connection with Patrick Kelly and his disappearance. I don't need to impress upon you the importance of this investigation, do I?'

She smiled grimly and answered him with false bonhomie. 'Will they be interviewing *you* at all, sir? Only you knew him personally long before I ever did.'

Ratchet slammed down his phone and Kate mentally chalked one up to herself. The two-faced bastard wanted to bury her and she knew it. Well, he could look elsewhere for his sacrificial lamb. She wasn't in the mood to let them cut her throat just yet.

She had dressed and left her house in fifteen minutes flat. It felt like the old days, before Patrick. She didn't dwell on the loneliness in those days. She knew that if she did she would be fucked. In more ways than one.

Mercedes was none the worse for her ordeal. Albeit pale and tired, she was smiling at all and sundry as she lay in her hospital cot being made much of by nurses, doctors and the police.

Kate was amazed by her beauty and wondered who mated with Kerry Alston to produce such a child. Whoever it had been probably had no idea she even existed. Kerry had been a fuck, an hour's interlude, a drunken shag. The thought saddened Kate but she knew she was right. It was how the job got you in the end. Cynical.

She shrugged off her gloomy thoughts. Robert

Bateman was by the child's bed and she smiled at him.

'Another one of yours?'

He shook his head. 'No, dear. I am here because the duty worker's on her hols. Probably got a drink in one hand and a waiter in the other as we speak! Gone to Greece, see, a big girl. She'll be easy prey for the bubbles.'

He took Mercedes's hand in his and she grinned at him happily. 'Poor little mare, isn't she?'

Kate didn't answer, simply asked: 'May we have access to the files, please, or have I got to get a court order?'

Bateman looked coy. 'Now you know the score. I'll give you access to the files by all means but they won't tell you anything. Names aren't permitted, you know that. It's like trying to work out a crossword puzzle at times. I'll give you an example. Recently two of my clients had a fight. I had to write that my client, who we'll call Joe Bloggs, had a fight with *another person.*'

He sighed theatrically, making Kate want to laugh.

'No, you won't get anything from them, but you can have them all the same. I always do me bit if I can. But we have to protect our clients, and while protecting them we watch our own arses.'

'Did anyone have any idea that these children were being used for pornographic purposes?'

Robert shook his shaggy head. 'Not an inkling. But it's hardly something you'd advertise, is it? None of the kids showed the classic behaviour but that could be because they were still pretty new at it. I can't really comment.'

He pulled Kate away from the bed and said gently, 'Kerry Alston was abused by her father. Awful abuse. Photos of her are still winging their way round the Internet, love. Along with the new ones, of course.' He waved his hand in a gesture of disgust. 'What goes around comes around, eh? We live cosy lives, Miss Burrows. Not everyone is so lucky.'

'I suppose so. But, Mr Bateman, if I had been abused I don't think I'd want to perpetuate it, would you?'

'That is something you can only answer through experience, love,' he said sagely. 'Not through thoughts or feelings. They are all victims, whatever way you look at it. Drop by the office and I'll have what you need, OK?'

'Thank you, Mr Bateman.'

He laughed girlishly. 'Call me Bobby, love – everyone else does. Did anyone ever tell you that you have a wonderful bone structure? I bet you take a lovely photo.'

Kate smiled at the compliment. 'Thank you.'

As he swept out of the ward with a backward wave she turned to the bed. Golding looked at her in disgust.

'I reckon he's a queer.'

Kate grinned. 'Takes one to know one, Golding.'

He kept quiet after that but Kate knew she had annoyed him.

Patrick's sister looked at him with contempt.

'I don't believe you, Pat. You got a woman like

Kate and you blew it? Honest, I wonder if any man born has ever had a brain in his head. You especially should have realised you weren't dealing with your normal tits and arse there. Christ, you should have been grateful she gave you the time of day!'

Patrick held up his hands in surrender. 'All right, Vi. We've had the Kate Burrows Appreciation Society for the last half hour, can we give it a fucking rest now? I dropped a bollock and I am paying for it, dearly. Happy? Shall I cut one of me hands off or commit hara-kiri? Will that prove I agree with what you're saying?'

Violet felt unexpectedly sorry for him. Her voice slower now, full of compassion, she said: 'I know you're in lumber, Pat, but for fuck's sake you're fifty odd years old. Leave all the ducking and diving to the younger chaps, eh? Enjoy life while you still can. Ooh, you make me angry! Just like when we were kids. Nothing was ever enough for you, was it? You had to have it bigger and better than everyone else. Even your bike was like a work of art! Streamers and all the rest of it. Mum was caught between feeling proud and having a strong urge to break your bleeding neck most of the time. Now look at you, up shit creek without a paddle as usual. But you'll get out of it. You always do.'

Despite herself she smiled at him. But he didn't smile back.

'Not this time, sis. This time I might just be in over me head.'

Violet blew a raspberry, grey hair bobbing on her

head as if possessed of a life of its own.

'I'll believe that when I see it, boy. Now get that grub down your Gregory and we'll see if we can come up with something between us. You know what they say, Pat, two heads are better than one.'

'Yeah but, Vi, that only counts if the two heads are above average intelligence. So, love, where does that leave you?'

She grinned. 'See, you cheeky fucker! Even with all this hanging over your head you're still making jokes. That Russian had better watch himself, mate. Then, when you've sorted this lot, Pat, do me a favour and fucking retire, will you? I can't take all this any more. I'm too old for it, boy. And without wishing to offend, love, so are you. There's loads more frosting on your bonce. Grey as a badger you are.'

Patrick chuckled. He loved Violet, nothing fazed her.

'Just because there's snow on the roof don't mean there ain't a fire in the grate, Vi.'

She rolled her eyes in exasperation. 'Shagging and fighting are two different things. The sooner you realise that the better off you'll be.'

He didn't answer her this time. There was nothing he could say. His show of unconcern was slipping and he knew it.

DI Jenny Bartlett was like a breath of fresh air and Kate was over the moon to welcome her into the team.

She and Leila sat and drank coffee as Jenny asked

them pertinent questions about the investigation. 'So, the dead kids showed no physical signs of abuse?'

Leila shook her head. 'No. The photos show them engaging in oral sex. It's the older kids who seem to have been used more aggressively. I think the adults concerned were aware that two- and three-year-olds would be outwardly hurt – bruised, cut et cetera. It's all been arranged very professionally. The mother of one child, Kerry Alston, was herself a victim of abuse, both ritual and parental. Her father handed her round to his friends as a party piece, evidently. There's no doubt in my mind that she enjoyed what she was doing, though she's trying to say now she was forced into it. That she's too scared to open her mouth. The usual old fanny.'

'Has a specialist interviewed the kids?'

'Not as yet,' Kate told her. 'We have a consultant psychologist coming from Aberdeen. He's an expert in the field and we want to cause as little trauma to the kids as possible. You must remember that at first these were treated as separate offences. Child endangerment and attempted murder. Now it seems the mothers are in cahoots. Honestly, it's the weirdest case I've ever worked on.'

Jenny sighed. 'The kids should have been interviewed by a psychologist before now. But there's nothing we can do about it now. Let's start on the mothers.' She looked at her notes. 'This Regina Carlton – what has she had to say for herself?'

'At the moment, she is under supervision in Rampton Hospital. We've nothing much on her since as far as we know her kids haven't been involved in anything else. They certainly haven't turned up in any photographs so far. We're pulling apart the Parkes girl's place as we speak. See if she has anything else that might enlighten us.'

'This latest kid, Mercedes, she was found in a place that had been thoroughly searched earlier, yeah?'

Kate nodded.

'So either the search team fucked up, or she had been kept somewhere else for a while? If the mother is involved with paedophiles then it's logical that she could have been taking her some place, isn't it?'

Jenny looked at the other two women and tried to explain what was going through her mind.

'I once worked on a case in Wales where kids were being taxied from playschool to paedophiles' houses. Even the cab firm was in on it. You can't underestimate these bastards, believe me. They walk through society invisible to the rest of us. They're from every walk of life, doctors and lawyers right down the food chain to roadsweepers. And they *all* cover each other's arses.

'We have no idea yet how big this network is. It could be small or it could be huge. What we *do* know is that the men in those photographs are *real*. They have names, dates of birth, and more than likely wives and kids of their own. We need to find out who they are and what they do for a living. Chances are there are other kids involved with them. Statistics prove that there's a paedophile in every street in the country. Scary thought, girls, isn't it? Over a thirty-year period the number of kids affected could be in the thousands and they keep at it until they drop down dead. We have to stamp on this and do it soon.'

Kate was impressed and it showed.

Jenny sipped at her coffee, her huge bulk overflowing the spindly office chair. She had a light in her eyes that pleased Kate, one that denoted energy and determination. She wanted these lowlifes as badly as Kate.

It was a good start.

'One more thing – when I interview the suspects you keep out of it unless I say otherwise, Kate. I know how to rattle them and trip them up. It's a knack I've developed over the years. Are you OK with that?'

She nodded her agreement. 'But remember, I have a few tricks I use myself!'

'Good. Then let's finish this coffee and get started, eh?'

Leila grinned. 'I warned you about her, Kate. She'll run you ragged.'

Jenny looked into Kate's eyes and said, 'But it's for the common good, that's the main thing. The sooner we clean the streets of this scum, the sooner I can get on to the next case and the next lot of nonces. And, believe me, they are legion. Fucking legion.'

Willy felt a presence near him and strained to see through the darkness. He was sore, and he was confused. They had put him in the dark, removed his watch and clothes, and left him tied to a small Z-bed. He wasn't sure if it was day or night, or how long he had been incarcerated.

He could smell a pungent aroma and realised it was aftershave.

'Who's there? Fucking get me up and fight me like a man.' His voice was hoarse from lack of water and disuse.

A heavily accented voice replied, 'We won't harm you, Mr Gabney, you are more like insurance to us. We want to use you to bargain with Mr Kelly. Please, put yourself at ease about everything, I beg of you.'

'Up yours, mate. Pat Kelly will take you and break you like a fucking child's toy! You don't know who you've picked a fight with, you don't. Well, you'll soon find out, mate. Quick smart.'

The voice was laughing now. 'I speak better English than you do, Mr Gabney.'

Willy said scornfully, 'Well, that ain't hard, is it? Everyone speaks better English than the English. The real English, that is. Ain't you ever noticed how everyone speaks English but we don't bother learning anyone else's language? Why would we? When prats like you bother to understand us, we don't need to learn nothing. But we teach good fucking manners, boy, remember that.'

Boris was impressed. This man, an *old* man by his standards, had put up a very brave fight. It had taken three men and eventually a gun to get him in the back of the van, and as they had driven him away he had really gone to town, knocking out one of Boris's best men with a single punch.

Now he had been kept prisoner for two days without food or water and he was still fighting. Boris envied Patrick Kelly this man's loyalty and devotion. But he would keep him without food, water or warmth for a good while yet. He didn't trust the prisoner's strength. It was abnormal.

'Mr Kelly knows we have you. I have heard from him and will be making a point of seeing him before very long. You need be patient for only a few more days.'

'Up yours, you Russian ponce!'

'The same to you too, Mr Gabney, I'm sure. I will bid you farewell.'

He left as quietly as he'd entered. Willy wondered where the hell he was being held. There was no sound, no smell, nothing. It was a completely dark and sterile environment. He felt better for the human contact, though. At one point he'd wondered if he was going to be left to starve to death. Maybe that's what they would do to him yet. He didn't know. He only knew the Russians were hard bastards. But then so was he, and more importantly so was Patrick Kelly. Pat would get him out of it if it was humanly possible, no matter what the price. Willy knew that as well as he knew his own name.

All he could do was wait and hope that things would turn out all right. He knew his boss would be moving heaven and earth to locate him. He only hoped Pat had talked to Maureen. She would have Willy's nuts and nail them to the wall over this little débâcle.

Kate listened to Superintendent Cotter and stifled an

urge to tell him where to get off. Politely, of course. The man had an arrogance that was almost palpable.

She listened as he droned on, obviously enamoured of the sound of his own voice. She observed him carefully, taking in every detail, from his sandy thinning hair to the beer gut hanging over his belt. She realised he wore a truss and this made her want to laugh out loud.

Cotter guessed what she was thinking and his shrewd blue eyes glared at her.

'I understand, Miss Burrows, and please correct me if I am wrong, that you have had an intimate relationship with the murder suspect for a couple of years.'

'I most certainly have. Mr Kelly and I had a full physical relationship until recently, when we both decided that our friendship had run its course – after which we parted company.' She shrugged. 'You understand how these things are, I'm sure.'

'Mr Kelly is wanted in relation to a recent killing in Soho . . .'

Kate interrupted him. 'I know. But Mr Kelly has never been found guilty of so much as a parking ticket or even given points on his licence before now, so I really don't see what all this has to do with me. You seem to be insinuating that I have somehow compromised myself but I have been in touch with my union and they assure me that unless Mr Kelly had any prior conviction, I was perfectly free to see him.

'I want you to understand, Superintendent Cotter, that I have always kept one eye on the job, *whoever* I was dating. Which is more than can be said for some of my male colleagues who seem to make a career out of escorting prisoners' wives around town, sometimes even marrying them. Now, if you're finished with me, I have a rather demanding case to investigate as I'm sure you are aware.'

'Were you with Mr Kelly last Tuesday night? Yes or no. As you are in such a hurry I will get straight to the point.'

Kate looked Cotter in the eye for a good fifteen seconds and he could see her battling it out with herself before she answered. She knew he wouldn't believe her. She could hardly believe she was saying it herself.

'Yes, I was. It was our last night together, so I could hardly forget. I can *categorically* state that Pat Kelly was nowhere near that club. He was a silent partner and had no involvement in the day-to-day running of it at all.'

She stood up and smiled. 'If you get this tape typed up, I'll sign my statement and we can all get on with our work.'

Cotter smirked. 'Not so fast, Miss Burrows. A Mr Thomas Broughton says that Patrick Kelly *was* at the club that night. How do you explain that?'

Kate paused for a moment before drawing breath. 'I can't. He's obviously mistaken. Now is that all?' Her voice carried far more conviction than she really felt.

'For the time being, Miss Burrows.'

She went straight to the canteen, saw Jenny alone at a table and grabbed a coffee before joining her.

'How did it go?'

'Not too good in all honesty. I think Cotter's after blood, preferably mine!'

Jenny laughed delightedly. 'He's a right arsehole, I've had dealings with him myself. You've heard I'm a lesbian? He tried to say I was as perverted as the people I put away. He's the one with the problem, not me. I'm happy. I like myself and my life and what I am. Not many straights can say that, eh?'

Kate admired her honesty. In a profession dogged by homophobia and racism it was hard to be yourself at times even when you were a white heterosexual. Admitting to being gay was tantamount to wearing a sign reading 'Kick Me'.

But it was getting better. Or at least Kate hoped it was. On the surface everyone was very politically correct but no one, not even the government, could dictate what people were thinking deep inside.

'Well, Cotter doesn't like me and quite frankly I don't like him. But I could do without all this at the moment, I really could,' she sighed.

'I've heard about Patrick Kelly.' Jenny laughed. 'A good-looking villain, by all accounts. Seriously good-looking if the gossip's true.'

Kate grinned. 'Who's been talking – Golding? He's worse than a woman, him. He'd find gossip at the Last Supper.'

'You've a good rep, Kate,' Jenny said warmly. 'You're respected by all the men here because you *caught* and *tamed* a lion. Never underestimate the power of gossip. It can do you a lot of good.'

Kate saw the logic in what she was saying. 'Thanks, Jenny. I needed a friendly word.'

'We all do at times. It's human nature, love. Now drink up and let's get back into the fray. We have to talk to Miss Parkes and see what we can get out of her, OK?'

Kate nodded but the lie she had told weighed her down. She'd done it not so much for Patrick but to give Cotter one in the eye. Was it going to backfire on her?

Patrick would have to be told she had alibied him. She wasn't sure if she was pleased at the prospect of talking to him or not. Told herself she needed time and space. She needed to sort her head out at some point and decide what she was going to do with her life, or what was left of it anyway. The last week had been full of emotional ups and downs.

Her nerves were shot and she was tired to the very core of her being. And on top of everything else she still had not phoned her mother.

Lenny Parkes walked into the Fox Revived and stared around him until he located the man he wanted.

Kevin Blankley was sitting with his cronies, Harold Carter, Les Smith and Davey Carling. They waved Lenny over and he mimed getting a drink and walked to the bar where he ordered a large brandy. Draining it down in one gulp, he ordered another immediately. He did this three more times until the landlady, Denise Charterhouse, a large woman with yellow teeth and a jocular manner, said: 'Who's rattled your bleeding cage then? Had a row with the old woman?'

He didn't answer her and she said brightly, trying to get him talking, 'Where's little Mary today? All the men have missed her.'

He knew on one level that she meant nothing by it. That she was just being friendly. As his wife had pointed out, he was always in the pub with Mary. She had been coming in here since she was a baby. But after all that had happened the words hit him full force and his last ounce of self-control disappeared.

Turning from the bar, he picked up a pint glass half-full of flat lager. The look on his face told Denise that something bad was going to happen. She watched in horror as he walked across the crowded room towards his friends. Before she could shout a warning, the glass was raised, smashed against a table and thrust with animal strength into Kevin Blankley's neck. The whole pub watched mesmerised as Lenny stabbed the jagged glass into the man over and over again.

Harold, Les and Davey jumped from their seats, Kevin's blood spraying all over them in a fine mist.

Kevin was on the floor now, his hands to his lacerated face and neck. Blood was pumping freely like a hose-pipe on a sunny day.

Lenny began kicking him, and then the shouting started. It came from his bowels, as he screamed his hatred at the man on the floor.

'Fucking touch my baby, you bastard! Touch my girl, would you? Make her like you, you fucking beast!'

Out of the corner of his eye he saw Davey go even paler, try to move away, get to the door. He saw the others looking at him in amazement and instinctively knew that Davey had been in on it as well.

Lenny turned on him like an animal. 'What you running for, Davey? Where you going – home? Got any nice pictures of my girl? That piece of shit I called a daughter? Who you lot took and dragged down to the gutter where you come from.'

He was walking towards Davey who looked terrified. Lenny glanced around the pub and said loudly, 'He's a nonce. A beast. I've seen the photos. And not just eleven-year-olds, oh, no. You're always saying how much you love kids, eh, Davey? Well, I've seen the proof with me own eyes. Old Bill are coming for you lot, but not before I get to pay you back for what you've done to my girl. Pay *her*, did you? Cheap at the fucking price, eh?'

Davey was a large man, heavy-set with a heavy job. He was muscular through and through. Challenged, he stood his ground and said nastily, 'Your Mary didn't need any teaching from me, Len. She's a natural. Look how she walks about, asking for trouble and getting it, mate.'

Lenny listened in amazement to his old mate and close friend. How could he not have known? How could he never have guessed what was going on? Davey wasn't that clever, surely.

He heard the distant wail of sirens and guessed, rightly, it was the police coming for him. Taking a carving knife from his belt, he held it before him and smiled. Davey tried to run. Lenny got to him as he reached the door. His hand was extended towards the heavy iron handle when the knife hit him in the back, tearing his skin but not doing as much damage as Lenny wanted.

The two plainclothes policemen Kate had sent to watch Lenny grabbed him as they saw their chance, while his back was turned and he was not expecting it. By the time the back-up arrived he was on the floor, handcuffed and subdued. One man dead, and another needing urgent hospital treatment. Lenny felt he'd done a good day's work.

It was over for him. He had done what he had to do and could finally relax. His wife and son would be moved away by Social Services and relocated in another town. That was the price he would exact for a full and frank confession. He knew the police would agree. He also knew that soon everyone would learn what his daughter had done; talk spread fast in a small place like Grantley. But he would be remembered as a man who had sorted things out. Done his duty. Removed the scum from the streets.

In short, he would be a hero.

It was shallow consolation, though. In truth nothing would ever make up for what his daughter had done. She had laughed at him, scorned all he had tried to be to her. The strangest thing of all was, already he felt nothing for her. Not even anger, hatred or disgust. It was as if Mary had never existed for him.

He knew as they marched him outside the pub that he was a dead man, inside, where it counted. If his body lived on until he was a hundred years old he would always know that for him death had arrived when he was thirty-eight. From this moment on, he would merely go through the motions. He would eat, breathe and shit, but he would never feel any real emotions again. Mary, once his pride and joy, his little daughter, had seen to that.

Kate looked into his eyes at the police station and he smiled back at her. Covered in blood and wild-eyed, he felt as if Kate Burrows and the heavy-set woman with her understood his actions. Understood what had made him do what he had done. They gave him tea, cigarettes and respect.

At least that's how it seemed to Lenny Parkes.

In her office Kate looked at Jenny with guilt and regret.

'I knew this could happen, but how could I have prevented it?'

Jenny shrugged and said breezily, as if she didn't give a damn, 'He took it to the extreme, I don't deny that. But he's led us to another paedophile we can interview, maybe find out more about how many are involved in all this and, more importantly, who they are. Paedophiles are passive, Kate. They're normally timid little men and women, terrified that someone will find out about them.

'They know what the normal members of society think of them, the disgust they engender. They know that a capture will bring down disgust, hatred, even death on them. That's why we have the VPU units. *Vulnerable* Prisoners. Pity they don't think about their vulnerable prey. I don't feel anything about the pub death, really, except that it was pretty horrific. But that doesn't make me any the less glad that another nonce has been removed from the face of the earth.

'I have seen the bodies of children that people like this have taken and tortured and killed. I lost any sympathy for them a long time ago. In fact, if I could get away with it, I'd nut them myself.'

She winked at Kate before saying, 'All that was strictly off the record, of course.'

Davey Carling looked ill. His breathing was laboured and his chest rattled. Golding was standing by the bed with a young police constable, and even he realised that the man was dying.

The doctor looked at David Golding and motioned him towards the door. Outside in the noisy corridor he explained what was happening.

'Mr Carling had a massive heart attack earlier this afternoon. He is in a deep coma and the chances of recovery are slight. The stab wound seemed to become infected overnight. It appears he was already suffering from chronic heart disease, which is not surprising. I already ascertained he was a heavy smoker and drinker, and from the condition of his outer body I knew he was out of shape.' He shrugged. 'If he hadn't been stabbed he would have died within a few months anyway. Keeled over, dropped dead. Probably while eating a large cooked breakfast.'

Golding was amazed at the young man's lack of

compassion. The doctor realised what he was thinking and explained, 'The way I see it, the greatest gift we have is the gift of life. When I see it wasted, it always makes me angry.'

'There's no chance of interviewing him?' asked Golding.

The doctor shook his head wearily.

'No. No chance. It's TLC from here on. He'll never utter another word.'

Golding walked away.

Davey Carling died with the young police constable as his only visitor. The PC was still stumped by the *Sun* crossword and didn't even realise he was gone until a nurse came in and quietly turned off the monitors.

Kate took the news calmly, one half of her glad that another paedophile had bitten the dust.

This was a death that no one was going to mourn. Least of all her.

Chapter Nine

'Hello, Kate.'

Patrick's voice was rich and warm, washing over her like a wave. As she sat beside him in his car she felt the old powerful attraction to him. Could smell his own particular smell that once had made her feel safe and secure. She had to force down a strong urge to put her arms around him for comfort.

'You did it then?'

She nodded imperceptibly. 'I lied if that's what you're referring to.' In the close confines of the car he seemed larger than ever. Bigger than she remembered him.

'*Were* you at the club that night? Tommy Broughton says you were.'

'Tommy's a liar then. I was nowhere near it, OK?'

She could hear the fear underlying his words and realised that Patrick Kelly was putting on a show of bravado for the first time since she had laid eyes on him.

'What's going on, Pat?'

From the tone of her voice, he knew that if he

could tell her the truth then maybe she would stand beside him after all. But he couldn't. She was away from him now and that was a good thing at this time. She must never know the danger he had already placed her in with Boris for just the simple reason that she was known to be close to him.

In all his life Patrick had never been in the position he currently faced. He had ducked and dived for years and it was finally all coming home to roost. He was out of the shit with Old Bill, though that could be strictly temporary. What he needed now was to keep himself and Kate safe.

'I appreciate what you did, darling. I know how much it took for you to lie like that.'

'Where were you, Pat? That night – who were you with?'

He looked into her eyes and sighed heavily. He trusted this woman more than he had ever trusted anyone before. Even Renée, his wife, had never engendered the feelings Kate Burrows stirred in him. But he could not tell her. Kate would want to sort it out, help him. Make him try the honest approach. She had never understood that with some people, the honest approach was fatal.

He admired her, though. To see what she had seen in the course of her work and still trust in human nature was to his eyes a wondrous feat. He barely trusted anyone, just a couple of very close friends, Kate being one of them and Willy the other.

As if he had put the words into her mouth she said, 'Where's Willy?'

He looked into her face and knew she half guessed what had occurred. 'He's doing an errand for me.'

Kate didn't answer, just stared into his eyes. Lying eyes, if she knew Pat Kelly.

'An errand? Pat, do I look stupid? I really need to know the answer to that question.' The sarcasm was back in her voice and it put his back up as she'd known it would.

'Leave it, Kate. Let it go, eh?'

She shook her head sadly as she watched him controlling his temper, but she knew he would not tell her anything about Willy.

'You'll never learn, will you, Pat? Still the hard man, eh?'

He turned to face her then, hostility in every line of his body. 'Nah, you're right as usual, I'll never learn. A fucking thug me, till I drop down dead. In fact, I love ducking and diving. Gives me a reason to get up in the morning, know what I mean? Only the same could be said of you too, couldn't it? Think about it, Kate. We're on opposite sides of the same fucking fence, love. Only you are a self-righteous pain in the arse . . .'

She smiled gently. 'And what are you then? How about a selfish bully boy who plays with other people's lives and affections? A ponce in every sense of the word. Living off the earnings of women . . .'

She saw his eyes harden and bit her lip. 'Have I hit a nerve, Patrick? Only that is exactly where you get your money from these days, isn't it? Why act so shocked at a simple statement of the truth?'

He wiped one hand across his face and she laughed.

'Are you by any chance ashamed? Is that it, Pat?'

He pushed her roughly in the chest. The car was like a coffin to him now; he wanted out of it. Wanted her away from him. He had enough on his mind without listening to her going on and on.

'Do you know something, love? You're beginning to bore me. I admit, you did me a right favour and I appreciate it big time. But I tell you now, Kate, you're getting to be a dried-up old cow. Always right, *always* got a fucking opinion about me and what I do. I sometimes wonder how the hell we ever got together in the first place. Well, let me tell you something, Kate. What I feel for you is beyond anything you could ever feel for me, lady. And shall I tell you why that is? Because unlike you I don't judge everyone. I take them as I find them.'

They looked at one another, antagonists now, wanting only to hurt.

Kate curled her lip and said, 'Did it ever occur to you that your outlook on life is exactly why you're in the shit now?' She waved one hand at him. 'Take everyone as you find them, eh? Well, I hope you learn from this lot, I really do. You sound like a schoolboy – a naïve and ignorant schoolboy.'

He was quiet for a moment and Kate was sorry for her outburst. Before she could speak again, try and undo some of the damage, he replied quietly.

'If I never clap eyes on you again, Kate, it will be too soon. I have finally seen you for what you are, love. Look down your nose at me if that makes you feel better – I couldn't give a fucking toss any more. As for your big lie: tell them you made a mistake. I can get fifty little birds to lie for me and they'd do it without a backward glance, OK? I don't need you or your help, lady. I don't need you full stop.'

'Oh yes, you do, Pat, because unlike the fifty little birds you can so easily get to lie for you, I at least would be believed!'

She got out of the car and walked away from him. Her heart was beating a tattoo in her chest and her anger was so acute she could have physically struck him for what he had just said. It seemed that overnight they had started to hate one another. How the hell had that happened to them?

She had never wanted to hurt another individual so badly in her whole life before, not even her ex-husband Dan when he had walked out of her life leaving her with a baby and no money because he had cleaned out the bank account. Not even when she found out he was living off his new woman, travelling the world and driving fast cars yet not giving her a halfpenny for their child. Not even then had she felt as angry and hurt as she did now. Over Patrick Kelly, a villain, a thug – and the most decent man she had ever come across.

She cried.

The child was quiet. The woman took his hand once more and pulled him gently towards the lorry park. He was a sweet kid with blue eyes and curly brown hair. He giggled as the woman smiled down at him.

'Mummy?'

'Mummy loves you, darling, you know that. But, you see, you get on Mummy's nerves. She can't do what she wants when you are around.'

The child didn't understand what was being said but the sing-song voice was pleasant so he assumed he was being told something lovely and he smiled happily once more.

No one saw them as they reached a large artic.

No one saw the woman deposit the child in the back of the lorry.

As she strolled out of the lorry park she saw two men walking towards her. They glanced in her direction and she turned her face away from them. Her long blonde hair caught on the wind and she pulled her jacket tightly around her even though it was still quite warm.

She was humming as she walked to her car. She felt lighter than she had in days.

Jackie Palmer was a good-looking girl. Her use of thick eyeliner and false eyelashes gave her a look of permanent surprise, opening her already wide brown eyes even further. The effect was striking to say the least. She was worth a second look, and she knew it.

As she sashayed towards her council house she grinned which marred her appearance somewhat. Her teeth, never her best feature, were a dull grey colour. Four children in four years had taken its toll on them.

She was happy, though. She had a new bloke, a few quid and a part-time job that more than paid the bills. She had been working in the massage parlour for all of three months and was not enjoying the work so much as the benefits it afforded her. New clothes when she wanted, a few recreational drugs for the weekend and some things for the home. She had to be careful what she bought, though, because she was still under a supervision order from Social Services. Jackie shrugged off her annoyance at the thought. In a few months it would be OK. She was giving them all the old fanny they needed to leave her alone and in peace to get on with her lucrative new way of life.

As she let herself into the house she was amazed by how peaceful it was. Her sister had started taking the kids to her house and it had been like a new lease of life to Jackie. She'd lied to Louise, telling her she got home two hours later than she actually did. That way she could bathe, have a drink and get herself something to eat before the four maniacs descended on her.

When she had had the first child at eighteen she had thought she was so clever. She got a flat and coped very well. But loneliness had set in and she started picking up men to while away a few hours. None of them stayed long but they generally left her with a new baby. At times she wondered how she could have been so stupid. She loved the kids, as much as they drove her mad, but it was hard to be young and attractive and to be tied down so early in life. Never having had a job, a proper boyfriend, or even a real family. All the kids had different fathers and it showed. Not just in their looks but in the colour of their skin and their different personalities.

She could still hear her mother's voice as she expressed her disgust and horror at yet another fatherless child, another pregnancy to leave her daughter drained and needing all the help she could get.

Her mother had recently met a man and gone to live with him in Kent. Jackie knew it was because of her, and her sister and brother never failed to confirm it whenever the subject of their mother and her defection from the family came into the conversation. Which it did, frequently.

Running a bath, Jackie made herself some tea and toast, taking off her make-up as she did so. She could do without the kids, she really could. But they were in the world and they were hers, her responsibility, as everyone kept pointing out to her.

Sighing, she tied up her heavy blonde hair and took the tea and toast into the bathroom with the newspaper and the radio for company.

This was her time, and she made sure she enjoyed it.

Jackie's sister Louise looked at the clock. Gathering up her own two children and three of Jackie's, she started the short walk to playschool to pick up little Martin. As she neared the gate she yawned. She was late as usual, and knackered. By the time she had got this lot into their coats and hats, and stopped them fighting, arguing and playing up, it was a hard job to get anywhere on time.

She stood outside and watched as the kids were taken home by parents and relatives. She smiled a greeting to a few of the mums she knew. The five children with her ran to the playground in the nursery yard and she watched them as they jumped boisterously all over the equipment. Mrs Walden would tell them off as usual and they would ignore her as usual.

Soon all the other mothers were gone and still Martin was nowhere to be seen. Walking to the double doors at the entrance to the church hall, Louise peeked inside.

Mrs Walden looked at her in surprise. 'Hello, Mrs Ashton, can I help you?'

Louise stared at her as if she had grown another head.

'You certainly can. You can tell me where little Martin is.'

'His mother picked him up a couple of hours ago,' Mrs Walden said, surprised. 'Didn't even come inside, just took him from the play area.'

The tone of voice said, 'Trust Jackie to do something like that without telling anyone.' She had a downer on Jackie, did Mrs Walden, but she wasn't alone in that and Louise was used to it. She actually agreed with people's opinion of her sister though she would never state that openly. Family was family, after all.

'She might have rung, I've been out,' she lied.

Louise turned and walked from the building. Collecting the kids, she swore that this time she was going to give Jackie a fair whack of tongue. Why hadn't she just rung up and let her sister know? That was Jackie all over. Selfish bleeding cow she was.

Louise's annoyance communicated itself to the children who walked sedately beside her all the way home.

Jenny and Kate were trying to make sense of the statements from Mary Parkes and Kerry Alston.

The Alston children were currently being interviewed but there wasn't much to go on from them. In fact they were well schooled in keeping things quiet and as secret as possible. It seemed they just wanted their mummy. Kate was constantly astounded at the resilience of small children.

Regina Carlton had lost it. The doctors said she had suffered a nervous breakdown. Her children were in the care of the courts and she was not fit to be interviewed.

'If this Kevin was one of the men, then he must have known some of the others apart from Davey Carling, it stands to reason,' Jenny said. 'Mary Parkes knew him, so the chances are she knew some of the others, too. Knew them well if the pictures are anything to go by. So we have to concentrate on her now. Kerry's too shrewd, that's the trouble. She knows she will go down but she isn't going down for everything if she can help it. So, what we find out, we use against her. Then she'll more than likely do a deal though I ain't offering her one just yet. Let her sweat for a bit.

'Most of the female paedophiles do deals,' she told Kate. 'One in three are women. Hard to believe, isn't it? That a woman is capable of doing something like that, especially with her own kids. They walk away from the courts because the male-dominated justice system can't comprehend that we are capable of such acts. Did you know, Kate, even the FBI think women need to be led into crimes like this? It's as if their very sex makes them innocent somehow. Yet some of the most predatory paedophiles I ever encountered were women. Look at Myra Hindley. If her voice hadn't been on the tape-recording of the rape of poor little Lesley Anne Downey, she would have walked away from it all as just a girl who'd been led into trouble by a man. Well, she was willing enough or she would never have picked up the kids for him, I'd lay my last penny on that.'

Kate listened to Jenny with morbid fascination. She was a walking encyclopaedia of sexual crime. It was her own personal crusade. Be it paedophiles or rapists, she had the facts, the stats, and anything else she needed filed away in her brain.

Kate's phone rang and she answered it. Replacing the receiver she announced: 'Mary Parkes's mother is outside, she wants to talk to us.'

Jenny raised her eyebrows. 'Let's hope she has new evidence for us. I'd love something over that little madam. You know, Kate, I never thought I'd ever say this about a child, but that girl is bad and I don't think it was just learned behaviour. I think she has a kink in her nature. Do you know what I mean?'

Kate nodded. She agreed with what Jenny had said whole-heartedly.

Five minutes later they were listening in amazement

to what Mary Parkes's mother had to tell them. Even Jenny was subdued as she took on board the full extent of the young girl's involvement in the crimes.

The woman was talking about her eleven-year-old daughter as if she was a mature and hardened criminal.

'It was something she said when I visited her to tell her about her father . . . about what he had done.'

Trisha's voice faltered and she sipped from a glass of water before continuing.

'She said to me, "It wasn't only Kevin he should have killed, it was his brother." Well, I wasn't even aware that Kevin *had* a brother. I visited my husband on remand and he told me there is one and that he lives in East London somewhere. His name is Jeremy Blankley but he uses aliases. Sometimes Carter, sometimes McCann. I don't know if this will be of any help to you, but I thought I should let you know.'

Kate saw the distress on the woman's face and her heart went out to her. Trisha Parkes had so much to deal with, so much to try and come to terms with, not least the loss of a child.

'I've told Social Services that I will not have Mary back in my home. I'm not visiting her, or having anything to do with her. My girl was raised to know right from wrong. She knew what she was doing all right. Just thinking about it turns my stomach.' The woman was unable to continue.

'We appreciate how difficult this must be for you, Mrs Parkes,' Kate said sincerely, 'but anything that you think may help is greatly appreciated by us.'

Trisha forced a smile, then said huskily, 'I thought I

had a good life in some respects. Lenny was a waster, but he was a good man for all that. My son Ian is a diamond, a good kid. But my Mary . . .' She shook her head sadly.

Jenny offered her a cigarette and lit it for her. 'Did Mary ever stay overnight anywhere?' she asked.

'Sometimes she stayed round her friend Sheila's, mainly weekends. Or so she said. But now I think she was staying at that Kerry's drum. But really you'd have to ask Mary where she was. She told me nothing, love. Well, she knew I was on to her, didn't she?'

Trisha looked straight into Jenny's face as she said seriously, 'I never cared where she was, to be honest. The house was so different without her there. Lighter somehow. That's a terrible thing to say about your own child, I know, but I'm glad I don't have to deal with her any more.'

She stood up abruptly. 'I have to go, I've said what I came to say. Now I just want to get on with me life.'

Jackie opened the front door with a wide smile on her face. Louise looked at her sister with a mixture of disgust and outright jealousy. Louise was older, and although she had a look of Jackie, she didn't have the latter's attractiveness. This hurt at times. She knew that her husband, Denny, looked at her sister in a way he had not looked at her in years. Yes, Jackie had it in the looks department. For all the good it did her. Dumped over and over again.

Louise pushed her none too gently in the chest and said loudly, 'Thanks a fucking bunch, Jack. Why didn't you give me a ring?'

Jackie saw the old animosity burning in her sister's eyes and pushed her back angrily.

'What the fuck would I want to ring you for?'

Louise ushered the children into the lounge. Opening her shopping bag, she brought out a bag of sweets and distributed them as she carried on talking.

'How about ringing me up to save me a fucking journey? Dragging this lot about is no joke, you know.'

Jackie stared at her as if she had gone mad. 'Who's rattled your cage, Lou? Denny on the missing list again, is he? And where's my little Martin?' Jackie's eyes were scanning the crowded room.

'What do you mean, where's Martin?' Louise said irritably. '*You* picked him up! That's why I'm so fucking livid. I walked all the way there with this lot—'

'What are you talking about?' Jackie interrupted her. 'I never picked up anyone. I assumed Martin was with you. That's what I pay you for, ain't it? To look after me chavvies while I work.'

Louise paled. 'Don't fucking wind me up, Jack. I just been to the playschool and that old witch told me you took him from the playground.'

They looked at one another then, all animosity forgotten.

'Tell me you picked him up, Jack. Don't fuck about, this ain't funny.' There was a frantic note in Louise's voice now. 'You are such a wind-up, Jack.'

She was trying to smile and Jackie was staring at her sister in utter dismay.

'Louise, mate, I ain't been near the playschool.'

There was fear in her voice. The children picked up on it and started to whine. Louise pulled her sister over to a chair and sat her down.

'I'll phone the school, they must have made a mistake. Now calm down and I'll sort this out, OK?'

Jackie felt her breath catching in her chest and knew she was near to panic. She had a pain in her stomach, a dull ache that was spreading all over her body. Something was dreadfully wrong, it was a mother's instinct. She knew her boy was in trouble. It wasn't a conscious thought, more a feeling that was growing stronger by the second. Martin was in danger somewhere and he wanted his mummy. She knew all this in a matter of seconds.

When Louise came off the phone she was quietly crying, big fat tears of anguish and terror.

'She said you picked him up, Jack. We'd better get Old Bill, eh?'

Jackie started sobbing. The other children gathered round her, upset themselves now at this show of emotion from their mother and aunt.

'You've read the papers lately, Lou. Someone's took my boy, my little Martin.' Jackie was hugging herself and rocking backwards and forwards. Her fear was tangible now, communicating itself to them all.

Louise phoned the police to a chorus of whimpering and tears from the younger children. She didn't start weeping again until she had put the phone down.

★ ★ ★

Jonathon Marcus drove slowly. It was a fine day and he had made a good start. He whistled along to the radio, trying to sing when he actually knew the words.

Jonathon was in love. He had met a man at last! A macho man, one with a hairy chest, a deep laugh and thick dark permed hair. Even his name was perfect. He was another John. They were already being referred to as the two Johns!

Jonathon had only been seeing him for two weeks, but they had so much in common. They liked the same films, the same music – even the same food. It was as if he had waited all his life for this moment.

The day seemed brighter, the world seemed lighter, and he couldn't stop smiling. He turned up the radio and listened to the sound of the Carpenters. He flashed another lorry and waved. If only the other drivers knew! But he managed to keep himself to himself even though he knew they referred to him as Queer John behind his back. He smiled again. They guessed, but no one had ever asked him outright what his sexual preferences were.

He was six three, well-muscled, and could have a row if he had to. He was twenty-seven years old and was what he liked to refer to as a New Gay man. He could take care of himself and people were wary of him. But he had proved himself to be a hard worker, a good bloke and a bit of a laugh. He had even recently been propositioned at work by another driver in the toilets at Granada Services, and that had cracked him right up. The man was OK and before John he might have been tempted. But not now.

He shook his head. He didn't need encounters like that any more. He'd just had a wonderful few days. They had gone to a party on the Friday night, had had lunch together on Saturday, and then – this was what he couldn't believe – they'd had lunch with John's parents on the Sunday, where the two men's sexuality was known, accepted and never referred to, just as if they were a regular couple!

That had never happened to him before. Ever.

He knew he should tell his family. His elder sister had already guessed but Elaine was good-hearted. She never said anything outright but let him know in her own way that it was OK by her. He knew she would love him whatever, but his mother and father . . . Now there was a different story.

His father thought that gays should see a doctor and get cured. He thought they were diseased. As for his mother! Jesus, whatever her husband thought, then so did she. If she asked Jonathon once more when he was going to find a nice girl he would scream. He had found his life-mate, he was sure of it. And after meeting John's family and experiencing their easy acceptance he had realised just what a lie he was living every day and how difficult that lie was becoming.

Only this morning his mother was going on about Lorraine Felton and how she was always after him. Even if he was straight he wouldn't give her a second glance. She was a big fat cow with a mouth like nobody's business! Talking through her nose and describing everything as 'phenomenal' in that Essex bloody twang.

Still, he knew his mother meant well.

He drummed his fingers on the steering wheel. He usually liked the journey to Cologne. Christ knows he had driven it enough times. He was dropping off for UPS and picking up sausages as usual. A nice easy run. Boat from Folkestone, over to Calais, on to Cologne and home again. Only now he was coming home to John!

Approaching the dock road, he slowed the lorry right down. It was heavy and he knew that the slope on the approach could really give you hassle if you were going too fast. Jonathon grinned at the thought of flying into the sea. Especially in his new Wranglers!

He turned the radio down and opened the window, loving the salty smell of the air. He was glad now that he had the curtain-sider; it was better than the container lorries in this weather. But sometimes the material caught the wind and that caused a few problems in itself.

When Jonathon saw another driver with a young man in his cab, he shook his head knowingly. It was a shirt-lifter's paradise at the docks these days. And this bloke was married, he knew. He glanced again at the boy, and sighed in exasperation. Rough trade, all right. He'd had his share of them over the years. Vicious little buggers some of them.

Now he had his John he didn't need anything like that any more. At least, he bloody hoped not anyway.

He yawned, rubbing his eyes. He was tired, it had

been an early start. But he would be in Cologne in under seven hours if the roads were OK. And if he loaded his return on time he would be at home and in bed with his new man by nine tomorrow night.

He started to crawl towards the ferry terminal, all the time on the look-out for people he knew. He wondered what unauthorised loads were on some of the lorries around him. He had been offered money recently to bring back hardcore porn but had refused. The money wasn't that good and the risk wasn't worth the hag. Though he knew a few drivers who had done it and not had a tug or even a search.

A bloke he had worked with for years, a grandfather of three, had been caught bringing in drugs. He was now doing a twelve-stretch which no amount of money could compensate for as far as Jonathon was concerned.

As he made sure his passport and papers were to hand he had no idea that he was carrying extra cargo himself: little Martin Palmer was asleep, worn out from exhaustion, hunger and thirst, on a pile of pallets in the back of the lorry.

Cologne airport was still a long drive away and, turning the radio back up, Jonathon sang along to Spandau Ballet's 'True'. His most favourite song of all time.

Martin curled up with his thumb in his mouth, his eyes red from crying and his body aching from the cold and the hardness of his makeshift bed. The wind caught the tarpaulin on the side of the lorry and the noise woke him up. He lay in the dark weeping softly.

Chapter Ten

Kate was worried. Another child gone, another mother in pieces and another phone call from Patrick Kelly, this time telling her that he would have all her belongings returned to her house as soon as possible. They were all neatly packed and ready to be delivered at her convenience.

Pushing her own problems from her mind, she looked at Jackie Palmer. She was an attractive girl with her brown eyes and blonde-streaked hair. At the moment, those brown orbs were red from crying. She was shaking as she lit yet another cigarette from the butt of the previous one. Unlike the others, this girl had a viable alibi which she was not frightened to give. She had been working at the Black Rose sauna and massage parlour and she could prove it. Once the other girls there realised what had happened they had rallied round and offered whatever help they could. In fact, Kate was impressed with the way they had all tried their damnedest to give as much information as possible.

They were a good crowd and obviously felt a close affinity with their colleague. As she listened to Jackie's sister explaining what had happened Kate was convinced that Louise was telling the truth. She wondered if this time someone else had taken the boy, because both women had alibis that were watertight.

The child had been taken at 10.15 a.m. Jackie had just left the massage parlour then. It was on the CCTV camera kept hidden so as not to scare customers. The girls there were more than aware of the dangers of the job they did and as the Black Rose was run by an ex-prostitute she made sure they were all kept as safe as possible. Kate brought her attention back to Jackie.

'I admit I am still under a supervision order, but that is only because I found it hard to cope at times. I have never neglected the kids in any way. I took a few drugs, had what were termed unsuitable friends, but my kids are my life. I flog me arse for them and I ain't ashamed of that fact.' Her pupils were dilated from the Valium given to her by the duty doctor.

Kate watched Jenny weighing up the girl once more and knew that she was feeling the same as herself. This was either a really good actress or she was telling the truth, though they could not discount the possibility she had asked someone else to pick the child up from the playground. She herself had rarely if ever picked him up there, apparently. The woman in charge was waiting to be interviewed and was going to get it in the neck.

She should have made sure of the identity of the

person picking up the child, even if they looked like a parent. In fact, she should have had the woman sign the child out as she was taking him early. It showed a lack of care that in the current climate was frightening.

People handed their most precious possessions over to strangers and assumed they would take care of them. They would give more thought to their cars or their pets!

Boris looked at the pictures of Kate in the newspaper and wondered that a woman who was so obviously straight could have a relationship with a man like Patrick Kelly. He looked out of the window of his flat in Soho. A girl was being dragged along the road by a man. He watched the little drama with amused interest. She didn't look trade so he assumed it was some kind of lovers' spat.

The girl wrenched herself free from the man's grip and kicked him hard in the groin. Boris winced and grinned as the man dropped to his knees. Now the girl was all concern, helping him up. Trying to make amends.

He shook his head pityingly. The man should have swung back his hand and beaten the girl until she was begging for mercy. That was all women understood. He knew that because he was a man who had experience of every type of woman, and basically they were all the same. They needed control. Respected it. Appreciated it even. It was part of their make-up. Women talked about being equal but that was as far as it went: talking about it. Inside, all women knew that man was the real aggressor. They wanted him to open the door for them, take care of them and protect them.

Whoever heard of a woman protecting herself? Even the girl in the street only kicked the man because he allowed her to.

The door opened and Sergei brought in his coffee and brandy. It was a daily ritual Boris enjoyed, the quick rush of strong coffee and alcohol. As Sergei placed the tray on an antique table, Boris seated himself on the leather sofa.

'How is Mr Gabney bearing up?'

Sergei shrugged, his heavily muscled shoulders straining against the thick material of his jacket.

'He is still fighting us. A worthy opponent in many respects.'

Boris nodded almost imperceptibly. 'I think the time has come to take Mr Kelly out of the ball game. Put one of the younger men on finding him. We will soon track him down – no one can hide for ever.'

Sergei nodded respectfully and as usual waited until his boss had sipped his coffee and indicated everything was fine before he walked from the room.

Jenny and Kate were eating a hurried lunch. The canteen was packed and the noise level high. Kate's head was splitting and the constant roar of voices, laughter, crashing cutlery and cigarette smoke were all taking their toll.

Jenny was sympathetic and concerned. Kate had confided in her about the current state of her personal life. She'd listened attentively and then made a request.

'Listen, Kate, can I ask you a favour?'

'Of course.'

'I know this is a bit of a cheek, but I really hate the hotel I'm staying in, and I believe you have a spare room available . . .'

She didn't finish. Kate gave her a tired smile.

'I'd love you to stay with me, Jenny. But I warn you, it's not Buck House.'

Jenny laughed loudly and all eyes turned towards their table.

'Look at them, Kate, all staring at the big lesbo! I frighten men. They think I want to be like them.' She flapped her hand. 'Fuck that for a game of soldiers! I have enough trouble being a woman, love.' She looked Kate in the eye. 'You don't mind about me, do you?'

Kate was stunned. 'Why would I?'

Jenny grinned. 'I'll rephrase that. You're not bothered at being around me? You'd be amazed the number of women who are.'

'Well, that's their problem. Move in whenever you like.'

'When it gets around the station we'll be the butt of a lot of jokes!'

'Good, I could do with a laugh myself.'

Jenny heard the sadness in her voice and gripped Kate's wrist. 'All relationships are crap really. Straight, gay, any of them. People are hag, Kate. Believe me, I know.'

They finished eating before Kate brought up the subject of the investigation again.

'I think someone is involved with all these kids, Jenny. There's something we're just not seeing here. Maybe if we go through everything again we can find a common denominator. Jackie says she's never heard of Mary Parkes, but she must have seen Kerry because they live only a few streets from each other. One thing I have learned from the estates is that everyone knows of or about everyone else. It's their way of life.'

Jenny nodded her agreement.

'We'll find the thread that links them, don't worry. We already know that two of the mothers were in the sex industry. We know that Jackie worked in the Black Rose and what her movements were daily. Someone else could easily have known about them too. In fact, I'd lay money that someone else *did* know. Annoyingly, we can't get any details about the working life of Caroline – she just won't let on about anything. I get the impression she's frightened. Maybe she works rough trade, I don't know. If so, we can't rule out the possibility that her kids may have been involved in what she was doing. After Kerry, we both know that's not impossible – right?'

Kate agreed, depressed to think of all the people who saw their kids as commodities, as opposed to little people they had created and should by every law of nature cherish.

'I think the time has come for some real digging. Did Social Services drop off the files at all?'

'Not yet. I went over there as requested, but they

refused me access until Robert Bateman was on the premises. But I'll go in later on, pick everything up then. We need Jackie's files now as well. All the children we've seen are either registered as at risk or under supervision. That's all they have in common, right? And that's what is bothering me. You don't think we have someone out there with a grudge against problem families, do you?'

Jenny pointed a fork in Kate's direction. 'That's assuming the mothers aren't involved, when I'm convinced that Kerry took her own child away. She's a proven abuser. As far as Caroline is concerned, we can't put her anywhere. Which makes me think she has to be lying in some way. I mean, her child is missing and she won't give herself an alibi? Please! And as for the first one, Regina, who can say what she was capable of? She was as mad as a hatter.

'I think you're looking for goodness in these women, Kate, when there isn't any. I'm not a mother like you so I don't have the same emotional reaction to what has happened. That's why I'm good at this job. I have a natural distrust of people and it seems to give me the edge in these kind of cases.'

She leaned forward. 'I'll tell you something else, love – all this maternal instinct crap and the other garbage women are dealt out is rubbish a lot of the time. I know, I see the opposite side of it on a daily basis. Some women have no maternal instincts whatsoever. I have dealt with women who have killed their babies and then are so terrified by their own action they actually get away with it. An ambulance arrives, they are hysterical and are then treated as the grieving mother. It isn't until the autopsy that we find there were suspicious circumstances and by then they have a story off pat.

'Don't take any of these women at face value, Kate,' she urged. 'Listen to my advice. Observe everything and anything. You'll be surprised at what was staring you in the face all along but your innate niceness wouldn't let you see it. These aren't women like you: good mothers, caring individuals. These are people struggling to survive and finer feelings sometimes go out the window.

'A child a week dies in this country through sheer neglect. That is on top of the ones who die from physical abuse. We still have kids with malnutrition in this country and we're nearly into the new millennium! Believe me, love, you cannot let liberal preconceptions affect your judgement in these cases. Suspect everyone until you know they're clean.'

'I hear what you're saying,' Kate told her gratefully, 'but I am working on a hunch, nothing more. Most prostitutes' children are very well cared for materially, you and I both know that. None of these kids, except Regina's, were under supervision because they were neglected as such. Most were there because of the mother's lifestyle – which is a completely different thing.

'Kerry's children were neglected but if she had not been known to Social Services beforehand, chances are she would have been left to get on with it. Where she lived, the neighbours aren't likely to ring up about child

216

neglect because their idea of neglect is completely different from ours. Dirty ragged children are accepted as part of their environment. Children playing out alone till all hours is normal behaviour. Babies of two with mouths like sewers are common, as are five-year-olds with an almost encyclopaedic knowledge of sex. Ask up the local school if you don't believe me.

'But then, I'm telling you what you already know. What I'm saying here is, we must not let this knowledge *taint* our thinking, that's all. There are many ways to look at this and we have to explore them all. Not every mother we see is bad. Some just don't know any different.'

Jenny listened carefully but Kate knew she didn't really agree. Jenny saw womanhood at its lowest ebb. It was natural that her thinking should be affected by it. But Kate could not bring herself to believe that *all* these women were predatory abusers. She believed once you accepted something like that as the norm then you yourself were tainted. Almost as if you were condoning it somehow.

She had seen plenty over the years but had made a conscious effort not to label people or assume anything about them because of their home, lifestyle or attitude. It was this that had kept her sane during George Markham's reign of terror.

She liked Jenny and knew how easy it was to become jaded in the type of job they both did. It was human nature. But there was still a part of Kate that saw the goodness in people. If it had not been there she would never have accepted Patrick Kelly as her lover.

Though, she reminded herself, he had turned out to be rather different from the way she'd imagined. He had let her down badly but she would still rather try and give humanity as a whole the benefit of the doubt until it was no longer possible.

She had learned a useful lesson from her daughter: never judge a book by its cover. Lizzy had taken an overdose when her mother had found out all about her and her activities. Kate had thought her daughter was still a virgin, waiting for Mr Right, when instead she was into all sorts of things, from drug taking to gang banging. But for all that she was still Lizzy, Kate's daughter, her own flesh and blood.

Some people looked and acted good but were nevertheless bad. Others looked and acted bad and were basically good. Kate had found that out the hard way.

When she had read her daughter's diary she had been devastated, as had her mother. Evelyn had been even more disgusted than Kate if that was possible. Lizzy had actually given local lads marks out of ten!

Reading it had made Kate feel sick, physically sick. But Lizzy was still her daughter. That was why she had found it in her heart to sympathise with Lenny Parkes. She knew the shock and horror of finding out a child was not only sexually active, but sexually active with anyone and anybody. It changed you, and it changed the way you perceived your child.

Patrick Kelly had learned that lesson too with Mandy. But why was she wasting her time thinking about him? He was a liar and a bloody cheat. Kate could have wept with the hopelessness of it all.

'When you're ready get your stuff and I'll give you a key, OK?' she told Jenny, who smiled her thanks.

Willy was given a glass of water and his parched throat eased slightly. As the cool liquid dribbled down it he felt almost high with relief. He was wasted and he knew it; his strength was all gone, and he realised that his captors knew this too. Untied at last, he was unable to move himself from the narrow Z-bed.

He listened to his jailer leave the room and lay in the darkness once more. At least they had given him something to drink and after nearly a week he was grateful for that. He was actually grateful to his captor for a small kindness and that troubled him. He should hate the ponce with a vengeance but he was too weak and too tired to get up the energy.

Willy wished Pat would get his arse in gear and get him out. He had a terrible pain in his kidneys and guessed this was something to do with being kept captive, lying down constantly and having nothing to eat or drink.

He tried, unsuccessfully, to raise himself. Nausea enveloped him like a shroud and he laid his head down carefully. He did not want to vomit and risk dehydration.

He'd not had the strength to talk to his captor, yet there were questions spinning around his head day and night. Was Patrick dead? That thought terrified him, but he was beginning to think it might be the case as he was nowhere nearer release than he had been and he knew it. His captor was too cocky, too sure of himself.

If Patrick was dead, then so was Willy.

Bile rose in his throat and he swallowed it down. He could smell himself now. He'd had to evacuate where he lay and was sore, dreadfully sore, all over.

Closing his eyes, he felt the sting of tears and fought them back bravely. He must not break down now. Pat might be negotiating his release even as he lay here in despair.

Turning his head, he saw a large rat peering at him through the gloom. Shaking his head, Willy decided he'd better start counting again. Anything to take his mind off what was happening. Because it was getting to him now, really getting to him. And he wasn't sure how long it would be before he started screaming or crying.

This frightened him more than anything. Being seen to be weak was something he had fought against all his natural life. Acting tough was in his nature, in his very bones. But William Gabney, hard kid and harder man, was finally near to breaking point.

Kate and Jenny were getting an update and both realised that 'demoralised' was too mild a word to describe how the team was feeling. Child murder was an emotive crime. Eventually it depressed even the most hardened officer.

Kate surveyed the glum expressions around her. Lenny Parkes's murderous attack on Kevin Blankley had somehow given them all a boost yet they knew they had lost in Kevin a vital witness for their investigation. And Davey Carling was dead, too.

Kate sometimes wished she could bring the bleeding hearts in to see the knock-on effect of a child murder or rape and then ask them to justify the release of the guilty parties. All the man-hours put in for free by dedicated officers. All their disgust at hearing the sordid details and having to follow up on them. The crawling of the skin that accompanied just being close to the perpetrators of these crimes. She knew most of the people in front of her now would say they would willingly act as hangman to scum like that if the law permitted it.

She listened to Jenny raising morale, saw how she made them all feel they were vital to the enquiry and doing a good job. If only they could find something to make the cases stick, they would all be celebrating overnight.

'If the women were ID'd how come we haven't enough to go with?' The young PC's voice was low and tentative, but Kate watched as the others nodded to one another in agreement.

'I mean, ma'am, all the mothers could be placed at the scene . . .'

She stood up to take the question.

'The fact that they are the children's mothers would naturally put them at the scene. Mums touch their kids all the time, so consequently they would share fibres and other physical evidence that we would normally use to place an unknown perp at the scene. And remember that one of them, Jackie Palmer, has a very good alibi. She could not have been at the scene as she is on CCTV at the Black Rose at the very time her child was taken from the nursery. So where does this leave us as regards her?'

Golding's voice was raised in reply as Kate had known it would be.

'But she's the only one with any kind of alibi. We've been all over the CCTV from Lakeside and we can't locate Kerry Alston who insists she wasn't anywhere near her kids all afternoon. The other bird won't even say where she was, and Regina Carlton is a piece of shit basically who had no qualms about leaving her kids on their own and pissing off overnight, or even for a couple of days, according to the neighbours. Yet we're still fumbling about trying to put them at the scene, even though anything we find that's forensic is basically a waste of time because, as you pointed out, they would all be in close contact with their kids anyway. But we have witnesses – that must mean something, surely!'

Kate could hear the underlying anger in his voice and privately sympathised. The others were murmuring and nodding their heads in agreement.

'Well, Mr Golding, you will come across cases like this a lot in your chosen profession, I'm afraid, and you need to bear in mind the absolute necessity of back-up evidence. Any good brief would piss all over forensics in his opening argument. "Of course my client has hairs, fibres, blood even, on them. It's only to be expected when they're caring for a child." No, you have to find more than the obvious, I'm afraid.

Look back over other similar cases and you will find in those that relied on this sort of evidence, all too often the accused walked from the courts. I do not intend to let that happen here, OK?

'We have photographs of the kids and I'd lay money there are videos too, somewhere,' Kate told the silent room. 'We need to track down Blankley's brother and check that out. The Met are getting back to me on him. I am picking up the social reports at long bloody last this morning. I will get them copied and then you will all be able to see what the social workers think of the clients and what we can gather from that.

'The child from the dump is still unidentified. We're contacting Interpol and trying to establish if he might be from abroad. As you all know that's not in the least uncommon. Two years ago, fifty-five foreign children, mainly Rumanian, were found in Amsterdam being used in pornographic literature. A few kids even turned up here. Christ knows there can't be more than one P-ring in Grantley – at least I bloody well hope not!'

Kate looked at her team and told them: 'I want you all to dig as deep as possible into the backgrounds of these women and their families and friends. We have to find something – *have* to. As for the witnesses, we've all seen what can happen to them, haven't we? That's why I want more and more evidence. A witness can be confused by a good brief, can be made to look unreliable. You all know this. I want to make our case as watertight as possible.'

Everyone nodded and murmured their agreement and she smiled.

'Right now I need some volunteers to help collate everything on computer. We want to try and put the mothers together at some time. I want to be able to prove that some of them knew one another, just in case this is a conspiracy of Ps and their victims.'

At this point Jenny broke in.

'And I want to hear from known sex offenders so I'd like to see if we can locate any from Grantley and try to get anything from them about these mothers and kids. The fathers are another worry as are grandparents. We have no idea who they are and the girls aren't telling. Now maybe they don't know who the fathers are, but maybe they do. We have to try and see if we can put any names about that might give us an inkling of how deep this ring goes and exactly who may be involved in it. Personally I think the kids aren't linked as such though some of the mothers are guilty as hell. But thinking and proving are two different things. One area where we can link them is the paedophile activity, but that is separate at the moment from the murder and attempted murder enquiries.

'This is deep, hard as fucking hell and confusing, but that is par for the course with this kind of case. Bear in mind that unlike blaggers, burglars, et cetera, paedophiles have more reason than any to keep themselves out of clink. They are as hated in there as they are out here. Fear keeps them quiet. Also, though paedophiles come across as passive, they are aggressive with one another, and use fear on the kids and also on the people they recruit to help them. Some groups use initiation ceremonies where a new recruit is filmed without their knowledge and then blackmailed afterwards. We will eventually uncover layer after layer of deceit, lies and confusion. This is how they work, and this is why it is so hard to pin anything definite on them. But if we persevere we will come out on top.'

'We'd better, ma'am. This is sickening me and everyone else. These women are fucking scum . . .' broke in a red-faced DS.

Kate took over. 'We have to keep an open mind, remember. A woman who neglects her kids must not necessarily be seen as someone who is capable of violating them. Remember that. Don't let your emotions muddy your thinking. Now, you all have an objective today. See if you can achieve it.'

Ten minutes later the women stared at one another glumly across the empty briefing room.

'Listen, Kate, this always happens,' Jenny assured her, 'so don't worry. It's the harshness of the case that causes this general depression. Once they make another breakthrough everyone will start to feel better. Take it from me, I see it all the time.'

'They're a good team, Jen, the best.'

Jenny smiled. 'I know, and they're learning something new which will stand them in good stead for the future. Now, we need to interview Caroline and get some information from her. She's hiding something and has been from the off. I intend to find out what she's so scared of and see if we can't put it into perspective for her.'

Jacques Vignon opened the back of the curtain-sider with a flourish. He had always regarded himself as having a special nose for smugglers. As he opened the door the driver looked nervous, but that wasn't unusual with the English. With all the trade wars going on between the two countries it was only to be expected.

But when he heard the little cries coming from the back of the lorry Jacques was amazed. By the light of his powerful torch he saw a young child sitting among the boxes of freight, his face streaked with dirt, snot and ink. He was clearly terrified.

Jacques, a father of six, was overcome with emotion as the little figure stumbled towards him, arms outstretched. He brought the child out into the salty air, hardly able to contain his emotion as he turned to face his colleagues. They were as shocked as he. In all their years they had never seen anything like this before.

The driver of the lorry looked equally stricken and had to grab the side of his curtain-sider to stop himself from fainting clean away.

'Where did he come from?' Jonathon's voice was higher than usual from shock and fear. He knew what the other men were thinking about him and he wanted to scream a denial. So many people mixed up gays with paedophiles, he knew that from listening to his own father and his cronies up the pub.

As they all stared at him he felt terrified denials springing to his lips, but dared not utter a word. It would only have made him look guiltier.

The child was crying now, loudly and heartily, as if the sunlight and salty sea air had given him a new lease of life. The Frenchmen were comforting him, wrapping him in coats to keep him warm. One even managed to find a bar of chocolate for him. Another gave him a drop of Coke from a can he had in his office. The child was thirsty and starving. He stopped crying to take the sustenance he so desperately needed.

The men all gathered around him, exclaiming at his beauty, his sturdiness and his predicament. Their hearts all went out to him and they looked menacingly at Jonathon as if they were going to lynch him at any moment.

The police eventually arrived in force. Jonathon was detained for questioning, and the child was handed over to a policewoman who spoke good English. He hugged her so fiercely it brought tears to the eyes of the onlookers.

Jonathon was terrified. As he explained that he had come from Grantley with his usual load and had had no idea that he was also carrying a child, he could see that he was not believed. He knew his very campness, which he tried so hard to disguise, was already making him a prime suspect and the thought made him feel sick.

Then a man from Interpol arrived with coffee and sandwiches. He explained that Grantley had been in touch already about missing children and that they really had no option but to try and rule him out of the enquiry. But Jonathon knew that they thought he *was* involved. He was a suspect in a child abduction case. He started to cry then, really cry, and the man let him.

The little boy was cleaned and dressed in borrowed clothes after a thorough examination by a doctor. His large blue eyes seemed interested in what was going on and he kept asking for his mummy. His French rescuers knew what he meant and he was showered with chocolate bars, toys and clothing from kind people who worked at the docks. He loved the attention and ate whatever he was given. He was flown home the same day, and that thrilled him too.

Jonathon, however, was kept in a cell until both the French and the English police had finished interviewing him. He made a statement and was released without charge but he knew it wasn't over yet. Not by a long chalk. He travelled home in tears, minus his lorry and his self-respect.

He wondered vaguely if he still had a job, let alone a relationship with the man of his dreams.

Caroline Anderson, mother of Christian and his murdered brother Ivor, was still vague about her life and lifestyle.

Kate was getting aggressive and lit a cigarette to hide her growing anger.

'Come on, Caroline, you know more than you are letting on.'

'I can't tell you anything about me job . . .'

Jenny interrupted her. 'Then that makes you more suspect, doesn't it? I mean, see it from our point of view. What would you think if you were us, and someone was sitting in a cell and not telling all they knew even though it was very important. It was about their kids.'

Caroline bit on her lip, she looked very young and very vulnerable.

Kate's voice was soft. 'Just tell us who you work for. We won't make trouble, I promise.' She could see Caroline was wavering. Fear was a great incentive, Kate knew that from experience.

'I know what you think of me and I don't blame you. But I am more scared of the man I work for than I am of you.' She was nearly crying. 'He would see me dead if he thought I had opened me trap.'

'We could guarantee you protection.'

Caroline shook her head in distress. 'Not from him.' She was getting hysterical, her voice rising and her hands shaking so badly she had to put them in her lap. 'He has the same access as you two. Inside or out he could get to me.' Caroline was crying, big fat tears rolled down her face and she made no attempt to wipe them away.

'How can anyone have that much power?' Jenny's voice was sceptical and that seemed to penetrate into Caroline's brain.

'Fucking think about it, lady. Don't you think I *want* to tell you?'

Jenny laughed gently. Then she said sarcastically, 'You're good, Caroline – I'll give you that much. You can act, love. You missed out on your vocation. Are you trying to insinuate it's a copper then?'

'I am not insinuating anything, and I ain't saying a word. I've probably said too much already. But you can lock me up, you can throw away the key. Put me on the fucking rack if you like. I *will not* utter another word.'

She refused to answer anything after that statement. Just sat and sobbed quietly. Later, when she had been removed back to her cell, Kate said to Jenny, 'She was trying to tell us something.'

But the other woman dismissed it with a wave of her hand.

'All people accused of child or adult sex crimes try on the Old Bill stance. If I had a quid for every time I heard an accusation like that I would be a millionaire by now. It's common practice. I mean, think about it. She has thrown the ball back into our court, hasn't she?'

Kate didn't answer and Jenny pointed out, 'Look, she has you wondering. So she's achieved her objective. While we wonder who the filth is, we stop querying her on the real issues, such as *why* she doesn't want to discuss where she was that night. I mean, was she in on what happened to those kids? Does she *know* what occurred? Attack is the best form of defence, remember that, love. Especially when it concerns *us*, what we are, what we believe in.'

'I can see the logic, but we can't dismiss it out of hand. Something is stopping her from talking . . .'

'A hard nut is what is stopping her from talking.

Nothing more and nothing less. Some villain, some piece of shit who uses and abuses kids. That is what is stopping her from talking. Some porn master, some scum making money from the degradation of others.'

'A paedophile isn't like a villain, Jenny. Normal criminals hate paedophiles and rapists, don't they. That's why they segregate them in prisons.'

They were silent for a few seconds. Kate realised that she was defending Patrick and his lifestyle, and the knowledge upset her. But Patrick like most of his ilk had an almost pathological hatred for what he termed 'nonces'.

But Jenny had hit a nerve. A painful nerve that Kate knew would always be exposed while Patrick Kelly was in her heart. The fact she was defending him spoke volumes.

Quiet now, they were both lost in their own thoughts.

Chapter Eleven

'This is getting weirder by the day, Miss Burrows.' Robert Bateman's voice had lost its usual bantering tone.

'Well, I have a feeling it will get weirder still before we're finished,' she replied dryly. 'Can you enlighten me further on any of the women?'

He shook his head. 'I only really have anything to do with poor Regina these days although I have to keep abreast of what's happening with the rest of my team's clients. You'd be better talking to the actual social workers themselves, I know they'll help all they can. But, like I said, they will protect other clients. It's in our code of conduct.'

Kate smiled and hugged the client files to her chest.

'I understand that. Have there been any other cases of abuse recently that we are unaware of? Or have any of the teams maybe thought there was abuse but couldn't prove it? You know what I'm talking about, Robert, I'm sure.'

''Course I do, dear, and this is strictly off the record,

right?' He went to the door and shut it theatrically before saying in a hushed voice, 'Kerry Alston and Jackie Palmer were mates at school. Both were accused of sexually assaulting another girl, but nothing was ever proved against them. The girl dropped the charges and moved away from the area. I remember because I was new here at the time and I was quite shocked by it all. I mean, two girls practically raping another one.' He paused for effect.

'The thing is, though, it was reported to the police and then nothing ever came of it. They were all minors, you see. Plus they said that the girl, whose name, if I remember rightly, was Pauline Barker – ring any bells? – had actually approached *them*. It was all very, very strange. I mean, these were little girls, love – eleven or twelve years old. But you won't find it on record anywhere.'

Kate was nonplussed. 'Why not?'

'Because the girl was a policeman's daughter.'

She closed her eyes and sighed, remembering how six years ago, DI Harold Barker had left Grantley suspiciously fast. Everyone assumed he had been caught with his hand in someone's till. He was certainly capable of it. Now she wondered if there was a different version of events.

'So how come you know all about it?' she asked.

'I was Pauline's social worker. Daddy was a bit too friendly at times by all accounts, but him being filth, it was all covered up and laid to rest in no time. Do you see now why I don't want my name mentioned in all this? Only I heard through the grapevine that he was part of a small ring. Mainly professionals. He ended up in the Vice Squad in Soho. But then, so many nonces do, dear.'

Kate's eyes had widened to their utmost. 'Are you telling me Harry Barker was a beast?'

Her voice was too loud and Robert flapped his hands at her in agitation.

'I'm not *telling* you anything, dear; I'm merely passing on information. But if you're going to shout it out all over the place then in future I'll keep my own counsel.'

'Who alerted you to him and his supposed friendliness with his daughter?'

Robert smiled at her obvious disbelief.

'His wife, love. Mavis Barker. A nice woman but nervous. You know, on mother's little helpers for years. She said he had been at it with all the kids. Pauline was the youngest of four but the other three were by his first wife who died. Mavis sort of inherited them with her marriage. She said that the elder girls had complained about him, as had his son. We could never get a word from any of them and nor could the police, by the way. In my view they were terrified. But what can you do? The elder ones were all over sixteen by then and unless they wanted to press charges there was nothing anyone could do for them. But, if I was asked for my professional opinion, I would say it was a definite.'

He looked deep into Kate's eyes and she saw how hurt he was by her reluctance to believe this of a fellow police officer.

'I have to see this on a daily basis, Miss Burrows. I have to listen to my team telling me this has happened to this kid and that has happened to another. But I tell you something, in cases like Kerry's and Regina's all that is happening is history repeating itself. Some abused kids actually fall in love with the abuser – that is proven fact – especially if the abuser is a family member. We teach kids to love Mummy and Daddy and they do. Whatever Mummy or Daddy does they love them. Kids are beaten unconscious and still they protect the parent. That is real life, dear.'

Robert paused for a moment and Kate waited to hear what he would say next. 'I see Kerry as a small girl with a big problem – the problem being her father who, as you know, abused her all her life. In fact, we know she still carries on a relationship with him, even takes the kids to stay with him. Kerry loves him, you see, Miss Burrows, whatever he has done. You're making the mistake common to most people who have never experienced abuse at first hand. It is the *norm* to them, remember. You learn what is right from your friends and family – mostly your parents, right? If they teach you wrong you don't know that as a kid, do you? And some kids become adults who *still* can't see anything wrong in what happened to them. Some talk about enjoying the feelings they experienced then. It was like affection to them. They were being singled out for this special attention. We even have cases where siblings are actually jealous of the abused child.

'Can you see where I'm coming from now?' he

asked Kate. 'Kerry and Regina, both of them victims, perpetuating what they learned from their own parents and family. You must temper your justifiable feelings of repugnance with pity for these girls and their children, Miss Burrows. They really can't help it; they were broken at an early age.'

Kate was sorry she could not wholly empathise with what this man had gone to such pains to explain. Half of her did understand. That half was desperately sorry for Regina and Kerry, for all the girls. But the other half was disgusted by them and she knew that nothing anyone said would ever make her change her mind. She felt Robert pick up on her thoughts.

'At least try, Miss Burrows. See it from another standpoint, eh? I understand your own daughter had problems at one time.'

Kate was stunned. 'How did you know that, Mr Bateman?'

'Robert, please. Mr Bateman makes me sound so old. I looked you up on my computer, dear. How did you think I knew? When your daughter underwent psychiatric treatment she was automatically assigned a social worker at the hospital.' He smiled to take the edge off his words.

'I can get access to all sorts, dear, and since the contretemps with Barker I make a point of finding out exactly who I'm dealing with in official circles. It's nothing personal, so do stop looking so worried. I just wanted to point out to you that many people have problems, some harder to deal with than others. *None* of us are immune.

'I just did what you do every day,' he said reassuringly. 'I know you routinely look people up to see their previous form or whatever. I do the same now because I have seen it proven over and over again that no one is ever exactly what they seem. I like to know who I'm dealing with, that's all.'

'So what, in your professional opinion, was wrong with my daughter?'

He leaned across his desk and took Kate's hand gently.

'From what I have seen of the case files, your daughter did not have a very good role model in her father. He was a womaniser and a useless lump. No offence, dear. It seems that nevertheless your daughter emulated him rather than you. It's not unusual, Miss Burrows – his lifestyle must have looked very exciting to her as a girl. This is only my opinion, of course. But I would say that he, as the parent who was often away from home, became more important to her. When she saw him it was stimulating, it was different from anything else she knew. It's only natural she would be enamoured. All girls love their daddies. They're important to them in so many ways. It's how they learn to interact with men.

'You, on the other hand, worked long hours and your mother brought Elizabeth up really. So she had lots of female role models and only one male. Unfortunately not a very good one.'

Kate was very angry and Robert Bateman realised that. He shook his head sadly, his large expressive eyes sad.

'Forgive me, please, if I have offended you. I didn't mean to. I was merely trying to make a point about socialisation.'

Kate hugged the folders to her chest and stared at the man before her.

'Maybe I'll look *you* up on my computer, Mr Bateman.'

'Do you mean to tell me you haven't already?' he said mischievously. 'I am disappointed, Miss Burrows. I had you down as much shrewder than that.'

He was laughing at her and she knew it. Then his expression changed, became serious.

'I feel such sorrow for my girls, I really do. I see their pain. See how they try to come to terms with what has happened to them. Please don't be too hard on them, Miss Burrows. Remember, they're as much victims as their poor children. Kerry Alston was so badly abused, you really couldn't imagine it in your wildest nightmares. Systematically violated from a baby until an adult. Read the files. They are as shocking as they are enlightening.'

Kate knew he meant what he said and admired him for it on one level even though he had hurt her with his insight into her daughter. It was as if he had opened up an old wound that had been festering for years. He knew all about her and knowledge always gave a person the edge. She knew that better than anyone.

'I'm a bleeding heart, me,' he went on quietly. 'Can't help it, love. Always for the underdog from a little boy. Maybe I'm a fool, I don't know for sure, but no one can help where their heart is, can they?'

Kate looked at him, from his scruffy clothes to his badly dyed hair, and found herself smiling. He was a good man in his own way. He still believed in rehabilitation, in helping people. For that alone she respected him.

'Read Kerry Alston's file, and then tell me if you think I'm a fool for feeling so sorry for her, OK? See if you could have coped with what she had to and come out at the other end. Try and feel for her, not judge her like everyone else.'

'I'll try, Robert. But don't hold your breath. I see a lot in my job too, you know. And I, like you, generally end up picking up the pieces.'

He grinned. 'See? We have more in common than you think.'

Kate drove back to the station slowly. She wanted to put her thoughts into perspective. First off, she rang Golding and told him to pull out the files on Barker, and on a whim she asked him to look up Robert Bateman, too.

She smoked one cigarette after the other. As she approached the station she saw the film crews and the gutter journalists and sighed. It was all pressure.

Driving carefully through the throng, she wondered briefly what the reaction would be if she arrested the lot of them for impeding a public highway. Consequently, she was looking smiling and relaxed in the late editions.

Jackie Palmer hugged her son to her. Jenny and Kate

were pleased to see the obvious bond between them. Martin was loving the attention. Sitting on his mother's lap, he held on to her hand with a vice-like grip.

He pointed with his free hand and said distinctly: 'Mummy kiss.'

Jackie kissed him tenderly.

'Why would someone put my Martin in a lorry?' she asked. 'And who is this blonde woman everyone's talking about? It makes no sense.'

Kate shook her head. 'That's what we have to find out. But witnesses have described someone very like you.'

Jackie was nonplussed. 'But the CCTV . . .'

Jenny broke in then. 'It shows you were at your job that day, but we can't locate you on it all the time, only going in and coming out. There's a back entrance and it's only five minutes' walk from the lorry park, fifteen from the playschool.'

Jackie looked stunned.

'You see, love, until we knew where he was we could take your word for it. But now we have other evidence that makes it look like you *could* have been out and back to the Black Rose in under forty minutes and no one can swear you were there all the time, can they? Only at certain times.'

Jackie shook her head slowly. 'I don't fucking believe you people. Are you honestly telling me that you think I could have done a cuntish thing like that!'

Martin squirmed as her voice started to rise steadily.

'You having a fucking laugh or what?'

The child turned on her lap and tried to put his

241

arms around her neck. She pushed him none too gently from her. Pointing her finger at Kate and Jenny, she said nastily, 'You've got it in for me, ain't you, just because I'm on the fucking game. Well, you ain't fitting me up, mate. I ain't Kerry Alston or one of the other pieces of dirt you've pulled in.'

Martin was crying loudly now. Pulling him up with her hands under his arms, she screamed into his face: 'Oh, shut up, you silly little fucker for Christ's sake . . .'

Kate and Jenny sat in shock as the screaming boy was forcibly removed from his mother by a WPC. Then Jackie Palmer started to cry like a baby.

Robert Bateman's words were still in Kate's mind and she found herself feeling reluctant sympathy for the confused girl before her. But as Jenny frequently pointed out witnesses were all they really had in each case. And more than one witness had put this woman at the scene. It wasn't far from her work and she was already in trouble for neglect of her kids.

Whatever they thought privately, no one could argue with the facts.

Kate glanced at the folder on her desk. As she leafed through it she quickly learned that Robert Bateman was a well-respected social worker, his senior status not hampered by his looks. In fact, he was seen as a leader in his field, which was child abuse. He was also an acknowledged authority on broken families. Broken people.

Golding brought her in a coffee without her asking

and the gesture pleased her. 'Thank you. I could just do with this.'

He nodded. 'I can't get anything on Barker. No a brass razoo. Seems Ratchet has had anything pertaining to him pulled in the last ten days. Doesn't that strike you as strange?'

Kate shook her head. 'Not really. Keep digging, Dave, see what you can find out through word of mouth and we can take it from there.'

'I have a few contacts meself, ma'am. Maybe I can have a little dig about. With your permission of course.'

Kate smiled. 'Of course. Don't worry – I'll take any flak from Ratchet.'

He thanked her and left the room.

Barker, it seemed, still had a few friends in the station. Now why didn't that fact surprise her?

But she would find out what she wanted.

She usually did.

Patrick saw the blue car as he pulled into Mortlake Road in Ilford. It had tailed him for the last fifteen minutes. He watched as it pulled over and another car took over. That was amateurish. Was he meant to see them following him?

He knew it was time to get away from the so-called safe flat. Driving into the traffic of Ilford High Street, he sat at the lights, his eyes glued to the black Granada four cars behind him. Inside were two men: one light-haired, one dark. Both in dark clothes, both nondescript in appearance.

When the motorbike came up alongside him he was not really taking any notice. He heard the roar of its engine, and as he glanced out of the window on the passenger side he registered the fact that the pillion rider was carrying a black bag and inside the black bag was what looked like a gun.

Patrick took all this in within a split second. His reactions were fast enough that when the first bullet hit him he was halfway out of the car. The second bullet caught him as he staggered and he slammed on to the road with a sickening thud.

He heard pandemonium break out before he lost consciousness, and saw a rather nice pair of legs as a young woman ran from the car behind him and, screaming her head off, dashed into the oncoming traffic. Her radio was still blaring out and Chris Tarrant's voice was loud in the warmth of the afternoon and the quiet that had suddenly descended after the shooting.

The bike roared off quickly, disappearing into the traffic. The Granada did a U-turn and drove sedately away, its occupants ready to swear that Patrick Kelly was a dead man.

Kerry Alston's mother was birdlike, with a lovely face and beautiful thick auburn hair. She smiled often, displaying small white teeth and pink healthy gums. Kate and Jenny were both surprised by her and she guessed that.

'Kerry is like her father.'

Her voice was harsh in contrast to her features and

sounded almost gravelly from too many cigarettes and too much booze. They knew she was an alcoholic. She lit a cigarette and pointed at the thick file on the table.

'I take it you want me to go over old ground again then? I've already spoken to you lot twice.'

Kate looked at the hard eyes before her and remembered what Robert Bateman had said about parents.

'Have you anything to add to what you have already told us?' Jenny wasn't holding out much hope and this came over in her clipped tones.

Donna Alston grinned. 'No. She's a little whore. Always was – her father made sure of that. Is she still spinning everyone then? You really should take a leaf out of my book where she's concerned and throw her out with the rubbish.'

'Yet you take care of your grandchildren. How do you equate that with the feelings you have for your daughter?'

'You don't know Kerry like I do,' the woman told them. 'Her father did some atrocious things to her, I don't deny that. But I also have to tell you that she ran away with him time and again when he was released from prison. Kerry is a waste of fucking space and if it was up to me, her kids would live here full-time. As it is I take them in when the social workers ask me to.'

She pointed her cigarette angrily at the two police-women.

'I would take them any day, poor little mites, but they won't let me. "Leave them with their mother," they say. "She loves them." Kerry doesn't know what love is, not real love. Not love for your kids. She sees them like her father did – as a commodity. Something to be used. I was terrified of that ponce for years, but Kerry still sees him, still has contact with him. Can you imagine how that makes me feel? Well, can you?' She stared into their faces. 'Knowing what he's capable of, she takes her kids to him for holidays. But you'll never find out where he lives from her. They meet at caravan parks and other places like that. She knows better than to let on to me where he is because if I ever find out, I'll go there and kill him for what he did. And that's no empty threat, ladies. One day I will have him.'

'Where was he from originally?'

Donna shrugged again and hawked deep in her throat, making Kate want to throw up.

'Originally from Newcastle or that way. But you can never get anything from him. Like talking to the wall. He has a southern accent these days but when I first met him he was a northerner. But then, it could have been another act. You'd have to meet him to understand what I'm talking about. Charm the birds from the trees him, and then wring their little necks without a second's thought. But I think Kerry probably knows where he is. He keeps in contact with her, I know that for a fact. She adores him, and I mean *adores* him. She spends her whole life waiting for him to get in touch.'

Jenny placed some photographs on the table. 'Do you recognise any of the men in these photos?'

Donna picked them up and looked at them. Kate saw her jaw tighten and her face go pale as she looked at her grandchildren and daughter in poses that definitely weren't for the family album.

There were tears in her voice as she said brokenly, 'No, I don't. But then, you can't see any faces, can you?'

They were all quiet. Only the rattling of the tape in the machine could be heard.

'I will get those kids this time, whatever that Bateman and his cronies say. They're victims now as well as her. Victims of their own mother, the dirty bitch! And I'll have them off her this time.'

'Have you any idea who the children's fathers may be?'

She shook her head and hawked again in her throat.

'The eldest is definitely her father's, I don't care what anyone says. He ain't all the ticket either, bless him. The other could be literally anyone's – and I mean anyone's. She'll fuck a table leg if told to. That's how he trained her, see. But I think it was in her anyway. Look at me other daughter, Mariah. She had the same and she's all right. Hates him for what he did to her. I tried to stop it all, tried my hardest. I had seventy-eight stitches where he sliced me open when I finally blew the whistle on him. Nearly died for them girls I did, but she hates me, Kerry. Hates me guts. And the feeling is mutual.'

Kate didn't know what to say.

'Now Mariah, she heard from her father a few years ago. Told him to fuck off out of it. She'll tell you that herself. In and out of the nut-house she's been, thanks to him. Cutting herself up, taking overdoses. Oh, the trouble I have had. But at least I know she felt something, do you know what I'm saying? She knew that what had happened was wrong. Not like Kerry. She seemed to thrive on it all.'

Jenny picked up the photos and held out her hand to the small woman with the tearful eyes and the inner core of steel which had obviously kept her sane through her harsh existence.

'If you can think of anything at all, anything that could help us . . .'

Donna smiled wearily. 'Don't worry, you'll be the first to know.'

Kate and Jenny arrived at Kate's at a little after 7 p.m. They had been interviewing the families of the accused all day and were both tired. Kate had the Social Services files under her arm and the dragging weight was a constant reminder of what lay inside their thick covers.

As they opened the front door they were assailed by the smell of a steak casserole and looked at each other in surprise. Then Kate saw her mother's rotund body bustling down the hallway to greet her and her mouth dropped open in shock and surprise.

'Mum!'

'I'll fecking Mum you, you villain! Right fool I made of meself going to Pat's and finding out from the housekeeper that you two were at each other's throats. Now get your coat off and get inside here and then I want to know what the feck has been going on here while I've been away!'

Jenny stood awkwardly in the doorway to the kitchen and Kate pulled her inside. 'This is my mother who's supposed to be in Australia . . .'

'Evelyn is the name, and you are? I suppose it's all your stuff that's in Lizzy's room, is it? Well, come away in and get this down the pair of you. I made enough to feed a family of culchies!'

Suddenly the house felt like home again and Kate realised what had been missing all along. Her mother brought the place to life with her ebullient personality and her love for living. Kate wished she had inherited that from her instead of the more self-contained personality she'd acquired from her long-dead father.

'I was fed up trying to get you on the phone so I thought to meself: if the mountain has to go to fecking Mohammed then it will. I jumped on a plane and here I am. Knackered, tired and shagged out, but still well able for likes of you two!'

Jenny was laughing in genuine amusement and Kate was glad. It was wonderful to see her mother standing in the kitchen with her apron on, her ruddy cheeks glowing with pleasure at cooking once more for the daughter she still treated like a schoolgirl.

The breakfast bar was laden down with food as usual: home-made soda bread, a thick casserole, carrots in butter and cabbage in vinegar. A real Irish dinner that would fill you up and send you to sleep with its heaviness. In the oven was a large apple pie, and home-made custard simmered on the gas stove.

'No Lizzy, Mum?' Kate's voice was wary and Eve sighed.

'Jasus, she's well in there, Kate. Men coming out of the woodwork and herself with eyes for only the one. Pray God in heaven she makes a good match. She loves it out there and they love having her there. Sure it has to be better than what's on offer for her here.'

Jenny picked up the underlying tension between them on this subject and helped herself to food in silence.

Kate hugged her mother tightly. 'Oh, Mum, it's good to have you back home, it really is.'

Evelyn pretended she was intent on tidying her neat grey perm as she said, 'And you can tell me what happened with himself later on, after we've eaten. When I got to his house this morning I nearly died! Anyway, I have all your bits and pieces and I've put them away for you so that's all done with. As for him, he hasn't been near or by the house for days according to that Mary Anne he calls a housekeeper. Anyway, enough! Eat that lot and I have a nice dessert for you both and a bottle of Australian Chardonnay to sample.'

Jenny was amazed at the little woman before her; she thought she was fantastic, and as they ate, they chatted as if they had known one another all their lives. But Jenny had a feeling that Evelyn made everyone feel like that. She was so open and so obviously kind it was impossible not to like her.

'Oh, Jasus! That eejit Ratchet phoned and said for you to ring him as soon as you got home. But wait until you've eaten. He sounds like a right sourpuss if ever I heard one. He can fecking keep.'

Jenny and Kate smiled at one another like conspirators. When Evelyn left the kitchen Jenny said sincerely, 'She's great, Kate. You're very lucky.'

Kate was pleased and it showed.

'I love her so much. I don't know what I would have done without her over the years. After Dan and everything that happened . . .'

'I wish my mother was like that. But we get what we're given in this life and nothing can change that. Look what we've had to deal with at work, eh?'

'Food for thought, I suppose. But do you believe that some people are born bad, like Kerry's mother seems to think?'

Jenny thought about it for a second.

'To be honest, I really don't know, Kate. Some people seem capable of great hatred and some of great love. All this about there being a thin line between them just muddles things, I think. One thing I do know, though, is that with Evelyn as a mother, you couldn't help but grow up well, eh?'

Kate didn't answer her, she just smiled.

Evelyn had been a major force in Lizzy's life too, and look what had happened to her. Kate suspected that though her mother had probably wanted to come home anyway, Lizzy was misbehaving in some way and this had spurred her on. It wasn't anything she could put her finger on, it was just a guess. And her guesses were usually spot on where her mother was concerned.

As Eve bustled back into the kitchen the phone

rang and Kate got up to answer it.

'Let the machine pick it up, child. I haven't seen you for five minutes and knowing that twit Ratchet you'll be off out the door in seconds!'

They all heard his voice over the answer machine and laughed.

'Hello, Kate. I really don't want to tell you this over the phone, but I'm afraid that Patrick Kelly was shot today in Ilford High Street. When you pick this message up could you please ring me? My home number is . . .'

They sat together in complete silence as they realised what he had just said. Kate looked at her mother. Her lips were moving but no words were emerging. It was as if she had gone dumb. She was shaking her head in disbelief.

'Pat's been shot . . . God in heaven keep him safe!' Eve blessed herself and poured Kate more wine. 'Get that down you, you need something, girl. Then we'll ring that fecker back and find out exactly what has happened.'

Kate was visibly shaking. It was as if her whole body was moving of its own volition. Her huge dark eyes were dry but filled with pain. Eve would have given anything to take that expression from them.

'Who the feck would shoot your man? It's getting like fecking Belfast in this place. Shootings and stabbings . . .'

'Evelyn, I really think we should get Kate a doctor.'

She passed out just as Jenny finished speaking,

slipping heavily to the floor. Evelyn was crying now, cradling her daughter's head.

'I knew it was time to come back, I had a feeling she needed me. Jesus Christ, she'll go mad with grief. The girl will go mad with grief. If ever a pair were meant to be, it was them. They were that close.'

She was still sobbing when Jenny picked up the phone and called Leila, explaining what had happened. They wanted to keep this as quiet as possible from their colleagues. Gossip would be rife enough without everyone knowing Kate had fainted with shock. Even in her grief she would want to keep something like that private. It was the way she was made.

Willy woke up when someone threw cold water over him. He was already frozen.

'Your boss is dead.'

He heard the words but was unsure whether to believe them. 'It would take more than you to waste Pat Kelly,' he said in a weak voice.

The unseen man laughed. 'Don't you want to know where this leaves you?'

'Not really. By the way, mate, thanks for the drink. I needed one.'

Sergei shook his head in amazement. He had seen some hard men in his time but Willy Gabney was as tough as old boots and the other man was impressed by his resilience.

'I shot him myself,' he boasted. 'Today, in his car. I watched as the bullets hit him and he bled away his life's blood.'

If Sergei was determined to get a reaction, he was disappointed.

'I don't believe you, son. Pat Kelly will take you and break you. For your sake I hope he is dead, mate. If he ain't, you'd better fucking run.'

Even in his obvious distress the man was still as hard as nails. The Russian walked from the cellar. Looking at the two men waiting outside the door he said in awed tones, 'Still he is fighting with his words.'

The younger men were as impressed as he was.

'I heard him talking to himself earlier. He was muttering on about Millwall or somewhere. And he was counting all night, one to a thousand, over and over again fast.'

They were all quiet for a moment, admiring Willy in their own way.

'Are we to kill him?'

The older man shook his head. 'We may need him yet. He knows much and we may need that knowledge. Feed him soon. Get him washed and then we will decide. Once he realises that his boss has gone he will see the sense in helping us at last.'

'Maybe not, though. Such loyalty is hard to buy. It is given through respect.'

They all admired William Gabney, yet any of them would have killed him at one word from their own boss. William Gabney's kind of respect for authority they understood. They shared it themselves.

They gave him food and a bottle of whisky. Somehow they knew that vodka would not be appreciated.

BOOK TWO

Virtue knows to a farthing what it has lost
by not having been vice.

> —Horace Walpole, Fourth Earl of Orford
> (*The extraordinary Mr Wilkes*, 1794), 1717–97

I was so young, I loved him so, I had
No mother, God forgot me, and I fell.

> —Robert Browning
> (*A Blot in the 'Scutcheon*, 1843), 1812–89

BOOK TWO

Chapter Twelve

Patrick's sisters arrived at St George's Hospital in Ilford together and slipped past the waiting press photographers easily. Grace, with her blonde hair and heavily made-up eyes, looked much younger than she was. Violet, on the other hand, looked older than her age. Unlike Grace, who had a face and skin made for foundation, Vi always looked like a garishly painted old woman when she wore make-up.

Neither of them spoke as they went up to the ICU together. A young Asian doctor with tired eyes smiled uneasily when he greeted them.

'How is he?'

'Very bad. I am afraid he is on a life-support machine.'

'Will he make it?'

The doctor shrugged. 'We really don't hold out too much hope. But he is strong, and he is obviously a fighter . . .' His voice trailed off.

Violet watched as Patrick's chest rose and fell every four seconds as the ventilator did its work. The noise was intimidating, the banks of machines scaring both the sisters. Seeing their Patrick, always so strong and full of life, reduced to this was shocking to them.

'Jesus Christ, Grace. What more can happen to the poor sod? Renée, Mandy, and now this. I told him not two days ago he was getting too old for all this. He looked rough, Gracie, really rough. He's going greyer by the day, and falling out with Kate ain't helped. But who can blame her? This is the last thing she needs with her job and that, ain't it?'

Grace took her brother's hand gently. 'Oh, well, God forbid he should interrupt her bloody work, Vi.'

Her voice was sarcastic and Violet bit her lip. Grace had always been a force to be reckoned with in their family. Both Violet and Patrick had automatically given way to her because she was so aggressive. But this was one time Violet was not going to let her call the shots. Pat loved Kate and she was good for him, whatever bloody Gracie thought. And Pat had come to Violet when he was down because he knew she would stand by him and not give him grief of the earhole.

'I mean, Kate's a funny fucker,' Grace went on. 'I know she looks down her nose at me and mine. Oh, she's never said anything, but I know . . .'

Violet grasped her sister's hand in hers. 'He loves the bones of you, Gracie, always did. But he had to have a life of his own as well. Kate was good for him, whatever you thought.'

Grace glanced around the room and sniffed. 'Well, where is she then? Miss high and fucking mighty . . .'

Vi left it. She knew how upset her sister was. She also knew she was dealing with a jealous woman. Kate had come in and usurped Grace's influential position in Pat's life and she wasn't going to forgive that one lightly. After Renée, he had relied on Grace and she had enjoyed that very much. Too much, in fact. But Violet couldn't say that because anything that could be construed as criticism caused all sorts of rows.

Grace was hard work, always had been.

Violet looked down at Patrick and felt frightened inside at the whiteness of his face. He looked like a waxwork, as if all his vibrant personality had drained away. He had taken a bullet to his neck and one to his buttock, something she knew would annoy the life out of him if he ever woke up.

The consultant had said on the phone that he was very poorly, whatever that was supposed to mean, and that the next twenty-four hours would be crucial. Patrick had severe trauma to the brain, apparently. Violet believed that doctors had enough on their plate without constant questioning from relatives. As long as they got her brother better she didn't care what they did to him. But looking at his beloved face, she didn't hold out much hope of that. He looked dead already.

'Shall I get a priest, Grace?'

Her sister turned on her like a lunatic. 'That's right, Vi, put the fucking mockers on him!'

Violet sighed heavily and sat down by the bed in silence, the only thing she could do that wouldn't make Grace even worse than she already was. It was like being a kid again and frankly, Violet was getting the pox of it. Always taking a back seat to her elder sister, always having to listen to her and what she thought everyone should do. When in reality Grace was useless at things like this, too emotional and too lairy by half.

Violet wondered sourly how long it would be before she got funny with the nurses, doctors, and anyone else who trespassed on her own private little world. In a funny way Violet envied Patrick. At least he didn't have to put up with Grace and her constant carping.

'I'm going to make a phone call, Violet. You stay here and try and collar a cuppa from one of these little girls parading round, disguised as nurses,' Grace said loudly, trying to catch a Staff Nurse's eye.

Violet closed her own in distress. Her sister was starting sooner rather than later.

Jenny looked into Kerry Alston's eyes and repeated her question, this time with added emphasis. The girl looked terrible, her fat face grey and dirty-looking. And Jenny could actually smell her. It was a sour stench of sweat and cigarette smoke, mingled with an acrid vinegary scent. In the heat of the interview room it was overpowering and Jenny knew that the young WPC sitting in on the interview was also affected.

'I really want an answer, Kerry, and I'm going to get one if it takes all day.' Her voice told the prisoner that she was running out of patience and the girl grinned, showing yellowing teeth.

'I'm impressed, but I can't answer that question. I don't know where my dad is and I don't know where Jeremy Blankley is either. Sorry.' The last word was said in a sing-song tone and Jenny stifled the urge to slap her hard for it.

'You really are a piece of work, do you know that? Do you realise how long you're looking at in prison? Well, do you?'

She was gratified to see a spark of fear in Kerry's eyes and carried on in the same low voice. 'And you won't do normal time, love, you'll be a beast. Now in a male prison that's bad enough. But in a female prison with women who are separated from their kids, kids they love like *normal* people, you will be in a very precarious position. Scalding water is the usual one, right in your face on the landing. They keep the boilers there, see, for night and morning drinks. You'll have to watch your back all the time. You see, you're not half as clever as you think, are you? In fact, if you're silly enough to refuse a deal, you'll be put away till you're an old woman. And you may think you're hard, Kerry, but you have to see some of the women in prison first – then talk to me about hard cases. Drunks, druggies, lunatics and murderers will all see themselves as far above you in the prison food chain. Have you thought about any of this? I mean, have you worked out how you'll survive?'

Kerry didn't answer her. Just stared at her with those washed-out eyes that had a feral light shining at the back of them. She looked mental, and she was going to act mental. But Jenny was determined that this one was not getting away with an insanity plea. Jenny would get fifty shrinks to declare her sane if that's what it took to get her to do real time.

'I admire you, Kerry, I really do. In your position I'd be shitting hot bricks and throwing them out the window. But there, you know best.'

She lit herself a cigarette and then said nonchalantly, 'Now then, this sexual assault when you were at school with Jackie Palmer. Could you enlighten me on that?'

Jenny was pleased to see Kerry's face tighten with shock. She mentally chalked one up to herself.

'That was never pursued, even you must know that.'

'Oh, I know that. I want to know *why* it was never pursued. Is it because your father and her father were buddies? I mean, you were very close to your father, I understand. Your mother explained to my colleague just how close you were – still are, in fact.'

Kerry didn't answer her.

'What's the matter, cat got your tongue? I thought you were good with your mouth.'

Kerry licked her lips suggestively, a lascivious look that turned Jenny's stomach. 'I could show you a thing or two, lady. I've got a feeling you would like it as well. All girls together, eh?' She sat back pleased at the knowledge she had made her antagonist really angry.

'Have you anything to say, Kerry?'

She shook her head slowly, a deliberate action of nonchalance. 'As I said, no one pursued those charges, so they are not relevant.'

'Just because no one pressed charges doesn't mean it didn't happen, Kerry. Her father was Old Bill, I understand. Did you ever have any dealings with him, in private like? I understand he knew your father very well.'

Kerry shrugged, her fat shoulders tense with fury, and Jenny realised just how strong this girl was.

'Why don't you fuck off?' she snarled. 'I know me rights. I ain't even got me brief here. You're fishing and I ain't got to answer fuck all unless it is relevant to the investigation.'

Jenny widened her eyes as if she was explaining something very simple to a small child.

'But it is relevant because Jackie Palmer is under investigation for the same reason as you. I thought you'd have known that by now? And it's true that you have been linked before, haven't you? I mean, when you sexually assaulted another girl at school. Do you see where I'm coming from now, dear?'

Kerry's arm was drawn back ready to strike when the WPC launched herself on top of her. It took the two of them to get the prisoner on the floor with her arms behind her back and the cuffs in place. All three of them were sweating from their exertions by the end of the scuffle.

'You lesbian ponce!'

Jenny grinned down at the heavy-set girl on the floor and said maddeningly, 'Ooh, temper, temper!'

Evelyn and Kate made their way up to intensive care, too nervous to speak. Evelyn could see the lines of worry etched on her daughter's face and felt a rush of maternal concern. The feeling never left a mother even when her child was fully grown. In her black trouser suit and red silk shirt, Kate looked slim and almost girlish from behind. Only the weary stoop of her shoulders gave the game away.

Her daughter was devastated and Eve knew it. She didn't care what they had argued about or how vitriolic it had been, those two had been closer than any other couple she had ever known. They adored one another even while they'd fought and argued about things that for most people would never even be an issue.

As they walked towards the nursing station Eve saw Patrick's sister Grace approaching them.

'What do you want?' Grace spoke in clipped tones.

'I beg your pardon?' Kate's voice was incredulous.

'You heard me, darlin'. What do *you* want?' Grace's usually cultivated accent had slipped into East End patois with her anger.

'How dare you . . .'

Grace held one immaculately manicured finger in Kate's face, her own a mask of anger and despair as she spat out, 'I dare? I dare when you look down that long fucking beak of yours at me and mine. You left him when he was at rock bottom, so piss off out of it now. Plain enough for you? Or would you like me to punch it right through to your brain? You ain't welcome here, lady.'

Kate looked at Grace, at her sleek dyed hair and over made-up face, and realised she was enjoying this.

Enjoying every second of it. She had always known Grace had a jealous streak but to give way to it now, when her brother was lying in a coma, seemed extraordinary. Grace was still standing there like a jailer, daring Kate with her body language to try and pass. She could see Violet's frightened face as she observed it all from beside Pat's bed.

But Grace had not banked on Evelyn. The tiny woman pushed past them both with the aid of a heavily laden leather shopping bag.

'Feck off, you! You'll not stop me going about me daily business, madam.'

She stormed towards Pat's bedside and Violet moved out of her way. Kate and Grace followed.

'When your man wakes up and tells us to go, we'll go. Until then, Grace, we'll do what the feck we please. Now, move out of me light so's I can get a good look at him.'

Grace did as she was told. Eve looked capable of blue murder and Grace knew of old that the little woman had a tongue that could cut through glass as and when the fancy took her.

Kate looked down at Patrick's face and felt the sting of tears. He looked so old. Old and haggard. His lifeless features so unlike his usual appearance that they frightened her. He looked broken and battered, so very white and quiet.

In a way she wished Grace *had* frightened them away – then she wouldn't have had to see this parody of Patrick Kelly that was lying in front of her.

The sound of the ventilator was unbearable.

A small part of her wished she had never come.

Jeremy Blankley walked out of the tower block where he lived, whistling contentedly. A tall man with a rangy walk, he fancied himself as a bit of a John Wayne. He had a long unshaven face, stubble well flecked with grey, and hideous false teeth. He dressed far too young for his age and consequently stood out from the crowd, gathering smiles from people that he wrongly assumed were friendly. It never occurred to him that he was being laughed *at*, not *with*.

Jeremy was with a young boy of twelve, Kieran Pargiter. Kieran was a rent boy used by the older man as bait. They went regularly to the West End, where Kieran befriended the young lads who were new. Runaways mainly. He introduced them to his 'mate' Jeremy, who offered them a place to stay. It was easy. Some of the smaller boys were never seen again.

As they walked towards a car, a dirty C-reg Escort that Jeremy used for mini-cabbing, they were approached by two men. He guessed immediately who they were and shouted out: 'Filth!'

He began to run. The younger of the two men had him in seconds. Kieran, however, got away.

When they had bundled him into an unmarked green Sierra Jeremy spat on the floor and said aggressively, 'This had better be good, mate.'

The beating, when it started, shocked him more than he had ever been shocked in his life before. When it was over he heard a voice say, 'Was that good enough for you, cunt, or would you like a finale? How about a drum roll and a pickaxe handle round the old loaf o' bread?'

The other man laughed then said in a music hall voice: 'Here, hold up, Harry, I do believe he's trying to escape again. What a wanker! Shall I stop him this time?'

The two men laughed heartily and a third man who was in the driving seat leaned back and said, 'We've been looking for you for a while, Blankley. Now you are going to Grantley to see some photos of you doing what you do best. Like little children, don't you?'

Jeremy's heart sank into his boots. He had thought they were after him for kiting – chequebook fraud. He'd never have believed in a million years they were after him for anything else. Surely they had all been too clever? Keeping it in the family more or less. What the fuck was going down here?

And, more to the point, who else had had a capture?

Boris was relaxed. He had showered, changed, and was having a drink ready to go out for a meal then on to a club he had recently purchased in Surrey. He was smiling as he walked down into the cellar of his house in Soho.

'How is Mr Gabney?'

His men stood up respectfully as he walked towards them. As usual his sheer physical presence was enough to command their attention.

'He has eaten much, and washed and changed his

clothes. He is thinner but still dangerous.'

Boris nodded. 'Open the door for me.'

They unlocked the steel-plated door and he entered the damp cellar as if it was the finest restaurant. Willy was sitting up on the Z-bed. He looked haggard and drawn, but at least he now had light and a few novels to pass the time.

'You are well, Mr Gabney?'

Willy guessed that this was the big boss and in spite of himself he was impressed.

'Are you ready to talk to me, Mr Gabney? Only I know you were Mr Kelly's number two and that you were party to everything he did.'

Willy looked up at the large man with what he described to himself as poofter's hair and sighed aloud.

'I will never tell you anything, mate. Patrick and me were more than business associates. I loved that man like a brother. You can burn me, bury me alive, rip me arms off – I'll not utter one fucking word other than a large "Ouch". Do you get my drift?'

Boris smiled and it completely changed his face. Willy knew that in other circumstances he would have admired, respected, maybe even liked this man before him.

'You are a brave man, Mr Gabney. I respect what you are saying. If only Mr Kelly had had more friends like you.' He raised his arms in a show of openness. 'But soon we will need to talk. Once I explain my own situation you will understand why I had to do what I did. I cannot be seen to be robbed, Mr Gabney, not even by your illustrious friend Mr Kelly.'

The sarcasm was not lost on Willy, who said quietly, 'Patrick Kelly never ripped off anyone in his life. Remember that for the future. Even if someone had a touch with *your* money in *his* club, you were barking up the wrong tree believing he was behind it. You could have found that out with a simple question. Patrick was looking for you, mate, to find out what the score was. He wasn't interested in what you had as such. He was just hagged that it was all going down on his fucking premises, without his permission or knowledge.'

Boris looked amused and Willy went back to his book as if the man before him was just a nuisance. He heard the Russian's shoes move away across the cement floor and breathed a sigh of relief. He was scared, shit scared, and just managing to conceal it.

If Patrick was really brown bread, then Willy had lost the person he cared for most in his life. Patrick was so generous, he had even shared his only child with his friend. Mandy had been the light of their lives after Renée's death. She had kept them both together, often joking that she had two dads. He remembered the looks they'd received at school evenings, the two big men with the tiny blonde girl. Willy knew his own appearance was unusual. In fact, he knew he looked downright scary. But Mandy had never noticed, she'd loved him with all her heart.

He felt the sting of tears but tried to console himself with the thought that Pat was with Renée and Mandy at last. Willy wondered how long it would be before he joined them.

★ ★ ★

Kate felt the eyes of the team upon her and ignored their unusual interest. She had seen the tabloid stories about Patrick's shooting around the station; noticed people reading the newspapers in the canteen and quickly putting them down when she walked by.

She didn't give a shit, and this came over in her attitude.

Most of her colleagues admired her but this was a hell of a thing to live down. Those who had met Patrick at different times understood the attraction, and knew it had been a genuine love match. Others relished the gossip that he had just been using her. After all, a DI in his pocket was a handy thing for any criminal. Especially one like Patrick Kelly. But they didn't know how Kate and Patrick had felt about one another, how hard it had been for them to follow their hearts. The trouble their different lifestyles had caused them.

They didn't know *anything*.

Golding, she knew, had often wondered what Patrick Kelly, with all his looks, money and kudos, was doing with a middle-aged DI. He'd left people in no doubt that he considered it some kind of business arrangement on Kelly's side, if not on Kate's. He constantly reminded them of Patrick's penchant for brainless blondes who were large on knockers and short on intelligence.

Now, as she looked around the dingy canteen, at the dirty cigarette-stained Formica tables and chattering men and women, Kate felt a feeling of unreality descend upon her. Pat was dying. He was going to die and she was as far from him now as if he was on the moon. He would never know how much she loved him. How much she still wanted him. How much he meant to her whatever their disagreements. Whatever their different lifestyles.

She felt Jenny take her arm and lead her gently from the room. A radio was playing 'Zoom' by Fat Larry's Band and the words seemed to blast away the last shreds of her self-control.

In her office she broke down, trying to keep her tears silent but occasionally giving way to muffled sobs. The other woman held her tightly as her shoulders shook and her whole body felt as if it would crumble from grief.

'Get it out of your system, Kate. Let it go, mate. Just let it all go.'

And she did.

Jeremy Blankley was so frightened he thought he might have a heart attack. In the cell, he looked around at the green-painted walls, at the pornographic graffiti everywhere, and smelled the usual reek of urine, old farts and badly cooked food. He felt the sting of tears.

He had done a nonce stretch once before, when he was younger. He remembered in vivid detail being asleep in his cell when the PO in charge had brought in three lifers brandishing broom handles in righteous anger. He had been used, he knew that. The lifers had been allowed to let off steam and he had been hospitalised for nearly three months.

This time, though, with little kiddies involved, he was a walking dead man. He knew that if they put him on VPU, the Vulnerable Prisoners' Unit, even the rapists would look down on him. And that was the best he could hope for. He would be the worst kind of beast, hated by everyone around him from the POs to the other prisoners. He would have to look closely at everything he ate; constantly be on his guard. There were a hundred and one ways to get at someone like him in a prison, from glass in his food or soap, to salt forced into his mouth, and rape with a blunt instrument.

He would have to look over his shoulder for the duration.

When the cell door opened he jumped with fright. He was pleased to see it was a woman, an attractive one with sad dark eyes and a tall slender figure.

Jeremy smiled tremulously. She looked him over as if he was so much dirt and her voice when she spoke frightened him with its intensity.

'I am Detective Inspector Kathryn Burrows and I am going to put you away for so long, Mr Blankley, that you will never again see the light of day unless it is through a barred window. Do you understand what I am telling you, you filthy piece of shite?'

Jeremy nodded, his eyes trained on the floor. He could no longer meet hers which were filled with contempt and hatred.

'Whatever prison you go to on remand, I'll make sure they know all about you. That is a promise, Mr Blankley, from my heart.'

She was quiet for a few minutes then and the silence crashed in on him as painfully as any noise.

'You had better think long and hard about what you are going to tell me in the next few hours, and you'd better get a damn good brief because I am going all out to get you, and I will. I don't care if you have friends in high places – I don't care who you think might be able to help you. I will have you, boy, and I'll enjoy doing it.'

She left the cell as quietly as she'd entered it.

The duty sergeant looked Jeremy over before shutting the door and then he heard a voice next door shout, 'Is he a fucking nonce? Am I celled up next to a nonce?'

Utter loneliness and desolation washed over him like a wave.

Kate sat in her office going over the files from Robert Bateman's office. She was amazed by the things social workers considered acceptable; the conditions in which they left young children because they were in the care of a so-called parent. Well, she would collate it all, and somehow she was going to match up these mothers and put them together in such a way that they would lose both their children and their liberty.

She wasn't so sure now that Jackie Palmer was innocent. It was beginning to look like some kind of conspiracy. Something that tied them all together . . .

As she stared at the reports and read the appalling things that had happened to the women she was looking at putting away, the memory of Patrick's near-lifeless form overlaid everything.

She exhaled sharply, shaking her head as if she could physically remove the image. She rubbed at her eyes, feeling the mascara crumble beneath her fingertips and not caring.

She would throw herself into work as she knew Ratchet would use any excuse to dismiss her from this investigation. Patrick Kelly was dying and the Chief Inspector wanted to distance himself from their association as fast as possible.

She didn't blame him; even understood him. He was like all rats that deserted sinking ships: he was looking after number one. Patrick would have applauded it, not taken it in the least personally, so why should she?

Now they had Jeremy Blankley she would concentrate on him, and what he was capable of, and what she knew he had already done. Every time she thought of those photographs she felt sick. That anybody could do that to a child, could *want* to do that to a child, was beyond her comprehension.

She pictured Patrick again and wondered if the Russian had any idea of the mayhem he had caused by his actions? She knew that Patrick had got into something that was over his head. That the lap-dancing club had proved a viper in his bosom. She wanted to do something about it all, but what?

Willy was missing, and there was skulduggery of Olympic standards going on all around her, and it all led back to Patrick Kelly. But she could not get involved, not officially. Unofficially she intended to find out as much as she could. But even then she could not let this investigation suffer.

These children came first – *had* to come first. Patrick himself would have insisted on that.

She stood up and stretched.

She was more than ready for Jeremy Blankley.

Chapter Thirteen

Kate looked into Jeremy Blankley's frightened eyes and grinned.

'You look worried, Mr Blankley. What on earth could be wrong?'

This woman terrified him. It was as if she could see right through him and read his mind. As if she knew everything about him. As if every dirty little deed he had ever committed was written on his forehead in a code that only she could decipher.

He lit a roll-up and his hand shook so much he had to grasp his own wrist to stop the trembling. 'Ever heard of the expression "innocent until proven guilty", Miss Burrows?' he said hoarsely.

Kate smiled, an easy, sarcastic smile. 'Save it for the jury, they're the ones who have to believe that shit. I'm going to make a case against you so tight a duck's arse will look like a gaping hole in comparison.'

She fanned out the photos on the desk before him in a theatrical gesture. 'Recognise anyone, Mr Blankley?' She grinned. 'Other than yourself, of course.'

He pulled smoke deep into his lungs and wiped at his mouth with the back of his hand. 'Are you offering me a deal?'

She shook her head. 'Never in a million years, mate. I want you put away as quickly as possible and for as long as possible. I just want you to cut the crap.'

Even the PC in the interview room was shocked by her aggression.

Jeremy Blankley stared at her for what seemed to him a long time.

'Imagine when the jury sees these photos and then recognises your tattoos in all their Technicolor glory. Same with your brother. My condolences, of course. Kevin was just unlucky, eh? You'll probably wish Lenny Parkes had got to you first by the time you're through.'

She laughed unpleasantly. 'You ain't got a fucking chance, mate. Not a chance. Any jury will want to hang you from the nearest tree. And who can blame them, eh? Most people, you see, the ones on the jury included, *love* their children. Love *all* children. It's the fucking *law*. So people like *you* – perverts, weirdos, shitbags – tend to give the rest of us *normal* people the hump. I do hope you haven't made any holiday plans because you won't be going anywhere for a long, long time.'

'I don't have to take this . . .' There were tears in his eyes, he was mortally afraid of her now.

'Oh, but you do. You have to take whatever I decide to dish out,' Kate sneered. 'Because, you see, in here I am the boss. I can make you do whatever I want. A bit like you, when you're abusing someone smaller than you.'

She opened her arms like a fisherman indicating a really big catch.

'This is all mine, you see, and I call the shots. You ought to bear that in mind, because I have a nick full of people who would give me hard cash to be alone with you for five minutes. That goes for prisoners as well as the policemen. I'm trying to save you from the hammering of a lifetime here. You need VPU and you need it soon, mate. Because when my patience runs out, you, boy, are on your own.'

She stood up, leaving the photos on the table so he could see them.

'Get a brief and get one soon. Then I'm going to take you apart and enjoy every bloody second of it.'

She left the room and the male PC watched her go with new respect.

When the door banged shut, Jeremy Blankley laid his head on his arms and cried like a baby. If Kevin had been alive he would have been in with a chance. He knew all the right people. Unlike himself, who had made too many enemies over the years. There was only one person who could help him, and Jeremy was too scared of the consequences to contact him without Kevin's presence.

The only other option was to grass. And that was no option at all.

He had to try and work out some kind of defence.

But what? That was the sixty-four-thousand-dollar question.

★ ★ ★

'Did you know Patrick Kelly's yard was blown up?' Ratchet's voice was hoarse and nervous.

Kate shook her head. 'I didn't know that, no. But I'll take your word for it, sir.' She shrugged. 'You obviously know more about it than I do.'

He looked at her closely. There was something different about her. She was obviously under a lot of strain, he understood that, but there was a distinct lack of respect in her tone and he didn't like that at all.

'Are you all right, Kate?'

She grinned and he was amazed at the change in her. She looked pretty again. The dour expression she had been wearing recently seemed to have lifted. He liked his women jolly, always had done.

'Oh, I'm great, sir. Patrick is being kept alive by machines. He has a nutter of a Russian after him who I assume you know more about than I do. I have a serious case of paedophilia to investigate and am being treated like a complete *cunt* by my superiors. What on earth could be bugging me?'

She stood up, gathering her files in her arms, then turned back to face her superior.

'If you're looking to dismiss me, sir, because I've become an embarrassment, you'd better think again. I have had it with you and all your blasted cronies! If I ever opened my trap I could remove more people from this nick than a strategically placed bomb. Now, if you're finished, I am going back to work. Remember that? I'm sure you must have done some at one stage in your illustrious career. It's not a bit like golf, you have to stay in the office a lot. Now, if you'll excuse me . . .'

At the door she turned and said loudly, 'Another thing: I need more manpower and I think you should make sure that I get it, don't you?'

'DI Burrows, you really can't expect to talk to me like that.'

Kate faced him down. 'But I just did, sir, didn't I?' She walked back to his desk and leaned over it. He was so amazed he sat back in his chair, almost in fear of her.

'You are a wanker, sir, a complete and utter wanker. In future I shall send a junior in to keep you up to date. Because, quite frankly, I can't be arsed to look at your face.'

When she left the room he was open-mouthed with disbelief.

'What on earth do you think you are doing to my client?' The young black woman looked positively incensed, bristling with anger.

'I beg your pardon?' Kate's voice was bored-sounding as she glanced up at the lawyer. 'Who let you in here?'

The woman was caught on the hop and it showed.

'You threatened Jeremy Blankley,' she blustered.

Kate held up her hand and said slowly, 'Did I? Was there a witness to this threat by any chance?'

They were both quiet for a moment.

'I didn't think so. Now, Miss Whoever, if you don't mind I'm busy catching nonces. Beasts, scumbags, clients . . . whatever you want to call them. Have you seen the evidence yet by any chance? The photographs?'

The girl couldn't meet her eye and Kate smiled.

'I'll take that as a yes then. Now listen to me: I am going to take Mr Blankley and destroy him any way I can. If you can bear to look closely at the pictures you will see children, distressed little children, and Jeremy Blankley with his brother right there in the thick of it with their home-made tattoos in full view. If your client can't take the heat he should have stayed out of the fucking kitchen in the first place, don't you think? Please forgive me if I cut this conversation short. I am very busy.'

The two women stared at one another and the girl looked away first.

Kate relented. 'Look, I know you have to give your client the best possible representation, guilty or innocent, and I respect that. You should afford me the same respect when I'm doing *my* job – which is putting away people like your client for as long as possible.'

When her office was empty Kate put her head into her hands and took deep breaths. When that girl had first come barging in, all self-righteous, Kate had wanted to let rip. It was as if another person was inhabiting her skin, a more aggressive, evil-tempered person. She knew this was the aftermath of her shock over Patrick and what had happened to him. Had happened to both of them. They had been estranged, but deep inside they had both known that it would not have lasted for ever. She loved him too well to ever stay away from him for any real length of time. Now she had no choice in the matter. He was a broken man, kept alive by machines and watched over by strangers. Every bodily function was usurped, every movement made for him. Patrick Kelly, the larger-than-life Essex wide boy she had come to adore, was lost inside a useless shell of a body.

How would she live without him?

Evelyn was cooking as usual. It was what she did when she was worried, depressed, happy or sad. As she peeled potatoes and sliced cabbage she felt the tension drain out of her. She was making a nice roast-lamb dinner for her daughter and that strange mannish friend she had staying.

There was more to that one than met the eye! But Jenny was lovely to have around and seemed to be what Kate needed at the moment. Obviously a very good policewoman as well.

Evelyn glanced at the clock on the cooker. She had plenty of time to get all this prepared then shoot up to the hospital to see Patrick. Her mouth set in a grim line now as she thought of Grace and her bolshie attitude.

When the doorbell rang, she bustled down the hall, a sprig of fresh mint in her hands giving off a wonderful aroma. Opening the door, she was amazed to see two very large men in overcoats. It took a few seconds for her to register the fact they were pushing past her and into the narrow hallway.

'What the Jasus are you doing?' Her voice was querulous with anger.

The men took her gently but firmly into the front room and shut the door on her. Evelyn stood in the empty room in shock, but something told her not to say a word. She glanced quickly at the phone on the table by the sofa, walked towards it and picked it up. It was dead and she wasn't surprised. Fear tightened her throat and chest. She sat on the sofa and stared down at her rough work-worn hands as she heard the house around her being systematically searched.

Ten minutes later the men walked into the front room and she watched in amazement as they began their search here as well. They were professional and quick. One even smiled at her and she found to her amazement she was smiling back!

It was then she realised she would not be harmed.

'Are there any things here belonging to Patrick Kelly?' The heavily accented voice was respectful and pleasant.

Evelyn shook her head in denial. 'Nothing – he never lived here. It's only my things and my daughter's. Oh, and my grand-daughter's but she is away, abroad.'

'In Australia, I understand?'

She nodded.

'A beautiful country no doubt.'

Evelyn nodded and smiled again. It felt surreal, chatting like they were standing in a bus queue. The other man took the cushions off the sofa and forced his hands down the sides and back.

'You'll find nothing, son. There's nothing here.'

He ignored her.

Then they talked to one another in a foreign language for a moment. The smiling man eventually told her, 'We apologise for any inconvenience we have caused you, madam.'

And seconds later they were gone.

Evelyn pulled out her good medicinal whiskey and poured herself a large glassful. She needed it to quell the rapid beating of her heart.

She looked around the room which seemed quite untouched, no different from when they had entered it. They had worn gloves so she knew that there would be no fingerprints, nothing. She realised after the second glass that she had been in the company of well-trained and probably highly dangerous men. Yet they had not intimidated her once.

She picked up the phone and was glad to find it worked once more. This did not surprise her either. She rang Kate and told her she was needed at home as soon as possible. Evelyn had a feeling she wasn't going to want this bandied about the station.

Then, already slightly tipsy, she went back to her medicine.

Jenny and Kate were in Grantley's most notorious pub, the Wheatsheaf. As they sipped their gin and tonics they looked around them at the usual clientèle. Kate saw a few double takes and suppressed a smile. She knew she was being recognised, which was exactly what she wanted.

As Michael McMann walked in she waved at him and gestured for him to join them. He did not look pleased at the prospect and Jenny and Kate glanced at one another with barely suppressed mirth.

'What the fuck are you doing?' He was looking at the two women as if they were aliens who had just materialised in front of him. 'Are you trying to get me fucking killed?'

Kate frowned. 'But you're a grass, Michael. Where else would we look for you if we wanted to put pressure on you other than where you work? We wanted to be seen, you see, and we are being, as you've probably noticed.'

The man was sweating; a fine film of perspiration was covering his ruddy face and his thin sandy hair was also dampening nicely. They could smell his odour of fear and anger.

'You are a right bastard, Burrows. I've done the Old Bill some favours in the past and you would do this to me?'

Jenny sipped her drink then replied, 'Yes, we would. Because we want a big favour. One that will make you the enemy of everyone you have ever dealt with. And you'll do it. Otherwise we will have to start hassling you. This is a bit of personal, you see. Not police business.'

She let the words sink in before saying brightly, 'By the way, does Jacky Gunner know you are a grass? Only you work for him as well, don't you?' At his silence she shook her head knowingly. 'No. I didn't think so.'

'Who the fuck are you anyway?'

Jenny looked at him closely and smiled. 'I, Mr McMann, am your worst enemy.'

'What do you two want?'

'We want to know about a man called Boris. A Russian. We want to know everything you can find out about him.'

'I don't know any fucking Russians . . .'

Kate interrupted him. 'No, but Jacky Gunner does – or so I understand. He has been bragging about his Russian connection – I heard that from another grass earlier today. Now you and Jacky are practically joined at the hip, so you were the natural choice to ask. You being a paid police informant, a grass.' She spoke deliberately loudly, to rattle him.

Michael licked dry lips and looked surreptitiously around the pub. 'I thought you was after the nonces. What's this, a side line?'

'As my friend said, it's a bit of personal.' She laughed at his outraged countenance. 'Where is Jacky these days, and what's his latest scam?'

Michael shook his head slowly. 'This is one time when you can lock me up, but I ain't saying a fucking dicky bird. This is way too heavy for the likes of me. I appreciate your man has been shot. I sympathise. But that, Miss Burrows, is as far as it goes.' He sat back as if he didn't have a care in the world.

Kate's voice was low and clear as she spoke. 'I will find out where Jacky is, and if it means shouting out all your past deeds in this packed public house then that is just what I will do.'

Michael knew she meant it. 'I am a paid informer, you can't do that to me. You would not only endanger my life but also a couple of ongoing investigations.' He sat back again, pleased with himself.

Kate leaned forward and growled, 'Like I give a toss. Now listen to me, Michael. I am going to get this out of you one way or another. I am Patrick's other half as you pointed out yourself. Remember that, because I am not playing games here.'

She leaned even closer to him. 'Fuck ongoing investigations, fuck it all. As I said, this is personal. I want to know now.'

'If I was you, Mr McMann, I would seriously consider telling her what she wants to know.' Jenny's voice was gentle, friendly and Michael looked from one of them to the other in obvious confusion.

'Are you two really coming the heavy with me?'

'Looks like it.' Kate stood and called across the bar loudly, 'Another round here, please. And whatever my friend Mr McMann is drinking.'

Everyone turned to look at him.

She glanced at her watch and said slowly, 'You have exactly two minutes before my trap goes louder than an air-raid warning. Are this lot aware of how many faces you have put in the frame over the last seven years?'

'He's in a safe house near Rettenden. Staying with Joey Partridge.'

Kate smiled. 'See, that wasn't too difficult, was it?'

Patrick's house looked deserted. As she opened the

front door, and stepped inside, Kate heard her own footsteps ring in the silence.

Jenny followed her in, hardly able to contain her awe. 'Bloody hell, this is some drum!'

'It is a nice house, isn't it? Patrick loved it. It stood for everything he'd worked for over the years.'

They walked through the entrance hall and into the drawing room.

Jenny stared around her without a word. From here they looked over the tennis court and the summerhouse outside. Inside there were heavy glass chandeliers and oil paintings on the walls, velvet-upholstered sofas and blue brocade curtains.

Kate opened a small locked cabinet and turned off the alarm.

'Jesus Christ, Kate, this is serious money,' breathed Jenny.

'Villainy pays well, that's what we learn at Hendon.'

Jenny blew out her lips and said seriously, 'I am in the wrong job, love.'

Kate smiled at her. 'This is legal enough, Jen. It just isn't what we would class as earned money. This lot came off massage parlours – places like that. Pat knew his market and he exploited it. Come on, let's see what we can find.'

It took them two hours to go through the place and Kate knew they would have to leave soon. The housekeeper would be back by 4.30 and Kate didn't want to see her. They'd found nothing that didn't pertain to Patrick's known business interests. There was nothing at all to do with Girlie Girls.

As they walked down the garden towards the summerhouse and pool room, Jenny exclaimed over and over at the beauty of the grounds.

'Jesus, Kate, I never guessed you'd been living like this for all that time. It's a fairy tale. A dream. You know, if you win the pools or something.'

Kate had stopped answering her over an hour before. She knew how Jenny was feeling, had felt like that herself at times, even when she lived here.

Lizzy had adored the place and had moved in without a second thought, enjoying it for what it was, inviting friends round and generally showing off. Unlike Mandy Kelly, who had been brought up to it, Kate's daughter had embraced her new lifestyle with an open enthusiasm that had looked out of place sometimes. She had even changed her accent to match her upmarket surroundings and that had grated on Kate at first. She had seen it as further proof of Lizzy's shallowness.

But as Patrick had said at the time, the girl had more than a trace of Dan in her under the voluptuous exterior, and blood will always out in the end.

Today, remembering the past while she had run her hands over his things, breathed in his special scent, Kate had felt an urge to cry.

Patrick was everywhere around here.

His dressing gown looked forlorn, hanging alone in the bathroom. Their bed looked huge and empty, with its unruffled covers and perfectly smooth pillowcases. Every trace of her was gone from the room and it hurt her. Hurt her deeply.

Her mobile rang and she answered it curtly. Sitting on a padded wicker chair in the summerhouse she said calmly, 'Fuck you too, mate.'

She turned the phone off and smiled at Jenny's blatant curiosity. 'Michael McMann didn't lose any time in telling the world what had befallen him. That was DI Thomas over in Harbridge. Not a happy bunny.'

Jenny shrugged. 'We'd better make our way to Rettenden, Kate. They might already have had a call from him.'

Kate shook her head and said gently, 'He can't afford to tell them anything, he knows we'll catch up with them eventually.'

'This Russian sounds intriguing, don't you think?'

Kate nodded. 'This place is clean. Patrick's too shrewd to leave anything incriminating around his home. Quite frankly I can't think where the rest of his stuff could be. His yard was blown, so anything there would be gone by now. Willy would know, but he's out of the ball game for some reason. So it looks like all we have at the moment is Rettenden.'

'We'd better get going, Kate. Can you imagine Ratchet's face if he knew what we were doing?'

Kate didn't answer. She looked out over the grounds and wondered if the Russian was having the place watched. She had assumed he was and wanted him to see her here. It might just bring him out of the woodwork.

'We'll drop by my house on the way and see how my mother's faring.'

The two officers strolled nonchalantly back, both enjoying the beauty of their surroundings. Kate asked herself if she missed the house itself and knew that she did and she didn't. Without Patrick it was empty. With him it had been a home.

Jacky Gunner looked at Joey Partridge. 'That's a hundred thousand pounds you owe me now, mate.'

Joey lit a cigar and blew smoke across the table. 'Business, ain't it?' He picked up the Monopoly board and emptied everything on it back into the box. 'Fancy a cup of tea?'

'Why not?' Jacky Gunner started to roll himself a joint. 'Did you hear about Laurie Simons? Caught with sixteen lumps of black. He tried to con the Old Bill it was bars of chocolate.'

The two men laughed.

'He's off his trolley,' Joey said. 'I heard he was being questioned by the Drugs Squad and when they showed him the stuff they'd found in his car, he opened the bag and blew into it. Fucking coke everywhere. All over the table, the floor – he really blew and all. The filth went mental and he was licking it off his face, 'cos it had gone everywhere like, and he told them, "That's good stuff, ain't been cut yet. Just what the doctor ordered." They went ballistic by all accounts.'

They laughed again.

'You ever seen his bird Big Lucy?' Joey sniggered.

Jacky shook his head. 'I've heard about her.'

'One fucking ugly fat bird she is, but she's so funny

she should be a stand-up comedian. There's something about her you can't help liking and she is well stacked and all. When they raided the house she got up out of bed stark naked, bent over and pulled the cheeks of her arse apart. She said to the Old Bill, "It's your choice – you can go in singly or in twos." Laurie said he was busting so much they couldn't cuff him. Their faces were a fucking picture. He'll be here later anyway, he's dropping some stuff off for me.'

Jacky lit his joint and took a deep toke on it. 'How much longer do you reckon we'll have to sit it out here?'

Joey shrugged. 'Fuck knows. Kelly should have died, the wanker. But he's on his way out by all accounts so we've that to look forward to at least.' He grinned cheerfully. 'I'll have to go to the funeral, won't I?'

Laughing, Jacky Gunner pushed his hair from his eyes. He was good-looking and he knew it. Even on his own he was always conscious of what he looked like. A lady's man, he liked to keep himself smart. Even now, locked up in a safe house with only men for company, he had dressed casually but well.

He watched Joey pouring out the tea and puffed once more on his joint. 'Can't we get a bit of skirt here tonight, Joe? I need a shag, mate.'

Joey gave a dirty chuckle. 'Fucking wear it out, you will, boy. I'll see what we can drum up.'

Just then the door opened and they stared in utter disbelief as a large black man walked into the room.

'Who the fucking hell are you?' Joey said, surprise cracking his voice.

The man's massive shoulders and heavy neck seemed to strain against his shiny skin. He was the biggest bloke that Jacky and Joey had ever seen in their lives.

Kate stepped into the room behind him.

'Afternoon, gentlemen. Any more of that tea going?'

'You're having a fucking tin bath, ain't you?'

She walked over to where they were standing and glanced around the room. 'This place is a bit of a dump, isn't it?'

The two men were silent, still in shock.

She smiled at their expressions and introduced herself. 'DI Kate Burrows. Or, as I am also known, Pat Kelly's bird the filth.'

She was pleased to see the two faces before her pale.

'And this is my friend, Benjamin Boarder. He isn't a policeman, but I think you might have guessed that much already.'

She rubbed her hands together. 'Now then, where's that tea we were talking about?'

Chapter Fourteen

Benjamin Boarder was thirty-nine years old. An East End boy born and bred, to a white mother and Jamaican father, he was the epitome of the New Man. Well-dressed, good-looking, well-groomed and the father of seven children, he was a thoroughly nice bloke.

Provided you didn't upset him, of course.

As he stood sentinel in the small bungalow in Rettenden he knew that his reputation had as usual preceded him. Jacky Gunner looked decidedly green around the gills, but then he would. They'd had a run-in many moons ago.

Benjamin was wearing the regulation enforcer's coat: leather, expensive and with a long pocket. He saw the two men's eyes trained on it and had to force himself not to smile. They both thought their number was up. If it was left to him, it soon would be.

He watched as Kate sipped her tea and chatted to them without any reference to her reason for being here. He could smell the fear in the air. The whole situation amused him.

Boarder liked Kate Burrows, always had. When Patrick had first taken up with her, Benjamin had agreed with a lot of the criminal fraternity that Pat's daughter's murder had turned his head. On meeting her though, he had soon come to like and respect her.

In fairness, as Pat had pointed out, everything he did these days was legal anyway, so he had no worries about being cuffed late at night, unless it was a sex game. Everyone had finally accepted her. Most people wondered if she was bent, and Pat never denied that. He only laughed. So eventually a lot of faces had just assumed it and Pat's rep had risen overnight.

'Sleeping with the enemy' has been one joke out of hundreds.

As he watched her now, fighting for her man's rights, Benjamin decided he would do anything to help her even if it meant falling out with mad Boris the Russian. A ponce of the first water and a foreign wanker they could all do without.

'All right, Gunner, stop trying to wind me up. You and I both know that you're due a final capture. It's the law, if you'll excuse the pun. So basically, I can pull you in now, or you can do me a favour. It's entirely up to you,' Kate was saying.

'You'd better pull me in then because I ain't got nothing to say to you, lady. Nothing whatsoever.'

She grinned. 'We'll go now then, eh?'

Gunner was frightened. As he looked nervously at Benjamin they could both see the confusion on his face.

'What, you taking me to the Bill shop then?'

'Maybe,' Kate said in a friendly fashion.

Benjamin looked at his watch as if he was in an enormous hurry and wanted to get going as soon as possible. This was not lost on anyone in the room.

Kate thanked God for her choice of heavy. Benjamin Boarder knew every trick in the book. They all watched as his hand went to his gun. It looked like a perfectly instinctive action and that made it all the more frightening to the two men sitting at the table. Boarder would use a gun for a price. Had used a gun for a price. Many times.

'Patrick is on the mend, did you know that?' Kate's voice was hushed now, as if she was letting them in on a big secret.

Joey Partridge was looking around the room as if expecting an escape route to open up before his eyes.

'You don't understand what you're dealing with,' he tried snarling. He looked from Kate to her henchman. 'Either of you. We're involved in something so big, lady, it would take an FBI team ten years to place just one face inside it.'

Benjamin watched impassively as Kate stood up and shook her head sadly.

'You don't half talk some crap, Joey. Who are you more scared of? Boris, Patrick or me? Only as I see it you're caught between a rock and a very hard place. Whatever I decide today, you are both basically fucked. Right or wrong? All I really want is a contact for Boris, that's all. Then I'll walk out of this door and forget I ever came here. But if I don't get what I want, I may have to start causing you hag. Then I'll have to tell people like McMann and others that if grassing was an Olympic sport, you lot would get the gold. Do you see what I'm trying to say?'

She paused and stared hard at the two men. 'Now if I can track you down here, I can track you anywhere. Unlike most of your peers, I can look you and all your mates up on a dirty big central computer. So let's cut the crap and make some sort of deal here, eh. I am a very busy woman.'

Jacky Gunner was not impressed. He wanted out of the country and he was going to leave within the next few days. Now he had a filth standing here telling him that he was either a captured man or a dead one.

He could feel sweat prickling on his neck and under his arms. He was clear and free but for this woman with her big expressive eyes and her flat tits telling him she had him whichever way he decided to turn. He thought of his wife Sheryl and his kids waiting for him in Tenerife. The bank account that only he had access to, and his girlfriend, Freya, living not a ten-minute walk from his wife's new villa.

It wasn't fucking fair. Life never was.

On top of it all he had Boris on his back. Big Bad Boris, who had more bloody contacts than AT&T, British Telecom and all the Internet service providers put together.

Jacky was in over his neck as usual. 'With Pat on the mend you two are in a rather precarious position because, being Patrick, he's going to want to know who set him up. He's funny like that, always wanting to know everything. It's what I like about him,' Kate said cosily. 'Now, once I give him the information he wants, you two can do what you like. Until then, you're mine. Take them to the car, Ben. This is starting to bore me.'

Joey jumped from his seat, his hands held out in front of him. 'Here, hold up. Where are you taking us?'

Boarder said quietly, 'Callum Norville is waiting for you both.'

'What! Callum is on to this?'

Kate heard the tremor in Jacky's voice and swallowed down her own fear. She had gone big, she knew that. The cost of all this was going to be sky high.

'Who else did you think we'd have called on? Patrick was his partner for years – I thought you'd have known that.'

Gunner looked at Kate. 'I ain't going nowhere.'

'You don't have any choice.'

He looked into her eyes. 'Oh, yes I do. I'll give you a contact number for Boris . . .'

'Leave it out, Jacky! What are you – fucking mad?' Joey protested.

Gunner waved him to silence.

'Fuck you, Joey. This was supposed to be a safe house – any minute now I'll have fucking Avon calling. Now piss off and let me do me own deal. You want to be a hero that's up to you, but I'm already in Callum's fucking bad books. I ain't going to see him for no one.'

Kate suppressed a smile. Patrick had said once that

just Callum's name was more frightening than anything Stephen King or anyone else could think up. From a bare-knuckle fighter to a paid torturer, his progress had been swift. He instilled real terror and would do so for a price. Hence he was the most hated and the most feared man in the smoke. He would nail legs to tables, burn the soles off feet, and laugh while he did it. On his own initiative, he had brought back facial scalping as his trademark. What's more, the man himself literally feared nothing. It was awesome to behold. Such was the reputation of Callum Norville.

'Give me the number and then I'll hand you to Benny here for the next few days. Once I establish contact with the Russian you can carry on as usual.'

Jacky shook his head. 'No way. I give you the number, lady, then you fuck off.'

Kate lit a cigarette, slowly and deliberately.

'Not being funny, son, but I think we've already established that I am calling the shots here. So just give me the number or I'll ask Callum very nicely to get it out of you. *Don't wind me up!*' she growled suddenly.

The two villains knew that this was a woman on the edge. The man she adored had just been left with gunshot wounds and a tenuous grip on life. She also had the backing of a serious and mentally disturbed face called Callum Norville.

There was no choice; they had to do what she wanted.

'I'll keep Norville away, don't worry.'

But it sounded a bit uncertain, as though she wasn't

sure she could really do that. It had the desired effect. Suddenly Boris took a back seat. He was scary, he was dangerous, but so was Callum Norville and he had the edge because now they were within his grasp.

As Kate saw the two men climbing into the van with Benjamin she sighed. She was in above her head now, had finally stepped over the fine line that separated law and order from badness and villainy.

She was disappointed in herself; had expected to feel much worse about it than she actually did. In fact, she had enjoyed it. But that was probably because she was doing something at last. She knew that Patrick Kelly would have moved heaven and earth to help her out if the boot was on the other foot.

She was just repaying the compliment.

Sarah Coltman got out of her car and stretched. She was tired out. Her whole body ached. She rubbed her large belly, felt the child within it move gently.

She loved living here, though everyone thought she and Max were mad for choosing to do so. There were only two other small cottages down Sunny Lane, but that was what they liked about it. The privacy and the quiet. Both born in Grantley on council estates, they had worked and saved to buy their dream home. Every time she looked at the cottage with its thatched roof and pretty garden Sarah felt a jolt of pure, unadulterated happiness. With the baby on the way, they had it all.

Sarah pushed her thick dark hair from her eyes

and looked out over the fields opposite. They would be muck-spreading soon and the smell would be atrocious, but that was part and parcel of going rural. A fly buzzed around her face and she brushed it away gently.

She yawned loudly and then opening the boot she took out her heavy bags of shopping, and lugged them towards her front door. Just then she saw a woman walking along the lane. The sight caught her eye because the woman had a stunningly beautiful child with her. The little girl had long blonde hair and blue eyes, like a picture of an angel come to life. But she was crying loudly, her face contorted by tears.

Sarah put down her shopping and walked to her gate. The woman turned abruptly as she saw her and dragged the child along the lane. The little girl was calling out, 'I want my mummy!' She was looking over her shoulder at Sarah, her huge blue eyes beseeching.

Opening the gate, Sarah followed them down the lane. It was instinctive.

As the woman picked up the child, Sarah found herself running behind them. The child was hysterical now, screaming.

'Stop! Excuse me, could you slow down, please? I want to talk to you.' Sarah's voice was louder than she had thought. It rang in her own ears as she ran, panting, down the uneven lane. She was praying she wouldn't lose her footing and fall over.

The girl was kicking and struggling now, holding out her arms to Sarah in supplication and Sarah knew in the deepest recess of her heart that this child was in trouble. It spurred her on. Even with her heavy belly weighing her down she made herself run faster. The sun was in her eyes and she was struggling to see.

The woman in front of her had long brown hair and she was running at a remarkable speed considering she was carrying a sturdily built toddler. Just then the little girl gave her a well-aimed kick and the woman stumbled. Sarah saw her and the child fall heavily to the ground.

She gained on them.

Then the woman was up on her knees and trying to snatch back the little girl. But the toddler was quicker. Fast on her feet, she ran blindly towards Sarah. Then the woman was up again and dragging the screaming child back by its bright red T-shirt. But she had been slowed down and with a final spurt Sarah gained on them.

The woman turned. Taking back her arm, she planted one fist straight into Sarah's swollen stomach. The blow doubled her up. She felt a heavy popping inside her and fell, stunned and in excruciating pain, on to her knees. With tears in her eyes she watched as the woman picked up the now quiet child and ran off down the quiet country lane.

Within seconds all Sarah could hear was the birds singing and the low drone of a tractor somewhere in the distance. She took deep breaths to try and still the racing of her heart and the heavy pain that was suffusing her heavily laden body.

Hearing a car door slam nearby, she remembered

seeing a black saloon car parked in one of the lay-bys as she had returned from shopping.

Rolling on to her side, she tried to pull herself to her knees. The pain was abating slightly and, praying under her breath, she attempted to stand. She started the walk back to her house, her body all the time telling her that she needed a doctor, and needed one soon.

It took her ten minutes to get back to her house. There she phoned an ambulance and the police in that order.

Kathy Collins was twenty-five years old, and she was an ancient twenty-five-year-old. As her four daughters ran around her, crying out for attention and fighting with one another, she sat herself down on the battered sofa and lit a joint. Kathy pulled the smoke deep into her lungs and let it out with a heavy, heartfelt sigh.

'SHUT THE FUCK UP!' Her voice was loud, but not that loud.

Her eldest daughter, Tiffany, started laughing. 'Shut the fuck up,' she mimicked. 'Shut the fuck up, shut the fuck up . . .'

The three smaller ones took up the chant and Kathy shook her head in mock reproof. They were four little sods.

'What do you want to eat?' Her voice was weary now as she heard the answer she heard every night of their lives.

'Chips. Chips and beans.'

They were running around again, the four beautiful

little girls that she loved or hated depending on what mood she was in. It was 7.35 p.m. and they had just come in for something to eat after a heavy day of playing out and generally being sods.

The front door stood wide open and Suzy Harrington walked straight in.

Kathy looked at her snidely. 'What do you want?'

'Can I borrow one of the kids, please? I have a client. Nothing too bad, just looking really.'

Kathy was unsure. She could do with the money, but she always felt guilty afterwards. Especially if it was the little one, Rebecca. She hated Suzy for doing this to her.

Suzy saw her indecision and pulled out a twenty-pound note and a small silver-foil package.

'Finest grade, not cut yet, so be careful, Kath. This is shit hot gear.' The girl's smile as she held out the package and the money was reassuring. 'It's only for an hour, love, and no touching, I promise. Just a few photos and a bit of fun. Straight up.'

Kathy took the money. 'Have you heard about Kerry?'

The tall girl shrugged. 'She's a cunt to herself. Always leaving them poor kids on their own. They're better off without her.' She was picking up Rebecca in her arms as she spoke.

Kathy suddenly wanted desperately to snatch the child back from her but the weight of the package in her hand stopped her. Inside she felt awful, but inside she was also craving the oblivion the heroin would give her. It was a vicious circle and she knew it. She wasn't stupid, though. She knew they never touched the kids because she had checked them over when they came back.

'Look, Kathy, it's OK. Like I told you before, this stops a lot of men from going out looking for kids. Now they can just look at the photos and get off like that. It's like prostitutes and rape. If there were more prostitutes there'd be less rapes. It's obvious.'

Kathy didn't really believe any of it, but she convinced herself she did. When it was convenient she could convince herself of most things.

'One hour and no more, right?'

The girl grinned, showing even white teeth. 'Probably sooner. This bloke is a real professional . . .'

Kathy held up a hand in protest. 'I don't wanna know, all right? Just get her back soon, she's hungry.'

Suzy knew better than to push it. She had the child, she had what she wanted, why rock the boat? She left the flat quietly with Rebecca in her arms.

Kathy saw the accusing gaze of her eldest girl and slapped her face hard. Then, giving the child the twenty-pound note, she sent her down the chippy for chips and beans. Soon she'd have them off to bed and indulge in her favourite pastime alone. The thought of oblivion had never been more welcome.

Sarah lay in the hospital bed with her husband by her side. He was gripping her small hand in his, tears in his eyes.

'Stop worrying, Max. I ain't in labour. I'm fine.'

A large man, he was totally in awe of his dainty wife

and her lusty determination to get the best out of life that she could. He adored Sarah, and she adored him. The child she was carrying was like a beacon of hope to him, the end of the long hard road they had travelled towards the good life.

He could not believe another woman could have punched her in the belly like that. It was anathema to him even to consider it. Sarah's heavy belly was bruised, but the child was fine, the doctors had told them. She had been more frightened and distressed than physically hurt.

'I keep thinking about that little girl,' she fretted. 'I mean, she was really scared, love. Terrified. I don't believe that woman was her mother.'

'Well, whoever she was, she'll get a slap across the face if I ever lay me hands on her.' His voice was low with menace.

Jenny watched them from the doorway. They made a touching tableau. The expectant parents. She felt a twinge of jealousy at their obvious happiness in each other. The man was holding his wife's hand as if she was made of fine china.

She stepped into the room with a big professional smile on her face. 'Mr and Mrs Coltman?'

They looked at her enquiringly.

'I am Detective Inspector Jennifer Bartlett. But you can call me Jenny.'

They both smiled.

'I understand you were attacked while witnessing an incident, Mrs Coltman?'

The woman in the bed nodded.

'I'd been shopping and I'd just got home. We live down Sunny Lane. It's really quiet there. You know, rural.' She sighed and took a sip of water. 'I saw this woman – tall, brown-haired, wearing a light raincoat and jeans. Well, it was really the child I noticed at first. She was a good-looking little kid, with really long thick blonde hair and blue eyes, aged about three. You know how hard it is to tell with kids.'

She was quiet for a moment, remembering. 'The kid was upset.'

'Go on, Mrs Coltman.' Jenny could hear the anguish in the woman's voice.

'She was crying, calling out to me. She was shouting, "I want my mummy." '

Sarah took another drink of water and her husband fussed around her, making her comfortable.

'Mr Coltman, could I trouble you to get me a cup of tea?'

He looked at Jenny strangely, then nodded his head.

'Thank you. White, no sugar.'

As he walked from the room Jenny felt the other woman relax.

'Thank you for that. Every time I talk about her punching me he gets more and more upset. I think he'd have took it better if it had been a man.'

'Can you remember anything more about the woman?'

Sarah closed her eyes. 'She was strong – and I mean strong. The child must have been quite heavy, you know. Yet she ran with her easily until she tripped. The kid was really upset, there's no way I misconstrued what happened, and when she hit me that woman really packed a punch. I mean, she brought her fist right back and the blow was very hard and painful. I thought it had brought the baby on.'

'Would you know the woman again?' Jenny asked.

'No danger. I'd know her straight off. The kid, though. It's her that's bothering me. Have any been reported missing?'

Jenny shook her head. 'Not locally, no.'

'I just hope it's got nothing to do with what's been happening in Grantley. All those poor children . . .'

Jenny smiled wanly. 'So do I. Can you remember anything else?'

'A black saloon was parked in the lay-by as I drove home. Whether they were in that car or not I really don't know, but I remember seeing it. I think it was a Ford.'

'When you go home I'll send someone to take a statement from you, OK? Can you try and think back, see if you can remember anything else that might help us?'

'I'll try. But I really don't think that woman was the mother. That wasn't a kid playing up to a parent. It was a terrified little girl.'

Sarah looked deep into Jenny's eyes.

'I know that woman wanted to hurt me, and I feel sure she was going to hurt that child. Call it female intuition, whatever. But her face was evil. Yet I can't really picture it in my mind.'

'Try and rest, Mrs Coltman. When you're ready, think back over it all. It's amazing what you recall the next day and the subsequent few days. Meanwhile, I'll see what I can dig up, eh?'

They smiled at one another.

'You were very brave to follow her like that, especially in your condition.'

Sarah shrugged. 'I didn't really think about it to be honest. I just knew that child needed help.'

'Well, whoever it is we'll have them on a serious assault charge to start with. Now you rest and then we'll see what else you can remember.'

Jenny turned to the man in the doorway. 'Ah, lovely, a cup of tea.'

She was worried, but it didn't show.

Kate stood by Patrick's bedside. It was quiet. All she could hear was the low hissing of the ventilator and the distant movement of the nurses on ICU. She took his hand in hers and squeezed it gently.

'Hello, Pat. I've missed you so very much. All day I think of you and hope you're getting better for me.' She kissed him gently on the forehead and lips. He felt cool to her touch and she wanted to slip into bed with him and warm him with her body heat.

'My mother sends her love, and Lizzy. She rang from Oz to say she's rooting for you.'

She leaned closer to him and whispered, 'I've pulled in Jacky Gunner and Joey Partridge. Well, not pulled in. I've had Benjamin Boarder put them into hiding until I can get to Boris the Russian. I'll sort this out for you, my darling, I promise. I should have listened to you. I shouldn't have been so quick to judge you. I am so sorry, Pat.'

A tear dropped on to his cheek and she watched it roll on to the pillow. It was soon followed by another and another.

'Whatever it takes, Patrick, I will get to the bottom of everything, OK? But you must get better, darling. You must get better for me.'

She straightened up. There was no response. Only the movement of his eyelids and the endless hissing of the respirator.

Kate felt an urge to rip out her hair with her bare hands, and scream her angst and desperate longing for him to the world. Instead she settled herself by his bed and whispered words of encouragement and love into his ear.

Jacky and Joey looked at their new abode then stared at one another in surprise. They had been blindfolded, trussed up and thrown bodily into a van. They had no idea where they were now.

In actual fact, they were tied up in a small Portakabin on Tilbury docks. They could smell sweat, dirt and urine. On the floor looking up at them were two Rottweilers. On the seat opposite sat a scrawny skinhead with bad breath, bad teeth and bad tattoos of extreme right-wing propaganda.

How this person and Benjamin had become friends was a mystery they didn't even want to contemplate.

The boy scratched his arm. He had a flea bite on one of his swastikas and rubbed at it furiously. One of the dogs gave a low growl and the boy kicked out at it with his officer-booted foot.

'Shut up, Bessie. You know you can't be fed when you're working.' He glanced apologetically at the two men. 'If they have to attack you, I prefer them to do it on an empty stomach. Makes the attack quicker and cleaner, like. Once I set them on this bloke and they'd eaten a great big dinner. Took them ages to do any real damage, see. I felt sorry for the bloke meself.' He began to roll a cigarette and the two dogs settled down once more.

Jacky Gunner looked around the cramped space. 'Do you live here?' he asked, genuinely curious.

The boy, whose name was Colin, laughed. 'Nah . . . live with me mum, I do. This is a shit-hole we use for dog baiting and attacks. That's what the horrible smell is. Dog-piss and blood. I fight these two, see, they're proper bastards. I bred the mother and the son and, fuck me, they're a mean pair of puppies they are! I have to feed them separate like or they fight for the meat. Yet once they're working, like all dogs they'll fight as a team. More than one dog is a pack, see. Do either of you keep dogs?'

He seemed really interested and Jacky and Joey both realised they were in the presence of a complete head case.

Jacky shook his head. 'Slept with a few, though.'

The boy screamed with laughter and the two dogs jumped up to see what was occurring. Their handler slapped them back down to the floor viciously and the dogs cowered, trying to lick his hand.

'I love dogs meself – the canine variety, I mean. Though my bird looks a bit suspect until I've had a skinful. She'll be here later to bring me some supper. I'll blindfold you while we shag. Have to observe the niceties, eh? Pity, really, she has fucking big tits. Not ashamed to flash them off either.'

The two men listened in open amazement.

'Has Benny-Boy explained the situation to you both by any chance?'

They shook their heads and the boy sighed heavily.

'Nor to me. But that's him all over. Nice bloke, though. All I know is, if you try anything I'm to let the dogs have you.'

He grinned. 'By the way, look at this, just in case you get any ideas.'

He opened the door and a blast of cool sweet air rushed in – along with about seven other dogs, Rottweilers and Dobermanns. He laughed at their fear, a high-pitched cackling laugh that seemed to come from deep within his bowels.

A few minutes later the door was closed, the smell was once more overpowering and the boy was rolling himself another cigarette.

It was going to be a long, long night.

Kathy Collins looked at Suzy with fear mingled with respect.

'Please, Suzy. Where's me little girl?'

Suzy smiled reassuringly. 'She's fine. Now look, here's a couple of ton.' She peeled off ten twenty-pound notes from a roll on her coffee-table and passed them to Kathy with a smile. 'You have a spend up, and I'll have her home by tomorrow – OK?'

Kathy took the money. 'Is she all right?'

Suzy looked angry. 'Of course she's all right, stupid. Have I ever hurt your kids?' She was peeved, upset. As if she was being accused of something bad and was going to lose her temper at any moment.

'I'm sorry, Suze. But you said she was only going for a little while . . .'

Suzy rolled her eyes at the ceiling in consternation. 'Do you know something, Kathy? You fucking amaze me. I am a mate, and yet you don't trust me.'

Kathy was distressed. 'Of course I trust you, but I want me girl home now. She has been gone ages.'

Suzy lit a joint and blew the smoke out through her loose lips.

'Take your money, keep your fucking trap shut and give it a rest, OK? She is being well looked after. Now *go home*.'

Kathy wanted to argue, but she was too scared. She stuffed the money into the pocket of her jeans.

As she walked to the door Suzy called out, 'Would you sell her for three grand?'

Kathy turned, her face white. 'Who to?'

'I know a couple who want to adopt.'

Kathy shook her head. 'No. No way. Sorry, Suze.'

Suzy shrugged. 'Fair enough. Bye-bye.'

Kathy was dismissed and she knew it.

Broken

When the front door closed Suzy allowed herself to relax. Where the fuck was the kid and how long before Kathy realised she had lost her? More to the point, what would Kathy do when she found out?

Chapter Fifteen

Jenny and Kate sat in her office eating toast and drinking tea.

'Are you sure you know what you're doing, Kate?' Jenny asked.

'No. But I know I have to do it, if that makes any sense. I have to make sure Patrick is safe. If he comes out of this alive I can't leave him in a position where he'll just have to wait for it to happen again. I spoke to the consultant and she says that even if Pat does come round he could be left partially sighted or even brain-damaged. They're monitoring a blood clot at the moment and as soon as they think he's able for it, they want to operate. But the op itself could do more damage. It's a typical Catch-22 situation.'

She smiled sadly. 'I remember when they operated on his daughter. They had to cut a window into her skull so the brain could swell unimpeded – not against the bone, you know. He willed that girl back to life, but it wasn't enough. For the first time ever he couldn't make something happen. I think it broke him inside.'

Jenny poured her more tea from a Thermos flask.

'We're all broken by something, Kate. I sometimes think that's all life is. A series of events: dramas, traumas, with a sprinkling of happiness thrown in to keep us on the straight and narrow. Look at that woman yesterday. She's having a baby, she's with a good bloke in a dream home, and then something like that happens to her. Punched in the belly by another woman. One who was dragging a small child along by the neck of her T-shirt. A woman, incidentally, about whom we have heard nothing since. Nor a word about a missing child. So it seems it's an everyday case of assault and child abuse. There's something really strange happening in Grantley, Kate. Something very, very strange.'

'So it would seem. One thing's really bugging me, though. Who is the child on the dump? How can a little boy be missing all this time and no one seem to know who he is? There's so much I want to know. Like how does Kerry Alston sleep at night? How does Jeremy Blankley walk the earth as a normal-looking person? How was all this filth going on in a block of council flats and no one any the wiser? How Mary Parkes and her cronies developed at such a young age into abusers?'

Jenny sipped at her tea.

'I was watching Mary when we were interviewing her. She was enjoying every second of what was happening. It's attention with her. No more and no less. I've seen it time and time again. Children who demand a lot of attention are like a beacon to paedophiles. Middle children from large families are often targeted by them. The attention paedophile. Some older children even enjoy it. A paedophile can wait three years before they pounce. In that time they gain the trust of parents, children, everyone. I often think for them it is part of the turn-on. The set-up is almost as exciting as the abuse.'

'It's a sick world we're living in.'

Jenny smiled to take the edge off the conversation. 'It's always been a sick world, we just talk about it more these days and that can only be a good thing, can't it, Kate? I mean, years ago an abused child wouldn't have received any help. Its parents would be terrified of people finding out what had happened. The abuser would either leave the area quietly, or the father would give them a slap. The police were not even informed so it was kept secret. That still happens, you know. People keeping it quiet. And what they don't realise is that they are giving that paedophile a licence to do it again with someone else's children.'

Kate nodded her agreement. 'I think we need to frighten Jeremy Blankley. I mean, really frighten him this time. Force him into talking. He's already terrified of going on remand.'

'Leave it to me, Kate. You go off and see what you can find out about our Russian friend and I'll keep everything going this end.'

'You're a good mate, Jen.'

She grinned. 'I know. I may ask you to return the favour one day.'

Kate gripped her hand tightly. 'You only have to ask.'

'I know that, love. I know.'

Robert Bateman looked at the little girl on his lap and smiled at her gently. She was small for her age with dark hair and expressive eyes. At eighteen months she was just about able to walk though with no real speech or co-ordination skills.

Her mother, Natasha Linten, known as Tash, brought in two cups of weak tea. Placing Robert's by his foot on the floor, she picked the child up roughly and plonked her back in her playpen. Then she put the small baby she had recently given birth to in beside her daughter and sat herself down to have a cup of tea and a cigarette.

The room was filthy. Like the rest of the place. It had a stale smell of neglect that a lot of the homes Robert visited seemed to harbour. The carpet was covered in stains: urine, faeces and vomit mingled with takeaways and biscuits trampled in by the older children.

The furniture was scuffed and smelly. One chair was soaked with urine and at this moment a little boy was sitting on it watching *Fireman Sam* with delight. Like the other children he even laughed quietly, his mouth opening but no sound coming out.

It depressed Robert just coming here.

'Look, Tash, you have to sort yourself out, love.'

She grinned, her brown neglected teeth horribly apparent.

'Fuck off, Batey. I just had a bleeding baby. I can't be expected to look after this lot *and* do the fucking housework.'

'But that's just it, dear, you don't look after the kids, do you? I mean, look around you. The kids are neglected; the house is too. There are maggots in the nappy bucket in the bathroom because you can't be bothered to empty it. Really, Tash, this isn't good enough, you know.'

She laughed. 'Drink your tea and stop moaning, for fuck's sakes. Me mum will be here at the weekend, she'll have a clear-up as usual and I'll get a proper rest.'

'I really have to write a report on all this, Tash. You have had chance after chance. We arranged for this new house for you so the other one could be fumigated and you promised me faithfully you were going to start sorting yourself out. But all you do is drink tea, smoke fags and gossip with your cronies. The children will be removed from you before long, dear, and I won't be able to do a thing about it. It will be out of my hands.'

The babies were crying, the noise loud and irritating.

Tash picked up her youngest and laid him on the settee. She took off his nappy and the acrid smell of ammonia hit their eyes, making them water. His bottom was red raw, and he was screaming now, his arms flailing and fists clenched in temper and pain.

Tash looked at him dispassionately.

'Hark at him, noisy little fucker.' She poked him in the buttock with the nappy pin, stabbing motions that made his roaring worse.

'Stop it! Stop it, Tash. That's cruel.'

'He likes it, all my kids do. Makes them hard for when they're older, see? Me mum used to do it to us and it never did us no harm.'

'That, my love, is a matter of opinion. If you're using terries, what are you doing with the disposables we're providing? Selling them, I suppose. Which means he's not getting his nappy changed often enough. It's a bloody vicious circle, isn't it?'

Robert's voice was deeper than usual, his eyes filled with pain as he tried to let this girl know that she was going to lose her children this time. That he had given her all the chances he could.

'We need to talk, Tash, and I mean grown-up talk. This is really serious. Malachi was reported by the playschool as having burns on his legs. He said they were caused by Eric holding him against the fire. He is three years old and he is bullied by your current partner. You go into one abusive relationship after another and your poor kids bear the brunt of it all. This is crunch time, Tash. I'm recommending fostering and maybe adoption, we'll see. But either way they can't stay here with you any more.'

She looked at him in stark incredulity. Pushing her stringy hair back from her face she said with utmost conviction, 'No one is taking my fucking kids.'

'I have no choice,' Robert said sadly. 'The police

will be informed, and you and Eric will be charged with cruelty. I mean, look around you, Tash. You are twenty-three years old and you have five children all born twelve months apart, like steps. They have different fathers, men who never seem to stay the course. This little one's father has five other children by five other women, none of whom he has ever stayed with or supported in any way. You are filthy, your children are filthy and neglected . . . it can't go on, my love. I like you, Tash. Always have, you know that. But I have a job to do and I'm afraid I'm going to recommend a care order, and put you from at risk and supervision on to my bad girl list. In short, you will lose control over your kids. I have no other option.'

She was staring at him now, her eyes enormous.

'I'll lose me money, won't I? I'll lose me few quid. How the fuck am I supposed to survive?' She practically threw the baby back into the playpen. 'Me muvver will have them. Give them to her for a while until I get sorted.'

He held up his hand.

'No way. Your mother doesn't want them, love. She has had enough and quite frankly no court would give them to her. Not even access. She beat you all and she's beaten the grandchildren in the past. It's over, Tash. We have done all we can for you.'

She was crying now, tears of rage and anger.

'You rotten bastard! You knew what you were going to say when you came in here, all nice as usual, you cunt. Well, you won't take them because Eric will be in soon and he'll sort you out, mate.'

'Eric is at his mother's. He knows, darling. He has already reported you twice. He's willing to give over custody of his son to Social Services. He wants nothing to do with the child. It's your own fault, Tash. What on earth possessed you to allow that bastard to hold a child against a fire? He must have been in agony.'

She kicked out at a teddy, covered in sweets and shit, sending it flying against the playpen. The impact shut the wailing children up.

'He was answering back as usual – he's a little fucker. It's all his fault, the bastard. I told him not to get flash with Eric but would he listen? Would he fuck! Just like his father.'

'He is three years old! What the hell do you expect from him? He's a child, Tash, a little child who should be protected, washed and fed regularly. He has a right to be treated with respect, love and kindness. But you can't provide any of that for your kids so they have to be taken to a place where they can at least receive basic care. That means food and clothes, a clean bed, toys, some decent treatment. I have explained this to you until I am blue in the face. You pushed it too far as usual and now your chances have run out.'

Tash sat on the settee and put her head in her hands.

'What about me money, though. How will I live?'

Robert sighed heavily and raked his hand through his hair, making it stand up. He looked eccentric and he knew it and didn't care a rap. He was heart sorry for this girl, but he knew she couldn't cope because she didn't want to. The course of her life was set and if the children stayed with her she would drag them down too. If he had his way he would force girls like her to be sterilised, though he never said that out loud of course.

But it drained him, dealing with the Tashes of the world. It was so depressing. And on top of that he had his sick father living with him who had just been diagnosed as suffering from dementia.

Robert wanted to help these girls so much but even he had to admit defeat at times and this was one of them.

He placed one hand gently on her bowed head, and sighed. 'I am sorry, Tash, really.'

She looked up at him, her faded blue eyes filled with tears. 'Fuck you.'

Which was what he'd expect her to say.

He took the cups out into the filthy kitchen and felt bile rise in his throat. A nappy, full of shit and urine, was lying in the sink on top of the baby's feeding bottles. Flies were clustered all over it and the smell was overpowering.

He stared around the room at the squalor and neglect and felt an urge to cry for the beautiful children she had produced and brought back from hospital to live in this hellhole.

He was getting too old for all this.

It had been a long time since he'd been able to leave it all behind at work at the end of a tiring day. Now, the fate of such kids entered his dreams. Preyed on his mind. Depressed him utterly.

He went back into the lounge and finished changing the baby. The other social workers would be here soon. Robert had done his job, and done it well. He had tried to soften the blow for Natasha. Tried to explain it to her.

But that did not make him feel any better.

Boris stepped out of his BMW and stretched. He attracted glances from people walking by but he was used to that. It didn't bother him any more.

His eyes scanned the pavement professionally before he walked slowly into the shabby mansion block in Maida Vale. His heavy footsteps echoed through the stairwell. It was dirty here and he made a point of not touching anything, not the walls or the banisters.

At the top of the stairs a girl was holding open the door to a flat, wearing nothing but a smile on her coarse-featured face. He walked past her, and once inside the flat he made for the good-sized lounge, decorated in pastel shades and looking much better than its counterparts in the building.

The room was full of naked women and girls. He looked them over expertly before accepting a drink from a small dapper grey-haired man in his sixties wearing a Versace suit.

Boris sipped at the vodka then said, 'Is this the whole consignment?'

The other man cleared his throat noisily before answering.

'Nah, the others were a bit ropey so I gave them to Christy. He's taking them over to Paddington. They can't speak much English either so they're better off out of it really until they can. I have this lot's passports and everything. They won't be any trouble. Sergei explained the score and most of them seemed like they expected it.

'No shrinking violets among them anyway,' he assured Boris. 'The tall redhead gave me a blowjob earlier and it was professionally done. With her skin and hair she'll make a small fortune. The Chinks like the reds, they do, and the blondes. Natural, though, which she is. The black-haired one with the big eyes is a bit of a fucker. Wouldn't trust her too far. Needs a hiding, I reckon, and she'll get one and all. But she's well-stacked and some men like a fight, don't they?'

He laughed at his own wit. The girls watched him warily.

'A couple of days without clothes will sort out the hardest cases. Usually does. I have a crew coming in later to service them so I'll be able to sort the wheat from the chaff, like. But I reckon we have a few good earners here.'

Boris looked them over individually. His eyes settled on a tiny blonde with a hand-span waist and big blue eyes.

'Bring her over to me tonight.'

The man nodded. 'Okey doke. But don't let Sergei have her, will you? He marks them and it takes days before we can shunt the fuckers out again. The last one needed eight stitches, Boris, and it's a pain getting in a bent doctor and all the rest of it. We don't need the fucking publicity.'

'I'll have a word with him, but you know what he's like. Each to his own.'

'True. But I can't abide the hag personally. I think they get a raw enough deal as it is, mate, without him launching himself at them. Not only that, they can't earn and that's the whole idea of the poor little mares being here in the first place. We've got over a quarter a million a year in this room. You can smell their muffs when it's hot. Make you throw up, some of them. The two dark ones sitting on the couch are at each other all the time. I reckon we could get a live show out of them and they'd enjoy it and all. That always brings in money. Punters can tell after a while when it's acted, and a real live show gives them the edge. Makes them spend more.'

'Where are they to go?'

The other man shrugged.

'I thought I'd put them in flats with established pros. They'll soon learn the ropes – they ain't stupid. I promised them they would pay off all they owe in two years. That gives them a goal, like. I tell them all sorts to get them working. But after a few years they're no good any more anyway. They lose that fresh look, start looking like whores if you know what I mean.'

Boris nodded. 'You have done well, Geoff. Where are the others going in Paddington?'

'Plain flats – you know, the cheaper end of the market – and a few will be taxied around the smoke, like. Bit ropey, as I said, but all right for what we want. A couple can go in the parlours. Beverley will train them up for a drink. So we didn't get a bad batch really. I've had better, and I've had worse, to be honest.'

The girls were watching the men dull-eyed. They knew what was being said even if they couldn't understand the language. Boris stared at them all again and they dropped their eyes under his penetrating gaze.

'Send the little one over and I'll speak to you in the week, OK?'

'Fair enough. Before I forget, did Sergei tell you about Julie?'

'What about her?'

'She had full-blown AIDS. One of the guys disposed of her Saturday. Her body won't be found – she was crushed in a breaker's in North London. He shoved her in the boot of a car. But we need someone to take over the parlour in Canning Town. I thought we could give the job to Amanda. She's pretty bright and already running the place.'

'Was Julie still working?'

'Oh, yeah, she didn't really look ill for ages. Then she started to look right fucking rough. I hate to think of the number of men she gave it to. But, as she said, if they wanted it with her, they had to take her as she was. Always had a sense of humour, right up to the end. But we had to nut her, she knew too much. Took it well by all accounts. I reckon she was probably glad to go, don't you?'

Boris shrugged, bored by the conversation. 'Bring me the girl later.'

He was humming as he got back into his car. A young girl walked past. She had long brown hair and a wiggle in her walk. He watched her in the wing mirror and smiled. He liked the young girls in England. They had a confidence about them that was attractive. He knew they all had an eye to the main chance and that intrigued him. Money was power in this country. Most people were willing to do literally anything to get it.

It amazed him.

He knew the girl had looked at him and toyed with the idea of driving after her and talking to her. But he couldn't be bothered. There were plenty more like her around if you knew where to look.

Jimmy Pierce was scared. He knew that Jacky Gunner and Joey Partridge were on the missing list and daren't tell Boris who would go ballistic.

He sipped at his Scotch, trying to make it last. He knew he should not be drinking but was so terrified he needed something to ease his nerves.

His wife looked at him through the serving hatch from the kitchen. She knew that something was wrong but couldn't get a word out of him.

'Have another, mate. Keep drinking,' she said sarcastically.

'Shut up, Shirl, you're getting on me tits.'

'Ooh, pardon me for breathing.'

Her sarcasm was lost on him as he drank and worried.

'Me mother's coming later. I hope you bleeding well cheer up before she arrives. You know what she's like – suss out anything her, and keep at you till you tell her everything she wants to know. Missed her vocation she did. Should have been Old Bill.'

When he didn't answer her with his usual disgusting comments about her mother she knew that it was serious. She walked through to the dining room where he sat at the table steadily drinking.

'Come on, Jim, what's the score? Should I be worried for the kids?'

He looked into her eyes. 'I've fucked up, Shirl. Big time.'

She sighed, looked down on to the balding head of her husband and said gently, 'What you done, mate? Tell me and we'll see if we can come up with something. Have you been gambling again?'

He tossed back his drink. 'Oh, that's you all over, ain't it, Shirl? Fucking blame me.'

She closed her eyes and said through her teeth, 'Well, unless you spill your bleeding guts, Jim, I can only assume that's it, can't I?'

'Where are the kids?'

'They're all out – why? Here, have you got another bird pregnant again? Only if you have I'll fucking have you spayed, Jimmy, I mean it. You can go in the vet's with the bleeding cat.'

He pushed her hard in the chest, nearly knocking her to the floor. 'No, Shirl, it ain't nothing like that. This is serious hag.'

'Any more little whores on my doorstep and I'll

show you what serious hag really is, mate. Our Sharon was disgusted last time.'

'Fuck Sharon.' He was quiet for a second, then grabbing his wife's hand he pulled her through the house and outside to the garage. Inside he locked the door and said to her gently, 'Don't scream – all right?'

She nodded reluctantly. Her skin was crawling and she wasn't sure she wanted to know what was going on now. He opened the boot of his car and gestured for her to look inside.

Shirley walked cautiously around the black Mercedes, the hairs beginning to stand up on her neck and arms. She looked into the boot and as she opened her mouth to scream her husband put one large meaty hand across her mouth.

'It's Tommy Broughton, dead and in the boot of my car, and I don't know how long he's been there but by the smell he's been dead a few days. Gunner and Partridge were at a safe house in Rettenden and they've gone on the missing list somehow. Boris the Russian is going to torture me and laugh while he does it if I can't tell him where everyone is once he realises they've gone. *That* is what is wrong with me, Shirl. Now, what dazzling ideas can you come up with this time to get me out of the shit?'

She knocked his hand away with all the strength she could muster.

'You ungrateful bastard! You bring home a dead body and expect me to take this kind of shit as usual. Well, boy, you take Tommy and you get rid of him. I don't want him near my children. Then I'll tell you what to do next, shall I? You, Jim, can fuck off out of it until you have sorted everything out. And if I don't see you ever again, quite frankly after this little lot it will be too soon.'

He pulled her into his arms. 'Oh, don't be like that, Shirl, I've got a lot on me mind.'

She rolled her eyes at the ceiling and for the millionth time wondered what the hell she had ever seen in this man she had married.

'You drive the car to Binky's yard for me. I'll follow on in a cab, OK?'

She blinked her eyes at him. 'Why have *I* got to drive there?'

''Cos the Old Bill don't hassle you, do they, love? I'll have to get it trashed and then report it stolen, like. That way at least we get the insurance.'

'Who do you think killed poor old Tommy?' Her eyes were once more drawn to the body in the boot. 'It wasn't you, Jimmy, was it? Promise me?'

'Why would I kill Tommy? I was doing a fucking right saucy scam with him, woman. Use your bleeding loaf. Kelly's topped him, ain't he? He'd obviously found out what was going on.'

'But Kelly's in hospital – he was shot.'

Jimmy rolled his eyes. 'Well, smell Tommy. He's as high as a kite, love. Been dead ages. Look at him, for fuck's sake. He's green. Look, he's even got mould on his boat.'

'No, thank you. I will take your word for it. Now shut the boot up, it's horrible.'

He slammed it shut.

'Well, will you drive over to Binky's or not?' he demanded.

She nodded. ''Course I will, but you owe me one for this, you fucker.'

He hugged her. 'You are a good old sort, Shirl. Salt of the earth you are.'

She frowned. 'Not so much of the fucking old, if you don't mind.'

They smiled at one another, on the same wavelength as usual.

'Here, wait till Sharon gets in, I have to drop her at East Ham anyway, she's going round her bloke's. I can drop her and Tommy off at the same time, eh?'

Her husband smiled. 'Fair enough. Now all I have to do is try and locate the other two and I'm back in the ball game.'

'See, Jim? A trouble shared is a trouble halved.'

'We'll see, girl, we'll see.'

Binky looked at the Merc and tutted. He hated having to trash the nice motors, so if possible he didn't – though he never told the original owners that.

After waving off Shirley Pierce he had looked the car over properly. It was a beauty. He had then made a few calls and a potential buyer was standing beside him at this very minute.

'What do you reckon then?' Binky asked.

'Nice motor, good mileage. I could ring it in a few days. How much you looking at for it? And more to the point, who owned it?'

Binky grinned, his little eyes almost disappearing into his fleshy face.

'You're getting a right nosy fucker, Simon, and no mistake. What does it matter who owned it?'

Simon shrugged his skinny shoulders. At nineteen he was at the top of his profession and he knew it. He could take a prestige car from anywhere in under a minute. No alarms could beat him, he was a natural born car thief. And unlike most boys his age he made a point of making money, serious money, out of his talent.

'I like to know its previous in case it ends up going back to them. I had a case like that before and it caused untold hag, mate. Whoever wanted this crushed had a reason, and I want to know what the reason was.'

He was serious now and the fat car dealer sighed noisily.

'A mate wanted it crushed for the insurance. As long as the bleeding thing disappears he's happy. You'll have to break in, though. He took the keys.'

The youth sniggered. 'He'd got your number, then. Didn't trust you, did he?'

Binky laughed but didn't answer. In fact, Shirley had told him that if the car didn't disappear tonight, he would in its place. But he wasn't too bothered by threats like that. Once Simon had it, it was as good as crushed. It would end up abroad more than likely. It was, after all, a brand new motor.

'Let me have a butcher's inside then.'

He popped the locks in twenty-five seconds. Binky was well impressed.

'You are good, Si, I can't take that away from you.'

The boy grinned. 'It's a knack, mate.'

He opened the door and looked over the interior.

'Nice bit of leather but it don't half stink, Binky. What have they done with it?'

The fat man shrugged, making his enormous belly wobble. 'Fuck knows.'

The boy walked round and opened the boot. The stench became heavier and they both looked down at the decaying body.

'Oh, for fuck's sake, Binky! Whoever wanted this crushed had good bastard reason, didn't they? Why didn't you check the motor over yourself?' Simon was holding a handkerchief to his mouth. 'This is gross.'

Binky stared down at his old mate Tommy Broughton and sighed heavily. 'I can easily shove him in one of the wrecks and get shot. But do you still want the car, Si?'

He shook his head. 'Do I fuck. Who is it anyway?'

Binky held up his hands. 'How should I know?' He slammed the boot and spat into the dirt, hawking deep in his throat. 'Ugh! Fucking stinks.'

Simon walked away from the car and opened his coat, flapping it as if to dispel the stench.

'Forget it, Binky. I ain't into all that.'

'Fair enough, I'll shunt it later, when it's dark. See you then, mate.'

Simon waved as he drove out of the yard at speed. Binky went into the shed that passed for his office. It was full of girlie photos and empty lager cans.

He lit a small cigar and puffed on it to take away

the foul taste in his mouth. Then, picking up his mobile, he dialled a number.

'Hello, Benny mate, Binky here. I think I might have something of interest to you. Can you nip down to me yard?'

He was going to make a few quid off this fucking car if it killed him. Plus, Tommy Broughton had been a mate. Whoever topped him had better have had a good reason.

Binky planned to find out what that reason was.

Chapter Sixteen

'It was Tommy Broughton all right. And from what I've heard it was Patrick who killed him.'

Kate listened to Benjamin with half an ear. She had already guessed that Pat was behind the killing. It fitted somehow with what she had already pieced together.

'I got Binky to crush him while I was there. The car belonged to Jimmy Pierce, the slag. He was working with Tommy on the tuck-up so he must be a worried man. He's lost two mates and found a third, all in twenty-four hours.' Boarder chuckled richly. 'Teach him to play with the big boys, won't it?'

Kate felt a sickness in the pit of her stomach. She knew Patrick was capable of murder, she had always known that. But now she was implicated too. She knew who had disposed of the body and how it had been disposed of. She also knew why.

She was an accessory after the fact.

Her stomach revolted against what she was doing, yet she knew she would carry on with it all. She had to, for Patrick's sake. Tiredly, she rubbed at her eyes.

Benjamin quietened. He had forgotten that she wasn't one of them. That she was a filth. He had assumed that as she had taken on Patrick's mantle she would automatically take the heat that went with it.

He studied her closely. 'You OK?'

She nodded.

'Listen, Kate, Patrick would have had good reason to do what he did, remember that.'

'I'll remember. So Tommy's gone then?'

'No one will see him again,' Benjamin promised. 'Patrick must have dumped him in Pierce's motor to teach him a lesson. Good idea really. I mean, if you want to make a point there ain't many better ways I can think of.'

'How are the other two faring?'

'They're in complete terror,' Benjamin grinned. 'Little Colin knows the score. He's keeping them on their toes nicely. We should have a result in no time. Boris is going to look for them, ain't he? Stands to reason. All we have to do is wait until he puts his face about then we can pounce.'

'Aren't you frightened of him? Everyone else is.'

The large man shrugged nonchalantly. 'The Russians don't scare me. They're just cowboys who think that London is another gold rush. Fuck them. We can work with them or without them. We know our job. Nah, they don't scare me, Kate, and they never scared Patrick.'

'From what I understand, this Boris is a psychopath.'

'Listen, they say that about me and Patrick, but we

ain't,' Benjamin explained. 'It's just a front we put on that gives us a bit of clout with other faces. It's good business, that's all. If people think you're a head case you get quicker results and get served first in certain pubs. End of story.'

Kate didn't answer him.

'Come on, let me buy you some lunch, eh? You look like you could do with a stiff drink.'

She smiled gratefully and followed him to his car. They were both unaware that they were being observed.

Natasha Linten was in the Wheatsheaf and she was drunk. Seriously drunk. As she poured yet another large Bacardi down her throat she felt an urge to vomit. Taking deep breaths, she steadied herself against the bar.

'Sit yourself down, love, before you fall down.'

The landlady, Marlene, was kind but wary. She knew that Tash could turn on a coin. Like most of the girls and women who frequented the pub, she was known locally as a dog and Tash certainly lived up to her namesake, from her poodle-like hairdo, long, streaked and scraped up on to the top of her head, to her baggy-kneed leggings and tight Lycra top. The ensemble was finished with a leather coat that had obviously seen better days.

She stumbled to a nearby table and sat down. The three men already sitting there started to move away from her, deliberately excluding her from their company and conversation. Tash was not so drunk she didn't pick up on the vibes all around her. She looked into the nearest man's face.

'All right, Billy?' Her voice was aggressive.

'Go home, Tash, you're pissed,' he said, not unkindly. 'Go home to your kids.'

'Ain't got me kids. Been took away. Rotten bastards.' Her voice was full of self-pity.

'Not before fucking time either, you slag.' Billy's son David spoke loudly as if she was deaf and might not understand him.

She tried to focus her eyes on him. 'Bollocks to you, mate. I loved my kids, they was me life.' She really believed this in her drunken state.

'Your poor kids are probably having the first decent day of their lives, Tash. Fuck me, you are in a state. Go on, piss off somewhere else.'

Oblivious to him, she took a crumpled pack of cigarettes from the pocket of her coat and lit one up. Drawing the smoke into her lungs, she gave an almighty cough and wiped her mouth on the sleeve of her coat.

The men looked at her in disgust.

'I got nothing left now. Lost me kids, me bloke . . .' She was on the verge of tears. 'Even lost me few quid, I have. Fucking social workers, why don't they go and look after the really neglected kids? Why pick on mine?'

David finished his beer and stood up. 'Another round?'

The men nodded.

'Mine's a Bacardi, thanks.'

David stuck his face close to Tash's. 'You'll get fuck all. Now piss off, you scummy whore.'

She looked up into his face and sighed. 'Fuck off, wanker. I don't need you lot to tell me what I am. I *know* what I am, mate, and I like being what I am. So bollocks to you.'

She stood up unsteadily. 'You make me laugh. I know all about you lot. I know everything about everyone.' She looked from David to his father Billy and sniggered. 'Oh yes, I know what you cunts get up to in Suzy's flat, remember that, Billy Reilly. You fucking better remember that I know that.'

She looked triumphant as she swayed precariously in front of them. 'Now, as I said, mine's a Bacardi.' She was staring at Billy as she said this and David Reilly looked at his father closely.

'What's she on about, Dad?'

Billy waved him away. 'How the fuck should I know?' he said irritably. 'She's off her face, silly mare. Get her a fucking drink and then she'll piss off.'

Tash listened and started laughing. 'I'll piss off then, will I, Billy? I'll piss off when I'm good and ready.' She belched and peered at the man sitting next to him. 'Oh, got Noncey Norman with you today. You'll miss my kids, won't you, Norman?'

Somewhere in the back of her drink-fuddled brain, Tash was aware that she was going too far. But the course was set now. She was going to pay back a few debts today. When she had first got drunk she had sought oblivion, a few laughs, but their snide remarks had turned her good-natured camaraderie into vindictiveness.

At least, that was how Tash saw it.

David felt the change in the atmosphere and looked from his father to his uncle.

'What's she going on about? Why will you miss her kids, Norm?'

The older man shrugged inside his donkey jacket.

'How should I know? Look at the state of her. Fuck off, Tash. Go home, girl, and sleep it off.'

'David, will you just go and get the drinks, please?' his dad asked, sounding annoyed.

David walked up to the bar and ordered but he kept an eye on the men at the table. Billy was leaning towards Tash and wagging a finger in her face. David couldn't hear what he was saying but he saw Tash punch his father's hand away and laugh defiantly. He came back to the table with three pints of lager.

'Where's me drink?' Tash's voice was even more slurred now.

'You get nothing. Now, for the last time, Tash, will you *fuck off*?' David shouted over to Marlene behind the bar, 'Why don't you bar her and her fucking cronies? Slags the lot of them.'

Wiping her large rough hands on a tea towel, the landlady made her way over to the table. She took Tash by the arm. 'Come on, love, let me get you a cab home, eh?'

Marlene was eighteen stone and known to have a punch like an Irish navvy. She needed a rep like that, running a hard pub, and she was respected by the men and women alike who frequented her establishment. She also kept a sawn-off under the bar like most publicans in the area.

Tash shrugged her off aggressively. 'Fuck off, will yer! What is it with you lot today?' She pulled out her purse and opened it with difficulty. 'I got money. I can buy me own fucking drinks.'

The older woman shook her head. 'Not in here you can't, not today. You have had enough, lady. Now don't make me throw you out, dear, I really don't want to have to do that.'

Marlene's voice was friendly but there was an underlying threat to it that was wasted on Natasha who was too drunk to care.

'They took me kids. Even me new one, what's his name . . .' Tash waved her hands around as she tried to remember. 'You know who I mean. He's lovely he is, right little hard man already.'

Marlene placed her hands under the girl's oxters and pulled her from her seat. In seconds Tash was standing up and being steered towards the door.

'Come on, love, we'll see you tomorrow.'

'Fucking bar her, the slag! At least those kids ain't got to put up with her any more.' David's voice pierced Natasha's alcoholic haze.

Throwing Marlene off, she ran back to the men's table. Pointing a none too clean finger at them, she said loudly, 'Shame on you.'

She stared at Billy and Norman. 'Tell him – go on, tell him about Suzy's place and then see what he has to say about me, you pair of old wankers!'

Billy was up and out of his seat in the blink of an eye. Taking her by her large topknot, he dragged Tash physically from the pub. He threw her through the double doors and she landed heavily on the tarmac of the car park. At that point he started kicking and punching her.

It was over in seconds. David and Marlene had pulled him off and Natasha lay bleeding and dazed on the ground.

'Who's rattled your bleedin' cage, Billy? The girl's out of her brains. You should have ignored her.' The landlady's voice was full of censure.

Billy spat on to the tarmac, breathing heavily. 'Well, she gets on my bleeding nerves. Drunken whore, with her big trap going all the time.' Then he stalked back into the pub, leaving his son staring down at Natasha who had fallen asleep where she lay.

'I'll get her a cab. Fucking pub's not worth the hag.' And Marlene went back inside.

David studied the young woman with her bad skin and teeth and the remains of too much make-up on her once pretty face. She started to vomit and turned on her side instinctively.

The sight made his own stomach revolt and he walked back into the pub hastily. There he sat with his father and uncle, drinking and chatting, but what Tash had said stayed with him for the rest of the day.

Evelyn wiped Patrick's face with a cool wet cloth and was gratified to see that he had a bit of colour in his cheeks. She hoped against hope that they would operate on him soon, so everyone could finally relax and get on with their lives.

Turning away from the bed, she pulled herself up a chair, just as a young man walked in with a chart and a fresh drip bag. Eve smiled at him and got out her knitting. She watched as he changed the drip and took Patrick's obs. Five minutes later he was gone.

Eve sat knitting and watched the ward around her. Through the glass walls she could see the life of the ICU. It was more interesting than sitting looking at Patrick who was, to say the least, not very good company at this time.

She was knitting herself a jumper, a bright red and green baggy jumper for the winter. It was double knit so it would wash well, and be exceptionally warm. As Eve grew older she found the cold less and less bearable – not like Lizzy her grand-daughter who would traipse out in six feet of snow in open-toed sandals!

Eve smiled at the thought, and stood up. Her legs were cramping – another sign of old age.

She walked stiffly out of the ward and down to the tea machine. As she put in her money, she saw the young doctor again, only this time he had taken off his white jacket and was talking loudly on a mobile phone. Eve could see signs everywhere asking people to turn off their phones because of the machinery in ICU.

'All right, mate, I'm on me way. Stop worrying, for fuck's sake. It's sorted.' The voice was all wrong. Everything about him was all wrong. Eve realised he didn't recognise her from Patrick's room, and for the first time in years didn't curse the anonymity she seemed to have taken on with old age. Hurrying back to the ward she went up to the main desk where a lovely young woman was sitting going through the files.

'Are you a doctor?'

The girl nodded. She was a student but didn't like to admit that unless she had to.

'Can you come and look at my son-in-law, please? He's desperately ill and I think someone has put the wrong bag on his drip.'

Even as Eve spoke she knew it sounded lame, but the fear in her voice communicated itself.

The student followed her down to Patrick's room. She checked the drip and then read his notes. Then she looked at Eve and walked quickly from the room.

Two minutes later there were three nurses and a registrar standing round the bed and pandemonium broke out.

Eve went out to the phone booth outside the ward and phoned Kate. She was sweating with fear, and relief. Then she saw Grace marching towards her and sighed. This was all they needed now with everything else that was going on.

Willy lay on the Z-bed half asleep. He was tired and disorientated from lack of rest and worry. They wouldn't tell him about Patrick, or about anything else for that matter. They just asked him over and over about Girlie Girls and what Patrick had done with their money.

It was getting physical now. They were continually torturing him in small ways. The cigarette burns on his arms and thighs were sore, but nothing Willy couldn't handle. He knew the next stage would be around his eyes and though he didn't relish the idea, he would have to swallow it. There wasn't anything else he could do.

Getting up carefully, he tried to count again but it was getting more and more difficult to concentrate. From feeding him and being polite they had turned to this. It was no more than he had expected, but he was getting older, and it was harder to take.

He decided that if he got out of this alive he was going to retire. Leave all this to the younger chaps. He'd had quite enough.

As the door opened Willy braced himself. He had only one thought in his head as they walked towards him with vodka for his burns – it made them smart like fuck – a large pack of Marlboro Lights and this time a small blow torch, the kind chefs used on cooking programmes to caramelise things.

Willy closed his eyes in distress and told himself: here we go again!

Kate was on her way to the hospital when she was waylaid by Leila. As she unlocked her car, she saw the pathologist running daintily across the car park towards her.

'What is it, Leila? I must rush.' Her voice was sharp

and this was not lost on her friend.

'Everything OK?'

Kate shook her head. 'I haven't time to explain, so can you be quick? I'll talk to you later.'

'Well, I think I've finally got the name of the boy on the dump.' She saw Kate's interest and went on: 'A woman, or girl actually, was found dead in Hartle, the next village along. She'd been dead a while. I think it's her son. She'd obviously dumped him then overdosed on heroin. I'm matching the DNA, but I'm pretty sure it will be him. It seems a smell was coming from her flat and eventually someone got the police. She had died leaning against a radiator, so every time the heating came on she burned that bit more. Maggot-ridden and stinking . . . what a way to go. She was twenty-three. Tragic, but at least we can rule him out now. It looks like she dumped him in a bin van then topped herself.'

Kate was nonplussed. 'So another young mum just decided to kill her kid out of the blue? This is getting weirder by the bloody day.'

Leila shrugged her slim shoulders. 'Sign of the times, perhaps? I don't know. At least we know who he is. He can be buried now. If we ever find the rest of him, that is.'

'Did she have any family, the girl?'

Leila nodded. 'Oh yeah, the youngest of six. Seems they gave her a wide berth.'

'Which means the child was abandoned, too, I take it. Poor little sod.'

Leila looked into Kate's eyes and said gently, 'At

least we can close this one.'

As she opened the car door Kate had a thought. 'Was this girl under Social Services, by any chance?'

'I assume so,' Leila said. 'As a registered addict, she must have been. Why?'

'Do me a favour and see if you can locate a picture of the child from somewhere – see if there's a file on him.'

'OK. I have to have a photo anyway. The police in Hartle are trying to locate one now. Are you thinking what I'm thinking then?'

Kate didn't answer, just waved and got into her car. Leila watched as she drove away at speed and wondered what was going to be the upshot of these cases. Perhaps the boy on the dump had been used in paedophile photographs as well. It seemed that was the direction Kate's mind was going on this and Leila wouldn't be surprised to find it was true. She wouldn't be surprised by anything any more. Like Jenny said, an addict would sell anything, literally *anything*, for heroin. Their own flesh and blood included.

Depressed now, she walked slowly back inside the concrete building. Why the hell did they have these kids if they didn't really want them?

It was something many people wondered on a daily basis.

Patrick had been given a large dose of morphine in the drip bag, enough to kill him, but thanks to Eve it had been removed before there was time for it to do any permanent damage.

Kate looked down at him, thinking how vulnerable he was, and how much he would hate to be like this. It was as well he didn't know.

She stifled a yawn with her hand. She was tired, so tired. Taking his hand, she stroked it gently, feeling the familiar sensation of the fine hairs on the back of it and almost weeping.

A shadow passed over the bed and she looked round to see a strange little woman staring down at Patrick.

'Can I help you?'

The woman smiled. 'I'm Maya, an old friend of Pat's. You must be Kate?'

She nodded and held out her hand. The little woman took it and her grip was surprisingly firm.

'How is he?'

'Not too good. But he'll get over it, I'm sure of that.'

The other woman heard the longing in Kate's voice and patted her arm reassuringly. 'He's hard inside. Always has been harder than anyone realised. Not that he hasn't a good heart, he has that too. He'll get over this if it's humanly possible.'

Maya sat down heavily on a plastic chair, her short legs barely reaching the floor.

'I remember him when he was an up and coming villain.' She grinned. 'He was a nice kid. I've known his family for years. Where is Grace, by the way? I expected to see her here standing guard over him.'

'To be honest, if I'm here she goes off and only comes back when I'm gone.'

'No change there then?' Maya chuckled. 'Renée, his wife, used to love winding her up. She was never jealous of Grace and her possessiveness over Patrick. But then, I think she guessed.'

Kate looked at her with interest. 'Guessed what?'

Maya looked at the man lying so still in the bed as she spoke.

'That Grace was his mother, of course. She was fifteen when he was born and so like most families did in those days, Patrick's grandmother took him on.'

Kate was staring at her in complete and utter disbelief. 'Is this just gossip?'

'Could be, but a lot of people believe it,' Maya told her. 'I heard it many years ago after his mother died. He was devastated. Adored her. But that was when I was first told she wasn't in fact his mother, but his grandmother. I never asked him – well, you don't, do you? I don't know if he ever knew or guessed, but she was a girl, old Grace. So was Violet. Both of them on the bash down at the docks. Haven't you ever wondered about the age difference between him and his sisters?'

Kate didn't answer. If what the other woman said was true, and Pat *had* known, then he'd kept it from her. This knowledge cut her to the quick. And all the time at the back of her mind a small voice was asking her what else Patrick had decided she wasn't fit to know.

Just then Benjamin Boarder walked in with another large black man.

'All right, Maya? Long time no see.' He looked at

Kate. 'This is Everton and he is going to look out for Patrick for a while, OK?'

Maya frowned. 'He needs a minder then? What's he been up to?'

Benjamin grinned easily. 'You are bad-minded, Maya. This is what we'd do for anyone like Pat, love. Everton's a gofer really for whoever else is here. Tea, coffee, a sandwich. No big deal. It's just a friendly gesture.'

Maya smiled, but she wasn't convinced. She looked down at Patrick again, her mouth a grim line. Her guttural voice was sad as she said, 'Poor Patrick, he would hate to be like this. Any strong person would.'

Benjamin steered Kate over to the door.

'I was shitting it, Kate. I heard they were trying to arrange police protection for him, and that's the last thing he needs. Make sure the idea is dropped and soon, OK? Patrick needs to be looked after by people who know the score and ain't in the pay of anyone we don't know.'

She nodded. 'I'll talk to Ratchet. But I'm warning you, Ben, this is getting harder and harder by the day for me. Why doesn't that Russian bastard show his hand?'

He hugged her to him. 'I know, mate, but at least we have a common goal – Patrick's best interests.'

He stared down at her white strained face. 'I have had the house in Rettenden watched. Not a soul has turned up there. Not a thing has happened. They are clever, very clever.'

They were quiet for a moment then Benjamin said,

'You need a long sleep and a good meal.'

She smiled sadly and said in a low voice full of emotion, 'I need a lot of things I can't have, love. Patrick Kelly being one of them.'

'It will all work out, Kate, I promise.'

He tried to sound more convinced than he felt. He liked this woman a lot. She had balls. Old Bill or no Old Bill Kate Burrows was all right. He wouldn't mind her batting on his team if he was in the shit, he knew that much.

Not forgetting that there was a chance that she might be able to do him a favour in the future.

A man had to look at all the angles.

Especially in his line of business.

Colin looked out of the window of the Portakabin and saw a large white van pull up outside the yard. The dogs automatically ran to the gate barking and he admired them from his vantage point. They were magnificent animals. They scared people and they were noisy, everything a good guard dog should be. They were trained to attack, but only on command. He knew the folly of not training a dog well, something stupid people only found out at their own cost.

Most dogs will turn on an owner, acknowledged fact. Shepherds were notorious for it. But he knew that if you loved a dog, and never, ever abused it, you had a friend for life. Colin loved his animals and he never abused them. Consequently they adored him and afforded him a lucrative living.

Most big faces took dogs from him after he had

trained them. They knew they were getting the best, better than any MoD-trained animal and that was a fact. His dogs were trained with simple phrases and kindness. They would die for him or their new owners.

Any scrapyards that had dodgy dealings got their dogs from him. Colin was the acknowledged genius of dogs, an accolade he treasured even though it made for some poxy jokes when he was out with his bird Rosalie.

When he saw three men get out of the white van, he admired the way the dogs' hackles rose in warning. His eyes widened as he saw the men had shotguns, pump-action shotguns, and as they started to shoot at the dogs he rushed from the Portakabin without a thought for himself. By now the gates were hanging off their hinges and his precious dogs were all on the ground, dead or dying.

'You bastards!' Colin's voice was thick with tears and snot. He was stunned by the carnage around him, too heartbroken to be afraid.

The noise of the gunshots had been deafening. Now all he could hear was the buzz of traffic from the A13. He saw a woman pull a pushchair up the kerb and deliberately not look in his direction. She hurried away as fast as she could, clearly not wanting to attract any attention to herself.

Then he saw the men going into the Portakabin. Just ignoring him.

Running to his car, Colin opened the boot. Inside there was an AK assault rifle he was looking after for a friend. He got it as far as his shoulder before he was lifted off the ground by a single shotgun blast and thrown on to the chain-link fencing, his stomach flying through the air before him. He landed heavily, hanging by his jumper, and twitched a few times before death finally overtook him.

The whole scene looked like an abattoir.

Jacky Gunner shook his head in amazement as they walked towards the white van.

'Fucking hell, Joey, this is getting out of hand.'

Partridge didn't answer, too busy wondering why their rescuers had not attempted to take off the handcuffs that bound the pair of them. He had a fleeting suspicion they were out of the frying pan but heading quickly towards a very large fire.

Chapter Seventeen

Suzy Harrington was tall, blonde and ugly, but there was something about her merry countenance that made people like her.

Suzy had a finger in every pie on the estate, that was a fact. She also had a finger in many other pies that no one here knew about. She could get you a bit of puff, a few Es or a nice bit of high-grade sniff. Her different businesses gave her a lucrative living and she dressed well, drove a nice car and went on foreign holidays frequently. Her flat was well decorated and always pristine. She was proud of her home, it was a real status symbol.

Today she was dressed to kill, and she knew it. As ugly as she was, and she had no illusions about that, she had good dress sense and used it well. In a dark blue suit, with sheer tights and black suede shoes and bag, she looked smart and sophisticated. Her long blonde hair was tied back demurely and her make-up was carefully applied.

She unlocked her five-year-old BMW and waved at

her neighbour in friendly fashion.

'All right, Sheila?'

It was the equivalent of hello to them.

'All right, Suze. You look nice. Going somewhere posh?'

She nodded and jumped into the car.

David Reilly watched her from his vantage point in the doorway of the flats opposite. He was frowning. When she'd driven off he stood for a while longer, smoking a cigarette. All the time his eyes were trained on the opposite entrance as he clocked who went in and who went out.

Robert looked at the children playing on the floor. Kathy Collins appeared nervous and he smiled at her in a friendly fashion.

'Where's Rebecca today?' he asked.

'Out playing.'

'Can I see her, please? You know I have to see each one of the kids for meself because of me report.'

Her eyes filled with tears. 'She's staying with me mate.'

'What mate?' Robert asked pleasantly.

Kathy leaped from her seat. 'Fucking hell, Robert, what's this – the bloody Spanish Inquisition? What's the problem for fuck's sakes.' She looked agitated, wiping a hand across her mouth over and over again.

'What are you on this time? A speedball, what?'

'Me usual skag if you must know. But I am stressed out today. That's why I let her stay at me mate's.'

'So who's the mate?'

Kathy licked dry lips and looked around the room nervously.

'Where is the child, Kathy, for the last time.'

Standing up, Kathy walked through to the kitchen. 'She is staying at me mate's. How many times have I got to repeat meself!'

Robert closed his eyes in consternation. 'And who is this mate then?'

Kathy stood in the doorway, wiping at her nose in an agitated fashion. 'You don't know her. She lives near me mum.' She warmed to her story. 'She was me mate at school. She offered to have our Becky for a few days so I could have a break, like.'

Robert smiled. 'So what's her name then?'

'Lisa Buck.'

She tossed her hair like a recalcitrant child as she walked back into the kitchen once more. She banged the kettle on to the counter after filling it and Robert sighed.

'Lisa Buck?'

There was a question in Bateman's voice which was not lost on Kathy.

'Ask me mum if you don't believe me.'

Robert followed her out to the kitchen and leaning against the door he said seriously, 'Don't worry, Kathy. I will.'

Sharon Pallister was in pain. She put a hand to her throat and felt the gaping hole there. She was too afraid even to cry. Instead she tried to crawl to the phone in the hallway.

The woman watched her, completely unfazed by the horrific injuries she had just inflicted on the girl. As Sharon reached up for the phone the woman kicked out at her, a heavy blow that landed in the girl's ribs. She bent over her victim, her garishly made-up face almost touching Sharon's.

'You are winding me up, you know. Why don't you just fucking die and be done with it?'

The young woman was beseeching her, gurgling her words, 'Please . . . please don't do this to me.'

The woman laughed cruelly. Then, walking to the bedroom, she took a small boy from his cot and walked back to his mother, the child snuggled in her arms. The woman jiggled him as if trying to comfort him, her face gentle as she looked down on to his soft downy head.

The girl watched as her life's blood drained from the many wounds on her body and she felt faintness overcoming her.

'Say bye-bye to Mummy, lovely.'

The woman held up the child's arm and waved it in a parody of goodbye. Then, after ripping the phone line from the wall, she opened the front door and was gone.

Fear of what would happen to him made Sharon's heart beat faster, which in turn sent the blood pumping more fiercely from her wounds. She lay on the carpet, eyes closed in resignation as she realised that she was going to die in her flat alone.

Lucas Browning was interviewing once more. This

time it was a young girl who was obviously still at school. He listened to her grating voice and gave her the once-over. He was tempted, very tempted.

He saw her lip curl in disgust and it angered him. He shifted one heavy naked leg and broke wind loudly, enjoying the look of utter disgust on the girl's face.

'Have you ever worked in this line of business before?'

She nodded, not so cocksure as she had been when she'd breezed in. He had seen hundreds like her. Schoolgirls who had got laid at twelve and lost sight of the real reason for having sex at an early age. They saw prostitution as glamorous and exciting. Saw it as a means of leaving home and making some real money. Oh, he was weary of it all.

He opened his legs and saw her eyes trained on his flaccid member. Lucas stifled the laughter that was bubbling up inside him. He knew she was scared now. Knew she had pictured sleeping with handsome businessmen who would shower her with gifts and secretly fall in love with her until she reciprocated. He thanked God daily for American TV and films, full of schmaltzy shite that was just the push these silly bitches needed to flash their little clouts and make him money.

But Julia Roberts this one definitely wasn't, though she obviously thought she was something special.

Didn't they realise that they were expected to sleep with anyone who had the money? And that meant old, young, smelly or ugly, or a combination of the lot.

He smiled gently. 'We expect our escorts to have a working knowledge of fellatio, that's sucking cocks to you, and also anal sex,' he told her. 'That's where the big money really is. I often have the girls give me a going over so I can judge them, see where they'll be best utilised. I take it you have practised safe sex?'

She didn't answer. Her face had taken on a greenish tinge and he suppressed the laughter inside him once more. He saw her look towards the doorway and grinned.

'You go, my dear, when I tell you that you can – and not before.'

She was really frightened now. It took the superficial maturity from her face and made her look just what she was: a little girl plastered in make-up, trying to be an adult. The worst kind of adult – one who would debase themselves for monetary gain.

'How old are you exactly?' he said nastily.

'Thirteen and a half.'

Lucas laughed aloud. 'And a half? A whole thirteen and a half? Why, you're far too old for most of my customers but I suppose I could fit you in. Have you discussed this with your parents? I take it they know you are here?'

She shook her head. 'I'm supposed to be at school,' she whispered.

'And where are you from?'

'Leicester.'

He smiled. 'I thought I knew that accent. So what time were you supposed to be home?'

She didn't answer. He looked at her for long moments.

'Are you in care, dear? You can tell me – I can find out anyway quite easily.'

She nodded almost imperceptibly and he grinned again.

'Well, why didn't you say that before! I have lots of girls like you and I take good care of them, believe that much of me.' He picked up his stick and banged on the ceiling. A few minutes later an old man walked into the room and the girl looked at him in terror.

'Take this one, Petey, looks like we've got a chicken ready for the pot. Get the make-up off and see what's underneath it.' Then, staring at the girl, he said, 'This is what you wanted, dear, surely? I always think it's nice to get what you want now and again, don't you?'

Petey was laughing as he dragged her from the room. Lucas watched her body language and sighed happily. She would be a good little worker, he had a feeling about that. The kids from care were always nicely desensitised well before he got hold of them. It was another perk to thank the government for, along with Social Security and housing benefit, both of which he claimed religiously every week.

Kerry Alston watched as the other women showered and preened ready for their visitors. Her own heavy build was gradually dwindling as she found it harder and harder to eat the slop that passed for food in the prison system.

'Ain't you going to shower again, you filthy mare?'

The voice was high-pitched and came from a spindly sharp-eyed woman under the last shower head.

Kerry didn't answer her, she knew it was useless. Instead she slipped past to walk back to her cell.

'What's the matter, nonce? Not young enough for you in here, I suppose, eh? Want to see some photos of me kids? Make you feel more at home like, you fat bastard!'

Kerry felt the hand of fear clutch at her innards as she realised what the woman was saying. She looked around her to see if anyone else had heard the jibe.

No one was taking any notice.

She scurried back to her cell and stepped inside – to find a reception committee waiting for her.

The hot water hit her in the face, blinding her, and the broom handles rained down on her prostrate body with the express intention of breaking bones. As she lay crumpled on the floor in fear and pain she heard a low chuckle. It was a PO on the landing outside observing everything through the spy-hole in the heavy metal door.

Kerry realised immediately who it was who had told everyone what she was in for. Even though she'd expected it, the shock was still enough to make her cry out in despair.

'Kerry was done in Chelmsford, have you heard?'

Jenny shook her head. 'I half expected it, didn't you?' she said to Kate.

'I suppose so. She's bad, though – burns and a hiding. Very violent by all accounts. But then, the attacks for molesting always are. I suppose it was a screw who grassed her?'

'Got it in one. Might make her a lot more amenable, though.'

'We can but hope.' Kate lit a cigarette and drew on it deeply. 'What else has happened?'

'I'll get some coffee and fill you in on the details. Are you around for a while?'

They were using a form of code with each other. Even the most mundane sentence had a hidden meaning that would escape any casual onlooker.

'Yeah, I've time for coffee and a chat. I want to have a final go at Jeremy Blankley today. Maybe this thing with Kerry will give us a handle, eh?'

'Could do. Can I get you a sandwich or anything?'

'OK.'

Kate smiled as the heavy-set woman stamped away. She liked Jenny more and more. She was a big woman in every way. Big-boned, well-padded and with a heart the size of the Albert Hall. She was also a loyal friend and that was something Kate needed desperately at the moment.

When Golding stepped into her office and shut the door, she looked at him quizzically.

'Can I help you?' Her voice was sarcastic and this was not lost on him.

'Ma'am, a young man called Colin Forbes was shot dead today in East London. He was a dog breeder. I thought you should know.' Golding's voice was loaded with meaning.

'What are you trying to say?'

He smiled and it changed his whole appearance. 'I didn't know you worked with Benjamin Boarder, ma'am. He's an old mate of mine from years ago.'

He walked from the office and left Kate wondering just how deep the ties between police and villains ran in her station. Not that she could say or do much about it; she accepted the fact. But it never ceased to amaze her. Look at her own life!

Then the full force of what he'd said infiltrated her mind and she groaned aloud. That meant she'd lost her two hostages, Jacky Gunner and Joey Partridge. And a boy had paid a high price for harbouring them.

The worst of it all was, she couldn't back out now no matter what happened. She was in too deep.

When Jenny came back with the coffee and food she saw a strained and worried Kate before her and wondered what could have happened in the last fifteen minutes to change someone's mood so radically.

Jeremy Blankley picked up on the change in his persecutor almost immediately. As Kate came into the small interview room, the first thing she did was send the young PC off for his lunch. Her face, normally good-looking and open, was like a closed book, and he could see she was just keeping her temper in check.

'Kerry Alston was seriously scalded and beaten today in Chelmsford women's prison,' Kate told him bluntly. 'They found out why she was on remand.'

She was savagely pleased to see him blanch.

'So you had better decide whether or not you're

going to open your trap to me. Wise up and maybe, just maybe, I'll have you segregated.'

He stared at her dull-eyed.

'I want names, dates, and I want them today. I want to know all about your brother and what you were both into. I understand you had a lot in common – a love of young children being the main thing. But first I am going to give you a few minutes alone with two of my younger officers. One is a body builder and the other is a PE instructor. They are going to give you a small taste of what you can expect in a big boys' prison, Jeremy. You'd better think hard while they do because I am at the end of my tether here.'

She pushed back the door and it clanged noisily against the wall. Two men walked in. Jeremy saw muscles and gleaming teeth as they smiled at him. Even though he called out Kate didn't look back. Instead she locked the door from the outside and walked slowly to the canteen.

As she passed her team they all smiled at her knowingly. Inside she was ashamed of what she had done even while a small part of her rejoiced. Blankley was getting his payback, and in this new world she was inhabiting it seemed that was what it was all about. Whether you were filth or criminal.

After today there was no going back to how it used to be. She had stepped outside every boundary and guideline now. There was nowhere left for her to go.

As she drank her coffee and smoked a cigarette she pictured Patrick's face and concentrated on that.

He was all she really cared about.

★ ★ ★

Jenny brought Robert into her office.

'What can we do for you?' she asked, smiling at him. She had taken to this man.

'I was hoping to talk to Miss Burrows as well,' he told her politely.

'She's really up to her eyes in it at the moment,' Jenny said, 'so you'll have to make do with me, I am afraid. Sit down and tell me what's wrong.'

'One of my clients, Kathy Collins, well . . . she seems to have mislaid her youngest daughter Rebecca. I can't locate her and I can't prove she has done anything with her. All I know for certain is, according to her she is letting the child stay with a certain Lisa Buck.'

He bit on his lips.

'Kathy is an addict – most of my clients are. She has four kids and she has trouble from the minute she gets up in the morning. Her life is a nightmare – although she stumbles through it somehow. But I have a bad feeling on me about her and about the child Rebecca.'

'Has she said the child's missing?'

He shook his head. 'No. She is saying the child's safe and well. Only I went to this Lisa Buck's house – she exists, there's no doubt about that – and no one knows where she is at the moment. There's no answer to the door and no one has seen her for days. The house is smart, a bought council house. It's locked up and the neighbours say she is on holiday. I don't believe for a moment that she has Kathy's child.'

'You want us to check this out?'

Robert nodded. 'Kathy is out of her nut most of the time. But she is not a bad person.'

He watched as Jenny's eyebrows moved up towards her forehead at an alarming rate.

'She isn't,' he insisted. 'Listen to me. Mad and bad are how women are portrayed all the time. Either one or the other. Kathy has problems, I do not dispute that, but in her own way she loves the kids.'

'I think this Kathy needs a visit.'

There was a finality in her voice and, seeing the look of sadness on his face, Jenny softened.

'Look, Robert, I know you care about the girls you deal with and I admire you for being so kind and for your dedication to them. But if a child is unaccounted for then we have to try and find out what's going on.'

He nodded. 'I know, that's why I came.'

'Don't feel bad, you have done the right thing coming here.'

He stood up slowly. 'I just hope I'm wrong,' he told Jenny, 'and that the child *is* with this Lisa Buck. But somehow I don't think she is.' He looked defeated and Jenny felt a small spark of affection for him.

'You are a nice man, you know.'

He grinned, back to his old girlish self. 'So they tell me.'

Willy had company.

Jacky Gunner and Joey Partridge were now guests of the Russians, too. As the three men looked at each other they all wondered separately how the fuck they were going to get out of this place alive.

Joey was lying on the floor, his arms screaming after days in cuffs. He knew that if they tightened them he could end up losing his hands at the very least. And by the shocking sight of Willy Gabney, that was a distinct possibility.

Unlike them, Willy wasn't cuffed.

'Well, well . . . if it ain't fucking Mutt and Jeff come to visit me.' Willy's voice croaked as if he hadn't used it in months. 'Who you tucked up this time then?'

Jacky Gunner was incapable of answering. His face was too swollen from a well-aimed kick with a steel toe-capped boot. But from where he was lying on the floor he could see the burns all over Willy's thighs and the stench of charred flesh made his stomach revolt.

Joey and he were well in trouble, serious trouble, and they both knew it. Not just from Boris but from the man sitting on the bed contemplating them thoughtfully. Willy Gabney had a score to settle and they knew that unless he was dead he would settle it, no matter how badly injured he was.

At the moment they were more scared of him than they were of the Russians.

Lucas Browning and Suzy Harrington were old mates. She had first worked for him when she was fifteen after running away from home and being introduced through a friend of a friend. The pair had got on like a house on fire straight away.

Suzy was one of the only few toms that Lucas had ever genuinely liked. They recognised each other as a kindred spirit. Both were completely amoral and both were violently opposed to any kind of regulation of them or their chosen form of business. They used each other as and when it suited them, both having contacts that could be useful to the other. It was a good arrangement and it suited them down to the ground.

In short, they were more or less best mates.

'You look well, Suzy.'

She grinned. 'You still look bleeding terrible and you smell worse, Lucas. You never change.'

He laughed like a drain, a loud rip-roaring laugh that was rarely heard outside the confines of his seedy flat. 'Only you would have the front to say that to me out loud!'

'So shall I make us a cuppa?'

He nodded. 'Unless you fancy something harder. I have a case of twelve-year-old Scotch in the bedroom.'

'Sounds good to me, mate. I'll go, it would take you a week to get there. You are really piling on the weight, Lucas. You wanna be careful. A strain on the heart, weight is.'

He wheezed as he lit up a joint.

'You want to get out more . . .'

'Leave it out, Suze,' he interrupted her. 'What are you, me fucking mother?'

She grinned as she collected the Scotch from the bedroom. There was a girl on the bed, half naked and in a deep sleep.

'Who's that then?'

Lucas flapped his hand. 'Don't ask. I'm trying out

this new drug, Rohypnol. Apparently it's great. You slip it in their drink and then the person does whatever you want. But the best bit is they can't remember for ages. If they're in a position to remember at all, of course. I'm thinking of using it for the more specialised films, if you get my drift.'

Suzy nodded, losing interest as she tried to locate two clean glasses from a small melamine cabinet by Lucas's chair. 'God, don't you ever clean up in here?'

'You know I don't. It's all part of the image,' he laughed wheezily. 'Now what is it you wanted to see me about?'

She poured them both a generous measure of Scotch and, taking the joint from his hand, took a deep toke before replying.

'I've got a right little earner and I think we could take it to the bigger boys,' she said seriously.

He sipped at his own drink. 'What is it?'

She looked at him for a few seconds before she said in a low voice, 'Kiddies. Little kiddies. Photos, whatever. I have a network of mums now who I did deals with to use their kids in photographs. It was strange, really, how it all started.'

She settled back in the chair to make herself comfortable.

'I deal a bit where I live, and one of me regulars came over for a bit of tick, like. You know the score – you get them in debt as soon as you can, keeps them coming, don't it? Anyway, she was a bit out of it and she was telling me about a girl nearby who was using the kids in photographs, for nonces like. I was shocked, but not as shocked as I acted. Anyway, I found out who it was and I paid her a little visit. It was pennies and halfpennies with her but I muscled in and now it's ready to go big. You see, I have got stuff on film and also on disk so we can look at a wider market. What I need, though, are the foreign contacts. I mean, these kids are lovely – blonde-haired, blue-eyed little angels – and the rub is, the mothers are up for it at a price.'

Lucas was looking interested. She leaned forward and told him: 'I also have a few adults who are willing to take part in the activities, and with all that, Bob can only be your uncle and I can only be your aunt. A rich auntie and all. Because there is wedge in all this stuff, serious wedge.'

Lucas picked up the excitement in her voice. 'You, little Suzy, are the lowest of the low.'

It was said with undisguised admiration and, laughing, she answered him, proudly.

'I know. Good though, ain't it? If we can get the distribution we're looking at real dough. And let's face it, Luke, even the advertisers on the telly know the value of kids. They're the new market. It's like all the beasts have finally come out of the woodwork.'

She didn't tell him that some of the people she had worked with were now in prison, awaiting trial. She was sure enough of herself to believe that they would keep her out of everything. Her reputation should guarantee her that much.

The fat man finished his drink in one gulp and poured another.

'I think I know just the bloke for you. He's a right Brahma, a really nice bloke, and he has contacts in the film industry. Well, our kind of film industry anyway.'

They both laughed uproariously.

'The only thing is, Lucas, I have a bit of a problem.'

Her voice was serious now and he picked up on it immediately. Smiling nastily he said, 'I get it. So now we come to the real reason you wanted me involved.'

'Oh, you are such a fucking tart at times,' Suzy chided him. 'Honestly, Lucas, I would have come to you sooner or later. I usually do.'

He acknowledged what she said with a small movement of his head. 'So what's the problem?'

She giggled uncertainly as she looked at him. 'I've lost one of the kids.'

Lucas stared at her for long moments. 'You've what?' She could hear the disbelief in his voice.

'You heard me. I lost a kid.'

His whole body seemed to convulse as the coughing fit hit him. And through a fine spray of phlegm and alcohol he roared, 'How the fuck have you managed that!'

Suzy relaxed back in her chair. 'I gave her to a bloke called Stanley Acomb and he fucked off with her. The mother is easy at the moment, but I don't know how long that will last. She's a skaghead – a piece of shit.'

Lucas raised an eyebrow. 'Well, it takes one to know one. I suppose you want me to get the kid back?'

She nodded.

He sipped on his drink again. 'Consider it done. But in future, Suzy, now I am part of the equation, you never leave any of the kids with clients alone. OK?'

She agreed, relieved that she had sorted out a problem and also that she had back-up. Big back-up to further her career.

'I'll drink to that, Luke.'

They clinked glasses.

'Now do me a favour and cover up your todger. It looks like a little baby mouse asleep on two Brussels sprouts.'

They both laughed uproariously again.

Kate stared into Jeremy Blankley's eyes and felt nothing. Not even pity. All she could see were those terrible photographs.

Blankley was lying in a holding cell, battered and bruised. She knew he would be pissing blood for days and that no one was going to get him a doctor. His face was unrecognisable and he would have difficulty talking. One arm was hanging limply at his side and for one awful second she thought it was broken. But he used it to wipe away the tears that were falling silently from his eyes.

'You've just had a small taste of what's in store for you daily if you go inside without our protection. So think hard about what you want to say to me, OK?'

He didn't answer her and Golding pushed past. Looking down at the broken man he said quietly, 'There's fifty more like that just waiting to get a crack at you. Remember that, Blankley. Keep that in mind.'

He followed Kate from the cell. 'He'll come through, ma'am,' he muttered. 'Let him get over the tears and the self-pity, because that's all it is. Then he'll want to save his sad arse and we'll have him.'

Kate didn't have the heart to answer and they were both silent as they walked back to her office. Jenny was waiting there. Kate saw from her expression that what they had done didn't bother her nearly as much as it bothered Kate herself. She felt more every day that she was stepping out of her usual self and taking on the personality of someone else.

Someone who was ruthless, utterly ruthless, and without a single shred of decency.

When she saw Leila laughing with Dave Golding outside her office window she wondered if what had happened was a good thing really. It seemed everybody else thought so. Kate just saw it as a means to an end. Or tried to convince herself of that.

She was changing inside, she knew she was. She sometimes wondered if Patrick was reaching out from his sickbed and putting all his own thoughts into her head, because he would have seen nothing wrong with what had occurred in this police station. In fact, he would have applauded it.

Everyone else seemed to see things in black and white. Maybe they were right. Christ, Kate wasn't sure about anything any more.

Jenny smiled at her sympathetically. 'Good news at last.'

Kate raised an eyebrow in half-hearted interest. 'What's that then?'

'They are going to operate on Patrick tomorrow – your mother rang earlier.'

For the first time in what seemed like aeons Kate felt herself give a bona fide smile.

'Thank God! At last something seems to be happening.'

'They are going to remove the blood clot and see what other damage they can repair. He ain't out of the wood yet, Kate.'

She put her hand up to her mouth in a gesture Patrick would have known meant she was about to cry though she was doing everything in her power to stop it happening.

'The other bit of good news is, your mother has made us another roast dinner. Beef this time, with Yorkshire puddings that are apparently like diddy-men.'

Kate began to laugh then, a high-pitched sound that bordered on hysteria. She laughed long and hard for what seemed like hours though it was in fact only minutes. But she felt the tension drain out of her with every painful breath she drew.

David Reilly watched as his father put on his coat to go down the pub.

'Are you all right, son?' Billy's voice was troubled.

David smiled. He was a good-looking man with thick blond hair and jutting cheekbones like his mother's.

'Why don't you come and have a beer?' his father persisted.

He shook his head. 'Nah, I'm knackered, Dad. Gonna have a few indoors and an early night.'

'Fair enough. I won't wake you when I come in then.'

Billy left the house a few minutes later and David watched him walk down the pathway. He looked around the room. It was smart and well-kept, with beige walls and leather furniture. The two men had bought everything between them, as they had lived together ever since David was a teenager and his mother Molly had died of cancer. Breast cancer. It had been a lingering death and he had shrunk from her pain even as she tried to hide it from him. Since then there had been just the two of them and it had been enough. His father seemed to have no interest in other women and at first that had pleased David, who was still mourning his mum. But as the years went on and he realised that Billy was still a relatively young man it had begun to bother him.

Then a few weeks ago at work – they both worked in an industrial park outside Grantley in a builder's yard – something weird had happened. One of the other blokes had complained that some photos of his kids he had put up in the canteen had gone walkabout.

They were nice photos, David had seen them. Three little kids on a beach in Greece without their kecks on. The usual sort of photos people took of their kids on holiday: sandy bums and large hats.

The funny thing was, though, the man said he had last seen them in Billy's hands. Billy had taken them down to admire them, apparently. Then he had put them back, or so he'd said. Nothing fishy about it, really.

Except after that conversation with the kids' dad, Billy had acted strangely. Nothing David could put his finger on exactly but he hadn't seemed right. Then all that with Tash in the pub . . .

David hated Natasha Linten – he hated all the slags who frequented the Wheatsheaf. At some point the women got passed round everyone. Except him, of course. He wouldn't touch them with someone else's let alone his own. But his father had usually been very tolerant of them.

The other day, though, Tash had issued what sounded like a threat and his father had taken it as such.

David walked slowly up the stairs and went to his father's bedroom. He felt disgusted with himself for what he was thinking. He couldn't believe he was, really. But if his father was a beast then he wanted to know.

He had heard about Lenny Parkes hammering a nonce in the Fox Revived. Everyone had been talking about it for days. Now word was out that Kerry Alston, who was always chatting to Dad and having drinks bought for her by Billy, was also inside for noncing. She'd been noncing her own fucking kids!

He wiped a sweaty palm across his face and started his search. He went through all his father's drawers and wardrobe.

Nothing.

David was feeling better. He had just put two things together that were no more than coincidences. But he pulled out Billy's divan anyway, just because he always did everything properly and that included searching his own father's bedroom.

Nothing – again.

He went downstairs and poured himself a beer, drinking it standing at the kitchen table looking out over the postage stamp of a garden his mother had loved so much. Then, after rinsing the glass, he went back up the stairs and into his father's room again.

David looked around him. It was a nice room, with heavy wooden furniture, flowery wallpaper and curtains to match. Taking off his jumper, he flexed his considerable muscles and physically dragged the wardrobe away from the wall.

Behind it was a large brown envelope.

David licked his top lip and tasted the acrid saltiness of his own sweat. Picking up the envelope, he sat on the bed and weighed it in his hands. He didn't want to open it, but he knew he had to.

He placed it on the bed, then put the wardrobe back in place. He smoothed down the counterpane and checked the room over to see if it looked disturbed. It didn't.

Then he went downstairs and poured himself a large brandy before he opened the envelope. He tipped the contents out on to the kitchen table and then he bit on his lip until he tasted blood. Sickness rose in him and he threw up in the spotlessly clean white sink, tears already flowing from his eyes. As he sat back down he gulped at the brandy to steady himself. Then, hands shaking, he looked through all the photographs one at a time.

He was still staring ahead of him when the sun set and darkness gradually crept into the kitchen.

He was still crying silently in the unlit room as he heard his father's key in the door.

Chapter Eighteen

Jenny had never felt such a fool in her life.

Kathy Collins had her daughter in her arms when they knocked on the door. The child was without a nappy and dressed only in a vest. She was half asleep. Kathy had looked at her askance, as if seeing the police on her doorstep was an unusual occurrence.

She smiled politely. 'Can I help you?'

A man appeared behind her. He was tall, of heavy build and he looked well groomed, smartly casual. It was only his eyes that seemed really alive. They were dark brown, almost black, and the DI felt as if he was looking through her.

'And you are?' she asked steadily.

He smiled at the question in her voice. 'Do you have a warrant?' he answered.

Jenny looked over him. 'Do I need one?'

He grinned, displaying white dentures. 'If you want to come in here, you do.'

'I was following up a report on a child. Rebecca Collins.'

'This *is* Rebecca. She is trying to sleep.' He grinned again. 'She's been staying with a friend, all right? Or is that against the law now?'

Jenny knew there was nothing she could say. The child was home, well and, as the man had pointed out, trying to get an afternoon nap.

'It's that ponce Bateman, ain't it?'

Kathy's voice was shrill and the child jumped in her arms with fright.

'Fucking wanker he is, snooping round all the time . . .'

The man pulled her away from the front door gently. 'Come on, Kathy, come inside. It's all over now, love.' He looked back at Jenny. 'If that's all, officer, we'll bid you good day.'

The DI nodded. Then she said courteously, 'What did you say your name was?'

He looked into her eyes a moment before answering. 'I didn't.' Then he pushed the door shut in her face.

Jenny was still smarting from the embarrassment. Bateman was going to get a bloody mouthful from her, a right bloody mouthful. Like they didn't have enough to do. And to add insult to injury, that man had made them look even more foolish than they felt.

She fumed all the way back to the station.

She would love to know who the man was with Kathy Collins. There was something fishy going on and she had a feeling that it went far deeper than anyone could imagine.

★ ★ ★

'So you are still not willing to tell us who is behind all this shit, Jeremy?'

The prisoner stared timidly at Kate and Golding said loudly, 'Fucking Blank by name and Blank by nature, eh?'

Kate saw that Jeremy's eyes never moved from her face. It was as if he was beseeching her to save him.

'Go outside,' she told the other detective.

Golding did as she told him without a word. Everyone seemed to do what she told them lately; she knew it was all down to the change in her. The change she couldn't stop, and wasn't sure she wanted to. If she hadn't made that change, she would have gone mad by now, she was sure.

Alone, she sat down opposite Jeremy Blankley. He was shaking, really shaking, and in a distant part of herself she felt a moment's compassion for him. What had made this man into the thing he was? When did he decide that children were preferable to grown women? He wasn't even into young girls. His preference was for babies, children still in nappies.

Sitting before her was every parent's worst nightmare; a nonce, a beast, a child molester.

Yet look at him, a wreck of a man. The power he'd wielded over others was gone. He looked as sad and pathetic as a beaten dog.

'Jeremy, whoever is in on this with you will eventually be found whether you grass them or not. If you're frightened about what will happen when you're put away – which you really should be – you need to think long and hard about helping yourself now. Or else I can arrange for you to be remanded with the general prison population and, believe me, you'll be there this afternoon if I don't get some answers soon.'

Kate paused to let her words sink in.

He sniffed loudly. 'You said you wouldn't do a deal . . .'

'I am not doing a deal, I am offering you the protection you are in desperate need of. I would offer that for a price to anyone in your position. What I *won't* offer you is the promise of a reduced sentence. That, I am afraid, would be defeating the whole object. You will go away for as long as possible – that's not in dispute. What is, is the level of comfort in which you'll serve your time. My arm is long, Jeremy. I can have you put in the Scrubs, the Ville, anywhere I want. And I can make sure that everyone knows why you're there. Funky Brixton should give you a sharp taste of what to expect once you're sentenced.'

Sweat was glistening on his top lip and Kate knew that she had him. His face held the feral look of a trapped animal and despite herself she felt a small thrill of pleasure to realise that she had broken him. But he surprised her.

'I want to tell you,' he said. 'Believe me, I do want to tell you. But it don't matter a toss how long your arm is or what you can arrange for me. It's nothing in comparison to what I'll get if I open me trap. I'll have to take me chances in nick. I don't really have a choice. None of us does.'

There was a note of resignation in his voice that

Kate picked up on. Whoever he was in league with had to be a very dangerous person because she had never met a nonce yet who didn't want to deal.

She stood up and stretched.

He looked up at her and said in a strangled voice: 'I want to help you. I don't want to do what I do . . . but I can't help it. I tell meself every day, it's finished, over with, I am going to stop. But I can't. Inside I know it's wrong. I do know that – I don't need anyone to tell me. But it's a compulsion that I just can't control.'

He was pleading for her understanding but Kate couldn't afford to take her eyes off the prize.

'Who is it, Jeremy? Who can frighten you even more than we can?'

His face was flushed, cheekbones jutting prominently. They'd given him the bare minimum to eat and drink. She could see him battling it out with himself, whether to tell her or not. But in the end his fear won.

He shook his head sadly. 'I have nothing more to say.'

She hardened herself then. 'In that case get ready for your transfer to the Scrubs, Jeremy. And God help you! Whoever it is who's frightening you will seem like fucking Santa Claus after a week on remand there.'

She walked from the room, heels ringing on the cement floor, drowning the sound of Jeremy Blankley's sobs.

Patrick was made ready for theatre. Grace and Violet watched everything in silence. As the porter moved him from the ICU they both took out their rosaries and started to pray.

Kate's mother Evelyn watched them impassively. Since they had removed the ventilator and Patrick had managed to breathe on his own there had been a general air of optimism. Now it was diminishing as they all realised the enormity of what he was about to undergo.

They had wheeled him away on his bed and the small side room looked strange without it and all the apparatus that usually surrounded it.

Walking down the ward Eve made her way to the public phone so she could give Kate the news as and when it happened. She knew her daughter was in turmoil over the operation but, whatever the outcome, at least they would all know more about what was going on inside Patrick's brain.

Deep in her heart, Eve hoped if he was going to be left unable to talk or fend for himself, that merciful death would take him on the operating table. Someone like Patrick Kelly, with all the heartache he had suffered in the past, did not deserve to drag out his existence in that state.

As she reached the phone she felt a tap on her shoulder. It was Grace and the two women sized one another up like boxers before a fight.

'You can tell your daughter that if she really cared about him, she'd be here with him now. When he most needs her.'

Eve pushed the other woman's hand away roughly.

'He doesn't need her now, he needs his mother – and I understand that's you. So stop acting like a silly adolescent and go and keep vigil for your boy.'

She saw Grace's lips form a thin white line, and for a split second regretted her own words.

'That's a rumour from years gone by, but hearing it from your lips does not surprise me. He's my own flesh and blood whatever you think he is, son or brother. And the truth about that is something you will never know. It's my business and no one else's.'

Eve didn't answer and the other woman stalked stiff-backed towards the ward.

As bad as Grace was, she was hurting deep inside and Evelyn acknowledged, with a touch of shame, that she should have made allowances for that fact. She was near to tears when she picked up the telephone.

Jeremy Blankley was on his way to prison and Kate was getting ready to go to the hospital. Depression had settled on her after her run-in with the prisoner. She felt isolated, cut loose from reality, looking on as if everything that was happening around her was happening to someone else.

She managed to smile as Golding launched into a lengthy explanation of why some of the case notes were missing, and even found herself nodding assent to Leila, without giving away the fact that she had no real interest in what they were saying.

She drove home from the station, forcing herself

to concentrate on the road. At home she changed her clothes and applied make-up without even looking at what she was doing. When she glanced up she saw a stranger's face in the gilt-edged mirror, pale and drawn, dreading what the day might bring.

She stood in the hall in her little red suit. Patrick had always loved seeing her in that. She had worn it just before the split, to a friend's engagement party. She checked herself over a final time. Applied some red lipstick, retouched her mascara.

She realised now she had never stopped wanting him. If he'd had fifteen affairs, she would still want him. She didn't even have to be with him to want him.

If he came through the operation and told her he never wanted to see her again, she would still thank God every day that she was at least breathing the same air as him.

She didn't care any more what he had done. Even the knowledge that he had murdered Tommy Broughton didn't concern her. Just to see him smile one more time would be more than enough for her. She wanted him back in the world even if she couldn't have him back in her life.

Walking out of the house, Kate slammed the door behind her as if closing it on part of her life. She got into her car, turned off the radio and her phone, and drove to the hospital in screaming, crashing silence.

His face was all that she could see. Seeing him smile at her again would more than repay every sacrifice she had made, every rule she had broken, just to save Patrick Kelly's skin.

Dave Golding took one look at the scene before him and stumbled, retching, into the back garden.

Lying across the kitchen table was the body of a man. He knew that because they'd received a call from someone named David Reilly who told them that he'd just killed his father. What he had not expected was to see someone beaten so badly it was impossible to say whether they were male or female, young or old.

David Reilly followed him outside and took a few deep breaths to steady himself. Golding knew that two PCs and the other CID were waiting outside for him to let them in. David had told him he wanted them to have a talk alone first. Now Golding was wondering if he'd made a big mistake in agreeing to it.

He breathed in deeply to calm himself and walked back inside, taking the blood-soaked floor and gore-sprayed walls. It looked as if a canister of red paint had exploded in the room.

David followed him in and gestured to an envelope sticky with blood.

'Look at these,' he said hoarsely. 'I found them in his room. He was a fucking beast, me own father.'

As Golding glanced at the photographs the body on the table gave a loud groan, making both men jump with fright. Golding was amazed to see blackened, swollen eyes open in that ruined face.

Running through to the front, he shouted, 'Get a fucking ambulance and get it quick!'

Then pandemonium broke out.

All the time David Reilly stared at his father as if he had never seen him before and couldn't for the life of him understand how this man had ended up on his kitchen table.

Underneath it lay a bicycle pump. It was rusty and broken. It was also covered in blood. As he noticed it, David remembered his father giving it to him one Christmas and then telling him that the bike that went with it, a Raleigh racer, was in the garage waiting for him.

He couldn't equate that kind generous man with the animal he now knew his father had become. He was bending down to pick up the pump again when Golding pulled him out of the room.

He put one arm across David's shoulders and said gently, 'We understand what you've done and why you've done it. Now you have to tell us all that you know, OK?'

David nodded. He still looked dazed, but he knew what was going on around him.

As Golding glanced through the photographs again he stifled a spark of excitement. Here was another link in the chain. Maybe this would be the break they needed to put away a whole herd of beasts. He wanted that so badly he could taste it.

When the ambulance arrived they let the paramedics into the house. No one had attempted any kind of help whatsoever though they were all trained in first aid as a matter of course. No one had wanted to even touch the victim, such were their feelings towards the man they knew to be a child molester. They were happier helping his son who, deep inside, they believed to be a bit of a hero. Though no one would admit that out loud, of course.

In the squad car Golding told him, 'You can smoke if you like, mate.'

David smiled. 'Thanks.'

'We'll get you a nice cuppa when we get to the station, OK?'

He smiled again.

They were quiet for a while then David said heavily, 'He was a good dad, you know.'

But no one answered him.

Jenny was over the moon with the new developments. It was as if finally, after all their work, a higher force had seen fit to give them a break.

David Reilly sat in a holding cell with a big mug of tea and a pack of cigarettes. He contemplated the graffiti-adorned walls. One wag had written *Kill the beasts* and his eyes strayed to it over and over again.

When Jenny came in he looked at her expectantly. 'Is he dead?'

She shook her head. 'No. But you nearly managed it, if that makes you feel any better.'

He didn't answer.

'How did you find out about him?'

David said tiredly, 'Ask Natasha Linten from the

estate. Those kids in the photos . . . well, some of them are hers.'

Jenny nodded. 'The duty doctor is going to talk to you. We must make sure you're well enough to be interviewed.'

He nodded. 'How's me fa— Billy?' He couldn't bring himself to use the word father.

'He'll live.'

David shrugged and sipped at his tea. 'I knew I should have finished the cunt off,' he said in a dead voice. 'But I suppose he's more use to you lot alive, eh?'

'Afraid so.'

'What will I be charged with?'

She put one hand on his shoulder and said gently, 'Let's wait and see, shall we? You've had a big shock, mate, and you need to get your head round what's happened. Don't commit yourself until you've talked to a good brief. I can recommend one if you don't want the duty lawyer.'

'Thanks.'

As she banged on the door for it to be unlocked he said in a brighter voice, 'He'll go away though, won't he? I mean, for a long time. He'll get what he deserves?'

'If I get my way, love, they'll throw away the key on the lot of them.'

David nodded happily and lit another cigarette.

Natasha Linten was frightened.

Robert Bateman was standing in her lounge telling

her that the police were outside and she was going to be arrested for child abuse, negligence, and a whole host of other charges relating to her children's use in pornographic literature.

Even his terminology frightened her.

Robert, her mainstay, the man she phoned when she was in trouble, the one who listened to her problems and always found a few quid to tide her over when she was skint, was looking at her now as if she was something he had found on the bottom of his shoe.

'What on earth made you think you could get away with it? Treating those beautiful children like that, allowing them to be used by grown men and women . . .'

She put her hands over her ears. 'Stop it, please. I only borrowed them out. I never knew anything was happening to them. Please, Robert, you have to help me! Believe me, I would never hurt them for the world.'

He pushed her away from him petulantly.

'Oh, save it for the police. I'm finished with you now.' He stared around her flat. 'Look at this place! A bloody dump has more class. I should have made sure you lost those kiddies a long time ago. You really are a piece of bloody work! Well, they're settled in with foster-parents now and are well away from you and what you dragged them into, though the repercussions will go on for years. And you will have yourself to thank for that, my dear. No one but yourself.'

Tash was hysterical. 'I didn't know, I tell you! Rob,

please, you must help me!'

He opened the front door and let in the waiting police. Kate, in her red suit, had been paged at the hospital and such was the atmosphere there she had been glad of the excuse to leave. As she looked at the sobbing girl before her she felt the now familiar disgust.

'You can't just come in here without a by your leave.'

Kate ignored Tash and watched as her men systematically tore the flat apart. She felt it was good for Natasha to watch the process. She wanted to impress on this ignorant girl that they were leaving no stone unturned in their quest for the gang of paedophiles.

As Natasha witnessed her home being destroyed she also heard their scornful comments about her slapdash housekeeping.

'This place is like a fucking tip!'

Kate watched the girl listen to all that was being said.

The children's urine-soaked beds were torn open with blades as they searched for anything that could make the case even tighter, though they all knew they didn't need much more.

Natasha was at breaking point.

She would talk.

David Reilly had taken Jenny's advice and got himself the brief she had recommended. Her name was Karen Lawson, a pretty woman in her thirties.

She was well aware that her client was something of a hero in the police station and this pleased her. At least she could communicate freely with CID now and wouldn't have to hide behind legal jargon and other tricks to get her client a good deal. In fact, they were already talking about bail on his own recognisance.

David Reilly was charged with attempted murder under extreme provocation. As he gave his statement, his voice was lucid and quiet. He had expended all his energy on the attack.

Kate and Jenny listened to him explain how he had tripped his father up.

'I had him lovely. He came in, he had had a few beers like. So he was well oiled – talkative. I asked him if he had seen Tash, and he laughed. Then I made a few jokes about her. I dropped her kids' names into the conversation, saying how I had seen her with them. And he starts telling me all about them.'

He lowered his head and took a deep breath. 'He forgot himself, see. Knew their names off pat. Told me how the youngest one had a real mind of her own.'

He wiped his hand across his face aggressively. 'I mean he *knew* them. And I said to him straight: "Are you a fucking beast?" But I knew the answer to that all right, and so did he. Tash had let the cat out of the bag and I told him and all. Dirty fucking bastards.'

He licked his lips and stared at the two women in abject disbelief.

'Can you imagine asking the man you loved all your life a question like that? I mean, to even *have* to ask it is unbelievable.'

'What did he say?' Kate's voice was low.

He looked straight into her eyes. 'He didn't answer me. He couldn't. That's when I lost it.'

They were all quiet now as he pulled himself together.

'I am glad me mum's dead. This would have killed her faster than the cancer, I can tell you.'

Kate looked at the man before her. A nice man, a kind man. A man who worked and had always been a productive member of society. Law-abiding, he had his own set of morals. Now he had tried to kill his own father and Kate knew he had done wrong. But somehow, she saw it from his point of view.

He had suffered the ultimate betrayal.

He had to live with what he had done; that in itself was going to be punishment enough. At least he could console himself with one fact. He had taken a predatory child-abuser off the streets.

She knew she was thinking like Patrick Kelly, but cases like this made everyone want retribution. Real retribution.

Kate lit a cigarette and placed it in his shaking hand. He nodded his thanks and took a deep drag.

'I should have finished him. But I didn't have the courage.'

She knew Patrick would have applauded him, and somewhere inside herself she did too.

'Another thing – he has a mate in the police force. Barker. Used to be here years ago. Don't let him use his contacts to get him an easy ride, OK?'

Kate and Jenny stared at the man in front of them.

He was like manna from heaven.

'Were they good friends?'

'Pretty much so. Still sees him now and again. His numbers and that are in his address book in the kitchen at the house.'

'Do you know him?'

He shrugged and answered Jenny's question with a question of his own. 'Do you think he might be involved?'

'What makes you ask that?'

'I often wondered what they had in common, to be honest. Barker always liked the girls – the old man used to joke about it. But now I think it was the kids he liked more than the mothers.' His voice was bitter. 'A bit like me father, eh?'

'What do you know about Kevin and Jeremy Blankley?'

He sighed. 'Not a lot really. Kevin drank with the old man. I never really knew the brother. All fucking nonces though, I suspect. I think the whole crowd of them was in on it. When Kevin was done by Parkes I half guessed there was more to it all than met the eye. But you don't want to think things, do you? Not about your own anyway. Plus me old man went on about it for ages. Cunting Blankley and calling him names.'

'Was Blankley friends with Barker?'

'I really don't know. I wish I did. *You'll* have to ask Barker, won't you?' There was a challenge in his voice now and Kate knew what he was thinking. If Barker was filth he would walk away. That is what was usually assumed by everyone, especially the general public.

'Can I get you a drink?'

He nodded. 'A coffee would be great, and can I have some more cigarettes?'

Kate walked from the room. She had a lot to think about and she wanted to set everything straight in her own head before she questioned the man further.

If Barker was involved then this was going to blow up in their faces at some point and she wanted to make sure it was tighter than a duck's proverbial before she set down one word.

She also wanted to bring it to the attention of Ratchet in such a way that he could not dismiss it without giving her a damn good reason. At last they were getting the breaks and she only hoped that this luck stayed with them, for she had a feeling they were going to need it.

Whoever was behind it all was obviously well protected. It seemed everyone was terrified to name the ringleader.

Evelyn and Grace sat together in silence. Violet was still in the hospital chapel, praying for her dear brother.

The two elderly women seemed to have decided on a truce, both realising this was no time for unseemly argument. Plus, each could clearly see the worry in the other's face.

Grace had her hair set immaculately, and was dressed smartly as always, though in a style that was much too young for her age: a bottle-green suit which made her look like a parody of an old-style secretary. Whereas Evelyn was wearing a navy-blue dress and her regulation fur-lined boots even though the weather had been marvellous.

A nurse walked towards them and they both looked at her with the apprehension hospitals always seem to induce. Fear of finding out what the score was could often be worse than the actual news itself.

The young woman clattered past them without giving them a second glance and Grace's lips thinned in anger.

'Might as well be fucking invisible in this place for all the notice they take of you.'

Evelyn nodded her head in agreement. 'Sure, once your face is lined you're finished. I can remember turning a few heads when I was a girl, as I'm sure you did. I understand you worked for years, Grace. What did you do?'

The other woman looked at her suspiciously to make sure she wasn't taking the piss.

'Didn't your darling girl Kate tell you about the family business then?'

Evelyn looked genuinely nonplussed and realised she had inadvertently opened up an old wound.

'I was on the game for years,' Grace said defiantly. 'It's well known, Evelyn, and I ain't ashamed of it. Me mother was ill a lot of the time after me old man went on the trot and I just sort of drifted into it, really.'

Evelyn tried her hardest not to look shocked.

'I was a good-looking girl, then a good-looking woman, then I was used up and dried out. It happens.

I never married or anything, just wanted to be on me jacksy like. I don't really like men very much but I don't think that was just because of my profession. Our generation had it hard really, what with the war and that. I had me moments then, too. I had a baby while I was unmarried and it died. But it soiled me reputation.'

She laughed bitterly.

'One girl in our street gave birth when she hadn't seen her old man for three years but she was married and that seemed to make it all right. At least these days women have a bit of a choice even if the silly bitches still marry a geek and produce one after the other till he gets sick of the sight of them all.'

The bitterness in her voice made Evelyn feel for the woman beside her. She saw Grace picking nervously at her skirt and wondered what made people take the paths they did. Even at an advanced age Eve could see the traces of her former beauty in Grace. Her fine bone structure was still evident and she had the look of a woman with money, even class, if she didn't open that cockney gob of hers.

She understood why Grace had decided to unburden herself today. She had assumed that Evelyn had known. That Kate would have gossiped about it. Most people would not have been able to resist it. After all, it was sensational and shocking. At least it was to Evelyn. But Kate, God love her, had never said a word and Evelyn, far from being miffed, admired her daughter's loyalty.

'We all did things we regretted. The shame of it is

when you get to our age you realise it doesn't matter a fuck. Sure, I regret more the things I never did, the opportunities I never took, more than I regret things I have already forgotten about.'

They were quiet together. Calm descended as they both thought back over the years and were reminded of things now far in the past.

'Still, I had some laughs,' Grace sighed contentedly.

Evelyn patted her hand. 'So did I, but I was lucky. I only ever had the one man and he was lovely. I had the two kids and devoted myself to them all. Some people would think that a wasted life. Especially today, women think you have to be rustling up dinner dressed like a fecking lingerie model, have a baby on the hip and sex all hours of the day and night while holding down a full-time job! Meself, I'd rather have it the old way. It suited me.'

Grace laughed with her.

A man walked towards them then in his operating greens. But they were clean and he looked relaxed. They both stared up at him expectantly. He smiled professionally and Evelyn listened to him talk even though the words were not penetrating properly. All she took on board was the fact that it was over. At last it was over.

When Grace began to cry she automatically put an arm around her shoulders, drawing her close.

'Whist now. Get it out of you, girl. It will do you the world of good.'

Grace cried harder. Her eyes were torrents of water and even her nose was running. Evelyn looked up at the doctor, who didn't seem embarrassed by this display of emotion. He was more than likely immune to it all by now.

'Did everything go well?' she asked.

He shrugged. 'The next twenty-four hours are critical. We will know more tomorrow.'

Eve nodded. She could tell from his tone that he did not hold out too much hope. She patted Grace's hand and kept her peace. Evelyn was a great believer in worrying when it was necessary and not before.

She was still gripping Grace's hand when Violet came up from the chapel.

Chapter Nineteen

Natasha Linten was still crying, only now it was a silly whine that was as forced as it was irritating.

'Oh, shut up!' Jenny's voice had an angry edge to it that Kate was beginning to recognise.

The girl did shut up momentarily. Then: 'I didn't know what they was doing, I only borrowed them out like . . .' And she started to cry again.

Kate sighed. 'Listen, Natasha, we might be able to help you, but you have to tell us who you *borrowed* your children to, OK?'

The sarcasm was not lost on the girl, who had the grace to look ashamed. Then she shook her head, her ridiculous poodle hair-do bobbing up and down.

'No fucking way. I ain't saying a dicky bird. You don't realise who you're dealing with, mate.'

Kate and Jenny were silent for long moments.

'Well, why don't you tell us?' Jenny said finally.

Natasha leaned back in her chair as if it had just occurred to her that she held all the cards. She had once heard someone say that knowledge was power,

407

and she suddenly saw what they'd meant.

'As much as I would like to help you, ladies . . .' she laid great stress on the word 'ladies', eyes boring into Jenny's, 'I don't really know meself. Only that they're well connected and you don't mess with them if you can help it.'

She smiled again, tears forgotten as she looked at them with an almost animal cunning.

'This bird used to knock at me door, slip me a ton and take the kids for a walk, see. I thought they was just taking photos, nothing more or less. Proper modelling like.'

'Where did you meet this *bird*?'

Natasha shrugged. 'I can't remember. I think she just knocked on the door one day, said she wanted some nice-looking little kids and my eldest is a right little looker. Put make-up on her and she looks like a grown-up . . .'

She realised she had made a stupid slip and shut up.

'Did you put the make-up on her or was it the *bird* who just happened to knock at your door one day and ask to *borrow* your kids?'

Kate thumped on the table and hissed, 'Don't fuck me about, Tash, I ain't in the fucking mood. Now you'd better open that trap of yours quick. We know all about Billy, see. David smashed his father's face in and he's coming after you next. Almost killed his dad. You should have seen what he did to him – nearly flayed him alive. Now David, who found out about his father over you mouthing off in a pub, was following you. We know what you were up to, lady, and you'd better think long and hard before you lie to us. Mess us around and we'll put you away for the fucking duration, if not longer. Do you get my drift, you piece of shit?'

Kate could feel her anger spinning out of control. Every time she thought of what Natasha and her cronies were capable of, she felt it burn inside her guts like a smouldering fire. Seeing this girl with her dirty nails, her face plastered in make-up and with that idiotic hair scraped up on her head in a brightly coloured band, she felt an urge to slam her fist right into the centre of her ignorant face.

She wanted Natasha to feel fear and pain, to know what it was like for her children when she gave them to someone to use at their whim.

She wanted to impress on her the enormity of what she had done in the eyes of other people. Those who didn't live in a twilight world of drugs, drinking, fucking and using others for their own ends, even their children. Their most precious possessions.

She wanted a reaction, but she knew she would never get one. The Natashas of this world live by a different code.

As the girl pulled open her packet of Benson's, Kate's hand flew out and knocked the cigarettes from her fingers with such force they hit the wall with a loud crunch. Natasha sat back as far as she could in her seat, fear on her face as she realised that the woman before her was poised to strike again.

She knew about police brutality; it was a fact of life

where she came from. Something to be discussed when talking about their nickings and their prison terms. Natasha had thought she was immune, and was suddenly conscious of the fact that she wasn't. She looked absolutely terrified.

'Don't wind me up, girl. I am on a short fuse and every time you open that ignorant mouth of yours the fuse gets shorter. Do not even attempt to take the piss out of me, lady, or I will rip your head off and ram it right up your jacksy!'

Natasha was really crying now and neither Kate nor Jenny felt any sympathy for her.

'I want a brief,' she whimpered.

'Well, you'll know what it's like to want then, won't you?' Kate said cruelly.

Natasha cried harder.

Willy stared around him in surprise.

Jacky and Joey were lying trussed up on the floor. After another two days of being tied up himself he had just been given a few sandwiches, a Thermos flask of tea laced with whisky and they had removed the ropes that had bound him.

As he sat waiting patiently for the numbness in his hands to subside, and the painful and tormenting pins and needles to arrive, he studied the two men who were gazing fearfully up at him from the floor.

Jacky was near to tears and Willy sneered at him. He was trying to rub his hands together to bring the circulation back as fast as possible. As he did so he spoke to the two men in a low sing-song voice.

'I'm going to enjoy meself, lads, and it will be at your expense.'

He was talking like a man who knows he is fully in control.

'I can smell me sandwiches, lads. Beef and tomato, cheese and cucumber. Know how to look after you, the Ruskies, eh? But then, you two treacherous bastards would already know about that, wouldn't you? Having tucked up everyone while you worked for them yourselves.'

He kicked out with one bare foot at Jacky's head, the blow landing hard and giving Willy total satisfaction.

'Where's all your mates now, then? Ain't got so much trap when you're on your Jack Jones, have you?' He was winding himself up now, aware that the Russians were either watching it all or listening in somehow. He knew he was being used by them and was glad of the fact.

'Enjoy tucking me and Pat up, did you? I bet you and Tommy Broughton pissed yourselves laughing at us, eh? Well, there's an old saying: God pays back debts without money. And look at what's happened here. You two have dropped into my lap like manna from fucking heaven and once my hands have a bit of feeling in them, I am going to take the pair of you apart.'

He laughed again and Jacky and Joey closed their eyes in despair.

Willy Gabney was a nutter of the first order. He was also Patrick Kelly's oldest friend.

They were dead men and they knew it.

'So come on, Tash, cut the waterworks and tell us the truth.'

Kate and Jenny had let her cry for a while, both sitting absolutely still, their eyes trained on her. It was a good act she put on, but an act all the same.

Eventually she picked up her cigarettes from the floor and amid much sniffing and coughing she lit one. Drawing the smoke deep into her lungs, she muttered, 'You bastards, you've always had it in for me.'

Kate rolled her eyes at the ceiling. 'Oh, change the bloody record for Christ's sake. No one has it in for you. The reason you are here, Tash, is because you allowed your kids to be used for degrading and immoral purposes. You were the cause of David nearly killing his father; you have made us have to arrest a man who unlike you is a decent and productive member of society. Thanks to you and Kerry Alston, we are having to put beautiful children into care and arrest their so-called mothers. So if that is having it in for you then yes, perhaps you were right. But I will get to the bottom of this, Tash. If I have to keep you here all night then I will.'

Natasha drew deeply on her cigarette once more.

'When was the last time you saw DI Barker then?' Both women watched as Tash's face blanched.

'What you on about? I ain't seen him in years.' Bravado was back in the voice now.

'That's not true and you know it.'

'If Bateman has been spinning you a line then you better watch out. Always had it in for me, him. Fucking big poof he is. Mincing round the place as if his shit don't stink and all!'

'What made you put Bateman's name up over Barker? Where is the connection?'

She shook her head as if they were stupid. 'Everyone knows Bateman hates him. They knew one another years ago. Bateman's like you, thinks everyone's a nonce.'

Jenny laughed. 'You mean you're *not* nonces – is that what you are saying? You gave your kids to a strange bird who put make-up on them and dressed them up as little women for photos and you see nothing noncey in that? Am I missing something here? Please explain to me the logic that you seem to live by.'

Natasha shook her head at the apparent skulduggery of the two women before her. 'You ain't putting words in my mouth.' She pointed a smoking hand at them, waving the cigarette around as she spoke. 'You two will have to get up very early in the morning to catch me.'

'Depends what you call early. From your social worker's notes that means us getting up before bloody lunchtime, love. Not too difficult, eh?'

Jenny laughed at Kate's exclamation and Natasha shook her head again, her ridiculous hair flying around her face.

'You will get nothing from me. I don't care what you say or what you threaten. I ain't seen Barker for years and I know nothing about him. Now I want a fucking brief.'

'What about Suzy Harrington?' Jenny rapped out. 'I heard she is involved in all this. Still mates with Barker, is she?'

'Suzy who?' Natasha's voice was full of wonderment as if the name was completely alien to her. 'Sorry, ladies, you've lost me. Never heard of her.'

'You are a liar and you know it.'

The girl shrugged. 'Sticks and stones, darlin', never hurt no one.' She was playing with them.

'Now, as I said before, I am entitled to legal representation,' she burst out. 'It's in the fucking Magna Carta or somewhere, innit? So until I have a brief I am going to shut me bleeding trap – OK? I stand by what I said. A bird I didn't know asked to borrow me kids. It's no different to a burglar saying he bought a video or a telly in a pub off a geezer. You can't prove otherwise. If you could I would have been properly nicked and you two could go home and scratch your bleeding fannies.'

What she said was true and it hurt hearing it.

Jenny stood up and looked down at the smiling girl. The blow took them all by surprise.

As Natasha was knocked from her chair to the floor she burned herself with her cigarette. She sat on the floor sucking on the burn, the smile still on her face. She looked into Kate's eyes.

'You two can't scare me,' she said triumphantly. 'Bear that in mind – you *can't* scare me. I will stand by what I said. I made a mistake and I am paying for it. I let me kids go off with an unknown woman and I will pay for that piece of stupidity. But that is as far as it goes. You can't prove fuck all.'

Jenny moved towards her and Kate pulled her back. A good hiding was exactly what Natasha wanted, and as much as she would like to oblige, she knew it would be madness.

Barbara Epstein knocked on the door loudly. Then, kneeling down, she opened the letterbox. A strange smell assailed her nostrils and she jerked her head back quickly. It was a sweet smell, like rotting leaves.

She stood up and looked around the lobby of the flats. Then, walking down the stairs, she knocked at a red front door with a well-polished brass knocker.

An elderly woman answered her knock.

'Have you seen Sharon from upstairs?' Barbara asked her anxiously. 'Sharon Pallister?'

The woman seemed to be in her seventies and her hair was a startling blue, her lips smeared with orange-coloured lipstick. She shook her head.

'I assume she's away. You normally hear that bleeding kid, but it's been quiet. So I think she has gone to her mum's. She does that sometimes.'

Barbara looked worried. 'I am her mum. I can't get her on the phone.'

'Oh, it's you phoning all hours of the day and night, is it? I can hear that bleeding phone as if it's in my own flat.'

The woman's voice was a relentless moan and, closing her eyes, Barbara interrupted her.

'I've travelled down from Edinburgh to try and see what has happened to my daughter. Do you know anyone who might have news of her?'

The woman shook her alarming head once more.

'Try one of the other unmarried mothers. Like a bleeding club round here it is. None of them married . . . it's a disgrace.'

The door slammed in Barbara's face. She turned to the one opposite then, taking a deep breath and knocking gently. It was opened by a small boy with fair hair and startling green eyes. He looked to be all of four.

'Me mum says she ain't in.'

Barbara nearly smiled then. 'Tell your mum, it's Sharon's mummy. Sharon from upstairs.'

A girl walked out into the small hallway. She had black hair in a long plait over one shoulder and even greener eyes than the child.

'Oh, hello. I thought you was the tally man come for his money, and I'm boracic at the moment. Come in, love.'

Her voice was harsh but friendly and Barbara walked in gratefully, even though the flat was hot and had a strange smell. As she entered the lounge she realised the smell came from a mixture of dirt and fresh paint. The kitchen, a shambles of boxes and tins, was in the process of being painted bright yellow. But the girl was so pleasant and Barbara was so tired from her journey that she accepted the offer of a cup of tea gratefully.

'How is Sharon?' the girl asked.

Barbara looked at her fearfully. 'I've just travelled from Scotland to see her. I can't get her on the phone and I'm really worried.'

The girl frowned. 'I assumed she had gone to see you again. Keeps herself to herself she does. Not a bad judge round here, I can tell you. Perhaps Suzy knows where she is, I know they're mates.'

'Where does this Suzy live?'

'Drink up and I'll take you over there, all right?'

Barbara nodded. 'Look, have you seen my Sharon in the last few days?'

'I ain't seen her for about a week, now you mention it. I ain't heard little Trevor neither. And he is one noisy little sod.' She was chuckling. 'He's a case him, ain't he?'

Barbara nodded but a terrible feeling was taking hold inside her. Opening her bag, she took out a mobile phone.

'I am going to phone the police,' she said shakily. 'I think my daughter has met with an accident or something. It's not like her to disappear like this.'

The girl shrugged and picked up a baby with a dirty nappy and a gummy smile. 'Round here, love, anything can happen to you . . .' She regretted the words when she saw Barbara's worried countenance.

'Yeah, you phone the Old Bill if it will make you feel better,' she said kindly. 'At least that way you'll feel like you're doing something, eh?'

Barbara nodded, but the fear was growing stronger now and as she looked around the cramped flat and smelt that strange smell she was reminded of the one from her daughter's home.

It was sweetly rotten, like something had died. Oh Christ. She could feel hysteria mounting inside her.

Sharon had been a difficult girl but never a bad one and she knew how much her mother worried about her. Whatever arguments they had had over the years, and they had been legion, Barbara knew that her daughter would not leave her all this time without getting in touch, because she knew she would be worrying.

As the girl got out a cold bottle of milk from the fridge to feed her baby Barbara was talking to the police. Turning off her phone she said quietly, 'They're on their way.'

Now that she had rung them she wasn't at all sure she wanted to know what was in her daughter's flat. She had a bad feeling about it. Had done for the last forty-eight hours.

She sipped tea from a grubby mug and watched the baby suck its milk with relish. It took her mind off what she was thinking at the back of her mind. *Sharon was dead, and so was her grandson.*

It wasn't a conscious thought, but it was there nonetheless.

Barbara was mentally preparing herself without actually admitting the fact that deep in her guts she knew it to be true.

Suzy Harrington sat on her leather sofa and raised one eyebrow as DC Golding told her she was under arrest.

'I beg your pardon?'

'We have reason to believe that you are using children from this estate for the purposes of immoral and degrading literature. You have the right to remain silent . . .'

She laughed scornfully. 'Fuck off.'

Getting up, she went into her bedroom and slipped on an expensive suede coat. Then she said snidely, 'I just have to make a call, OK?'

She dialled a number and after a few seconds said: 'I am on my way to Grantley police station, accused of child pornography.' Then she replaced the phone quickly.

She did not say another word all afternoon.

Kate took a call from her mother and relaxed slightly. Patrick was over the worst. All they could do now was wait, apparently. As she sat at her desk, face lined with tiredness and hands trembling, she received a summons to Ratchet's office. Her mind on Patrick, she assumed the Chief Inspector would want an update on his progress.

Instead he was standing by his window stiff-backed. He didn't turn to face her as she waited in his office like a schoolgirl in trouble with the headmaster.

'I've had a call from Above and they have told me that you are to let Suzy Harrington go without further discussion.'

Kate thought for a few seconds that the lack of sleep had affected her hearing. 'I beg your pardon?'

He sighed heavily. 'You heard me, Burrows. She is to be released without charge.'

Kate had to press her hands against his desk to control a desperate urge to slap him round the back of his practically hairless head.

'On what grounds?' she demanded. 'If this woman is part of an ongoing investigation then we want to know what it entails.'

He said loudly, 'I do *not* have to explain anything to you! I have issued an order and you will carry it out without further comment.'

His face was pale and his eyes were shifting about as if he couldn't bear to look at her.

'I'm sorry, sir, but I need to know why we have got to release someone who is central to our investigation of abused, missing and murdered children. I can't convict without her, she's the linchpin of what we have been investigating, and I want to know what authority is stopping me from carrying out the job I am so badly paid for.'

Her voice was heavy with sarcasm and disgust. 'This stinks, Mr Ratchet. It stinks to high heaven.'

He seemed to deflate before her eyes.

'Listen, Kate, if you value your career, let this go. You must! This has come from the top and I can't do anything to help. Do you understand what I'm saying?'

She shook her head.

'By Christ, how the mighty have fallen. You honestly think that I'm going to lie down and swallow this? After all the snide remarks and the bloody innuendo I have had to endure from you over the last few years, you have the brass bloody neck to stand there and talk to me about *my career*. Practically threaten me, then expect me to tug my forelock and say "Yes, sir"!'

For the first time ever she saw Ratchet frightened.

He was begging for her understanding.

'Look, Kate, I'm as upset about this as you are. But I have to follow orders too, you know, and this one came from the highest source, believe me. If it hadn't I'd have told them to take a flying fuck myself. I have the newspapers on my back, too, don't forget. This is a high-profile case and we need results fast. So I can understand what you are saying. But I can't go against direct orders and neither can you.'

Kate laughed. 'We'll bloody well see about that,' she said angrily. 'Can you imagine what my team will say when I present them with this little gem? Great work, guys, but we can't actually convict Suzy as she seems to have friends in high places. But, hey, you did a good job anyway.'

'I never said that, Kate. I never said she had any friends . . .'

Kate laughed again, this time loud enough to attract glances from beyond the glass walls. She and Ratchet were now the focus of interest for the whole team.

'You didn't have to,' she said tersely. 'Right – I want to know where this came from and I want to know now. Who is the culprit, sir?'

Ratchet sighed and sat at his desk. He suddenly looked old.

'I cannot divulge that information, but if it makes you feel any better I went above him and was told the same thing. To let it go.'

There was a finality about his voice that spoke volumes.

'You have enough to convict the others, Kate – just leave Suzy out of it. Those were my orders and now they are yours.'

'And if I don't do what you ask?'

He sighed and raised his hands in a gesture of helplessness. 'Then I'm afraid I can't help you and this conversation never took place.'

He softened. 'Come on, love, it's not like it's the first time something like this has happened, is it? It's how the whole world works. I scratch your back and you scratch mine.'

'Bollocks, sir. If I ever had to rely on you to scratch my back I'd know that I'd hit rock bottom.'

Inside she was sorry for him. He was weak and he was stupid. But what else was new?

'This is about Barker, isn't it?' she raged. 'He's in this little lot up to his neck. I can't get a statement from anyone in all this. Some big guns are involved and you know who they are.'

She shook her head. 'I can't even believe I am hearing any of this! I knew you were bent, knew you ducked and dived with Pat, but I never had you down as a nonce-lover. Well, Mr Ratchet, as soon as I have enough evidence, Suzy is nicked and so is Barker. He's like a bad smell turning up when you least expect him. I will have them both and I will do it in such a way that the DPP himself will have to issue the arrest warrants.'

She turned and walked from the room, slamming the door behind her so hard it rattled in its frame. She could taste her own anger. It was burning her mouth and her chest like vicious bile. Her hands were shaking so much that when she got back to her own office she had trouble opening the door.

Jenny listened in amazement as Kate related what she had just been told. Then they both watched helplessly as Suzy came walking cockily past, a wide smile on her over made-up face.

She wiggled her fingers at them in a parody of a wave as she said happily, ''Bye, ladies.'

Boris was listening to all that was being said in the basement of his house. He knew that Willy Gabney would probably kill the two other men but didn't care. In fact it would save his men a job and he liked to think the troublesome duo were being paid back. They had caused him a lot of problems over the last few months and he was sick of them. Men like Gunner and Partridge were basically ten a penny. Hard nuts in their own little manor, normally a small estate of some kind, but nothing when they were mixing with the big boys like himself. He could replace them in minutes if he needed to and so he was quite happy to give them to Willy.

He still liked the big man, respected him. Most men, his own included, would have broken long ago. But Willy had taken what they had dished out and had still kept silent, only reiterating that his boss had known nothing of the club's other activities and that his trust had been abused by so-called mates.

He had also pointed out that Patrick Kelly had more than enough money of his own without needing to take what wasn't his. Not unless he was bankrolling an armed robbery – which he hadn't done for years because he had turned semi-respectable to keep his woman happy, the woman in question being a police inspector whom he loved like nobody's business.

Boris had to admit that it sounded plausible enough, and guessed that if he put Jacky and Joey in with the big man then he would get the exact truth.

Which he had.

He had also found out that Patrick's woman was bent when need be. Something else that interested him. Everyone needed bent police on their side and she seemed like the perfect candidate for what he had in mind.

All in all it had been a good few weeks.

Barbara Epstein stood on the landing outside her daughter's flat and listened to the commotion inside. The police had broken open the door and the smell had hit them all at full force. She could feel her heart beating a tattoo in her chest.

She heard one of the policemen say, 'We have the body of a female, dead maybe a week.' Waited until he walked out to her then said in a frightened voice, 'My grandson . . . little Trevor. Is he in there?'

The policeman shook his head.

'Then where the hell is he?'

Her voice was rising hysterically and she felt as if she was filling up with hot air. As she fainted the young man caught her clumsily and tried to lay her on the floor as best he could, then arranged her in the recovery position.

Then he went back inside and called out to his team, 'Looks like another missing kid. Better get in touch with CID, tell them a child is missing and we have a murder victim.'

He looked down at the body of the young woman they knew was Sharon Pallister. Her eyes were staring up at them sightlessly. A milk whiteness seemed to have taken over her whole body. Her lips were a dark blue and the stab wounds in her throat looked like something from a slasher film.

He wondered why he wasn't retching as usual. It finally occurred to him that he was a veteran at last. They all talked about when they had finally become hardened and he'd secretly believed it would never happen to him. Last winter when they'd broken down a door and found the decomposed body of an old-age pensioner he'd had to have a week off work with pretend 'flu. But now he could stomach it, could take it without flinching.

It had taken him ten years.

'You are still under caution – remember that, Natasha.'

The girl was sweating profusely now. She had thought her last run with them would have it finished. She was determined not to say a word and she knew that providing she kept to her story there was nothing they could do.

They had woken her up from a well-deserved nap

and she was still feeling groggy. To cap it all, Jenny and Kate had kept repeating the same questions over and over again. It was finally getting to her.

'So, once more. Is Suzy the bird you supposedly gave the kids to? Only we think she is behind it all. Kerry Alston hasn't got the brains to do it on her own; she's like you – thick, stupid, needs someone to lead her by the hand. They knew what they were doing. Probably laughing up their sleeves at you. You gave them babies away cheap if you only knew it.'

Natasha listened to Kate in distress. 'I really don't know what you mean about Suzy. She's me mate.' Her arrogance was gone now, worn down by their constant questioning.

'Do you know Sharon Pallister?' Kate asked.

Natasha shrugged. 'I know her face, yeah. I don't really know her as such, why?'

'She was found murdered in her flat today. Her little boy is missing. I wonder if we can tie you into this lot as well, only she was seen talking to you last week by a neighbour.'

The news devastated Natasha. 'I want a brief please.' She was green-gilled with fear.

Kate softened her voice. 'You'll get one, don't worry. Now is there anything you want to tell me about Trevor Pallister? He's in some of the photos with your kids, isn't he? In glorious Technicolor. Also, the little boy murdered recently, who was found on the tip – he's in the photos too. I mean, it seems to me that there are an awful lot of kids *you* know about that *we* need to know about, if that is simple enough for you to take on board. It all points back to you, Tash. Now Suzy has in effect walked, it looks like it's all down to you, doesn't it?'

'I mean it, Burrows, I want a brief.'

'You will have one when we see fit to let you have one,' Jenny said impatiently. 'Now answer our fucking questions! A child is on the missing list and we need to know where he is. He might be dead, then again he might not. But I have a feeling that wherever he is, you know more about it than we do. Now then, what were you talking about to Sharon last week?'

Natasha licked her cracked lips. 'Can I have a fag?'

Jenny looked at Kate who nodded. They watched the girl light it, saw her trembling hands and heard her nervous cough. They knew they were rattling her.

'She did the same as I did – borrowed her kid out. Trevor is three and he's loud, so they were getting fed up with him. He's quite an aggressive little boy and the playschool had told her that he was going to be excluded for his bad behaviour. That's what we were talking about, I take oath. Plus I've just had a baby and she was asking me about that. The usual women's things.'

'Usual women's things?' Kate jeered. 'What kind of woman gives her kids – oh, sorry, *borrows* her kids – to paedophiles? Talking of babies, aren't you wondering where your newborn is?'

Natasha shrugged.

'He's all right, Robert will make sure of that. He's good, is Batey. All the girls love him. Poofy though he is, he's a real kid-lover and tries to help when he can.'

'You've changed your tune. He's not too happy with you, is he?'

Tash shook her head. 'Nah, he goes like that sometimes. Honest, though, he'll see me kids all right. He always does.'

The girl's careless acceptance of her children's plight appalled Kate.

'In fact, I want him here while I talk. I am under supervision and can request a social worker if I feel I don't understand the questions,' said Tash craftily.

Kate shook her head and laughed.

'You really are a piece of work, do you know that? You're looking at fifteen years and still you can find it in your heart to have a joke. I admire you for that. Don't you admire her, Jenny?'

Jenny nodded and laughed as well. 'I'd have thought you'd have been trying to help yourself, not putting yourself further and further in the shit. But then, you're not exactly the brightest bulb on the Christmas tree, are you?'

She held up one hand and counted off on her stubby fingers.

'One, we have evidence that you spoke to a woman who was later murdered. Two, we know through David Reilly that you were aware that his father was interfering with your children and other people's. Three, you admit that you knew Sharon's son Trevor was being *borrowed*, for want of a better word, to the same people. And four, you also knew that Suzy was the brains of the whole operation. On top of all that, Billy Reilly is in hospital and everyone round your flats knows why so we'll have loads more statements putting your face in the frame, and yet still you sit there like you haven't a worry in the world.'

There was a knock at the door and Golding popped his head round.

'May I see you, ma'am?'

Kate nodded. As she walked from the room she heard Jenny asking Natasha solicitously if she would like a cold drink. She smiled. Jenny was going to start tripping the prisoner up – not before bloody time.

In her office she raised an eyebrow at Golding.

'Is it true, ma'am? That we can't question Suzy Harrington?'

'According to my superior, yes.'

Golding smiled. 'Suppose I was to find out where that order came from – would it help?'

'It would. Can you?'

He took out a photocopied sheet of paper and placed it on her deck.

'This is a list of the calls Ratchet has taken today. From what his secretary says, he was OK until early this afternoon when he took a quick call from the Home Office. I'm guessing that this was the one that gave him the bad news.'

'How did you get this?' Kate asked. She had to hand it to him – it was good work.

He held up his hands and said, 'A policeman never divulges his sources.'

They shared a laugh together and Kate found herself pleased that she had Golding on the team. He had amazed her in the last week and yet she had never liked him before and had thought he did not like her.

'How's Mr Kelly, ma'am?'

She shrugged. 'He has had the clot removed and now we all just have to wait.'

Golding put a hand over hers and said kindly, 'Well, we're all rooting for him, ma'am.'

This solicitude, especially coming from Dave Golding, was nearly her undoing. Sniffing loudly, she turned away and looked out of the window.

She had put Patrick out of her mind all day. Now, such was the intensity of her emotion, he could have been in the room with her. When she composed herself and turned back to Golding, she saw the office was empty.

She sighed heavily and picked up the sheet of paper he had left on her desk, looking through the names.

Wondering once more at the kindness people could show when you least expected it.

Chapter Twenty

Evelyn was tired out. Her eyes felt as if they had been sprayed with hot sand. She was trying not to nod off in the chair by Patrick's bed but it was difficult. The room was so hot it induced sleepiness within minutes of sitting down.

Violet and Grace had left, both happier than she had seen them for days. In fact, everyone seemed more relaxed, even the nurses.

Patrick's hand moved gently, his fingers half clenching, and she smiled to herself even though she knew it was reflex rather than deliberate movement. Everything seemed to indicate that the worst of it was over and Patrick was on the mend. She hoped against hope that was the case.

Kate was due later and Evelyn would be pleased to tell her that everyone seemed optimistic. In a way it was for the good that her daughter was so busy. However demanding her work was, if it took her mind off the plight of the man lying in his hospital bed then Evelyn was grateful for it.

In fact, she hoped Kate was detained for a long, long while, until something happened with Patrick. Something good.

As she rubbed her eyes and adjusted her skirt to make herself more comfortable, a man walked into the room. He was big and heavy-set with long thick black hair and a handsome autocratic face.

He glanced at her briefly, smiling as if he knew her, before walking to the bed.

Inside, an alarm bell was ringing, telling Evelyn that this man could be trouble. But his relaxed attitude belied that and she found herself politely smiling back at him.

'How did you get in, son?'

He seemed surprised that she should address him – perhaps that she should dare to. Turning towards her, he looked her over from head to foot and Evelyn received the distinct impression, though his expression never changed, that he found her almost beneath his notice. She felt her hackles rise.

'You have to speak to the ward sister before you can come in here,' she said sternly.

He just stared at her so in a softer voice she said, 'Do you know Patrick? Only I can't remember seeing you before.'

He held out a large well-manicured hand and a smile transformed his face as he said heartily, 'You are Patrick's mother?'

He had the same accent as the men who had searched Kate's house. She looked at the door to see if Everton was sitting guard outside as usual but he was gone.

Evelyn laughed nervously. 'Jasus, no. I'm a sort of ex-mother-in-law.'

She saw the confusion on his face and flapped a hand at him. 'Take no notice of me. Me mouth runs away like a drunk with a Giro!'

He was still smiling, but she noticed he didn't offer his name in return.

'I am Evelyn, Kate's mother,' she explained. 'Kate is Patrick's girlfriend, or partner as they say these days. Though meself I thought you only had partners in a business. Then, I suppose a lot of marriages *are* businesses these days, eh?'

He nodded, looking perplexed, and then glanced back at Patrick. Evelyn watched as he stared down intently at the figure in the bed.

'He is much better now?'

She nodded. 'Well, he seems over the worst but we have to wait and see how he reacts to the operation. He had a blood clot removed from his brain, you see. He's having another CT scan in the morning, if he doesn't come out of his coma, and they'll know more then.'

The visitor was silent as he contemplated the man on the bed. He looked at all the tubes and the drips, eyes lingering on the catheter bag that hung down by the bedside. The sight made him avert his eyes as if he had been burned.

'But he seems to be doing well? They think he will regain his strength?'

Once more Evelyn shrugged. 'He's like all of us, son. In the hands of God Himself. Only He can decide our fate in the end.'

He nodded agreement then, bowing slightly, he said courteously, 'Thank you for the information. If he awakes tell him his Russian friend visited him.'

He went to walk from the room and Evelyn pulled his arm gently. 'Shall I give him a name, son?'

He shook his head and bowed once more. Jasus but he was attractive, she found herself thinking.

'He will understand my message.'

Evelyn watched as every nurse, male or female, followed his progress from the ward. She herself stood and stared until he passed through the large double doors. Then she glanced at the bed.

Whoever that was, he was almost certainly on a par with Patrick Kelly. She could tell just by looking at him that he was not a man to cross; she felt that unlike Patrick, the visitor's natural authority wasn't tempered by an innate kindness. In fact, for all his courtesy to her she'd known instinctively that he would have slit her throat without a second's pause if she had somehow got in his way.

Evelyn was thoughtful as she sat down and waited for something to happen – disconcerted without fully understanding why. When Everton wandered back to his chair outside the door, she wondered if she should mention the man's visit. But she had a feeling he already knew about it. Though why she thought this she didn't have a clue.

Patrick had been gunned down in the street in broad daylight, yet Kate had not mentioned whether anyone was to be arrested for it, or if they had any idea who had done it. In fact, the more Evelyn thought about it, the stranger it seemed.

With hindsight she wondered if her daughter knew who had shot him. And if so, why had she done nothing about it?

Curious now, Evelyn settled herself back in her chair. She would get to the bottom of it all, let no one be in any doubt of that. Kate owed her a few explanations and once she thought the time was right her mother was going to insist on hearing each and every one of them.

Suzy was a busy girl. In fact, she hadn't had two minutes to herself since leaving the police station. Aware that she might be followed, she made her way cautiously to London where she went to see her old friend and confidant Lucas Browning.

Once inside his flat she finally relaxed.

He was sympathetic about her arrest and laughed with glee when she told him about her speedy release.

'Good,' he beamed. 'I told you I had friends in high places, didn't I?'

Suzy was smiling like a Cheshire cat, so pleased with herself she was practically preening. In fact, for the first time in her life, she felt indestructible. It was a heady feeling. She had always known they enjoyed a level of protection, but the fact that it extended so far and in the face of such serious charges amazed and excited her. She was literally untouchable and she gloried in it.

'So who did you use to get me a tug out of there?'

Lucas shook his head reprovingly. 'Never you fucking mind. You'll mouth it all over the place if I tell you.'

She grinned. 'Really? Do I know them then?'

He laughed loudly at that, throwing his head back and wheezing, 'Everyone bleeding well knows him!' Lucas wiped at his streaming eyes. 'At least, anyone who's anyone knows him. But for all that he's a touch and I'm grateful for that.'

'Ain't we all!'

They both celebrated their good fortune. Then Lucas remarked in a low voice, 'I heard about Sharon Pallister. One of yours, wasn't she?'

Suzy wasn't laughing now. In fact she was annoyed. 'How did you know that?'

He smirked. 'I get to know everything, Suze – remember? That's what gives me the edge.'

'Well, fuck you and your edge! I have no idea who topped her. I reckon she might have been on the rough trade a bit, I wouldn't put it past her. She was always after money. Honest, she'd be at me daily to try and earn a bit more and, I mean, I pay well, Lucas. You have to for what I expect for my clients. But it was never enough for Sharon, yet she weren't on drugs, I'd take oath on that. No bloke that I knew of either so it was a bit of a mystery. Now she's brown bread no one will ever know the score, I suppose.'

'Is all your stuff safe? I mean, they might still seize it. We can't stop them doing that.'

'Don't worry. It's well hidden,' she teased him. 'Right under their noses, in fact.' Then she laughed uproariously again. 'One of me clients is Old Bill. He keeps it locked in the evidence room for me. He can make it appear or disappear. Whatever I want, he does. For a price, of course.'

'If only they knew . . .'

She lit a cigarette and coughed herself red in the face.

'I must give these fuckers up, Luke. They'll be the death of me.'

'Have you any idea where Sharon's little boy is?'

Suzy looked at him askance and said nastily, 'What is this? The fucking third degree?'

Lucas sighed as if she was boring him. 'I just want to know, is the boy off with anyone you deal with?'

Suzy sighed dramatically. Her voice was heavy with annoyance as she said, 'Not that I know of and that's the God's honest truth. Sharon was a weirdo even by our standards. She was up for anything. Christ knows where the kid is.'

She puffed on her cigarette and thought for a few seconds. 'Whoever killed her stabbed her over and over. They was well upset. I can only assume they took the bleeding kid. Little fucker he was and all. Mouthy little git! All noise and aggression. But, like his mother, he would do anything for a chunky Mars bar and a can of Coke.'

Lucas relaxed back in his chair.

'I think it's strange, that's all. I've been thinking . . . I mean, all the girls who've been nicked have worked for you over the last year or so, right?'

She nodded, frowning now.

'All the women were from your estate basically or nearby. Yet you, it seems, have no idea who could have started off all this crap – which, I might add, brought the filth to your door. I didn't realise just how deep it was till you asked me to come in with you and I agreed to do some merchandising. But I did a little digging on me own – as I said earlier, I like to know what's going on – and I found out that you were less than honest with me, weren't you? Only you let me think that everything was hunky-dory when it fucking well wasn't. You must have known the filth would start sniffing round at some point.'

Suzy was getting annoyed and swallowed her temper with difficulty.

'Have I ever got you a capture yet?'

He didn't answer her, just stared at her lazily.

'Well, you fat bastard, have I?'

'That ain't the point, Suze, and you know it. I certainly don't want one, thank you very much. Now I got you out the shit today, but if this keeps on and child abduction or murder comes into it, I can't guarantee you my continued assistance. It'd be out of my hands. The papers are all over this like a fucking cheap suit, and my contact is getting worried. He did us a right favour then he finds out that the girl he put a word in for, put his neck on the line for, is maybe not just into noncing, a pastime he rather enjoys himself, but is also a contender for the big M. And of some kids, if you don't mind. Kids, incidentally, who are caught up in a big abuse enquiry. So, Suzy love, you tell me all you know and you tell me now, dear heart, before I get upset. If I have put meself out to distribute videos and pictures of dead kids I'll break your fucking neck.'

'Well, it wouldn't be the first time, would it, Lucas?'

He looked at her with his cold eyes and all at once Suzy had trouble meeting his gaze. When he was like this he was dangerous, she knew that better than anyone. He drew you in with his jokes and his camaraderie, but she knew he could kill her without a second's pause if he needed to.

'It would be the first time I did it knowingly, love, that's the difference. The films from Rumania and Amsterdam were already well in circulation before I started shunting them out. Plus, I only provide the fuckers to the distributor, I don't even watch them. Young girls are one thing, but kids are different. And anything to do with kids brings out the worst in everyone, ain't you noticed that yet? I have judges I supply with everything from fucking drugs to boys and trannies, but they keep well away from little kids. Do you get my fucking drift? The man I asked for the favour today needs my assurance that you are sound and I mean to give him the truth, Suze. For all our sakes, yours included.'

She was seriously frightened now.

'You see, Suze, I have no morals. But I get them when my boatrace might be put in the frame, see. So now I am looking at the situation from a different standpoint. I am seeing it as others see it. Others who are not as enlightened as us. Now if you have half a brain in that head of yours you would start seeing things from *my* point of view. Dead kids cause hag and you are up to your neck.'

His sarcasm was not lost on her.

'So, if you know anything about the kids, you should share it with me. I might be able to make some sense of it all and prevent a catastrophe.'

'I promise you, I have no idea what happened to them kids. I swear it on me mother's grave.'

Lucas sniggered. 'Your mother is alive and well and playing bingo in Bournemouth.'

Suzy grinned mischievously. 'Same difference. Might as well be fucking dead.'

'Same as her daughter will be if she tucks me up, eh?'

Suzy raised her glass defiantly. 'Up yours and all, mate.'

'This is fucking ludicrous! Where the hell can the child have gone?'

Kate didn't answer.

'Jesus, in all my years in this job I have never come across anything even remotely like this,' sighed Jenny. 'It's just too weird. I mean, we have all these women who have tried to kill their kids, then we have a woman murdered and her kid missing. We find a child on a rubbish tip – a fucking rubbish tip! – and his mother dead at home, OD'd. Now I am thinking, did she OD or did someone, somewhere, help her along? Because either we are dealing with child abusers who murder their kids or we have a murderer out there who targets women and children who are abusers or abused. Fucking Freud would be hard pushed to make sense of this lot.'

Kate stubbed out yet another cigarette and pushed open the window to let some air into the office.

'Suzy is the answer to all this, we both know that, Jen. She could lead us to Barker.'

Her friend nodded. Her usually cheerful countenance was disconsolate and she looked deathly white. Her eyes were ringed with black and her mouth curved down continually. At her best she wasn't a beautiful woman but this last week she had begun to look haggard.

'But how can we get to her if we've been warned off?' the big woman fretted. 'I mean, if it was a Home Office call then we're talking big league here. Seriously big. And whoever gave the nod, considering the severity of the offence they must be pretty bloody sure of themselves to go out on a limb for her.'

Kate smiled smugly. 'I know who the call came from, Jenny. It was from Jeffrey Cavendish.'

Jenny sat down in amazement, her mouth a small O of disbelief. 'Are you sure?'

'Sure as I can be,' Kate said. 'Golding got a printout of calls made to Ratchet. Cavendish rang him ten minutes before he called me in to warn me off. Why else would Cavendish contact anyone in Grantley?'

Jenny looked out of the window at the car park and sighed inwardly as she saw Natasha's solicitor arriving accompanied by Robert Bateman.

'But he's the big wig there at the DPP,' she objected. 'He wouldn't lay all that on the line for a trollop like Suzy Harrington, surely? There must be someone else involved, someone in on this with her. She can't have *that* much clout. Anyway, from what I've heard, when she was told she was out she was as shocked as we were. No, there's more here than meets the eye, Katie, but what the fuck it is I don't know.'

'Someone knows, Jen. We just have to suss out who that might be. Golding has offered to keep the beady on her if we give the say-so. He's been following her since she left here. I'm waiting to hear from him, but he's not ringing here. We decided it was too dangerous. Who knows if we are being listened to? Plus the calls are taped routinely these days.'

She stretched. 'How I miss the old days without all this blasted technology to fuck everything up.'

'Tell me about it. Now for more bad news. Tash's solicitor just arrived with that Bateman. I suppose we'd better go and give them a welcome committee.'

Kate stood up. 'I want to get to the hospital today, Jen. If it's OK with you, I'm going to shoot off about five.'

'Go whenever you want,' Jenny told her. 'I can deal with things here.'

'There's loads of food in the freezer, you know what my mum's like.'

'I think she's great. Here, this'll make you laugh. She told me that she'd just read this article in Reader's Digest about a Greek island where all the lesbos go.'

Kate smiled and groaned. 'She means well.'

Jenny was chuckling. 'I know that, mate. I think

she's priceless. Her age and religion make it hard for her to understand me and my lifestyle and I respect that. But she did make me laugh, I don't know how I kept a straight face.'

They were both smiling as they walked from the office to the interview room. As they passed through the main reception area Kate saw Robert Bateman and found herself smiling even more widely.

He was dressed in a bright pink shirt and lime green trousers. Over the shirt he had a red and yellow cardigan, and wore brown cowboy boots with the ensemble. He looked like a refugee from a circus. He waved at her, wiggling his fingers and smiling widely. He'd had his hair dyed recently and it was now a nut-brown colour that made him look like Barbie's boyfriend Ken's father.

'Hello, Robert. Have you come to see Natasha?'

He nodded. 'Oh, she makes me so angry, that girl. But I never could refuse a damsel in distress. Even if the distress was of their own making.'

As she walked him through the door to the interview room, Kate said in friendly fashion, 'Some of the case-notes you gave me were incomplete. Was that deliberate?'

He stopped and looked at her shrewdly. 'Clever girl, how did you know?'

'Call it an inspired guess. Just a feeling, really. Why did you do that?'

'None of it was relevant to the case in question . . .'

Kate interrupted him. 'Why don't you let me be the judge of that, Mr Bateman? If it pertains to lifestyles

443

or friendships, appropriate or otherwise, then it is of interest to me.'

He rolled his eyes. 'I apologise and I'll make sure you have the relevant information as soon as possible. But it was only stuff we had discussed, things they had done. Nothing that would interest you. Really.'

Kate held the door open for him and ushered him into the interview room with her usual politeness.

'As I said, Mr Bateman, let me be the judge of that.'

'Natasha isn't the one you want, Miss Burrows. I think the big fish have slipped the net. At least, that's what I hear on the grapevine anyway. Tash has lost her kids, she'll go down no doubt about it, but the real villains will walk away scot free as usual.'

'You sound very sure about that.'

He sighed. 'I am. I've watched this stuff go on for years, dear, and time after time I see little people like Tash go away while the king pins carry on doing what they do, day after day. It's how things are. I accept it because I can do nothing about it. But it doesn't mean I like it, dear, does it?'

Kate got the distinct impression he was trying to tell her something, but what it was she couldn't for the life of her work out.

'I wish you'd level with me,' she told him.

'Not here, dear. I couldn't talk here.'

'Where would you?'

'Ring me at home tonight. I'm in the book.'

Kate couldn't answer him as Jenny and the brief came into the room together just then.

'Did you get signed in all right?' she asked the lawyer, who nodded.

After the preliminaries, Kate left Jenny to start the official questioning. Her own mind was working overtime.

Evelyn saw a strange woman walk into the ICU and glance about her. She stood up to greet the figure in the black suit and dangling earrings.

'Can I help you, love?' she asked pleasantly.

She could see Violet and Grace coming up the ward out of the corner of her eye and was grateful. This woman did not look too happy. As she stood by Patrick's bed and stared down at him Evelyn had the strangest feeling that he was in danger again, and when Everton came into the room she was relieved.

The visitor was stocky, well-made, and looked fit to burst. Suddenly she pursed her lips and spat into Patrick's sleeping face.

'Here, what the fuck you think you're doing?' Grace's voice was harsh.

The woman turned on her. 'Murdering bastard! My Tommy's gone. He's on the missing list and, believe me, he wouldn't fucking dare do that to me. I heard a whisper on the street this cunt had him topped and I came to see him get his just deserts.'

Her voice was breaking with emotion.

'Now my kids are fatherless and I am without a breadwinner. You'd better hope he don't wake up, lady, because if he does I'll swing for him.'

She pushed Grace forcibly in the chest to get her to stand aside.

'I can't even bury my Tommy, don't know where he is. He could be anywhere: holding up a fucking motorway or slipped in East London crematorium with a legal stiff. I can't mourn him, can I? I just have to go through the rest of me days wondering if he was tortured or frightened or scared. Did he call my name or the kids' before he was topped . . .'

She wiped her streaming eyes with taloned hands, the long nails stained crimson to match her lipstick.

'You tell Kelly I'll have him. I will have that ponce. My memory is long, and I won't forget he robbed my kids of their father. You tell him I want me comp and all. I have school fees to pay and a house to keep up. You tell him he owes me. Big time.'

She stumbled from the room on her impossibly high heels, grasping at the door for support. They were all left in shock. Violet made as if to follow her but Grace grabbed her sister's arm.

'Leave her, Vi. Let her get it out of her system.'

Pondering what she had seen and heard, Evelyn sat back down. Suddenly she felt very old and very stupid. *Was* Patrick a murderer? And was her daughter aware of that fact? And torture – in this day and age?

She knew Patrick was not one hundred per cent kosher, but a murderer?

Violet was voicing these thoughts, too, and Grace hissed angrily: 'Don't talk out your arse, Vi! 'Course he ain't done nothing wrong. Her old man's probably gone on the trot. It happens. Imagine listening to the ravings of a deranged trollop like her. Compensation my eye! When he's back on his feet Pat'll laugh at this little escapade, you mark my words.'

Neither Evelyn nor Violet answered her. Their silence spoke volumes.

Willy was in his element. He had battered Jacky to within an inch of his life and was now happily eating the last of his sandwiches and drinking his tea.

No one had been near or by them. It seemed the Russians were leaving him to get on with whatever he wanted. If they topped him afterwards, he didn't care any more. He was paying those two bastards back for everything that had happened to him and Patrick.

Joey, huddled on the floor, was trying his hardest to turn round so he could look Willy in the face. He hoped to talk him round. It was a long shot but he still had a few cards up his sleeve.

Now Jacky was out of the ball game he was hoping to save himself. If he could sweet-talk Willy, there was always the chance he could persuade the Russians to go easy as well. He had always been an optimist.

Joey heaved himself round and as he finally made it on to his left-hand side, Willy's foot hit him square in the chin. Joey's mouth filled with blood. It was acrid, tangy, and then everything went black. The last thing he heard was Willy's laughter.

Kate was on her way to the hospital when she realised that she was passing Robert Bateman's house. It was after 8 p.m. and she was late, but part of her dreaded each visit to the hospital and what it might bring. When she saw the turning for Bateman's street she drove into it, crawling along until she found his number. She parked her car and locked it while observing his home.

It was a large detached house in an area that had once been select but was now rundown. Most of the houses were converted into flats. The others all seemed to be up for sale. But Robert's home, though dilapidated, had a well-kept garden, not concrete off-street parking like the other houses, and there was a warm glow coming from behind the curtains.

Kate rang the bell and waited. She heard him call out, 'Who is it?'

His voice sounded querulous and she wondered if she had come at a bad time.

'It's me, Kate Burrows. I hope I'm not intruding. I was just passing . . .'

His voice changed to its usual high-pitched cackle. 'Hang on, dear, let me get decent!'

She found herself grinning. He was a case. Five minutes later he opened the door, a wide smile on his face.

'Come in, come in.'

She followed him through a bright yellow hallway into a lounge with walls painted burnt orange. It was like being in a kid's painting. Everything was so bright, the sofa sky blue and the skirting board a deep red. It smelt gorgeous.

She saw him looking at her. He was smiling indulgently.

'I like a bit of colour,' he explained. 'Christ knows, this world is bloody boring enough.'

Kate thought he had a point.

'So it seems at times,' she agreed. 'This is vivid, but it works.'

He seemed pleased. 'It's because it's all so modern-looking. That's the secret. Modern furniture can take colour. The older style can't.'

Kate heard his computer buzzing and said, 'Have I interrupted you?'

He was busy shutting it down and shook his head.

'Glad you came. I work too much, really. I am a sad bastard when all is said and done. Can I get you a coffee?'

She shook her head. 'I can't stay too long, I'm on my way to the hospital.'

He nodded his head sympathetically. 'So I heard. Is your chap any better at all?'

Kate was surprised by his knowledge but just shrugged it off. She knew how gossip spread around the station and Robert Bateman seemed to know everyone.

He must have read her mind, for he said in a friendly way, 'It was the desk sergeant, Camilla Holder. She can't resist a chat if you know what I mean. And be fair, dear.' He rolled his eyes in mock horror. 'She's fifteen stone and with that nose, my God, she gives new meaning to the word drab! No wonder she gossips, eh?'

Kate put her head back and laughed aloud. He was priceless.

Robert put his hand gently on her arm.

'You're a nice woman, Kate. Sit down and have a quick G&T. One won't kill you.'

He was already at a large Art Deco cabinet, taking down glasses and mixing the drinks. Kate watched him. He was camp as a row of tents and yet he had an air of assurance that was wholly masculine. As he passed her the drink he smiled and his even teeth and fresh complexion made him look almost handsome.

He grinned at her. 'Drink up, love. A slug of alcohol never did anyone any harm. Though of course you didn't hear it from me. Most of my clients think that life is unbearably boring unless they have a bottle of vodka, fifteen joints and a few sniffs of the okey-doke nightly!'

Kate laughed again, aware that he was studying her closely. She took a gulp of her drink.

'Down the hatch!' Robert encouraged her.

A loud crash from upstairs interrupted their jollity. Robert seemed unperturbed by it.

'It's me father, he's bedridden. Won't be a sec.'

He hurried out and Kate sat down again. The crash had made her jump out of her seat, heart beating like the clappers with shock. She took a few deep breaths to steady herself. Five minutes later Robert was back in the room.

'He has senile dementia. I have looked after him for the last nine years. I have a woman during the day.' He chuckled at this. 'To look after me father, of course!'

'It must be difficult, Mr Bateman.'

He rolled his eyes. 'It is, dear, believe me. It's like living with a stranger.'

Kate didn't know what to say. Another thump from above brought him to his feet again. Placing her glass on the small table by her side, Kate stood up.

'Look, I'll let you get on. Have you the missing paperwork from the files?'

'I'll get it all to you tomorrow, OK? Can you see yourself out?'

He sounded distracted, looked harassed now and drained. Kate felt an enormous liking for this dutiful son and pity for his plight.

'Of course, Mr Bateman.'

'Oh, for Christ's sake, would you call me Rob? I feel like an elderly neighbour when you call me Mr Bateman!' Then he rushed upstairs.

Kate placed her glass in the kitchen sink and glanced around her at the chaos of someone else's life. As she walked through the hall on her way to the front door she could hear him talking loudly, as if speaking to a child, and her heart went out to him. She shut the door behind her, thanking God her mother was still hale and hearty at seventy years old.

It occurred to her that, like Robert Bateman, she might one day be left with someone completely dependent on her. It was a sobering thought.

Chapter Twenty-One

Bernice was pretty in a childish way. At twenty-one she looked about fifteen and she knew it. As the man approached her she grinned coquettishly. For a split second she thought she had a punter, a live one, which would have been handy for her. She had had a shit shift that day. But she recognised this man and he never paid for sex. Arm in arm, they walked along the darkened road.

Inside her flat she pulled off her coat and put on the kettle. As she made the coffee she lit a small half joint, bemoaning the fact that she had no puff left. Lately there'd been a dearth of good grass, and all she could get was poor quality solid. Bernice was a grass smoker, preferred its lift to the stoned nonchalance of black.

Pouring a hefty measure of vodka into her coffee, she carried the two mugs back into the lounge. Her friend was sitting on the sofa with her little boy on his lap. He was telling him a story and as she watched the tableau she felt a moment's sorrow that her son had never had a father figure to look up to.

She wished she had had one herself. Her mother said once that her father was a nice man with nice eyes, but she was fucked if she could remember his name. All her numerous brothers and sisters had different fathers so it didn't matter too much. At least that is what she had told herself all her life.

She was still speeding and she hoped the joint would bring her back down; if it didn't, she would have to ask a neighbour for a couple of Valium.

'Good night's work?'

She shook her head. 'Nothing spectacular, a couple of wanks. The parlour is shit these days. I'm thinking of going up the City. Suzy reckons I could earn much more and work less hours. All the City gents are after a quick flash before they go home to the legal. I don't know though, the travelling is the pain, ain't it?'

The man nodded in sympathy. Then: 'Don't you ever tidy up? Shall I phone the council and get them to drop off a skip?'

She laughed uproariously at his wit. 'It is a bit of a shit hole, ain't it? But I can't be bothered with it any more.' She ran her hands through her cropped hair. 'Mind you, I never could be bothered, could I?'

The man laughed with her. 'Bet you was a slut even when you were a girl, weren't you?' Now his voice was cold, hard.

The girl looked at him in complete outrage. The last thing she needed tonight was this visitor jumping on his high horse.

'How dare you? If you just want to give me a hard time then you can piss off. I can get that fucking anywhere.' She was hurting and it showed. Her tiny heart-shaped face wore a frown, making her look her age for once. Her eyes, a deep brown, were full of anger.

She looked at the man before her and said contemptuously, 'What is it with you lately? One minute you're all sweetness and light and the next you're a right arsehole. Well, listen to me, mate, I don't fucking need this shit from you or anyone else.'

She was standing now. Her short skirt had ridden up and exposed her pale thighs. By the harsh light of the naked bulb the cellulite was glaringly visible. Her high heels were worn down at the sides so she rolled her ankles to compensate and her tiny breasts were quivering with annoyance under a bright orange crop top.

'You're no different from the punters, mate. You think you know it all, just like them. Well, you bleeding well don't. I know what you want – a blow job. That's what you always want. Well, you can piss off. The freebies stop here.'

She was angry.

A night of strange men demanding outlandish favours and arguing over payment had taken its toll. The speed had made her paranoid and she had argued with another of the girls, coming off worst to the amusement of the onlookers. It had rankled. Tina was only seventeen and already a loud-mouthed slut who had gradually taken over as the wit of the massage parlour, a position that had been Bernice's until recently. She was not a happy bunny and hearing her degradation exposed by the man sitting opposite her was the last straw.

'I mean, what makes you think you're so great anyway?'

She was glaring at him, her eyes deep pools of annoyance and uncertainty. Her son was cuddling into the man, obviously frightened of her, and somewhere in her drug-crazed brain she knew she was over-reacting. Going too far. She should be used to abuse by now. The punters handed out enough, God knows.

Picking up her son, Mikey, she tried to comfort him. As she held him close and whispered soothing words in his ear he pushed her away, his strong little hands making her aware in no uncertain terms that he wanted nothing to do with her.

Which only induced more anger in her already muddled brain. She dropped him unceremoniously on to the chair she had just vacated.

'You little fucker!'

The man was grinning at her.

'Temper, temper, Bernice. You left him alone this evening as usual. Now all he needs is for you to have one of your tantrums.'

The child was staring at her with a mixture of fear and undisguised dislike. She was so wasted from the drugs and the drink and the nagging sense of failure that had dogged her young life that she felt a sudden urge to kill him.

It was irrational, she knew, but everything was too much for her lately. Her job was getting her down, no one to tell her what to do or praise her when she did something right. Although, as she reasoned in her darker moments, how often did *that* happen? She was too busy earning enough to keep herself so out of it she had to ask what day it was.

Bernice suddenly felt an overwhelming need to cry. Everything about her life was crap, complete crap, and now someone she'd regarded as a friend was telling her so to her face. Telling her something she tried to hide from herself with yet more drink and drugs.

Mikey was walking to his bedroom, his little body in its Postman Pat pyjamas looking so small and vulnerable she wanted to pick him up and comfort him. But she knew it was too late for that. At three years old he had well and truly sussed her out. Everyone did eventually, why should Mikey be any different?

'Out, you. I want you out now.'

The man was lounging back on her sofa, long legs stretched out in front of him, seemingly quite at ease. Then he stood up and put out one big hand to ruffle her hair.

'Calm yourself down, girl, I was only joking. Winding you up.'

She smiled uncertainly. Hoping it was true. He was the only friend she had.

'You are a cunt!' she said, almost affectionately.

When the knife slid into her belly she thought at first she had been bitten by something. It was only when he repeated the action that she realised he had stabbed her. She dropped to her knees, her face a picture of shock. She pressed her hands over the wounds and watched the deep red blood running through her fingers.

He looked down at her, his face blank.

'I never really liked you, Bernice. Why would I? You are a fucking whore, like all the others. I only befriended you so I could observe you at close quarters. Marvel at the inborn ignorance that put you on the game. I knew I would do something to you at some point, but I wasn't sure when. That's always the hard one, don't you think? *When* should you do something? When will you get the appropriate response to your carefully thought out actions?'

She was doubled over in pain as he brought the knife down again, this time between her shoulder blades. She slumped forward and he knew she was dead.

He sat and stared at her for a few moments. Then he wiped his hands across his face as if he had just woken from a short nap and started to weep. It was a cold, lonely sound.

Mikey could hear it as he watched late-night erotica on the colour portable in his bedroom.

He ignored it.

His mother cried all the time; it was a safe sound to him – it meant that someone was in for a change.

That he wasn't alone.

Kate was alone with Patrick, who looked better. His face seemed to have some colour in it and as he lay there he looked so heart-wrenchingly handsome it took all her will-power not to kiss him over and over.

How many times had she watched him sleep? Especially when they were first together. She had never quite been able to believe that she had captured such a prime specimen of manhood.

He had reached her on every level, and that had been frightening at first because after Dan she had sworn never to let herself go again. Always to keep a small part of herself back. With Patrick that had been an impossibility. Murderer, whoremaster, she didn't care. She could forgive him anything.

Was that how his Renée had felt about him? It must have been, Kate decided. He had been faithful to them both in turn, she was as sure of that as she was of her own name. He had been lucky enough to find two loves in his lifetime.

She only hoped that lifetime wasn't over.

A noise outside caused her to look quickly towards the doorway. Her mother had told her of the strange man's visit and it had bothered her. But she consoled herself with the fact that if Boris had intended any harm, he had had ample opportunity to inflict it and hadn't done so. She would go and see him at the first opportunity, Kate decided. See if they couldn't sort something out.

She had had a call from Jenny saying that an old friend had told her that Patrick was going to be charged with Tommy Broughton's murder if he regained consciousness. But Kate had guessed that one for herself.

She shuffled in her seat, trying to get comfortable.

She had been sitting by the bed for over three hours
and now it was coming up to midnight she knew that
she should make a move.

But she couldn't. After putting off the visit, now
she was here beside him it was like being asked to
leave a newborn child with strangers. She just couldn't
bring herself to do it.

She pressed her lips to his fingers and was
astounded to feel him grip her hand. She nearly
snatched it away in fright. Then, looking at his face,
she saw that his eyes were open. Patrick was staring at
her but it was a blank stare.

He closed his eyes again and made a guttural
sound in his throat. For a second she wasn't sure if
she had imagined it. Had wanted it so badly she had
hallucinated it.

Now he was quiet again, his eyes closed and his
breathing regular. Kate pressed the buzzer to call a
nurse. She was praying that he was on the mend.
Somewhere at the back of her mind she knew she was
here for the night now. She couldn't go home and
leave him after this.

She slipped off her shoes and settled herself more
comfortably in the chair. If he did come out of it all,
she would more than likely have to visit him on
remand until he was sentenced on a murder charge.
That's if they could make it stick. She had already lied
for him once. She wondered what they would make of
her part in it all. She would lie again, on oath if
necessary, she knew that as well as she knew her own
name.

She would protect him as he would have protected her in the same situation.

As a nurse came into the room Kate stood up to greet her, an uncertain smile on her face. 'I think he squeezed my hand.'

The nurse nodded and went to adjust a machine by his bed.

'Don't get too excited,' she said quietly. 'It could just be reflex.'

Kate nodded, but inside she was already convincing herself he was on the mend. Willing him to wake up and recognise her.

If the power of thought was as strong as it was reputed to be, then Patrick Kelly would be up and about in no time.

Jacky and Joey were on their last legs. Willy knew that and the fact didn't bother him one iota. As far as he was concerned, he was just paying them back. Not for himself but for Patrick.

When Boris came into the cellar Willy was scared, but didn't show it in any way. He was expecting to be finished off and was hoping they would do it cleanly. He'd had plenty of time to think over the last few weeks, and he regretted only one thing. He should have got himself a woman sooner than this and had a few kids. It was what male and female were put on this earth for: to procreate. To make children and give them the best that life could offer. Not necessarily money or worldly things but a lust for life coupled with a sense of decency. Of wanting to live as one with the rest of the world.

If he had not taken the path he had chosen, he would not have ended up in a cold cellar, tortured, beaten and waiting to die. Praying it would be quick.

It was a waste though. All those years he had been grateful to Patrick Kelly for giving him part of his life, allowing him to share his daughter, when Willy should have had a daughter of his own. Should have had someone else to care for, to work for. To cherish. How many times had Patrick told him to get himself a decent bird over the years? To go out and get a real life.

Willy was disappointed in himself.

If they topped him now at least he would die in the knowledge that life was of your own making. People only did to you what you let them do. How many times had his mother said that to him as a kid? Too many. In the end he had exasperated her with his lifestyle and his wild ways. But it had taken all this to make him see what had been staring him in the face since he was a boy.

Everyone needed someone.

Shyness with women had always been his downfall. Now he had someone, and he loved her. Maureen was a sort, bless her. But she was a good sort and at the end of the day what did it matter what she had done in the past? It was the past that made you the person you were now. Maureen had been round the turf more times than Red Rum, but that was her prerogative. She was grown up and had lived by her own lights. She had had a few knocks, was battered round the edges, but she had genuinely cared for Willy and he had felt cared for.

Had felt wanted.

For once in his life he had been half of a couple and it had felt good. He had been comfortable with Maureen. Liked her conversation, even her irascible temper. She had made him laugh, really laugh, and he had enjoyed that.

Now that he had finally sussed out what it was all about, Boris was standing in front of him with a gun and a smile. Willy decided to take whatever came with good grace. There wasn't much else he could do.

'You did well, Mr Gabney.'

Willy didn't answer him. He could feel the cold now, it was seeping into his bones. He wasn't sure if it was fear or the dampness of the cellar.

'So Mr Kelly was innocent all along – but he was losing his edge. Once that goes, vultures like our two friends here are quick to take advantage.'

Willy shrugged. 'Pat trusted Tommy. Had no reason not to.'

Boris nodded. 'I suppose not. I am sorry for the attempt on his life – I am sure he will understand it was just business. He would have done the same in my shoes.'

'If Patrick had ordered a contract it would have been carried out properly, you can take that as gospel. He never suffered fools gladly and there'd have been no half measures with an order of his.'

Boris smiled at the far from subtle put-down. He was not insulted, merely amused. Old-style villains like Gabney were dying out. The real money nowadays was in drugs and the older faces tended to steer clear of that fiercely competitive market. The Russians were not so choosy.

Boris jerked his head at the two men on the floor. 'Why didn't you kill them?'

Willy shrugged. 'To be honest, mate, I couldn't be arsed. They're your prisoners, like I am. I think the ball is in your court at the moment, don't you?'

Boris squatted down and placed the gun by the side of Jacky's head. He pulled the trigger. Brains and blood showered over Joey who had opened his eyes and was now in a state of catatonic shock as he looked into Boris's calm smiling face. After a few seconds he shot Joey, too.

He threw the gun on to the Z-bed and adjusted the immaculate lines of his Armani suit.

'Can we drop you off anywhere, Mr Gabney, or would you prefer us to call you a cab?'

Benjamin Boarder was outside the hospital. He had been watching Kate since Jacky and Joey's abduction. He knew who had them and he also knew that the chances were, Boris the Russian would be back at some point.

Benjamin owed everything he had to Patrick Kelly, who had given him his first few quid to start up a debt-collecting operation. He had been nineteen years old then and full of bravado and pride. Patrick had liked him, and after an introduction by a known face, had given him five grand to buy a debt. Benjamin had collected it from a well-known Welsh dog breeder and lunatic and his reputation had been set.

He had met his wife, a tiny redhead with a quirky sense of humour, in a night club when he was bouncing to earn extra money. She had been a virgin, which had been a shock in itself. Another shock was her family's ready acceptance of this large half-caste man who obviously adored their daughter Chantel.

Seven children later he had never looked at another woman and didn't want to. He still wanted to touch her every second of the day, still found her exciting. Before Chantel he shagged anything that moved and was remotely fuckable. Since Chantel other women had ceased to exist for him.

He had seven fabulous kids and a blinding house, a big car and plenty of money – if not in the bank at least in holdalls hidden throughout the South East. He had left a letter for Chantel telling her where all the money was hidden in case it went pear-shaped.

He owed it all to Patrick Kelly and was willing to put his life on the line to repay that debt.

So he watched the hospital, and tried in his own way to take care of Kate Burrows. It was all he could do for Patrick Kelly.

He hoped it would be enough.

Suzy was out of her brains, blazing with drug-induced camaraderie. When she heard the ring of her doorbell she stumbled out to answer it, giggling. The man at the door looked familiar. She screwed up her eyes and finally recognised him.

'Hello. Long time no see.' She pulled the door

open and the man walked inside.

'You look well, Suze.'

She grinned at him. 'I am out of me fucking nut, mate.'

He laughed with her. 'Tell me something I don't know!'

He followed her into her spotlessly clean lounge. Even drugged out of her brains Suzy managed to keep everything tidy. It was a kink in her nature that came from being brought up like an animal and rebelling against it at an early age.

Suzy had no qualms of any kind; she would do anything for monetary gain, but she hated dirt and squalor. They had played a major role in her childhood and she had learned early on that you could be as scummy as you liked so long as you didn't look it. Provided you dressed right and drove the right car, the majority would accept you at face value. It was one of the most useful lessons of her short childhood.

She liked to see people's faces when they came into her home, enjoyed the admiration and envy of the less well-off. Nowadays, of course, it was an advert for how much she earned and that made the girls and women she dealt with more convinced than ever that they were on to a winner with Suzy.

Now a blast from the past had called on her and such was her drug-fuelled confidence that she didn't find it strange that a man she had not seen for years should track her down and come calling unannounced.

'Want a drink?'

He nodded. 'The usual, Suze. I assume you remember what that was?'

She laughed girlishly. ''Course I do. Sit down and make yourself comfortable. Fuck me, I was just thinking about you not two days ago.' She poured him a large brandy. 'Ain't that weird?'

He took the brandy and sipped it. 'As long as you weren't *talking* about me, Suze.'

She sat down and crossed her skinny legs. 'Why should I do that?' She sounded genuinely interested.

The man shrugged inside his crumpled C&A suit. 'Well, you was nearly in the shit, wasn't you, Suze? I heard a little whisper that you were nearly banged up on a lifer. Scary prospect that. Grass up your own granny you would if that was an option, eh?'

Suzy was annoyed. 'Listen, Barker, I know how to keep me trap shut. Fuck knows I ought to after all these years. And, with respect, if I had wanted to toss you off at any time I had ample opportunity over the years, didn't I?'

The man sipped his drink.

'I have been here tonight sorting out old business, Suze. Now you can tell me in minute detail what has been going down here.'

Suzy shrugged. 'Where do you want me to start?'

'From the beginning – but first, Suzy, I need to know why you went to Lucas. Why didn't you come to me? Were you hoping I wouldn't find out when you know I used the girls as well? You've muscled in on me, my dear. I gave you a little taste and you abused it. It seems me and you are treading on each other's toes now. You see, Lucas contacted *me* to get *you* out of the shit. So I think you had better understand from the off that I know more than you may think. Plus, you owe me. I had to go as high as the DPP to get you out.'

Suzy sipped her drink. 'I appreciate it.'

Barker laughed gently. 'You are a cunt and no mistaking. First I give you a taster, ask you to do me a favour for old time's sakes. Then you set up your own operation. Now do I look a twat?'

Suzy was scared. 'I was under the impression you were out of it now. None of the girls mentioned you at all.'

He shook his head at the skulduggery of the girl before him.

'Well, they wouldn't, would they? Unlike you they have the sense to be too scared to mention my name or indeed tread on my toes. But people now think you have Old Bill on your side. You have been asked about me by Burrows, I understand.'

'I never said a word, I take oath on that. I wouldn't.' She was pleading with him. 'Why would I, Mr Barker? I ain't stupid. I have been paying off Clive Hamlin from Soho Vice – as you probably know he is a touch. And I also have another Old Bill but it's someone at Grantley.'

'I know. Lucas told me. Now I want to know who that is.'

Suzy took a deep breath. 'I'll tell you anything you want, Mr Barker.'

He relaxed back into the luxurious seat. 'See? Life

can be so easy.' He looked around the flat. 'Looks like you have got yourself *another* partner, doesn't it?'

Suzy nodded. She tried to look pleased.

But she wasn't successful.

Maureen was missing Willy. She had heard a whisper that he was dead. Knew someone had done the dirty on Pat Kelly and that he was fighting for his life in hospital.

Since the news she had gone into a decline. Her hair needed dyeing and styling, her nail varnish was chipped and her face, devoid of make-up, looked old and haggard. In fact, her son Duane was seriously worried about her. In the last few weeks his mum had gone downhill at an alarming rate.

He had even resorted to lying to cheer her up, telling her that his mate's dad had thought she was his sister. Usually something like that would have lifted her spirits for days. Instead Maureen had looked at him with those hollow eyes and said disdainfully, 'You what! Got a white stick and a fucking dog, has he?'

Still he was feeling sorry for her. He knew she had been bounced around by blokes before and he had accepted that. *She* had accepted that. Taken the blow, picked herself up and brushed herself down. Maureen's natural good humour always seemed to cushion the shock. But this time it had been more serious.

Willy had by all accounts been kidnapped. Maureen had explained to her son how they had been having a right nice time at the fight when he had simply disappeared. At first she'd thought he had blanked her, then she'd heard rumours. The circles she mixed in, she got to hear a lot of things. Duane tried to point out that not all of them were true. And she had forcefully asked him what he was trying to say? That she had just been dumped then?

He couldn't win.

He wanted desperately to help her, but he didn't know how. So he brought her cups of tea without her asking and had stayed by her side, forgoing his usual evenings out on the rampage with his mates. He was genuinely worried about her. For the first time ever she wasn't strong and he was scared inside. His mother had always been strong for them all. She had to be. A succession of useless bastards had seen to that much.

He wondered if Willy's body would ever turn up and if it did, what would be her reaction.

Duane, who had until recently taken his mother completely for granted, had finally realised just how much she did for him, just how much he needed her. Loved her even. Silly old bag she was, he hated seeing her so down and lonely.

When the doorbell rang, Maureen didn't move from the settee. She had the TV on and Ricki Lake was ridiculing a bunch of women who had had babies by their sons' friends.

In the old stained and ripped candlewick dressing gown she seemed to live in these days, and with a Superking dangling from her lips, Maureen shouted, 'Get that, Duane. And tell whoever it is to fuck off, I ain't in the mood.'

He sighed heavily and walked to the door.

Two minutes later he watched as his mother's face sagged in shock, seeing Willy standing in the doorway like a bruised and battered ghost. She shot from her seat like a bullet from a gun and hugged him to her as if her life depended on it. Her voice was drenched in tears as she repeated his name over and over again like a mantra.

He finally pushed her away from him and said gruffly, 'Fuck me, girl, you do look rough!'

Maureen wiped the tears from her cheeks and said loudly, 'You ain't looking exactly the dog's knob yourself, mate!'

Duane saw that Willy was in pain and pulled his mother away, helping the big man to the sofa.

'Shall I run you a bath, mate, and get you a bit of scran?'

Willy nodded gratefully. 'That would be a touch, son, thank you.'

Duane went out to the kitchen and put the kettle on, feeling extraordinarily pleased to be doing these mundane tasks for Willy. Just seeing his mum's happy face and hearing her running a brush through her tangled hair was payment enough for him.

Unlike all the others his mum had taken up with over the years, Duane had a feeling Willy Gabney was going to stick around.

Chapter Twenty-Two

Girlie Girls was packed again. Boris looked around him at the women who were paying hard-earned cash to have a young man dance at their table.

One of the bouncers was joking: 'Give me the blokes any time. They have a fight and that's it. But the women . . . they're like animals!'

Boris smiled. He had heard it all before.

As the women squealed with delight at the young men in thongs and baby oil he pushed his way through to the offices. Inside he was greeted by Pascal, Patrick's runner. He was keeping the club ticking over until Kelly could formally agree to sell it to the Russians. Boris had no doubt that Patrick would agree to the sale. After all that had happened he would see that it made good business sense.

Boris knew that everyone was amazed at his taking over the operation but he also knew they would not question him about it. He was too well connected these days.

Pascal was going over the books with his usual

worried expression. It was a look he had perfected over the years to keep anyone from guessing what was going on in the razor-like mind he kept carefully concealed, just as he hid his sharp eyes behind thick-lensed glasses.

He, unlike most of the people in the club, did not see Patrick Kelly just rolling over and handing his club to the Russian. It didn't add up. If Patrick ever got up and about again he'd want what was his, in Pascal's opinion. And that included the club. So he was doing two sets of books, one for the Russian and another for Kelly.

It was the least he could do, and whatever happened he wouldn't lose out. But he would rather keep books for Patrick – he felt more relaxed with him. These Russians made you feel that if you pushed them in any way at all you were finished, in more ways than one.

So Pascal worked out the real earnings and the bunced-up earnings and what the difference was and where it was to go. A foot in each camp – the safest option until things were finally sorted out.

Kate was amazed to see Golding standing outside the entrance to the ward. He looked nervous and she hurried out to meet him. It was 6.35 in the morning and she was still half asleep after spending the night dozing in a chair.

He smiled at her and she smiled warmly back. He had come up trumps lately and it had shaken her that she could have been so wrong about someone.

'Sorry to barge in like this, ma'am, but we have another murder and another missing child.'

She closed her eyes in distress. 'Who?'

'A little bird called Bernice Harper. Pro, works in a massage parlour. Kid called Mikey, another one that was borrowed. She'd been stabbed to death. Twice in the belly, but the one between the shoulder blades seems to be the one that did the trick. Her kid is three and he's gone missing. She was another one who was under supervision. She had a record, mainly for petty offences – obtaining money by false pretences, kiting and shoplifting, and the regulation ones for soliciting. The first soliciting offence goes back to when she was thirteen. Pretty girl and all. Shame really.'

'If she was working last night then maybe the child is still with a neighbour or a friend?'

Golding shook his head. 'A woman who lives next door said she heard a commotion late last night, crying and everything, but it was par for the course so she didn't take any notice. But no reports of anyone going in there or being seen nearby. Whoever this is came and went without attracting attention.'

Kate sighed. 'I'm not surprised. It seems another thing these women have in common is that they all seem to live such complicated lives that nothing they do attracts undue notice.'

He pushed a hand through his sparse hair. 'We've alerted the next-of-kin but the mother didn't seem too surprised, by all accounts. Didn't even ask about the child. I took a photo of the lad from the scene and guess what? He's in the photograph we seized from Kerry's.'

'Get me a copy of the pictures and then meet me back here in about an hour, OK?'

'I have a set in the car, ma'am. Can I drop you home to get showered or anything?'

She shook her head. 'I have my car.'

He went to walk away.

'On second thoughts, I'll meet you at the police station at nine,' Kate told him. 'I have someone I want to talk to first.'

'Fair enough. How is Mr Kelly?'

'Bearing up, like the rest of us.'

Golding smiled a goodbye and she watched him walking away, her mind already completely focused on the new development.

This was someone who was able to get about completely undetected. That meant they were either very clever or very well known. Well known – meaning frightening. That was all it could be. Gut feeling said Suzy knew who it was, and they were trading together in kiddie porn. It fitted, made sense. But who the hell could it be and how was she to find out with a block put on questioning Suzy?

There was only one person she trusted enough to ask and she was going to do that now, before she changed, washed or ate.

Kate could tell that Robert was surprised to see her, but his wide smile of welcome made her feel better about calling so early in the morning.

'I hope you don't mind, Robert, but I really need your help.'

He grinned. 'Come away in. I'd just made some coffee.'

She followed the delicious aroma into his kitchen which was now spotlessly clean. 'I was up half the night cleaning. I find it so hard to keep up with everything, don't you? After all these years with my father I can really sympathise with working mothers!'

He poured her a mug of fragrant coffee and she sipped it gratefully.

'My one extravagance,' he explained, 'but I refuse to start the day with crap coffee. And tea! My dear, my stomach has to be awake for at least three hours before I can take it.'

Kate smiled.

'So, what can I do for you, Miss Burrows, or can I call you Kate?'

'Kate will be fine. I want to ask you a few things, off the record. We've had another murder. Bernice Harper.'

She saw his face pale at her words and his eyes fill with tears.

'Dear God, not poor Bernice! How did it happen? And how is little Mikey? Shall I arrange care . . .'

His voice trailed off at her expression.

'Mikey is missing, I'm afraid,' Kate told him. 'That's the second child in a week since Sharon Pallister's son hasn't been found yet. For your ears only, we have literally nothing to go on other than

Natasha and Suzy – and Suzy has friends in very high places.'

'I'm not surprised.' Robert smirked nastily. 'Always made sure she was covered, did Suzy. I knew her before I came here. I was in Wales years ago, ran a care home for girls there. She was a skinny, ugly kid with a ruthless streak even then. If I told you what she'd do for a Kit-Kat it would blow your mind. But then, her mother was a *thing*. That's the only description I can give, a positively disgusting *thing*. They were living in Tilbury then. Her mother was the worst kind of Dock Dolly. Take on anything after a few drinks in the Anchor and expected her daughters to do the same. I know Suzy gets up everyone's nose, but considering how she was brought up, it's no surprise really. I mean, put yourself in her shoes for five minutes. Where would she learn compassion, caring, how to love, if no one showed her?'

Kate knew he was right but she couldn't share his feelings. To her, excuses didn't count when someone was a whoremaster of children.

'As far as I'm concerned, Robert, after that upbringing she should want to make sure that other kids are spared the same experiences.'

'There speaks the product of a decent home and a decent upbringing. I know everyone thinks I jump on my soap box too readily about my girls but *someone* has to care for them. *Someone* has to try and get through to them and put them on a better path. My job is thankless, I am fucked off out of it twenty times a day. But I keep trying and every now and again I make a small impression. I get a girl to see what she's doing. Get them to put their kids first. The public give so much money to good causes – the poor kids in Rumania, whatever. Yet here two neglected children die per week, with babies more likely to be battered to death than toddlers or school-age kids. We have women who are pushing out kids like a conveyor belt with practically no back-up. Paedophiles find certain council estates havens for their covert activities. Some abuse can be traced back generations to grannies and great-grannies, all of them abused by relatives or a family friend.'

Robert paused for breath and looked at Kate, who was listening intently. 'I see myself as a small cog in a dirty great big wheel,' he explained, 'and I try to help them instead of ridiculing them – make them see their bad points themselves without pointing them out as glaringly obvious like everyone else they come into contact with. I try and make a friend of them instead of treating them like the dirt they are to so many people in this world. In short, I try to give them a bit of self-respect. That, to me, is the key to dealing with society's rejects.'

Kate had listened to him, but Robert knew he still had not wholly convinced her. But he would carry on doing what he had to do. Someone must help these people and it might as well be him. At least he genuinely cared about them.

'Are there any more girls you think might be a part of the paedophile ring – who might be allowing their kids to be used?' Kate asked him.

'This is off the record, isn't it?'

She nodded. 'Of course. I swear I will keep it to myself, but if you can think of anyone at all who might be able to help us, or better still, someone you think might be involved with Suzy . . .'

'As I said before, look up DI Barker when you can. He had a gang of kids when he was at Grantley. Most of them are still around and he had them well trained. No one could touch him, he made sure of that. Suzy was one of his, and Kerry Alston. Tash when she was a small girl. Quite a few of them. He was pulled over for it, but nothing was ever proved against him. Instead of being ostracised as you might expect would have been the case, he went onwards and upwards. Yes, Barker's the only common denominator I can think of.'

Kate frowned, realising the enormity of what he had just said.

'What do you know, then, that isn't in a file anywhere?'

'Look back to twelve years ago, when a young girl was raped and murdered. Lesley Carmichael. Off the Bentwood Estate, like the others. See what you think about that.'

The name rang a bell and Kate smiled her gratitude. 'Thanks, Robert.'

He raised his eyebrows delicately. 'One tries to help if one can, dear. But that was off the record, remember. I don't want anyone coming after me for what amounts to gossip really.'

Kate finished her coffee and didn't refuse the refill

he offered her immediately. 'I knew Barker through some of the girls I worked with in the homes,' Robert told her. 'He would visit them. When I came to Grantley I was surprised to see him here, to be honest. But he was on his way out even then.'

He shrugged dismissively. 'Never liked him but that's no crime, is it? Being an arsehole, I mean. And he is an arsehole, believe me. Now he's in Vice he should be able to indulge his passions freely. Eleven- and twelve-year-olds are plying their trade in London as you well know. Though of course he has the lovely Debbie waiting for him at home. What a slag she is.'

Kate heard the weariness in his voice and empathised with him.

'Barker went deep. There were a good few involved with him – some in the so-called caring professions too. A GP and a director of Social Services. All of them walked away. The GP is still practising in Grantley but the Social Services type took retirement and a pay-off. The usual when things are hushed up. Ratchet, your superior, could tell you more about it than me. He headed the investigation then watered it down and tidied it up like a good boy. It was all internal. The girls who made the complaints were portrayed as liars. Well, they were from "problem" families. Basically they didn't have a chance. If you talk to Camilla, she'll tell you who they were. Her father was a beat cop here years ago. He'd know more about it than anyone.'

Robert paused significantly before continuing.

'But Ratchet, now, he's the one you need. He knows all about it. Mr Ratchet's a funny man. The ·

cover-up basically made him what he is today and we *all* know what that *is*, don't we?'

He saw Kate's eyes widen, and laughed.

'Don't quote me on it, but gossip often has an element of truth. Remember that.'

'Wouldn't surprise me if you were right.'

Robert looked gratified.

'Thank you, Robert. I really appreciate all this. Especially the coffee.'

He pushed his hand through his hair. 'I'm considering going blond, what do you think?'

Kate suppressed a smile. 'You have the skin colouring, maybe you could get away with it.'

'We'll see. How's that man of yours?'

She was happier to be on more familiar ground. 'I thought he had made a breakthrough last night but the nurse says it might not mean much. He opened his eyes and squeezed my hand.'

Robert gripped her arm gently. 'I think after what happened to him, that can only be a good sign, don't you, dear?'

She nodded, her eyes filling with tears at his kindness.

'He'll be OK, Kate. I have that feeling.'

She gulped at her coffee again to hide her distress.

'I'd better start breakfast. My father will be awake soon and then all hell will be let loose. That's why I like to get up early, have a bit of time to myself even if I haven't had much sleep in the night. It's what keeps me sane.'

'Is he very bad?'

Robert nodded vigorously, his hair flying in all directions with the force of it.

'Imagine a really spoiled toddler and a really foul adolescent and times it by twenty and you'll get an idea of what I have to deal with on a daily basis. But I can't home him, I just can't. He is my father when all is said and done.'

He squirmed in his seat and the action made him look very young and insecure.

'The strange thing is, Kate, if I was dealing with a client in this situation, I would advise them to put him away for their own sanity. He's as daft as a brush, God love him, and yet physically he's as healthy as me or you. And the strength of him! My God, the strength of him.'

He got up and rinsed his mug under the tap at the sink and Kate took it as a sign that she should go. So making her goodbyes, she left him to look after his ailing father who didn't even know who he was, and nurse his deluded belief that he could make headway with girls and women like Suzy and Natasha.

In a strange way, as over the top as he could be and as effeminate as he came over, Kate found herself admiring him. She wished she could be so whole-hearted about her job and personal philosophy as he was. It took guts and a certain quiet strength to make a stand against the prevailing opinion. It put her own problems into context and she felt lighter at heart than she had for a long time as she drove to meet Golding at the station.

There she concentrated solely on the dead women,

the missing children, and on dreaming up a way to get to Suzy without anyone in authority knowing. The first thing she wanted were the relevant files on Barker and on the dead schoolgirl, Lesley Carmichael.

She also wanted Jenny and Golding to track Barker down and see what else they could find out about him. Some up-to-date gossip on his track record in Vice would be good, too. She was going to pull in a few favours herself, to get that.

She was going to crack this case whatever Ratchet and his cronies thought. They believed that because of her association with Patrick who was under suspicion of murder she'd fall in with anything they said to safeguard her career.

She smiled grimly. They were wrong about that but she wouldn't make her stand yet. Not until she had enough hard evidence to convict the pornographers. If they were guilty they were going down. She didn't care if she had to appeal to the DPP direct, she was going to ensure that the culprits were slaughtered, in prison and out of it.

Kate realised she felt much better than she had in weeks. Thanks to Robert Bateman she had new information and an ally. Now all she needed was to sort out Patrick's problems and she could finally relax.

Ratchet looked at Kate and sighed.

'I cannot give you access to the files on Lesley Carmichael. I am sorry, Kate. And I am sorry that Harry Barker's file has gone missing. But these things happen in a busy station.'

Kate looked at him for long seconds without saying a word. When he dropped his eyes she finally spoke.

'I know you are bent, Mr Ratchet, I know that for a fact. I also know that you are hiding the files from me. If Patrick was up and about you wouldn't dare because he would move heaven and earth to get me what I wanted in order to close this case. Now you listen to me, sir, and you listen good. I am taking this higher – I mean it.'

Ratchet interrupted her. 'Are you really stupid, Kate – only I never had you down as cranially challenged. This isn't anything to do with *me*. I am on orders now, as I was then. It is not a matter of what *I* want or what I don't bloody want. Unlike you I only have a few years left. I want my pension and I want out. I got involved twelve years ago in what amounts to a cover-up. I had no option then and neither do you now. So stop all this Famous Five crap and get into the real world. One day Barker will push it and then CIB will have him. Until then he is more protected than Yasser Arafat on a day trip to the wailing wall. Stop seeing me as the obstacle in your way. I am only the fucking messenger boy – OK? Now shut the door on the way out.'

Kate was sorry for him because she knew what he was saying was the truth. But it was all wrong, so very, very wrong.

He relented. 'I know how you feel, love, I feel like it myself. I have to live with what I did twelve years ago and believe me, if I had the opportunity over again I would have thrown the book at him and hang the consequences. But Barker was a collector of information. He knew too much about everyone, including me, and that is the edge he still has. This goes up so high, Kate, it would make you dizzy. Stick with what you've got, take a few good collars and leave him out of the equation. It is all you can do.'

He let his words sink in.

Then: 'By the way, Gunner and Partridge are dead. How is Patrick?'

He saw her blanch and smiled gently. 'Life has a funny way of panning out, don't you think? We all have things we want to hide.'

Kate turned away and walked from the room.

He had her, and he knew it.

Julie Carmichael lived in a small terraced council house not far from the Bentwood Estate. It was clean and well-decorated, though the furniture was shabby with age. Julie herself had greying hair, cut short in a severe mannish style, and a wide open face with faded blue eyes and a strong jawline.

Kate liked her on sight. There was something about her that engendered trust.

Julie made a pot of tea and Kate sat at the kitchen table and watched the woman as she pottered about. It was obvious from her nervousness that she didn't have many visitors.

'So you're here about my Lesley then?' she asked.

Kate nodded. 'I would like to ask you a few questions, yes.'

Julie smiled derisively. 'Reopening the enquiry, are they?'

Kate bit her lip and saw Julie Carmichael shake her head despairingly.

'I didn't think so. No one gave a fuck before and they don't now.'

She became aggressive then. It was in her stance, her every movement. She slammed the tea pot on to the stainless steel draining board and the sound rang through the kitchen.

'I think about her every day, my Lesley. They found her up by the woods, she'd been raped and murdered. They'd buggered her, more than one man at work. I know that because the pathologist told my Jack. He worked in the hospital. Was a porter, man and boy, at Grantley General. He knew everyone, well liked Jack was. But then later, at the hearing, the coroner said it was the work of one man and that she had not suffered. All the face-saving crap you can imagine. No one was ever brought to book for it and shall I tell you why that was, love?'

Kate didn't answer.

'Because he was one of your lot. A bleeding policeman! Bastard Barker as he was called. I saw her with him on many occasions. I trusted him. Knew his wife.' She shook her head at the iniquity of the man.

'He actually came into this house and commiserated with me over her death. Told me that he was going to find the culprit. And I believed him. I didn't know then, no one did, about him being investigated. About the complaints made against him. That my

Lesley had threatened to tell on him for interfering with her and some schoolfriends.'

Julie closed her eyes tightly. 'She wasn't a good girl, my Lesley, but she didn't deserve to die like that. If it had happened to an animal everyone would have been up in arms. But when it happens to a person, it's just news for a few days until something bigger comes along.'

'Who else was involved in it all? I mean, which other girls?'

Julie sighed and poured out the tea. It was thick and brown and Kate knew it would taste stewed.

'There were a few I knew of. You see, I found Lesley's diary so I knew more than I let on. But when Barker was pulled in, I didn't know she was writing about him. She had used the abbreviation "B", you see. *No* real names there. I only put two and two together later from the things the other girls said. But then the diary was taken from me. I gave it to them in the belief that it would bring Barker to justice. Never saw it again. No record of its ever having been seen by anyone, apparently. But that nice man, that Mr Ratchet, *he* had definitely seen it because I gave it to him when he came here.'

Kate had read the file five times. All it said was that a girl had been murdered, that the usual enquiries had been made, but that no one had ever been caught. The murderer was believed to be a traveller or vagrant. A one-off. There was nothing in writing to say there had ever been an internal enquiry, that a policeman had been suspected of the crime. It was a blatant cover-up. But looking at Julie Carmichael, Kate knew this woman would not have had the strength to make waves. She was a victim of her own ignorance and fear. Fear of the police and the establishment.

'Social Services must have been involved?' Kate probed.

Julie nodded. 'Oh, yeah.' She lit a cigarette and sat at the table with her rough hands clasped together, nails bitten down to the quick.

'Les was under Social Services because she was in trouble at school. Truanting. Being rude to teachers. Nothing over the top. It was par for the course with her little crew. But it was when she started hanging round with that Kerry Alston that she really went off the rails. Kerry came here for her that day, the day she died. I still believe she was in on it all. Her and Barker set my baby up.'

Julie was visibly distressed now.

'At Lesley's funeral, Kerry was crying and I told her to piss off out of it. She was using it to get attention for herself, I could see that. She even came here asking if she could see Lesley in her coffin! I thought she was just being a kid, you know. Then I cleared Lesley's room, and that's when I found the diary. I took it to Mr Ratchet who was in charge of the case. He held on to it and told me he was going to investigate further. I'd realised by then, see, that she'd meant Barker because I had seen him with Kerry and that little mare Jackie Palmer. He used to pick them up on the corner of the Bentwood Estate, where the waste ground is. It was common bloody knowledge. But not my Lesley. Or at least that's what I thought, until I read the diary. It was sickening, Miss Burrows. Can you imagine what it was like for me to read about her private doings with men?'

Kate looked down at the scuffed table. She could image that better than anyone. She had done it herself with Lizzy. She knew the trauma it caused to find out that your daughter, the child you'd reared, loved and adored, was being used by people as a plaything and was perfectly happy for it to happen. In fact, they seemed to think it made them special somehow.

Julie stared out of the window, smoking silently, her mind a world away from the cramped kitchen.

'Not just with men either, that was the hardest part. Goings-on with the other girls. Little girls they were – twelve and thirteen years old. Some even younger than that. I was devastated. It killed my Jack. I tried to hide the worst from him, but losing her had taken its toll. I buried him eight months after we buried Lesley. He took an overdose while I was at work one day. Never knew the whole of it and for that much at least I'm grateful.'

Kate was puzzled. 'You kept it from your husband?'

The other woman nodded. 'I know it sounds strange but, you see, Lesley was his life. He could never have coped with what she had become. I only ever had her. I had a couple of miscarriages first and we thought we'd never get a baby. When I fell with her and everything seemed to go well, we were over the moon. My Jack adored her. Absolutely adored her.

I couldn't have told him what she'd become, it would have killed him.'

Julie laughed weakly. 'Well, you know what I mean. He was distressed enough. How could I, in all honesty, make it even worse for him by telling him about her other life?' She stabbed out her cigarette and immediately lit up another.

'Did no one take you seriously?'

'Oh, they pretended to. But you see, it was like Mr Ratchet said. Did I really want everyone to find out about my daughter and her activities? Especially as I couldn't prove it was Barker behind it all. When I thought about it, I didn't. Not just because of what people would say but because of Jack. And then when he killed himself, I couldn't desecrate his memory so I left it. But believe me when I say it was hard, bloody hard, because I'd let that bastard walk away, and when I asked for the diary back, I was told there had never been one. That I was under too much strain and didn't know what I was alleging. I had to see me GP, Gordon Browning, and shall I tell you something? He was in on it and all.

'I tell you, Miss Burrows, this place is fucking rotten with it. Nonces coming out the woodwork and no one cares. I changed me doctor, kept me head down and me trap shut. Because no one wanted to know, and I mean *no one*.'

Kate felt ashamed of the treatment this woman had been meted out by the police. Knowing what she already did about Ratchet, she found the story believable. And didn't she know from her own experience how close the police and the villains actually were?

But to hear that your own force had overlooked a paedophile amongst its ranks . . . and not only over-looked him, but let him go on to join Vice where underage prostitution came with the territory! It made her wonder if *anyone* could be trusted any more.

'So what brings you here to see me?' Julie asked. 'It's not just a follow-up, is it? You look as if you actually believe what I'm saying for a start.'

Kate sipped once more at the strong sweet brew. She was trying to choose her words. She so desperately wanted to tell this woman the truth but she wasn't sure if that would be wise at this stage.

Suppose she was blocked again? Suppose she was pushed out of her job? But looking into the devastation on the other woman's face she decided on the truth. It was about time Julie Carmichael got a fair deal.

'I believe every word you've said. But I'm afraid this is strictly off the record.'

Julie nodded, her eyes sceptical. 'Go on. I'm listening.'

'I'm investigating Barker myself. I am a DI, as you know, currently working on another case and his name keeps cropping up. I heard about your daughter and that's what brought me here today. But I swear to you, Mrs Carmichael, that if I can bag that bastard I will. But I cannot promise anything. I am in the same position as you, coming up against some powerful vested interests, and if I pursue this enquiry to their detriment I could be drummed out of my job. But, I assure you, I will do the utmost I can to bring him to justice.'

Julie seemed to fold in on herself with the release of tension. Her whole body sagged with relief. She held her bottom jaw tightly with one hand as if trying to contain her emotion. Her eyes were glistening with tears.

'Just to tell someone and be believed is more than enough,' she said shakily. 'But to hear you say you are going to try and do something is more than I ever imagined. The worst of it all was that everyone I dealt with looked on my girl as just a tramp. Beneath their notice. It was as if they thought she had asked for what happened to her. But whatever she was, she was led there by someone. And that someone was Barker. He was a guest in my home. His wife Mavis was my mate. He knew my little girl. Knew her and used that to get to her.' She was crying openly now.

Kate gave her a clean hankie and tried to comfort her. But how could you comfort a woman who had lost the two people who were most precious to her through the callous betrayal of a police department? The very people who should have been protecting her family had been working against them from the start.

How the hell are you supposed to comfort someone who knows that to be a fact and that no one else will ever believe her?

But Kate tried, though it was the hardest thing she had ever done.

She looked around her at the photos of Lesley and

her parents everywhere. At the votive candle alight in front of a photograph of a small girl with gap teeth and an innocent smile. And Kate herself wanted to cry until there were no more tears left.

Chapter Twenty-Three

Willy felt better than he had in days. Maureen was looking after him like a favoured child: cooked breakfast, a doctor for his burns, and as much affection as he could cope with. Ensconced in her large soft bed with its pink nylon quilt and padded headboard, he finally relaxed.

Duane had rolled him a small joint for medicinal purposes. Willy had binned it, secretly, because he knew the boy meant well and didn't want to hurt his feelings.

Now, though, he had to think about his next step. Visit Patrick and see what the score was, then get his arse round to see what was happening with the club and the businesses. He also needed to see Kate but he had to tread warily because he wasn't sure what Pat had told her and he respected her too much to lie to her face.

Maureen came into the room, her hair freshly washed and set, nails gleaming and her ample cleavage wobbling from her exertions. She carried yet another tray laden with food and drink.

Willy smiled at her fondly, his moon face a picture of contentment. She was a good sort, old Maureen, and he owed her for these last few days. Really owed her. She had asked him nothing but what was relevant to looking after him. She knew the score. Another woman would have nagged the life out of him for explanations, but he had told her only what he wanted her to know and Maureen had left it at that. That kind of trust was not given to everyone, and for that reason alone he was a happy man.

As he tucked into yet more good home-cooked food he found it in his heart to wonder what the next few weeks would bring and whether he would be able to get through them without involving Maureen and her son.

He hoped so. But the way things were, he might soon be putting his life on the line again for his old mate.

Maureen smiled at him and he recognised the gleam in her eye as she said huskily, 'You up to a bit of how's your father yet, Willy?'

He wolfed down a large piece of succulent steak and smiled winningly. 'I don't see why not, girl.'

They smiled at one another and Maureen sat on the bed and watched him eat as if her own life depended on it.

Kate looked again over the files from Robert Bateman. Kerry's made particularly depressing reading, but there was no mention anywhere of her being involved with anyone other than her father and his friends. Barker's name was nowhere to be seen. Kate had had to disguise her shock at hearing Kerry Alston's name being mentioned in connection with Lesley Carmichael and her murder. She had not wanted Julie to know that she was already investigating Kerry and Jackie. But names were recurring too frequently for it to be merely coincidence, not just in her enquiries into the paedophile case but in Lesley's death as well.

It seemed that Kerry was implicated in one murder at a young age. What if there were more than one? Kate would have to visit her soon, tell her what she'd found out and see what effect her words had on the girl. She didn't hold out much hope, though.

The phone rang and she answered it. 'Burrows here.'

A deep rich Irish brogue oozed along the line like melting butter. 'How are ye, me darling girl?'

Kenny Caitlin's voice lifted Kate's spirits at once.

'All the better for hearing from you. Any chance of a lunch?'

He picked up the hesitation in her voice and chuckled.

'How about I ring you later and we arrange it properly? I understand you're interested in a colleague of mine?'

She didn't answer and he chuckled again.

'I'll be in touch at eight tonight, make sure you're in.'

The line went dead and Kate replaced the receiver gently. She had better tell her mother to set another place for dinner; it sounded like Kenny was coming to see her himself.

One thing with Kenny, you could rely on him for the truth no matter how bad it was or who it offended. When she thought of her initial dismay at having to work with him on the Grantley Ripper enquiry it made her smile. He had been fantastic. He had also become a good friend which was why she had called on him now.

If there was any way to smoke out Barker, then Kenny was the man to do it. Kate felt easier just for talking to him. Picking up the files, she walked from the office. She would look them over at the hospital. As she passed Golding she told him to arrange for her to see Kerry on remand, then she left the building.

On the way to the hospital her mind was on Lesley Carmichael and her mother, the children who were missing or dead and the quest for the common denominator that linked them all.

She had trained herself not to think too much about Patrick. She was going to wait until they knew if he would make a full recovery before considering whether they still had a future. Until then she had enough on her plate without going looking for more.

Evelyn was just leaving the hospital as Kate arrived. Kate explained about dinner that night and saw the pleasure on her mother's face when she heard it was Kenny Caitlin who was to be their guest.

'I have a nice piece of pork I could roast to a dream!'

She went off planning the night's menu and Kate wondered how she had not put on fifteen stone with the amount of food she now polished off at her mother's insistence. Jenny was already up half a stone and counting, but she didn't seem to care. In fact, Kate had a feeling that Jenny would become a permanent fixture in the house if she could. It was strange how even grown women needed mothering at times.

As she settled herself into the chair by Patrick's bed and grasped his hand, a wave of weariness overcame her. She detected a strong aroma of Estée Lauder and turned to see Grace and Violet as they came into the ward.

'How's he seem?'

Grace shrugged. 'OK. No real change. The consultant says he can be moved to a general ward soon so that's something. He breathes on his own and has reflex actions but that's about it.' Her voice was resigned, manner offhand as usual when she spoke to Kate.

Violet smiled kindly. 'You look tired, love. Too much work?'

'As usual,' Kate replied. 'Still, Vi, someone has to do it, eh?' Her voice was light and seemed to offend Grace.

'Someone has to be a filth?' she snapped. 'Are you having a tin bath? Who in their right mind would want a fucking job like that? No one I know would even consider it.'

Kate's patience snapped too. This was the last in a long line of insults and snubs.

'Well, for your information, Grace, decent law-abiding people *like* me and my job. If you only mix with thieves, liars, con men and ex-prostitutes, you *would* be biased, wouldn't you?'

As soon as the words came out of her mouth she regretted them. But Grace and her silly innuendos, her constant sarcasm and bitchiness, were getting her down. With everything else she had to think about, it was the final straw.

'There are more bent people in the police force, darling. You take my word for it. I *know*.'

Kate couldn't really argue with what Grace was saying. Not with what she had just found out. But all the same she answered her.

'You *know*? You know everything, don't you? Well, Grace, let me tell you something: you know nothing, do you hear me? All you do is shoot your mouth off from a position of complete ignorance. But if you got burgled, the police would be the first people you would ring. If a child is killed, if a bank is robbed . . . the police step in. It's what keeps this country from descending into fucking anarchy. Think what it would be like if we had no laws, you silly bloody bitch! Think about it. Anyone and everyone, all doing exactly what they wanted. Why don't you look at the big picture for once?'

Violet, ever the peacemaker, said stoutly, 'Right and all, love. Really, Grace, you are a pain at times. The girl is only doing her job.'

Grace turned on her sister and shouted, 'Girl? *Girl*? She's in her bleeding forties! She ain't a girl, she'll be catching up with us soon. You don't half talk some crap, Vi.'

'You vicious old bitch!' Violet shoved her sister in the chest. 'She'd be hard pushed to catch up with you. Seventy-two you are, lady, and I can prove it. Bloody woman, driving us all mad with your nasty tongue and your miserable boat. Even the nurses can't stand you, you wicked old cow!'

'Can I have a drink?'

The quiet voice was ignored as Grace shoved her sister back, none too gently.

'Now it's all coming out, ain't it? We know whose side you're on. Don't we? Sneaking round after her, making her cups of tea . . . I've seen you! Even though she dumped our brother and left him on his Jack Jones. Soon came back when he was shot, though, didn't she? After a cut of his dosh . . .'

Kate was mesmerised by what the woman was saying. Her mind registered that the row was being listened to by everyone in the vicinity and as this was the ICU she expected a nurse to come in at any second and tell them their behaviour was out of order.

Instead Violet shrieked, 'I am sick of you, Grace! All me bleeding life I've had to listen to you. Well, let me tell you something – I think Patrick had a touch when he met Kate. I like her and I always will. And her mother. Pat was out of order – he told me that himself when he came to see me after she went on the trot. He regretted doing what he did and now he is paying the price. So why don't you shut your trap and give your poor arse a chance now and again?'

Grace was puce with shock, anger and embarrassment. She could take anything from Kate Burrows, but to hear her own sister say those things was beyond her comprehension.

But Violet wasn't sorry at all for speaking up. In fact, she was glad it was finally out in the open. Grace's constant harping and bullying were getting her down. Violet was as upset as anyone but Grace, as usual, made out she was suffering more than any of them.

Kate and Violet glared at her now. Violet had even walked over to stand by Kate's side which made it even worse for Grace. She was defeated and she knew it.

Her carefully made-up face crumpled. She looked years older and close to collapse as she turned away from them and stormed out of the ward. It was quiet suddenly and both Violet and Kate were shaken and upset by what had just taken place.

Then a voice made them both jump as Patrick said hoarsely, 'She'll be all right. Now, if you two have quite finished, can I have a drink of some description, please?'

They both turned and stared at the man in the bed as if they had never seen him before in their lives.

Then a scream from Violet brought the nurses running in. They had been listening to the argument, too frightened to interrupt Grace and her harangue. Now, though, seeing her storm outside, they felt brave enough to enter the room. As one nurse had remarked, that old bird's voice could raise the dead. It seemed it had done the next best thing and had roused Mr Kelly from his coma. But no one said that in the room, they saved that little gem for their tea break. They just enjoyed seeing the happiness on the faces around them and their own sense of justifiable pride that he had recovered in their care.

Kenneth Caitlin's voice was loud and betrayed the fact that he had already had a drink before arriving.

Jenny had heard of him but never met him. She had prepared herself for an irascible old bastard and was pleased to find he was a charming elderly man. The large breakfast bar in the kitchen was laid with care and both wine and food were superb thanks to Evelyn who greeted Caitlin like a long-lost relative.

After being served with a large roast dinner and exclaiming that it would keep him going for a week, he looked at Kate and got straight to the point.

'So, Katie, what's your interest in Barker?'

'He was accused of paedophile activity when he was at Grantley. A young girl was murdered and he was investigated in connection with it. Then everything was dropped – the investigation, I mean. He was never charged. It seems that it was Ratchet who pulled the plug on it all. And now I have a paedophile ring involving young women corrupted by him, the murder of a child twelve years ago which I believe he was in on, two more children dead, and three more missing. I believe he's in on it all.'

She looked Kenneth in the eye. 'I have no proof that he's still active in this area, though – it's just a hunch. Paedophiles return again and again to their haunts, as you know. If they find an area where they are welcome and not found out, they will keep going back to it. I think he *has* to be in on this latest child abuse, somehow. I recently tried to arrest a girl called Suzy Harrington and was warned off by Ratchet, who apparently had a call from high up. Very high up, in fact – the Home Office itself, no less. But the person who made the call was a crony of Barker's and we can prove that . . .'

Caitlin interrupted her, a mouthful of pork crackling in his mouth. 'Who was the Home Office grass then?'

'Jeffrey Cavendish.'

She saw Caitlin's eyes widen.

'Jasus! They have everyone, don't they?'

'So it would seem,' Jenny agreed. 'We have so many people involved in this it would take all night to go through them all. What we need from you is everything you know about Barker. We need your assessment of him. Is he evil enough to be behind all this?'

Caitlin finished eating, then, pointing his knife at Kate, he said seriously, 'Barker has had a cloud over him for years. It started here and it followed him to the smoke. You can believe me when I say he's tight with someone big. Very tight. He's a known jobber with the younger girls, but then that's nothing unusual in a Vice cop. With him, though, it's out of control. He's a vicious thug on the wrong team yet no one seems able to get shot of him. His wife Mavis was terrified of him, when I knew her, as was his youngest girl, Pauline.'

Kate interrupted. 'I thought his wife's name was Debbie?'

He shook his head, and Kate was puzzled for a moment before letting it go.

'No. His wife is Mavis. His daughter is called Pauline.'

'Pauline accused two of our suspects, Kerry Alston and Jackie Palmer, of sexually assaulting her when they were all at school. The charges were dropped, and it seems it was forgotten about.'

Jenny's voice was low as they were all by now aware of the appalled expression on Evelyn's face at hearing their conversation.

'What we can't understand is why the charges were dropped or why they were even brought in the first place. But we can't ask Pauline Barker, can we? Her father would hear of it in no time and realise we were after him.'

Kenneth was quiet, thinking hard.

'I know he has divorced his wife Mavis and lives with a younger woman these days. I don't know her name. Perhaps it is this Debbie you spoke of. If you can track down the wife you might strike gold there but she was fecking terrified of him in the past. Everyone I spoke to has an opinion about Barker and they'll give it to me freely enough but it's always off the record. Suffice it to say that they all believe he's bent, he's bad and he's protected. He is also dangerous to know. Very dangerous. Has no fear of anyone or anything.'

Kate and Jenny were listening attentively.

'I can't believe this, can you?' Jenny's voice was high with wonder and disbelief. 'I mean, how the hell can one person have so much power? How can Barker walk away from everything that he's done without anyone cottoning on?'

'You tell me, my little pickaheen,' Caitlin said soberly. 'Because we all know he has. This goes to the top of the fecking tree or I'll eat my boots.' He looked at Evelyn. 'Though, if you cooked them, missus, I think they would be eminently edible.'

She didn't smile at the joke, she was too stunned. Listening to their conversation she had realised for the first time that her daughter was dealing in children's lives. It was forcibly brought home to her just how many women were willing to sacrifice their children for monetary gain. She could hardly credit that such wickedness went on.

Kenny tactfully changed the subject. 'I still can't believe Patrick has come round at last.'

Kate brought him up to date as they finished their meal. Patrick was sleeping now, but at least they knew he was better. He had been lucid this afternoon, still had his memory and all his faculties. Now she just had to get him out of the large hole he had dug for himself.

'Ratchet is willing to let him take the rap for murder, but I think I may have to inform my superior that Pat was with me that night. I am ready to give a statement to that effect and if they want to call me a liar I may have to bring up Mr Barker's case and Mr Ratchet's involvement in it.'

Caitlin shook his head. 'Don't you dare! You need to talk to CIB, Kate. That's the only way you're going to get any answers here, surely you realise that much? But don't even involve them until you can finger the fucker. I will help you all I can. I am due a bit of leave and I might just take it.'

Kate smiled widely and grasped his hand. 'Thanks, Kenny.'

He looked serious then and his voice was grave as he told her, 'Don't be too quick with the thanks, Kate. I have a price like all men.'

She frowned. 'What is it?'

He grinned. 'A few more dinners like this and a bottle of good Irish whiskey now and again.'

Kate relaxed. To have him on board was like a dream come true.

'You, Kenny, can have what you want,' she told him.

'Now, Katie, you should know better than to make a statement like that to a poor old fella like meself!'

Evelyn laughed for the first time in what seemed ages.

'You dirty old sod! Now then, who's for a great shive of apple pie and custard?'

Everyone groaned their acceptance and she laughed again, but after everything she had heard tonight she wondered how any of them could find it inside them to crack jokes and be merry. She knew their conversation would haunt her in the small hours as she tried to sleep tonight.

★ ★ ★

Patrick lay in the hospital bed, his mind working overtime. He had awoken in more ways than one. Now that he had heard the ins and outs of everything from Kate he knew he was going to be up for murder. The thought didn't bother him as much as it bothered her, but he knew he was on dodgy ground.

As pleased as Kate was at his recovery, he had the sense to realise that she wasn't going to be so over the moon once everything came out.

He wiped his hand across his face. His head was still aching, but the doctor had told him he could expect that after such a trauma. He was still trying to get over the fact that he had been shot in the first place!

He was furious to hear that he had actually been shot twice. The buttocks wound was the final straw as far as he was concerned. He wanted nothing more than to retaliate by shooting that Russian cunt in the face. At least, that was what he told himself. But he was so weak he knew he wouldn't be capable of picking up a gun, let alone firing it.

Which wouldn't stop him paying someone else to do the deed. Patrick was a great believer in delegating.

He opened his eyes, fighting the sleepiness that kept trying to overtake him. He wanted out of this place and he was going to make sure he left as soon as possible. Even if he had to go private and pay for his freedom.

He grinned. It wouldn't be the first time he had paid for that.

He closed his eyes as sleep welcomed him once more. He would not admit that part of his fear of sleep was that he might not wake up again.

'All right, Pat?'

His eyes flew open at Willy's voice. The two men looked at one another and then Willy bent down carefully and embraced him. It was the nearest either man had ever come to the other.

'Am I glad you're on the mend, boy!'

Patrick watched as Willy gingerly tried to lower himself into a chair by the bed.

'What happened to you?'

Willy waved one hand dismissively. 'Plenty of time for all that fanny when the doc says you can be aggravated. Until then I want to know how you're feeling?'

'Obviously a fucking sight better than you do, mate,' Pat joked feebly.

Willy chuckled. 'You're a boy, Pat, and no mistake.'

It was all that would be said on the matter but each knew the deep joy the other felt to see their friend still alive and more or less whole.

The woman pushed back her shoulder-length red hair. It was a very feminine gesture and she smiled seductively as she looked at herself in the mirror.

'You are going to break a few hearts,' she said to her own reflection, then picked up her bag and tripped out of the room on high heels.

At the bottom of the stairs she smiled at the little boy who stood beaming up at her. 'Ready?'

He nodded.

She picked him up in her arms and left the house,

slamming the door behind her. In the car she put on a tape. Kylie Minogue. She sang along with it, heavily painted lips enunciating every word. When the little boy was falling asleep she turned the tape down.

'Thank God for Valium!' she sighed.

Twenty minutes later, she arrived at a derelict building. Parking the car, she got out and picked up the little boy who was snoring softly. She pushed open the old wooden door to the depot.

'Goodbye, little chicken, goodbye.'

She whispered the words into his ear as she placed him on a broken-down sofa. Then she quietly left the building.

She drove off with a squeal of tyres, just missing the canal bank that skirted the building. The water was filthy, full of old bedsteads and car tyres. It was also stinking.

'Straight into the water, boy! My own little water baby!'

The woman was laughing out loud as she drove away.

Kate got to the hospital at 10.50 that night. Patrick was awake as she'd guessed he would be. He was over the moon to see her.

'I love you, Kate. Whatever you think of me, don't ever forget that, will you?'

She shook her head. 'I love you too. I missed you more than I thought possible.'

They were quiet for long moments.

'About the club, Kate . . .'

She put a hand gently over his mouth. 'It doesn't matter, Patrick. None of it matters now. I know everything and I want to help you any way I can.'

A nurse came in and smiled at them. 'How's the patient?'

'I'm OK. Did you do what I asked?'

She nodded, looked over her shoulder and then said quietly, 'Dr Tarbuck will be here to see you first thing. You should be moved by ten-thirty in the morning.'

'What's going on?'

Kate's voice was cold and Patrick grabbed her hand.

'I am exercising my prerogative to go private, that's all. I got the nurse here to phone a mate of mine and he's sorting it all out.' He saw her sceptical look and said loudly, 'Tell her who he is, Nurse, before she starts questioning me. She's Old Bill so she can't help doing that. It's a bad habit she's acquired over the years!'

'Dr Tarbuck is a very respected neurologist. He has a private practice and Mr Kelly is going to be moved to his hospital in Brentwood, Essex.'

Kate's mouth was a grim line.

Patrick pleaded with her. 'Come on, Kate. I can't take up a bed in the Health Service that could go to someone who really needs it when I can pay and get Sky Sports and a proper drink in me room!'

She laughed reluctantly. 'You are definitely on the bloody mend.'

He shrugged. 'Find a decent cup of coffee for this one, will you, love?'

The nurse left the room.

'I can't stay here, Kate,' he hissed. 'Fuck me, they offered me a salad tonight that looked more in need of fucking doctoring than I do!'

She laughed despite herself.

'I need a bit of space, love. When you go home will you bring me in some proper pyjamas and that?'

She didn't answer him.

'You are back home, Kate?'

She shook her head. He closed his eyes and sighed.

'Please don't leave me to get over this alone. I need you, Kate. More than ever before. I am frightened to go to sleep in case I go back into a fucking coma.'

His voice was harsh and the fear in it communicated itself to Kate.

'Let's get you back on your feet, eh? Take one day at a time. I'm there for you twenty-four seven. You know that, Patrick.'

'I don't know about getting me back on me feet. I wouldn't mind laying you on your back . . .'

She put her hand over his mouth again. 'Like I said, darling, one step at a time, eh?'

He grinned and her heart melted. How could she ever have imagined she could live without this man? What did it matter how he made his money? As he had pointed out from the start he had never pretended to be completely kosher. She had known what he was and had still loved him. Now she could not imagine being without him.

Even if he had committed murder.

That fact frightened her more than anything. It

went against everything she believed in, but it was a fact and Kate dealt in facts.

She kissed him hard on the mouth and with that gesture sealed both their fates.

Chapter Twenty-Four

Tristram McDavey thought of himself as a hot-shot estate agent. He was vain, he was gelled and he was dressed in designer clothes. He prided himself on being able to sell anything, absolutely anything. As he drove his client, John Larvey, towards the old Lux factory, Tristram was already selling him the property.

'It's ideal for what you want. There's ample parking for lorries, and the old depot itself is over four thousand square metres. More than enough for what you want and still enough space for further offices if you need them.'

He laughed gently, showing perfectly capped teeth. 'And let's face it, the way you're going you *will* need them.'

'Do you think the owners will come down on the price?'

Tristram nodded vigorously. 'Without a doubt. I've had this place for a while and between me and you they won't get the asking price.'

He negotiated a steep turn flamboyantly in his

BMW Cabriolet, making Mr Larvey's face go pale with fright.

'I have told them over and over that it is a sought-after property but it has to be realistically priced. If you are interested – and I think you will be when you see the location – I shall put myself out on a limb to get you a substantial discount.'

He drove through a muddy puddle and looked at himself in the mirror, checking his hair.

'I'm sure we could come to an arrangement,' he murmured.

Tristram didn't tell Mr Larvey that he often overpriced things so the buyer felt they had got a bargain when he supposedly haggled the price down to a realistic level. It was good psychology as far as he was concerned. No one could resist a bargain.

As they pulled up outside the dilapidated building, Tristram checked his hair once more. He was a great believer in making a good impression and made a point of always looking well groomed and in control.

He had parked in the least filthy part of the large yard before the building, having been caught out here before, getting out of his car and stepping straight into a puddle of mud and rust, ruining an expensive pair of shoes from Brown's. A mistake he was not going to repeat.

The air was crisp as they stood admiring the imposing building. Tristram extolled its virtues as they walked the perimeter, carefully steering his client away from the smelly canal.

'It certainly seems to be what I'm looking for.'

Tristram preened himself in the knowledge that he was in for a good chunk of the sales commission. He was determined to get shot of this place and in doing so, to prove to his bosses what a shit-hot salesman he was.

'It is rather out of the way, though.'

Mr Larvey was wavering and Tristram said carefully, 'With respect, I'd have thought that was part of its charm. You will have lorries?'

'Artics, actually.'

'Artics then, leaving here at all hours of the day and night. In an area of residential streets that can cause problems. Out here, who is going to complain? Certainly not the wildlife!'

He laughed loudly at his own wit and Mr Larvey was quiet, pondering what he'd said.

'You never see anyone round this way, or at least very rarely. It's very quiet and private here. You could be dead and no one would know for months!' Tristram joked.

He had the sale, he was convinced of it. Mr Larvey looked sold. It was an expression he had come to recognise. People tried to look nonchalant and that told him, clever dick that he was, that they were interested. More than interested.

He carried on with his carefully planned sales pitch.

'I know the roads aren't too well maintained in the immediate vicinity, but it's only a mile or so and with the tyres on your lorries not such a problem. I think the great thing about this place is the fact that you will be bothering no one. In these days that is such a bonus. All you seem to see on the news lately is people protesting about noise from industrial areas.'

Mr Larvey sighed his agreement. It was the reason he was looking for new premises himself.

'Come inside and let me show you the *pièce de résistance*!' Tristram pushed open the broken door, registering the fact that someone had been there since he'd last visited. The door was jemmied open and he cursed himself for not checking the place over yesterday. All they needed now was to encounter New Age travellers or tramps.

But Mr Larvey was not registering the broken door, he was too busy staring at the large expanse of floor. Probably seeing it bustling with his own busy workforce. Tristram smiled smugly and mentally chalked up one more big commission to himself. Then he realised what Mr Larvey was staring at.

A small boy was standing in the middle of the floor, urinating.

The two men looked at one another when the child said in a high piping voice, 'Where's the lady gone?'

Boris walked up the narrow stairs. His normally impassive face looked worried, something he rarely allowed.

The girl who had opened the door to him was weeping. She knew she was in trouble.

'Please, I couldn't do it.' She was almost incoherent with fear and Boris looked into a pair of deep brown eyes that pleaded for his understanding.

He stared around the room. The cameras were still

set up. The lights had made the place like a hothouse and the girl's face was beginning to bruise around her left cheekbone.

Boris looked at Geoff Marchant, his face hard now. 'Who arranged this?'

Marchant was nervous and it showed. His forehead was beaded with sweat that had nothing to do with the heat from the lights.

'I thought it would be a good idea.'

Boris stared at him and Sergei knew that trouble of the worst kind was brewing. He could read his boss like a book and Boris was near to blowing. Geoff Marchant, however, did not know the signs and was obviously hoping to talk himself out of deep shit.

Sergei smiled to himself. Would these English never learn?

'Have I got this right?' Boris looked at Geoff with raised eyebrows, as if desperate for his opinion, and Sergei cringed inwardly. 'You were making a film here with this young lady . . .' He looked at the girl enquiringly.

'Soraya. My name is Soraya.'

Boris smiled widely, making his whole countenance seem benevolent, caring. '. . . with this young lady, Soraya.' He smiled at her as he spoke. 'And you decided to introduce a German Shepherd dog?'

She started to cry again.

'I'm not being troublesome,' she snivelled, 'but I'm not doing that! I don't like it here and I want to go home.'

'I thought it would make it different,' Marchant

said arrogantly. 'I didn't realise I had to discuss the film's content with you.'

Marchant was being clever now or so he thought. Sergei marvelled at the man's stupidity. Boris looked at him like a fly he was thinking of swatting.

'Fuck the content. I understand that her screaming brought the police to this door. They came here for the first time ever.'

Geoff could no longer meet Boris's piercing gaze.

'I have a house full of prostitutes from all over Europe and *you brought the police to my door*. Do you think I can overlook something like that?'

Geoff looked at Soraya, who was cowering on a white leather sofa, hiding her face in her hands. Her shoulders were shaking and she looked very small and very frightened. He felt a momentary urge to slam the silly bitch against the wall and crack open her head.

'If you are so stupid, or more to the point if you think *I* am so stupid as to allow someone like you to bring the police to my premises, then I don't think we have anything more to say to one another. Do you?'

Geoff felt his heart sink. He knew he was dealing with a dangerous man here. Knew he was making the Russian richer, too. But men like Geoff Marchant were eminently expendable in this industry. Pimps and porno film-makers were ten a penny in the smoke and he realised with a sickening lurch of his stomach that his job was not as important as he had led himself and others to believe.

He had known while he was pushing Soraya into doing what he wanted that he should have left it.

There were plenty of women who would do things like that for the right price. In fact, he knew one girl who said she preferred it to strange men, a statement he had never asked her to explain.

But he had had a lot of coke, and as usual, that had been his downfall. He had pushed it. He was renowned for pushing things, and usually it didn't matter. These girls were lower than scum. They expected to be treated badly. He often forced them to do things they had never done before. But this bitch had been adamant, becoming more and more hysterical. Eventually she had lost it and that was when the trouble started.

Now he was in a position where he could not, in all honesty, justify what he had done. When the police had arrived he had been terrified. Not of them, but of the fact that they had come to Boris's safe house, a house where he plied more than one trade and paid heavily for the protection not just of himself but of his customers. Most of them were wealthy businessmen and other high-profile people who paid for discretion and a bit of sex that was out of the norm.

Soraya was led gently from the room. She would be taken care of by Sergei. Geoff was left alone with Boris and one of his larger henchmen, a huge Chechen called Olaf. When Boris bowed and left the flat Geoff knew he was saying goodbye to the world.

He tried his best to take it like a man.

But he didn't manage it.

Soraya listened to it all wide-eyed. Sergei decided she had been frightened enough; she would keep her mouth shut. He gave her a few downers and let her sleep it off.

But he was as aware as Boris that their lair was now tainted and they would have to think fast about finding another. It was always something silly, like a noise complaint, that brought you to the attention of the authorities. Better to cut your losses than to wait around and hope for the best.

Geoff Marchant had cost them dearly and he had paid dearly.

Such was the world they lived in.

Kate was over the moon. It seemed they had found Trevor Pallister, and unlike the other children he was a good talker. She watched him with his grandmother and smiled.

Barbara Epstein obviously loved the child and was going to take custody of him. It had been hard explaining to her that her daughter had allowed him to be used by paedophiles. It had taken her a while to even take on board what they were talking about. But seeing him, hale and hearty, had pushed the other thoughts from her mind. Trevor was in her arms and he was alive. After what had happened to her daughter she was so deeply grateful for that.

Kate knew that as more and more emerged, Barbara Epstein was going to have to come to terms not just with the death of her daughter but with the horrific implications of Sharon's lifestyle. Trevor would be scarred for life by what he had seen and had done to him. He was safe but quite possibly his young life was already ruined.

Robert Bateman had sent a young social worker called Karen Dillon to oversee Trevor's interrogation by Jenny. He had not been able to come himself, he explained, due to pressure of work. Karen was pretty and gentle, just what the little boy needed.

Eventually he was seated on a small sofa with his grandmother and the social worker. Kate and Jenny sat on another sofa opposite. They were low and uncomfortable for everyone except Trevor.

Jenny had already chatted to him and made friends. He was an outgoing child and rather mischievous. He was also aggressive, there was no doubt about that. He used bad language as part of his everyday speech, and on top of all that he was as bright as a button. He knew that something was going on and that he was to be the centre of attention. In short, he was in charge and he knew it.

Kate was saddened by his knowing demeanour and sorry every time she heard him swear. He was a beautiful child, yet it seemed he had been dragged up to fend for himself. It was heartbreaking.

Jenny smiled at Trevor as he ate a Milky Bar.

'Who took you from Mummy's house?'

He stared into her eyes for long seconds before answering, 'The nice lady.'

Kate and Jenny exchanged glances.

'What did the lady look like?'

He licked his lips as he thought over the question, his tongue snaking as far over his cheeks as his muscles would allow to gather up every crumb of stray chocolate.

'She had a nice smell like apples and nice hair.'

'What was her hair like?'

'She had lots of different hair. Hair for every day of the week, she said.'

'Pretend hair?'

He nodded. 'All in a cupboard in the man's bedroom.'

'The *man's* bedroom?'

He nodded vigorously. 'The man in the toilet.'

'The toilet?'

He grinned. 'He was funny and he tried to kiss me.'

No one laughed and Trevor was quiet for a minute.

'He was a nice man. I liked him. He liked me.' Then his eyes filled with tears as he asked, 'Where's my mummy? Is she still on the floor?'

He was crying now and Barbara hugged him to her. His eyes scanned them all warily, like a small-time creeper who has been caught red-handed in someone's home and doesn't seem to understand how it all happened. How the hell he ever ended up in someone's bedroom stealing their jewellery and their memories. Kate felt great sorrow that any child should be like he was. It seemed as if he was waiting for them to ask him something else. She rose from her seat and left the room. She couldn't listen to any more, would watch the video of it. Somehow that made it less personal.

She didn't know how Jenny could listen to stuff like this on a daily basis. It was all she dealt with. Kate could never have borne that.

In her office the phone was already ringing. She ignored it. Taking out the statements of all the women, she began to read through them once more.

Regina Carlton was now well enough to be interviewed, apparently, and Kate was going to visit her that afternoon. She was going to systematically revisit each and every person arrested for their part in the paedophile scandal. Each and every one of them would be questioned about Suzy Harrington and DI Barker.

Someone was going to let something drop, she was sure of that.

Jeremy Blankley was going to get a surprise tonight in his prison cell courtesy of Kenny Caitlin and Kate fervently hoped it might jog his memory.

She was using tactics Patrick would normally adopt – but she didn't allow herself to dwell on that. This case had to be sorted, for the sake of the children of Grantley. She wanted to wrap it up and let everyone get on with living their lives. Then maybe she and Patrick could get back to the way they once were.

She wanted Barker and she wanted Harrington, and she was determined to get them.

Patrick was tired.

The move to the private nursing home had taken it out of him. As Dr Tarbuck had explained, it was still early days and although he felt that he was on the mend his body had suffered a major trauma.

Even the private ambulance and the care of its highly trained staff had not stopped him from suffering a raging headache and complete exhaustion. But now he was out of the ICU and in a room that looked like a

Martina Cole

comfortable hotel bedroom, all chintz curtains and cushion covers and tasteful prints. Nothing spectacular but certainly better than the cracked ceilings and flaking paintwork of the NHS!

Even the bed was more comfortable and his Sky channels were in working order. He had his privacy, with a full en-suite bathroom. He also had access to two phones, a computer and fax. All in all, it was a much better deal – although, as he reasoned, at over a grand a day they should have thrown in a secretary with big tits and long legs.

Closing his eyes against the pain, he relaxed back into the cool pillows. Migraine could become a regular feature of his life according to good old Tarby. But even if that was the upshot Patrick was grateful to be alive.

He knew that the Russian had not banked on his being around after the shooting. But, from what he could gather from Willy, Boris was sorry for that now. It was a misunderstanding, nothing personal, just business, apparently.

Well, Patrick would give him fucking business when he was finished with him! Boris had more front than Brighton if he thought Patrick Kelly was going to roll over like a good little doggie after someone had had the flaming audacity to have him shot.

Business or no fucking business.

Every time he thought about being shot, in broad daylight and in front of a herd of shoppers, he could cheerfully get out of his sick bed and shoot the Russian ponce himself.

Boris had also told Willy that any charges made against him would never stick. He could have them dismissed at the drop of a hat. Patrick had no doubt that what Boris said was true. He just wondered who was on the take, and were they also on the take from him?

There was so much to find out, and to do it all he had to be well and truly back on his feet. He wanted to face that ponce with his usual strength and bravado intact. It was, in fact, something he *needed* to do. Just to prove to himself, and to everyone else, that he still had what it took to run his empire. If he didn't, every little grifter with a dream of the big time would be out after him.

Patrick had a lot to think about and a lot of catching up to do, but he would get there in the end. He always did.

He tried to stretch over to the buzzer and the effort it took reminded him of just how weak he still was.

Outside the door were two men, handpicked by Willy to keep an eye on him just in case the Russian decided on a repeat performance. The knowledge irritated him even though he knew that what Boris had said was true. It wasn't personal, it really was just business.

He hoped to fuck that if he had to waste Boris, the Russian would be just as fucking understanding.

Patrick had tried to talk to him. The Russian had in effect blanked him. That still rankled. Now Boris was running Patrick's club, and creaming it for all it was worth. He could not, in all honesty, swallow much more. There would be a showdown, and it would be sooner rather than later.

Willy said that for all they had put him through, he had not disliked the Russian boss. He said Boris was a real old-time villain and Patrick respected Willy's opinion. Nonetheless he would be looking out for himself and his own interests.

Boris had had him shot like a mad fucking dog in the middle of Ilford High Street. It rankled still and Patrick knew it would rankle for a long, long time.

At least until he had faced the man down once and for all.

Regina Carlton looked at the woman opposite her and wasn't sure whether to laugh or cry. In fact, she wondered if she was hallucinating.

'Long time no see, Reggie.' Her visitor's voice was husky.

'What do you want here? I promised you I'd never tell anyone about you. Why have you come here?'

Regina's voice was rising in panic and the woman grinned in a friendly way.

'Calm down, my love. I am just concerned, that's all. After all, Reggie, you're an old friend. I've known you since you were a child. And I knew your babies, didn't I? How are they? Have they taken them off you again?'

Regina didn't answer.

'I've brought something lovely for you, dear. Have a guess what it is?'

She shook her head, fear evident in her eyes even

though she was pumped full of drugs and relaxants.

'Oh, go on. You used to love surprises, didn't you?'

The falseness of the woman's voice made Regina remember things she would rather put out of her mind.

'You look like my mother,' she said.

The woman grinned, showing pointed white teeth.

'I know. Isn't it a fabulous look? I love a wig, as you know – I always have. They're my trademark, you see. I can walk around and be whoever I want in a wig, can't I?'

Regina didn't answer; she was still staring at her visitor fearfully.

'Relax, for Christ's sake! Anyone would think you'd never seen me before. I just wanted to make sure you were OK. I am, after all, a very old friend.'

'You are no friend of mine, mate.' Regina was trying to look past her visitor but couldn't get the attention of the nurse outside the room. A large hand came across the table, nails painted red, and gripped her wrist until she yelped in pain.

'Listen to me, Regina, and I'm not joking. I can make you or break you, lady – I always could. Now I have been a touch to you and you had better remember that when that filth comes sniffing round. And she will. She's going to visit you today. See how much I can find out when I want? I'll know everything you said to her within hours. Do you get my drift? If anything about me or our little scam comes out, *I will know*. And then I'll be back and that is when you'll really need to start worrying, isn't it? I know you dumped your kid on that building site . . .'

Regina was shaking her head now, in distress. 'I never did. I wouldn't do that!'

The other woman laughed. 'Fuck off, dear. You don't know what you're doing half the time.'

But Regina, off the hard drugs and on to anti-depressants, was a lot more aware than she had been for years. Her mind was fragile but it was clear enough.

She leaned across the table and hissed, 'I know who you are, remember that. You can't hurt me any more. I know what you do and what you get out of it. So listen, *mate*. You leave me and my kids alone, do you hear me? I've had enough of your sick fucking games. You can't frighten me any more. I can sort meself out, the doctor said.'

The red-stained mouth curled in contempt.

'Listen to it, for fuck's sake! The doctor said what? You couldn't work out your own fucking age, you silly bitch, if someone didn't remind you. Once out of here the safety net is gone and you'll be back on the skag in a week. People like you are born, girl, not made. You were born to be destroyed and if someone like me or your mother doesn't do it, you'll do it all on your own. Don't talk to me about what you can and can't do! What you will do, Regina, is what you always did, and that is what you're fucking told, OK? Do I make myself clear or shall I punch it into that thick fucking head of yours?'

It was the voice she hated, the voice that could

reduce her to a quivering wreck. It was the voice of her mother. It had the same timbre, the same clipped way of speaking, and all the same exasperation and disgust.

Regina quailed under the assault.

'I haven't come all this way to *discuss* this, I have come to *tell* you what you are going to do. I wasn't aware that I had *allowed* you to even have an opinion on the matter. Have I missed something here?'

Regina was sweating. It was running down between her breasts and under her blouse on her back. As she looked into the painted face before her she saw visions from her childhood and from her children's short lives. She closed her eyes tightly and hoped against hope that when she opened them the visitor would be gone.

'Tell them nothing about recent events or about Jackie Palmer and that cunt Caroline. So now you know what to do, don't you?'

That laugh again, lighter this time. 'See you again, sweetheart.'

Regina watched as her visitor left the room, smiling and greeting people like a queen acknowledging her subjects.

Regina went back to her cell and lit a cigarette. She sat on the bed and smoked it. Then she went into the bathroom and smashed a safety razor so she could get to the blade.

Tears rolling down her face, Regina ripped open her arms. The stitches had not healed properly and the skin opened quickly and painfully.

Then she sat down on the floor and watched as the life's blood ran from her body.

Kate arrived two hours later and made her way to the psychiatric wing of Grantley Hospital. She had brought cigarettes and fruit, wanting to make a good impression. When she asked on reception to see Regina she was told to wait until a nurse could speak to her. Fifteen minutes later she was taken into a side room where, after establishing who she was, the nurse looked at her sadly.

'Regina is back in hospital, I'm afraid. On the general side. She tried to commit suicide again – we don't know why. She really was on the mend. She opened up her arms again. This time she's had to have an operation to stitch them back up.'

Kate was perplexed. 'I thought she was still under constant supervision?'

'She was, but she had a visitor by all accounts – a Suzy Harrington. She seemed quite happy to see her. It was directly after the visit that she cut her wrists.'

Kate was amazed. 'Did you see her?'

The nurse shook her head. 'Sorry, I wasn't on. I'm only doing a late today – my shifts are all over the place lately. The duty nurse saw her. Shall I get her to call you? She's gone home.'

'Can I catch her there now?'

The other woman smiled. 'Well, you might, but she's gone out with a crowd of other nurses and their partners to see *Cats*. They go every now and again, by coach. You can book it through the local paper. She's back on duty in the morning.'

'Can I have her address, please? I might have to see her before then. And who can I talk to concerning Regina and her prognosis?'

'You'll have to see her consultant, Mr Manners. He's over in A&E at the moment, as he's the duty registrar as well.'

Kate thanked her. The name Suzy Harrington had been enough to give her a buzz.

Suzy had finally made a mistake. She had finally come out of the woodwork.

If she was involved with Regina, it meant she was involved with them all. Smiling at the woman's stupidity, Kate made her way to A&E.

She hoped that Regina would be able to talk soon but didn't hold out much hope. She had already been well over the edge, Kate knew that herself. The move from Rampton back to Grantley had been surprising and Kate wondered now who had arranged it.

She was puzzled about it all, but also elated.

If she could get a witness to say that Suzy had been here, she could place her once and for all with one of the mothers. Before and after her arrest.

It wasn't much, but at least it was a start.

Chapter Twenty-Five

Janice Hollington was dressing for work when she saw the police car arrive. She'd looked out of her bedroom window to see who was being visited. Janice was a gossip, and like most dedicated gossips, what she didn't know she surmised and what she surmised immediately became fact.

Her penchant for embellishing stories had caused her trouble over the years at Grantley Hospital where she worked on the psychiatric wing. At fifty-two she was nearing the end of her nursing days and she knew it. She liked the job which paid enough for her to have a good holiday every year with her husband George, but her habit of sifting through the most mundane of conversations and sensationalising them had made her colleagues wary of her.

Janice started gossip and embroidered it until it fitted her mood at the time. She knew this, but it didn't stop her from indulging in her favourite pastime. Consequently, she was given a wide berth and treated rather distantly by her fellow members of staff who had experienced her troublemaking at first hand.

When she saw a uniformed policewoman and another in civilian clothes walking along the pavement outside she nearly had a seizure, convinced they had finally come to arrest Mandy Clarkson's son, Thomas, for drug dealing or similar.

At last, it was happening! She'd known by the way he dressed and that stud in his nose that he was breaking the law somehow. You only had to look at his long hair and baggy trousers to see that much. Art student indeed!

Then Janice saw the women hesitate at her gate. Her mouth was a perfect O as she realised they were coming to see *her*. The uniformed woman stayed put. To see a plainclothes policewoman walking up her path was a terrible shock. There could be only one reason to bring the police to her respectable doorstep.

Her husband must have died.

On her way downstairs Janice wondered how she felt about that, and was amazed to find that she didn't actually feel upset. But, she reasoned, no one had actually told her that he was dead yet so maybe she was still due for a shock.

She opened the front door, a hesitant smile on her coral-painted lips.

'Mrs Hollington?' Kate enquired pleasantly. 'May I talk to you for a moment, please? DI Kate Burrows, Grantley police.'

Janice registered the ID card with the woman's picture on it and thought it didn't do her justice. She looked like a convict herself in the grainy black and white photo.

'Please. Come in.' She took Kate through to her pristine lounge with its burgundy Dralon corner unit and large overfilled MFI cabinets.

'Now – how can I help you?'

Kate noticed the gleam in the woman's eyes and realised she was enjoying the drama.

'Can I get you a coffee? Or tea perhaps?' Janice asked.

'No, thank you. I am just going to ask you a few questions about work yesterday. I understand you were on duty and brought in a visitor to Regina Carlton. A certain Suzy Harrington?'

She saw Janice Hollington visibly relax.

'Oh, you scared me. I thought me husband was dead and I was already spending the insurance in me head!' She laughed nervously and Kate laughed with her, though she wasn't sure if it was an actual joke. It sounded more like a statement of fact.

'Can you remember her?' she asked politely.

Janice grinned. 'How could I forget? What's he done?'

Kate was nonplussed. 'I'm sorry, who are you talking about?'

Janice shook her head knowingly. 'It was a transvestite, that Suzy, I'd lay money on it. We've had a few of them on the unit over the years.'

Kate was still unsure what she meant.

'Can you start at the beginning?' she asked. 'Tell me exactly what you saw.'

Janice pointed to a seat and Kate sat down. Janice perched on the end of the corner unit and crossed her legs at the ankle.

'I knew it was a bloke straight off. But then, we get so many strange cases these days as I'm sure you are aware. So I just acted normal like. He was a tallish man, in a wig and heavy make-up. He was dressed smartly, though. Not over the top. From a distance he could probably get away with it. Nice eyes.'

'You're sure this was the person who came to see Regina Carlton?'

Janice nodded vigorously. 'No doubt at all, she gets so few visitors. Mainly her solicitor or Social Services. Not only that, he was so outlandish you couldn't help remembering him really.'

'You are sure it was a man?'

Janice grinned again. 'Look, love, I *know* it was a bloke. He had great big feet and hands. Even without the obvious, you could just *tell*. Nice eyes and nice teeth, I remember that much, but the make-up was overdone. Heavy foundation so he ain't had any hormone treatment. Definitely a TV not a trans-sexual.'

Janice laughed, launching into one of her stories.

'We had one on the unit last year – right nutter. He used to walk around the streets late at night dressed as a woman. His wife had had enough and in the end he was talked into going into hospital voluntarily. He was a barrister and all, but there you go. It affects all sorts. I still see his wife sometimes, you know, around town. I have to laugh. She never acknowledges me like, but she knows I know. You being a policewoman would probably know him if I said his name . . .'

Kate didn't like the way the woman was practically confiding someone else's private business in her. She knew that if she asked for the name she would get it. Instead she stood up.

'I'll send round a PC to take a statement from you. If you remember anything else that might be of help you can tell them, OK?'

Kate knew she was being petty, just dismissing the woman, but Janice's sort got on her nerves.

Janice stood up uncertainly. 'Well, it was a shock as you can imagine. But after what I read in Carlton's notes . . . I mean, is it really surprising she'd mix with that type of person? I wonder, could I ask why you are enquiring about her? Is it to do with her kids and that?'

The last was said in a low, concerned voice as if they were in a room full of onlookers. She was letting Kate know that she was in on what was happening.

Kate ignored her. 'Thank you for your help,' she said, and was out of the house almost immediately. People like that really did leave a bitter taste in her mouth.

Kate knew her visit would be a hot topic of conversation for Janice, in the hospital as well as with the neighbours. Regina didn't need any more on her plate than she already had, but thanks to the Janice Hollingtons of this world she was going to get much, much more than she'd bargained for.

But if Janice was telling the truth about the visitor

being a TV, which Kate felt she was, then this case had taken on yet another strange dimension.

As she got into the back of the police car it gave Kate food for thought. All the mothers, though admittedly involved with the paedophile ring, had sworn they personally had not done anything to their children. This was a long shot, and she knew it was, but what if someone had dressed as them? Trevor had said something about pretend hair . . . hair for every day of the week. And he was too small to understand about men dressing as women, would have assumed it was a real woman. He'd also said the person smelled of apples and that had struck a chord in Kate's head though she couldn't think why.

Had someone else said it? She would have to comb through the statements again.

Whoever had visited Regina had distressed her enough to make her try once more to end her life. So what had they said? Regina was under heavy sedation, pushed over the edge again. She had been the catalyst for their investigation, the first mother to be arrested. She had also sworn over and over that whatever she was guilty of, she had not tried to kill her son.

If someone else was behind it all, then whoever it was knew about the paedophile ring, knew the children were being abused and knew the mothers. Every movement of their lives. Someone had watched them and had taken opportunities that were as dangerous as they were sinister.

Maybe the mothers had been telling the truth all along. Maybe they had *not* abandoned their own children. Maybe whoever had taken Trevor and little Mikey had also killed their mothers. It would have been a logical step if they'd been opposed while trying to snatch the kids.

This was quite a story Kate was spinning herself but it was all she had. That and Barker.

She needed to talk to his wife and she needed to do it soon. She was also due to see Kerry Alston today and wondered what fresh revelations that might bring.

She lit another cigarette and stared out at the passing scenery without seeing it. All she could see was Suzy Harrington walking away from arrest.

Well, not for long. Not if Kate Burrows had anything to do with it. Suzy's days of being protected by an influential pervert were strictly numbered.

Boris ate slowly as usual. He savoured food, enjoying the taste and the texture of it. Sergei usually knew better than to question him while he was eating but today he decided to chance it.

'Have you thought any more about Patrick Kelly?'

Boris looked at him for a few moments before answering.

'What is there to think about? He is an intelligent man. He understands. I will take the club from him for a fair price. What has he to worry about?'

Sergei, for the first time ever, wondered if his friend and mentor had become overconfident. It was almost inconceivable, admittedly, but there was a first time for everything. How to hint as much without causing offence was going to be difficult. Boris was always on his dignity, looking for slights where none were intended and constantly questioning his men, trying to gauge their opinion of him. He needed their reassurance that he was respected by everybody. And, if Sergei guessed rightly, so did Patrick Kelly. He had a feeling that once Mr Kelly was back on his feet, he might well come looking for retribution. Boris would. Sergei himself would. Why was his boss so convinced that Kelly wouldn't?

'It will be seen to have been done, though. It will be common knowledge among his peers . . .' Sergei's voice trailed off mid-sentence. He knew better than to push it. Just to plant the seed of doubt was usually enough.

Boris shook his head in a friendly way. 'He's not a real villain. Too soft now. He was looking for an out at some point. I mean, he was a sleeping partner, for God's sake. No, he'll let it go. Once Mr Gabney has explained the situation Kelly would have to be a lunatic to try and do anything to us. We blew up his offices. We went to his woman's home. We shot him in the street like a dog. He knows our strength – he'd be crazy to try anything.'

Sergei didn't answer and Boris, aware that his orders were being subtly queried, carried on talking. He wanted to justify his position.

'Patrick Kelly is an also-ran, as they say here. At home he would have been murdered long ago, you and I both know that. It's why we came here. We knew that our kind of operation would clean up in Europe. They can't control us here. Aren't geared up for our ruthlessness or our immense strength. We have the money and we have the power to take over. In five years we will run this country as we do our own.'

He laughed at the picture he was painting.

'Look how easy it was to walk in here, buy a house for cash in Holland Park costing two million, then mortgage it to the hilt. We had clean money in under a month. This country was ripe for a killing and we obliged. Don't worry about Kelly. He will know by now that I have in effect taken over London and I didn't even have to fight for it.

'The money everyone earns for me and for themselves is enough to guarantee their allegiance. We are invincible. I let Kelly live as a sort of public relations exercise. Everyone knows he was defeated and that he took it like a man. It will be a very clear example of what we are capable of. What we are really about.'

Boris looked at his number two and smiled, his handsome face brimming with confidence.

'So, Sergei, stop worrying and let me eat, eh?'

Sergei saw the sense in what he was saying but the uneasy feeling remained with him. From what he had heard about Kelly he was very much like Boris: fair but hard. But unlike Boris, he would not take any chances. He would take out the opposition even if he liked and respected them.

It was good business sense and Sergei was inclined to go with Kelly on that one. But of course he didn't say this to his boss. He was aware that if anything *did* happen to Boris, he would be expected to take everything over.

There was always that to take into consideration. After all, a man had to look after himself, didn't he?

Kerry looked terrible. Her eyes were black-ringed and she looked as if she needed a good bath. Kate could smell her across the table, a mixture of hand-rolled cigarettes and sweat. She looked back with a sneer on her mouth and a set to her shoulders that told Kate she was not in for an easy time. But she didn't care. She could play the game, too.

She started it by lighting a cigarette. Kerry stared at it with undisguised longing. Kate pushed the pack across the table and the prisoner lit up with alacrity.

'I miss the tailor-mades more than anything.'

'More than your kids, I should imagine, knowing you like I do.' Kate made sure she sounded nasty and was gratified to see the expression of bewilderment on Kerry's face.

She quickly recovered herself.

'You sound happy today, Burrows. Your boyfriend getting shot must have given you the right hump.' She laughed at Kate's dark expression, at her obvious shock that someone on remand knew so much about her.

Kerry drew deeply on the cigarette. 'You make me laugh. You're trumping a known face and *you* look down on *me*?'

Kate was aware of the PO listening to all that was said.

'A sewer rat would look down on you, Kerry. At least they take care of their babies.'

The other woman looked smug. She knew she had Kate on the hop and she was enjoying it.

'Patrick Kelly, eh? Bit of all right and all, him. Do you help him with his work at all? I mean, with your knowledge of the law and that . . .' She was smirking again, revealing yellowing teeth coated with tobacco and tea stains.

Kate had had enough. 'Think you're so clever, don't you, Alston? But knowing what you do about Patrick Kelly, aren't you nervous of insulting his bird? Only he can be very unpredictable where I am concerned.'

Kerry looked uncertain now.

'I mean, I have pull in here, but not half the pull that he has. He knows everyone who is anyone, my Pat.' This was said in a low confidential tone of voice.

'He also had a daughter murdered, as you probably know, so a case like yours makes him all the angrier. Funny that, isn't it? He worshipped his daughter but she died. While you . . . you try and kill your own kids. You hand them over to paedophiles and transvestites without a second's thought. Like me, Patrick finds that weird. Thinks people like you should be hanged. And let's face it, love, in here anything could happen, couldn't it?'

Kerry was so astonished at Kate's threats that she let the cigarette burn down until her fingers began to smart.

'Fuck you, Burrows.' She looked at the PO, and

whined childishly, 'She's threatening me.'

The PO grinned. She was an old hand. She knew what was going down and she laughed as she said, 'Good! Save me a fucking job, won't it, nonce?'

Kerry glanced from one woman to the other, deflated now.

'You bastard, Burrows.'

Kate smiled. 'I have come here today to help you, as a matter of fact. But let's get one thing straight, shall we? I'm not taking any more shit from you, OK?'

Kerry watched her warily, puffy eyes gleaming with cunning. 'Pull the other one. It plays "A Hard Day's Night".'

This time Kate was the smug one.

'Oh, but I did. I came here to say that I actually believe you aren't guilty of trying to kill your child. Guilty of being a nonsense certainly, but not of attempted murder. You see, I think you know very well who took your kids but it wasn't you.'

Kerry screwed up her face. 'What the fuck are you on about?'

Kate heard the hesitation in her voice and knew she was halfway there.

'Well, I heard a snatch of gossip that there's a transvestite involved. Someone you all know. This person has been to visit Regina Carlton, and just have a guess who the TV said he was?'

She smiled before carrying on, watching the changing expressions on Kerry's face.

'He said that he was Suzy Harrington. Wore a wig, had make-up plastered everywhere. Except the nurse was convinced he was really a man.'

'So who was it then?'

Kate shrugged and played her ace.

'Could it have been DI Barker by any chance?'

Kerry stared at her for a few moments and then she started to laugh. She couldn't stop herself. She was absolutely screaming with laughter. Her eyes were watering and she was waving one hand at Kate as if trying to tell her she couldn't take another joke like this.

Kate watched her stony-faced.

Between gales of laughter Kerry kept saying, 'Barker! Dressed as a woman!' It would set her off again.

Kate waited, smoking quietly, until she'd calmed down. Wiping her eyes with the back of her hand, Kerry sniffed as she said seriously, 'Barker? You honestly think this is something to do with him?'

Kate nodded.

'You are so far off the wall, lady. Barker's a cunt but he ain't got nothing to do with all this. At least if he has, and this is the truth, it's only something to do with Suzy. Now that's all I am willing to say and it's off the record. You never heard it from me. I hate him, and I mean *hate* him, but I fear him as well. His arm is a damn sight longer than yours or that poncey bloke you hang around with. Take it from me, lady, that is a fact.'

Kate was inclined to believe her. She didn't know why.

'So Suzy could be involved with him then?'

'Could be, probably is. But about the other business . . . If he was involved, the kids *would* have died, take it from me. He don't know when to stop.' She had said too much already and she knew it.

Kate pushed the cigarette packet across the table again and Kerry took another, lighting it slowly, pulling the smoke into her lungs and blowing out a perfect smoke ring.

'So who is the TV then?'

Kerry shrugged. 'No idea, mate, and that's the truth. But it ain't Barker.' She was on the verge of laughter again.

'How about Lesley Carmichael? What do you know about her?'

Suddenly the humour was gone from Kerry's face.

'I know even less about that, love.'

She was on the hop and Kate knew it.

'We are reopening that enquiry – you should get a visit soon.'

Kerry didn't answer her but said brightly, 'Bobby was in to see me last week. He said that you were all right. I was surprised, he don't normally like Old Bill.'

Kate smiled gently. 'You like Robert, don't you?'

'He's all right. Bit of a pain at times.'

'He's got you out of enough shit, I understand. He's very protective of all you girls. The only person who has ever stuck up for any of you.'

Kerry shrugged. 'He has reason to. Good reason.'

'What do you mean?' Kate frowned.

Kerry leaned across the table and picked up the cigarettes. 'I'll swap you a bit of info, OK?'

Kate nodded and Kerry took the cigarettes and placed them in front of her on the scratched table.

'He gets his rocks off with us all.'

Kate was puzzled and it showed. 'In what way?'

'Well, I used to suck him off, you know. For a few pounds or help with stuff I needed.' She was staring at Kate now, her face a mask of glee at the shock she saw registered on the woman's face.

Kate shook her head in denial. 'I don't believe you. He's gay.'

'No, he ain't. In fact, now I think about it, *he* dyes his hair. Wears make-up sometimes, too. But I can honestly say I have never seen him dressed as a woman.'

'But you have sucked him off, as you put it?'

Kerry nodded. 'On more than one occasion, dearie. We all have at some point. He calls us his girls. It's one of his things that you have to put on lots of red lipstick so it goes all over his cock and his underwear. It's what he gets off on. That and Appletise – he drinks it all the time. Been to his house? He has this thing about apples. The smell is everywhere.'

Kate's numb mind was already registering where she had smelled apples. It was at Robert's house! That was what Trevor had remembered.

As the enormity of what she was thinking hit her she felt sick. She had actually been round to his home and spoken to him and the chances were that Trevor had been there all the time.

But then she was dealing with Kerry here. Hardly a trustworthy witness. And Kate couldn't afford to let her see what a shock she had just been dealt.

'So, you have nothing to say about poor little Lesley? I thought you were her mate.'

'I ain't got no mates, Miss Burrows, never did have. Ain't you sussed that one out yet?'

Kate opened her mouth to comment and thought better of it. Instead she asked: 'Would Mary Parkes have had anything to do with Barker or Bateman?'

Kerry shrugged easily, as if she were in her own home with a mate, chatting about inconsequentials. 'Dunno. You'd have to ask her.'

'Don't you care what you've done, Kerry?'

It was said seriously and the girl had the grace to think for a while before answering.

'To be honest, no.'

It seemed to Kate that her attitude summed up all the rottenness at the heart of this enquiry.

Kate arrived home to find Kenneth Caitlin and Jenny sitting in the lounge drinking her mother's Holy Water: a litre bottle of Black Bush whiskey from duty free.

They were all pleased to see her. She took one look at the bright eyes and merry faces and regretted that she was going to have to piss all over their alcoholic fireworks.

She sat down and sighed. Took a large sip of the drink they'd poured her and stunned them all by saying, 'I think I know who it is. And I think they still have a child on the premises.'

She looked into their eager expectant faces. 'I think it's Robert Bateman.'

No one said a word for a few seconds.

'This came from Kerry?' Jenny questioned her.

Kate nodded. 'I went to see the nurse from the psychiatric wing this morning. She said the person who called herself Suzy Harrington was a man. A TV. She said they had the wig and the make-up but it was definitely a man. Now Suzy, ugly as she is, is definitely a woman, right? She's well-built with curves in all the right places. Then I saw Kerry and, according to her, Robert asks the girls for sexual favours.'

She saw the look of surprise on Jenny's face and shrugged.

'That's what I thought. Then she said he has some weird hang-ups and one of them is his love of apples. His house smells of apples, I noticed it when I was round there. When Trevor said something about an apple smell it bugged me. But in Robert's house it's an underlying smell, if that makes sense. You don't notice it immediately, it's just *there*.'

She watched them look at her in amazement.

'He also told me about Barker, and about Barker's wife being named Debbie not Mavis. Well, I phoned Ally Palmerston . . .'

Caitlin grinned. '. . . and she told you what she had told me. That Barker's *new* squeeze is called Debbie. An ex-child prostitute from Lancashire.'

'How the fuck would Robert *know* that unless he had seen Barker recently or dealt with people who had contact with him? I think we have the murderer and abductor of the children, I really do. It all makes sense. We have to go and get a warrant now.'

'We have no real evidence, though,' Jenny objected.

Kate looked into Kenny's face. 'There are still children missing. I think that's enough.'

'I can't believe it, can you?' Jenny was completely poleaxed. 'He was the one person who looked out for the girls, he was there in front of us all that time.'

Kate nodded. 'I know. But we have him now.'

Caitlin replenished his glass. 'When you're finished I'll give you all I've dug up on Barker. It makes an interesting story, as Jenny already knows.'

Kate pushed her hands through her hair.

'I'm still going to see his ex-wife, Mavis, ask her about the murder of young Lesley Carmichael. See if he's in with the girls and our paedophile ring. I still want him. I want them all.'

She finished off her drink and stood up.

'We'd better go. Robert Bateman can't be left at liberty for another night.'

Chapter Twenty-Six

Robert Bateman was rinsing his father's hair in the bath. The old man was emaciated, his body a mass of bruises and scratches. As Robert looked down on him he felt a great tide of emotion wash over him. Sometimes he loved him so much. So very, very much.

After all, he was the child now.

The thought made Robert frown.

Not that Dad had cared very much for his own child, of course. He felt angry then. Dad had used him, beaten him and hurt him whenever he'd felt like it.

Robert was shaking his head now, as the bad thoughts began taking him over again. Oh, he had not been a happy bunny when he was young. Tears stung his eyes and self-pity overwhelmed him.

His mind wandered back to his first memories of his father and mother.

He had been very small, sitting on the bed watching as his mother had carefully applied her make-up. She would take ages drawing a lip line, making her mouth look far poutier than it was. She would then paint it a vivid red, a blue-based red that made her even teeth look whiter than ever. Then she would smile at herself in the mirror.

He would clap his fat little hands and she would put some lipstick on him, smiling as she painted his face. Brushed his hair and painted his toenails. Then she would envelop him in her slim arms, a wave of cheap perfume washing over him, livening his senses.

He loved the feel of her, the way her soft large breasts bunched up as she hugged him, showing the cleavage she was so proud of.

He loved the way her merry eyes watched him as he played in the park. He loved the way she attracted attention wherever they went, from women as well as men.

He had adored her.

But his father hadn't adored her or his small son. He had given them grief, so much grief. He had attacked his lovely young wife. Beaten her. Abused his son. He had been like a dark cloud hanging over the household.

Robert would wait patiently outside the bedroom while she had her fun. He would listen to her laughing and joking, hear the noises from the men she had fun with. Then she would bring him into the still warm bed and hug and kiss him. She would squeeze him to her naked body and make him laugh. What he'd felt for her was adoration.

The man in the bath was whimpering now and

Robert felt a moment's guilt. He glanced at his watch. The water must be freezing. He'd lost over an hour again. It was happening more and more lately.

He helped the old man up and wrapped the emaciated body in a towel. At that point his father started shouting, pushing his son away, lost in his own world.

'Bethany, you whore, where are you?'

Robert closed his eyes in distress. 'Stop it, Dada!'

The old man looked at him, a cunning look in his eyes.

'She was a whore – slept with everyone. My boss, my friends, everyone.'

Robert didn't want to hear this.

'She used my child, you know, in her games. Used him against me. Tried to make me accept what she did with threats of taking him from me.'

The voice was old, high-pitched now. Gone was the deep threatening bellow from Robert's childhood. Gone was the strength that had accompanied it, too. He remembered running to his mother and wrapping his arms around her legs, to try and protect her from his father. He remembered her laughter as she would pick him up and sneer in her husband's face.

'No one could satisfy her, she was insatiable. Man after man she would have. One after the other, sometimes two or three in an afternoon. She was a whore. A whore who looked like an angel.'

The voice was quieter now, as if Dada was talking to himself, telling himself the story. Robert wiped a sweaty hand across his face. He was sick of listening to this. Since his father had gone senile he had dragged up all their old life. The life they had lived before his mother had left them to go off with the tall man, the one with thick black hair.

The man who, it turned out, had been a pimp.

The man who had wanted her to leave her small son with her husband. But he couldn't cope with a child because his own grief at the loss of her was still too acute, still far too painful. He didn't know what to do with the little boy who cried constantly for his mother. Who pushed him away with pudgy hands and refused to acknowledge him. The same child who constantly tried to get out of the house so he could search for the woman who had in effect abandoned him.

Robert relived the final dreadful scene again as he had every day of his life: Bethany, her face a mask of disgust as she looked at her husband.

'Give him to me, Johnny. I'll take him with me. He'll soon adapt to another life.'

But his father had refused, even though Robert was fighting him, trying as hard as he could to tear himself from arms that gripped him like steel bands and run to his mother.

'Take him off with your pimp, Beth? Take *my son* and bring him up in your filthy world? Never! Not while I have breath in my body.'

She was laughing then, lovely head thrown back, eyes bright.

'OK, you have him. I can have more children if I want them. I can have anything I want from life. I've already proved that to you. Have him. Keep him. He's yours.'

Robert had listened to this, stricken, and over the years he had rewritten it all to make his mother the heroine. He never saw his austere father as the man who was trying to protect him. He saw instead someone who was trying to take him from his mother – the only person to ever really love him. Living with his father and his grandmother, a woman who saw him as the fruits of sin, was a bleak existence. Gone were the hugs and the leisurely mornings in his mother's warm bed, eating toast and having sips of tea. Gone were the afternoons rifling her make-up bag and waiting for her friends to leave. Gone were the intimate baths and the love she gathered round him like a warm moist cloak.

In its place was school, prayer, and a cold, cold house. Food was plain and lukewarm, breakfast a quiet solitary affair. And John Bateman was a broken man. A broken and bitter man who looked at his young son as if he couldn't work out where the hell he had come from.

Robert's natural ebullience died a slow death in their company. His mother became the focus of his existence; she grew into a beautiful and longed-for stranger.

He missed the way she used to light up his life. Forgot the times she'd left him alone to fend for himself or slept leaving him beside an unguarded fire. He forgot the times she didn't feed him properly, plying him with sweets to keep him happy while she entertained the latest man friend. Forgot the times she slapped him – hard, stinging slaps – because he wasn't quiet enough for her. He even forgot the times he had peeped at her, sprawled naked on the sofa as a strange man assaulted her roughly and without love. He would hear the groans and run in thinking she needed help.

Or thought he had forgotten. But these memories would assail him sometimes. He would wrestle them away, forcing himself to see something different.

He forgot the times his father had walked him to school, made sure he had pocket money, taken him on long and interesting bike rides. He had been determined not to love his father and it had worked.

He also forgot the times his grandma had taken him to church and watched him proudly as he made his First Communion, his Confirmation, or read the Gospel during Midnight Mass.

They had loved him but he had forced that love away in his quest to keep his mother's memory alive.

Then he had found her and it had been the turning point of his life.

Robert heard the knock on the front door. Put his father naked on the bed and placed the restraining straps on his arms.

The old man looked at him pitifully. His body was like that of a victim from a concentration camp. All ribs and bruises.

'Don't . . . please don't leave me.'

The voice was thin, quavering with fear. He hated the cold so much. Sometimes Robert ignored him for days at a time. Then guilt would force its way through and he would go in and deluge the old man in care and attention. Until he wet the bed again or defecated while Robert was in the room with him. Then that temper would emerge, the violent temper that made his son into a demon of anger and hatred.

This had been the pattern of their life.

Walking down the stairs, Robert picked up his can of Apple Tree room spray and he sprayed it everywhere, savouring the smell.

Enjoying the memories it evoked of his mother, of her perfume.

When he saw Kate through the glass he put a smile on his face and answered the door.

'Hello, dear. Come in. I was just dressing my father.'

He saw Golding and Jenny behind her and his expression altered. Without a word he walked back inside and through to the kitchen. He was putting the kettle on when they came to join him. Turning around and looking at Kate, he said gently, 'You know, don't you?'

She nodded.

'I'm glad, to be honest. I don't think I am very well really.' He pointed to his temple. 'I hurt, in here.'

Against her will Kate felt sorry for him then. He looked so harmless, so forlorn, that he engendered only pity in her heart at that moment.

'Where are the children, Robert?'

He shrugged and turned to the small window that overlooked the garden. 'They died. So I buried them.'

Kate closed her eyes.

'Shall I make us all a nice coffee before we go?' Robert offered brightly.

Patrick lay in bed, his eyes open and his mind alert. He was tired but otherwise he felt OK. He lifted his head from the pillow and waited until the dizziness had passed before sitting up carefully.

He caught his reflection in the mirror and surveyed himself dispassionately. He was greyer, thinner in the face, looked older. The image depressed him. He put one hand to his jaw and gently squeezed the loose skin. Then he relaxed back against the pillows, registering the fact that whatever he'd thought before, he was finally getting old.

He could remember being shot now. He remembered the fear, the noise and the humiliation he had experienced. He remembered that he had evacuated himself at the final moment, from fear that he was going to die in the street like an animal.

He closed his eyes to try and blot out the images. Felt the trembling begin once more in his hands.

He knew that emotionally it was going to take time to recover. Physically, he was already on the mend. He was strong, very strong. He had proved that by his incredible survival.

But he still broke out in a sweat if he remembered that day's events. Still shook inside and out as he remembered the stinging sensation of the bullet hitting him. The terror that he was going to die without ever telling Kate he was sorry, or Willy that he'd always cared for him like a brother.

Patrick was aware for the first time ever of his own mortality and that was a frightening thing.

He closed his eyes and tried to picture Kate. He found that if he thought about her and her calmness, he relaxed. When she touched him he felt revived, happy inside. She gave him the constancy he needed. Had given him the feeling of security he craved from a relationship. He always felt complete when he was in her company.

From the first time he'd met her, when his daughter was missing and he was terrified to think what could have happened to her, Kate had been able to calm him. It was just part of her considerable charm.

The last few years had been the happiest of his life in many respects because in her company he had finally and irrevocably relaxed. No longer worrying about what he looked like or having to consider everything he said.

They had talked all the time, travelled together, loved each other. One thing he had realised early on: he needed her in order to be happy. Without her he was adrift and he knew it. Nearly losing her had finally made him realise that he had to prioritise his life. He had to put her first.

But that could only happen after he had sorted out his Russian friend.

He knew inside that until he had paid back Boris he would never feel anything even remotely like peace. He had to get his revenge on the Russian bastard who had put him in this hospital, though it could just as easily have been his coffin.

This was personal now.

Boris needed a real kick up the arse and Patrick Kelly was just the man to give it to him. Once he had taken him out of the ball game Patrick was going to retire.

He picked up the phone and dialled nine for an outside line. He was back on form and working. His recovery was nearly complete.

Robert seemed changed. It was as if the fact he'd been found out had broken the brittle thread that had held him together. Even his body seemed different. It was sluggish, looked fatter, deflated somehow. He stared into Kate's eyes.

'It was Bethany, see. I had finally seen Bethany.'

Kate nodded; she didn't speak.

'I loved her so much, I really did. She put the idea into my head.'

'Who is Bethany?' Jenny's voice was soft.

Still looking at Kate he answered, 'My mother.'

'What had your mother to do with the children?'

He closed his eyes.

'I saw those women . . . the way they treated their children. They were like her. They had all those lovely little boys and girls and didn't want them any more. When they could dress them up and play with them, take them out and show them off, they were happy. Once the kids had a mind of their own, an opinion, the mothers didn't want them.

'But I guessed what they were doing with them, you see. It was Trevor who alerted me, displaying the classic behavioural symptoms of an abused child. Sharon Pallister even told me what had been going on. She was quite upfront about it. Didn't care. Saw the child as a way of making money. I played at friendship, but I killed her in the end. I knew I would at some point, I just didn't know when.'

He was talking in a sing-song voice.

'It was all down to Barker, you see. He'd taken the mothers as children and had made them into what they were. I had no choice, I had to decide what to do. If I'd put those little kids back into the same system, they would have ended up being abused by everyone. It's how it works. At first I just wanted to attract attention to them all. Try to frighten their abusers into stopping what they were doing.'

Jenny looked at him hard. 'So you went into Regina's house and you took her son and left him on top of a building you knew was about to be demolished?'

Robert nodded. 'Oh, yes. I had keys to their houses, all my girls' houses. They didn't know that. I took them over the course of time, just in case I needed to have a look around when they weren't in. I've often done it over the years with clients. Lots of social workers do.'

He was lying, trying to justify a small offence in the face of the greater ones. Kate was amazed that he should worry about a breach of his work ethic when he had been responsible for so much more.

But he wasn't in the same world as everyone else. He was gone from them now.

'I liked Regina, but Suzy got to her. She was on my agenda of things to do. I should have taken her out first, but I didn't. Suzy took those children and dragged them through the same degradation that my mother wanted for me. You see, I saw Bethany in them all. I dressed as them – I've often dressed as a woman. Copied their clothes, their hairdos, their walks even. You see, I knew them better than anyone. I was all they had.'

'Where is Bethany now?'

Robert closed his eyes again and sighed, making a small wheezing sound from his chest. He was back in time, here in this house, looking forward to seeing his mother. He had cleaned the place from top to bottom and had made a beautiful meal. Chicken salad and minted new potatoes. A large raspberry roulade and a cheese platter.

He had spent hours rubbing the chicken with garlic and salt. Letting it marinade so that it would be fragrant and crispy. He had enjoyed waiting for her to arrive. Her voice on the phone had been so beautiful, exactly as he'd remembered it.

When she had knocked, he had felt as if his heart would explode with happiness. After all those years she was back, she was once more with her beloved son.

But time had not been kind to her. A grossly overweight woman had emerged from the voluptuous figure he recalled. Puffing and wheezing her way into his home, she had criticised everything from his décor to his dress sense. It had been nightmarish. She had insisted on seeing her husband and finally he had taken her up to see his father.

Bethany had stood at the end of the bed and enjoyed seeing her husband's disintegration. Robert had found her disgusting then, this travesty of the woman he had once adored. The woman he had recreated in the comfort and privacy of his own bedroom.

Her voice a cracked whine, she told him story after story about how life had done her down, how unhappy she had been, her pendulous breasts heaving, her breath stinking of cigarettes and brandy.

Then had come the bombshell.

She was short of funds, and this house was obviously worth a few quid. She pointed out that as she had never divorced his father she was still entitled to half, and she *wanted* it.

Needed it.

In fact, according to her, she *deserved* it.

Robert had been terrified then, terrified of what she could do to him and his life. She wanted to move back home. In her twilight years she saw it as a refuge from the hell that her life had become.

All those years of adoring her from afar and now he had seen with his own eyes what his father had realised years before.

She was a whore, the worst sort, one who would drag her own child into her trade. Those innocent cuddles remembered from his childhood were not so innocent any more. The men who had given him sweets and caresses were finally seen by Robert for what they really were. In fact, it was as if a light had come on in his head and illuminated all the memories he had repressed.

This parody of motherhood was actually telling him how much she had loved and missed him. How she was looking forward to being with him again after they had put his father into a home.

It was an assault to his sensitive ears, listening to her grating voice, and to his nostrils, smelling her over-ripe body.

He had refused. Told her outright that none of her plans were remotely possible. He had tried to be reasonable but she had taken his acquiescence for granted. She was *telling* him, not asking. She was sitting in his pristine kitchen, a living reproach to motherhood, and telling her son what she had decided he was going to do.

He forced the picture from his mind.

He knew he had stabbed her then. Was aware of it on some level. Until today he had pushed it from his mind and replaced it with the better memories. The ones where she was still lovely and smelled of apples and loved him desperately. The ones he had embellished over the years to suit his moods and the games he played with himself.

It was why he liked the Reginas and the Kerrys and the other whores. When they had placed their red-stained mouths in his lap he had been close once more to his mother. The one he had created, not the one sitting in his home smelling of degradation and decay.

He finally opened his eyes and reluctantly said to Kate, 'She's in the garden, dear. There's a few of them in there.'

Kate was nonplussed. 'What do you mean, a few of them?'

Robert grinned then, smiling boyishly at her naivety. 'A few bodies. You see, I have a habit of killing people who irritate me. Plus, I sometimes picked up young men in Soho and brought them home with me. Of course, I was always sorry afterwards. I should never have even contemplated it, they were all so *young*. But afterwards I couldn't let them go, could I? I couldn't let them tell anyone, and me a respected social worker.'

'So what you're saying is you killed an unknown number of people and buried them in your garden?'

He nodded now, eager to help. 'Oh, yes! Lots.' He clapped his hands together in glee. 'Lots and lots. People who offend me do tend to end up dead.'

He was so pleased with himself. Thought he was doing them all a big favour by telling them things. Just like a child hoping to be rewarded for telling the truth.

Jenny heard Golding say, 'Jesus Christ!' under his breath.

'There's about fifteen people buried there. Women, men and the children. I was sorry about the kids – I was very bad that day, but I never could stand crying.'

Robert frowned, thinking about what he had said. 'Yet *I* cry all the time, at sad films, things I read in the newspapers. Over things I've done, even.' He shrugged. 'They'll put me away, won't they?'

No one answered.

'You see, I had to do those things because if I didn't then someone else would have. It was like the kiddies, I knew I had to help them.'

He was in deadly earnest. 'You do understand that, don't you?'

His eyes were pleading with them to tell him he had done the right thing. He slumped down in his chair.

'Could I have a cup of coffee now, please?'

Kate nodded and Golding got up to do it.

'Is my father OK? Will someone take care of him for me?'

'Of course they will. He is being cared for even as we speak.'

Robert nodded gratefully. 'I wasn't very kind to him, you know. And he wasn't as black as he was painted. I realise that now.'

No one said anything. All were waiting for him to get it out of his system so they could put what he said in some sort of order. He gnawed on his thumbnail, his usual calm gone.

'I had a feeling it would be you who sussed me out, Kate. It was your eyes . . . they saw straight through me from the first. So I looked you up on the computer. I read about Lizzy and her overdose. She was under us for a while after her suicide attempt. I knew then that you knew how I was feeling. That you understood disappointment. That you would fight for what you thought was right the same way that I did. You had had experience of a whore first-hand and would understand my feelings of anger and jealousy.'

He leaned on the table and said in a voice that was supposed to be conspiratorial but was in reality shockingly loud, 'She slept around and had had an abortion. Did you know that, by any chance?'

Kate realised he was mocking her, and closed her eyes to hide the distress she knew was registering in them.

He shrugged disarmingly. 'Sorry, have I let out a secret? My big mouth will be the death of me.'

He laughed aloud. 'We have so much in common really but you won't see that for many years, my love. Now, after the coffee, I'll tell you what *really* happened to little Lesley Carmichael. I should know, my dear, I was there.'

He couldn't control his mirth.

'Get a warrant. I think you might just have found out all you need to know about Barker. Me and him go way back. But talk to Mavis. She'll give you the real lowdown. Silly of me to mention Debbie, wasn't it?'

'How did you kill the children?'

He sobered up then, his whole body stiffening.

'I sent them to sleep, my dear. Don't you worry, they didn't suffer at all.' This was said self-righteously.

'I would never intentionally hurt a child. Not when I am being me anyway. When I am their mother . . .' He shrugged again. 'Well, then I am allowed to do what I want. Do you understand what I am saying?'

He was cunning and clever, one step ahead of their thought-processes all the time.

'I won't even get to court, my dears. Won't be fit to stand trial, which is a pity really.' He wrinkled up his nose. 'I'd have enjoyed the notoriety.'

He carefully tidied his hair.

'Now I need a brief. After my coffee, I want to make a call. Is that OK with you?' He smiled tauntingly. 'Don't forget to tell Barker I have the goss on him, will you?'

Kate looked into a madman's eyes. Robert Bateman was so far over the edge he was never coming back. What frightened her more than anything was the fact that she had liked him. Had truly liked him. She wasn't sure exactly what that said about her, but it worried her greatly.

Jenny and Kate drank coffee and smoked with him. They knew better than to try and force anything from him. Robert had the upper hand and he knew it.

He smiled when he was charged. Smiled all the time. But it didn't always reach his eyes.

Patrick Kelly was awoken by the pressure of Kate's lips on his. He opened his eyes and smiled. Slipping his arms around her, he pulled her on to the bed with him, both of them amazed at his strength.

As he kissed her and ran his hands over her body she relaxed against him. This was what she needed. Human contact. Love. Understanding. This was all that made life bearable.

Then, pulling away, she dragged herself from his embrace. 'Suppose someone comes in?'

He grinned. 'That's why I went private, girl. Lock

the fucking door and get in here now.'

She did as he asked her, and he was overjoyed, for he could see that she needed succour as much as, if not more than, he did.

She trailed her nails down his torso, staring at him as if she had never seen him before, and suddenly he was frightened. He knew he looked different. Knew that in the harsh light of the hospital room he looked grey and ill.

He looked at her breasts above him as she leaned across to turn off the overhead light. In the half-light from the open bathroom door they gazed into each other's eyes.

'I love you, Kate.'

She smiled then. 'I love you too. Are you sure you're up to this?'

He pulled the blanket down and said hoarsely, 'Well, I'm obviously up for something, girl. See for yourself!'

She laughed huskily. This was what she had missed so much. She lowered herself on to him gently, concerned about his wounds, worried that she would hurt him. He thrust up his hips and dragged her on to him at the same time. The feeling was at once painful and exciting.

She lowered her face to his to kiss him deeply and felt him begin to shudder beneath her. She rode him harder, catching up with her own orgasm just after he had come.

Afterwards they lay together, their bodies sweaty and limbs entwined, and after everything that had happened in the last few weeks, Kate Burrows finally felt at peace.

Patrick sighed happily. 'Fuck me, Kate!'

She looked into his eyes. 'I thought I just did?'

He started to laugh and she laughed with him. They were roaring as if it was the funniest thing they had ever heard.

'Marry me?'

He wasn't sure he had heard her correctly. 'You what?' he asked.

She sat up, disengaged herself from him and gently caressed his body.

'You heard me, Patrick Kelly. Marry me.'

'Are you sure about this?'

She nodded.

Then the nurse started rattling at the door and they began to laugh again. They had needed to relieve the pressure of being apart and managed it triumphantly. It was what had always made them work, had been the thing that had kept them going for so long, and now they both knew without a shadow of a doubt that no one else would ever give them the peace they brought one another so easily.

Chapter Twenty-Seven

'You've done well, Kate.'

Ratchet's whole body seemed to be smiling. He was over the moon to have the case settled.

'And how is Patrick?'

She felt an urge to tell him where to get off once and for all. Instead she forced a smile.

'He is on the mend,' she said politely. 'What was the news you had for me?'

Ratchet was feeling pleased that she had not forced any real conversation about Kelly.

'It's about Barker. It seems he's gone missing.'

Tell her something she didn't know.

'Do you think someone might have tipped him the wink about what was going down here?' she asked.

Her superior shook his head. 'He's been missing for a week. But because of his working habits no one realised until now.' He handed her a slip of paper. 'Here are two addresses – of his wife and his ex-wife. You can talk to them.'

'Thank you, sir. Oh, and Patrick wants to know

when you are going in to see him. He says he needs to talk to you about Smallbridge Holdings.'

She saw his face go pale.

'I didn't realise you were a director in the business. It almost makes us related.' Christ, how she enjoyed watching him squirm. It was worth every second spent in his company just to witness it.

Pocketing the paper, she left the room.

Five minutes later she was on her way to Robert's house. They had found the first bodies a few hours ago.

Things were finally coming together.

Boris looked at Kate's photograph in the daily papers and despite himself he was impressed. She was obviously a good policewoman but he still thought she was bent.

Bent for Kelly.

Which meant she could be bent for him.

The more he thought about it, the more it appealed to him. He liked the look of her. She was what he thought of as wholesome. Sexy in a muted womanly way, but wholesome also fitted the bill.

He decided he wanted to meet her and put his proposition personally. She wouldn't refuse, he would make sure of that.

Sergei watched his benefactor and mentor perusing the newspapers, looking for more pictures of the dark woman, Patrick Kelly's woman, and wondered if he was going to try and use her. It certainly made sense. She was being fêted by everyone at the moment. She had closed a case that had shocked the country – had shocked the world, in fact.

Kate Burrows was now famous and her private life would come under scrutiny soon. Unless Kelly made sure it did not.

Boris sipped his coffee, which was black and strong. He savoured it with his eyes closed and his mouth pursed. But he was picturing Kate Burrows beneath him, imagining himself making love to her.

He had a feeling that it would be a very rewarding experience.

Maya stood by the hospital bed and laughed.

'Only you could get shot and end up looking better than ever!'

Patrick knew she was lying but he was pleased. It was after all meant kindly.

'Sit down, girl. Can I get you anything? Coffee, tea, a drink?'

She shook her head. 'I'm fine.'

'I wanted to see you about my getting shot but I expect you guessed that already, eh?'

She nodded. 'I know it was the Russians.'

Patrick was amazed by her acumen. Maya sussed everything, but then that was what had kept her on top for so many years.

'Clever girl.'

'Not clever, love. Nosy. It was the word on the street.' She shrugged. 'I didn't have to ask around much to find out. You've trodden on a few toes. Or shall I rephrase that? You were set up to look like you'd trodden on a few toes. I tried to warn you, remember? Look to your workforce, I said.' Her guttural accent was thicker as it always was when she was excited.

'You knew Micky was ducking and diving then?'

She nodded. 'I couldn't get involved, Pat. I have dealings with young Boris myself.'

He nodded. He had guessed as much.

'I am going to take him out of the game,' he said slowly.

Maya thought about this for a while before she nodded. 'Good. Can I be of any help?'

'You certainly can. I need to know a few places he visits regularly. To find out his movements. Can you do it?'

'Of course. Leave it with me. I'll have all you need in a few days.'

'OK. Now, how are you, me old china?'

They chatted happily about nothing very much. When Patrick's sisters turned up Maya made a move. As she walked slowly from the room he was reminded once more that they were all getting older and remembered his promise to himself that after this was resolved he was going to retire.

He was definitely too old for all this ducking and diving. It didn't excite him any more. Nothing did these days. Except his Kate.

Film crews and journalists packed the pavement outside Robert Bateman's home. Kate pushed through and refused to comment, but she had brushed her hair and repaired her make-up in the car. It always paid to look your best on TV.

In the back garden it was pandemonium. Two officers were still digging carefully, placing the dirt on to trays ready to be sifted. It was a long hard job and Kate wanted it over as soon as possible. She sat on a folding chair and was given the lowdown on what they had found already.

'We have a new body, ma'am,' a young officer told her. 'You are never going to believe this! We believe it to be DI Barker, of Soho Vice Squad.'

Kate looked almost comically surprised. The PC took her to a body bag and unzipped it.

It was Barker.

'See, ma'am? He's still got his ID in his pocket.'

'How did he die, do we know yet?'

'Looks like he was stabbed. Leila will tell you more after she's looked at him. There's bodies everywhere. Bateman just dumped them in on top of each other and replanted. The road is so deserted these days he had no real neighbours overlooking him. He could basically do what he wanted.'

'Have you found the children?'

'Not yet.'

'Right.' She went into the house. The place was being torn apart systematically.

'Anything here?' she asked in the lounge.

WPC Joanna Hart nodded, her face grim. 'Look at these, ma'am.'

They were videos.

'The children are all on them. Christ knows where

he got them from.' Her voice was disgusted. 'We have something else interesting on this first one.'

Kate looked at her askance. 'What's that then?' she asked, almost dreading the answer.

'We have Suzy Harrington showing the kids what she wants them to do. We've got her, ma'am. Bang to fucking rights.'

Kate closed her eyes in ecstasy. At last she had her! Now that Baker was off the scene she had been free to go after her, but with evidence as well it was all a foregone conclusion.

'Give that to me and I'll take it back to the station with me. I want it viewed and a warrant sworn as fast as I can get one.'

Kate could not hide her elation. Suzy had obviously been the brains behind the operation. Now they could find out who was bankrolling her, and more importantly, who was distributing the stuff.

She looked around her and felt a moment's satisfaction at a job well done. Patrick was on the mend and life was getting easier all the time. She finally felt that there was a light at the end of a very long and very dark tunnel.

Boris walked out of the club. Willy, sitting in a coffee shop opposite, had a prime view. As he sipped at his coffee, he saw a young man simpering at him and he scowled in return. One of his most frightening scowls. He had already ordered his drink and taken a good seat before he'd realised that this place was full of gay men.

Willy sat back in his chair and took the registration of Boris's car. There was an outside chance it would be registered to an address, though he had a feeling it would be linked to a business.

Sergei was scanning the street and it made Willy nervous. He lifted his copy of the *Sun* and pretended to study the tits on page three. The young man smiled again and Willy toyed with the idea of giving him a well-earned slap. Reading his mind, the other man dropped his eyes and carried on drinking his iced tea. It was a shame; he liked the older, ugly ones. They were always so grateful.

When the BMW pulled away Willy got up, threw a fiver on the counter and walked over to the club. Inside he saw Pascal, and the two men grinned at each other.

'He's gone to his drum in Paddington. More hag there, Willy, by all accounts.'

Willy shook his head. 'Women on the slide always cause trouble. It's why they end up on the game. Out for attention, most of them. Out for fucking hag.'

Pascal agreed, then offered: 'Want a beer?'

Willy nodded and followed him to the bar area. In the harsh light of day the place looked seedy, and carried a strong stench of old beer and cigarettes.

'Fucking dump this is.'

Willy had never liked the clubs even as a young man. The sight of degradation always pissed him off. Knowing that, as ugly as he was, he could still pull there had always depressed him whereas other men loved every second of it.

Willy was glad he had his Maureen these days. She was a touch, a diamond, he might even marry it if she was good. She had all the attributes he wanted. She was a good cook, she was a laugh, and she liked a bit of the old rumpy-pumpy. He was fond of her son as well, which had been a surprise. Duane reminded him of himself when he was younger. A tearaway looking for the right angle. The life of most young boys on a council estate.

Willy was going to buy a house when all this was over. A nice drum for the three of them, in a better area. But he was going to get professional decorators in. As much as he loved his Maureen, he wouldn't let her loose in B&Qs without a bodyguard.

He would take the boy under his wing, too. Duane had the size for a bit of protection or maybe even collecting a few debts.

'So, he still thinks Patrick is going to roll over and leave him the club then?' Willy said aloud.

Pascal nodded. 'He is priceless, Willy. Has so much fucking front. Waltzes in here like the big I fucking Am, takes the money without a by your leave. He's a Russian cunt and I am looking forward to seeing him get his comeuppance, I can tell you.'

He lowered his voice as if there were onlookers.

'You know Patrick is still paying all the bills?' Pascal shook his head at the effrontery of it. 'Straight up. The bills are still going out on Patrick Kelly's standing order. I mean, please, is that the ultimate piss-take or what? He comes in, takes Pat's living, half kills his best mate, sets him up – and still he's nicking what amounts to pennies and halfpennies from him. I tell you, Willy, that ponce needs a serious sorting out.'

He sighed. 'I mean, where the fuck does it leave me, eh? I can't do nothing and he knows it. I'm strictly numbers and accounts, me. Never was the heroic type as you know. But even I have felt the urge to administer a few fucking slaps, I can tell you.'

Willy nodded. 'Relax, for fuck's sakes, Pascal. It will all be sorted in a few days.'

'That Maya was here again last night. All fucking sweetness and light. They have a scam going or I am the fucking Duke of Edinburgh. She takes an envelope every three days so it's a touch of some sort. But then, she deals with the European birds and all. You want to see some of them he brought in here to lap dance. Fucking G-ropes they should have been wearing, let alone strings. Looked like fucking Russian shot putters. Right hefty birds. Needless to say they were not the most popular dancers we've ever had. One of them offered a blow job in full view of the punters. We don't need that, whatever protection Boris thinks he might have. He's asking a lot about Kate Burrows as well these days. I think he has ideas in that direction. It don't take a fucking Einstein to suss out what he wants her for, does it? Old Bill and well-connected.'

Pascal laughed. 'If he knew what a slag I am where he's concerned he'd kill me. But Patrick is an old mate and I can't put meself first on this. Whatever happens I have to see Boris out the fucking door. This is personal now, as you know.'

Willy's hand went unconsciously to his thighs, which were still healing and were very painful. A reminder every time he woke up of exactly what the Russian was capable of doing.

'You can't steal a man's livelihood and expect his mates to sit back and let it happen. If Boris thinks that then he's a bigger twat than I first thought.'

Willy nodded his agreement.

'What has Maya got going with him then?'

'She was supplying the drugs for Micky, so I assume she's doing the same for them. That was why she wanted the coon out of the way. She had Leroy wasted, I know that for a fact because it was Harry Price and Dicky Campbell who took him out. They reckon his place in Docklands was the dog's knob. Right upmarket. Poor little fucker, I never minded Leroy, he was a grafter if nothing else.'

They were quiet, reflecting on the murder, when Pascal said quietly, 'Patrick is sorting all this, ain't he?'

Willy nodded. 'Don't worry, mate. He'll see you all right. Any addresses hanging around?'

Pascal grinned. 'I thought you might ask that.' He took out a cheap notebook and passed it to Willy. 'That's all I have. But there's a few addresses there. A few numbers too that I took from the phone bill. Might come in handy.'

Willy was pleased. He had always known that Pascal was trustworthy.

'Well done, mate. Right – I better get going before someone comes in and sees us having a mothers' meeting.'

'No worries. All the CCTVs are off, I made sure of that. We're as safe as houses. Plus Boris assumes I'm too scared to do anything. He thinks he's invincible though I reckon his number two wouldn't mind a look in now and again. That Sergei is the loose link in his chain and he can't or won't see it. You know what I'm talking about, don't you? I accept the Eastern Europeans are a force to be reckoned with but they have to understand that we won't sit back and watch like they're used to in their own fucking countries. I mean, we may be villains but we're British villains. It has to count for something don't it?'

'Too right, mate. Be seeing you.'

Willy left the club patting the small tape recorder in his pocket. He wanted Patrick to get that lot first hand. They had a lot to think about.

Evelyn replaced the phone and sighed. As she looked around the small hallway she saw the scuffed paintwork and the well-worn carpet. Patrick wanted her to pack all their stuff and move them back to his house and she was tempted, very tempted to do it. But she knew that Kate had to make the decision for herself.

Evelyn knew that Patrick was a rogue. She never used the word 'villain' when thinking of him. To her mind that was not the right epithet for him though she knew it was used by many others. She saw him more as a likeable rogue. After all, as he had always pointed out, his businesses were *legal*. They might not be what she would call respectable but they *were* legal.

She felt an urge to pack up and go back to the sheer luxury of his home, with or without her daughter. She was honest enough to admit that her suite of rooms at his house were calling her. She had everything there, from Sky TV to a small well-stocked mini-bar. It was like staying in a high-class hotel.

But more than that, she had seen her daughter content there at last. After years of scrimping and saving and working her arse off, she'd been relaxed and happy, cared for by a real man for once in her life.

Evelyn laughed to herself.

Kate would go through the roof if she ever said that to her. Feminism was all well and good for those who could *afford* it, but most women with a herd of kids and a meagre wage-packet needed a man, and so for them feminism wasn't always an option. Kate had never understood that. She was a grafter all right, but at times Evelyn wondered what her daughter would have done if she, Evelyn, had not moved in and taken over the house and Lizzy. Career women with families only functioned when someone else assumed their parental responsibilities. Without her mother's help Kate would have ended up in a right old state.

In fairness, her daughter had paid for the house and done her best. She had carved out a career for herself. But it had taken herself, Evelyn, to make that possible. Now she wondered what she should do. Kate would be spitting feathers if she just upped and packed, so she would have to be diplomatic about it all.

But if that daughter of hers wasn't careful she would find herself right back where she'd started.

Because Patrick was a man's man, and all the feminism in the world wasn't going to change *that*. If he wanted her back home, as he put it, then that was where Kate had better go.

Evelyn looked out of the lounge window and saw the journalists who were dying to get an insight into the woman DI who had taken down a paedophile ring and a second serial killer.

Maybe she could use that as an excuse? But by the same token it occurred to her that Kate's being known to live in the home of a man who was the acknowledged king of Soho sleaze would not endear her to the public, her bosses or her colleagues.

There was all that to consider.

Evelyn thought of her lovely suite of rooms again and sighed. She missed them.

She went back into the kitchen and looked around it. They had had many a happy meal in this room, three generations of women against the world. Now she was finally admitting that she was getting too old for it all. She wanted comfort, peace and a good long rest.

Suzy Harrington was already at Grantley Police Station when Kate arrived; the young woman was dressed like a schoolmistress and devoid of make-up. Kate left her sitting there and went to her office.

'Has she said anything?' she asked Jenny.

'Not a word, Kate. Just said she wanted to see you and only you. She has news for you apparently.'

'Did the press see her arriving?'

Jenny shrugged. 'I don't know. I assume so. She came here in a limousine.'

'You are joking!'

'There's something going down here. Either she's going to spill the beans and look for a deal or she's going to have an out. I'd bet on the out myself.'

'Until she hears about the videos, of course. That's when we really have her. She can't know we have them yet. I want to see her face when we tell her!'

Kate was looking good today and she knew it. Patrick was on the mend and she had solved her case, got more than she bargained for and made the headlines. She had every reason to look and feel on top of the world.

'Let's play it by ear, Jen, see what she has to say then surprise her with the tapes. I want to see that fucker squirm.'

Jenny laughed. 'Don't we all?'

Five minutes later they were sitting opposite her. Suzy looked steadily at them, her eyes holding secrets.

'Miss Burrows, I think it's about time we talked. I have brought my brief with me and he is going to sit in on the interview if that's OK?'

She was smiling now and Kate saw the girl she could have been if she'd ever been allowed a childhood. It depressed her and her mood of elation faltered.

'I want to set up a TV and video if that's OK by *you*?'

Suzy nodded graciously. Kate knew she thought it was so they could tape whatever she said. She didn't disabuse her of this notion.

She left the room again, enjoying making Suzy wait, making her nervous. She drank two cups of coffee and smoked a couple of cigarettes before she made her way back to the interview room fifteen minutes later.

The equipment had been set up in a second room and they brought Suzy in with her solicitor, a small elderly man in a cheap suit. She saw the paraphernalia and smiled knowingly.

'Without tape first, please.' It was said gently, as if she was in charge of the whole operation.

'Why?' Kate's voice was bored-sounding and this was not lost on Suzy or Mr Millan her solicitor.

'Because I want to get your reactions to what I say first.'

It was an honest answer and Kate agreed.

'I warn you, though, Suzy, we have evidence and we will be charging you.'

She didn't answer for a few seconds, just carried on smiling that self-satisfied smirk.

'OK, shall we start then?' Kate asked everybody.

'I'm ready when you are,' Suzy told her.

'Well then, how about you telling us why you are here today?' Jenny began, her voice heavy with sarcasm.

'I want to do a deal . . .'

Kate interrupted her. 'No way. We have video evidence to put you right where we want you.'

'You haven't let me finish, have you, Miss Burrows?'

Kate watched her warily. There was something wrong here. The girl looked too sure of herself. She definitely had something up her sleeve.

'I will hold me hand up to whatever in exchange for a minimal sentence. You'd better say yes because I have the goods you need so badly. I know who filmed the kids, who edited the videos, and more importantly – who the distributor was.'

'Really. And you want us to give you an out, do you?' Jenny said heavily.

'Quick learner your mate, ain't she, Burrows?' Suzy lit herself a cigarette. 'Did she learn at the same place you did, Kate?'

That was when they realised there was something drastically wrong. This girl was playing with them, and given what they had on her she should be shitting hot bricks and throwing them out of the window at regular intervals.

'So who's the Mr Big then – or the Mrs Big as the case may be?' Kate kept her voice and demeanour casual, but Suzy knew she was getting to them.

She opened her eyes wide. 'You mean, you don't know?'

'Are you going to lay all this at Barker's door?' Kate's voice was low. 'Only it isn't going to work, I can assure you of that much, lady.'

Suzy finished her cigarette, her pale painted nails looking babyish on her long slim fingers. Other than her face, she was a stunner. Each part of her body was perfect from her hands to her breasts to her legs. It was only above the neck that she let herself down.

She looked from one to the other.

'You really don't know, do you?' She was grinning

in triumph and it was all Kate could do not to go for her.

'I thought you already knew. I really did.' Suzy was shaking her head in apparent disbelief.

'We know a great deal,' Kate bluffed.

'But, Miss Burrows, surely *you* know who's behind it? After all, you live with him, don't you?'

Kate felt fear gripping her heart even as she was telling herself she had no reason to believe this girl.

'What are you on about?'

'The distributor of course. It's Patrick Kelly.'

Kate was out of her chair and round the table in record time. Her hand flew out and she grabbed the girl by the face. The feel of her fingers digging into warm soft flesh was wonderful.

As Suzy fell from her chair and collapsed to the floor Kate felt hands dragging her away. She was so angry she was spitting hatred and rage from her mouth like a madwoman. She kicked out as Suzy lay on the floor. It took three PCs and Jenny to finally drag her away from the crumpled figure.

'You disgusting sick bastard! You will *not* get me like that, you hear me?' Kate could hear the terror and the shock in her own voice and hated herself for it. 'You piece of shit!'

Suzy sat up, dazed. She looked at her brief and said in a pleased voice, 'I want to press charges.'

Kate watched her drag herself from the floor and lean against the table as if she was in pain. But she was still smiling.

'I thought you knew, Miss Burrows. I realise it must

be a shock, him being shot recently and everything.'

Kate was standing unrestrained now, her arms hanging limply by her sides.

'You had better be able to prove this allegation.'

Suzy picked up her cigarettes and looked at Jenny when she replied.

'I'd hardly come here if I couldn't, now would I?'

'You are a liar. You know you are and I will prove it. I *can* prove it,' Kate cut in.

Suzy smiled again. 'Can you? We'll see.' She wiped a hand across her face. 'I can understand you wanting to protect your man. That's why I never helped you before. I knew I couldn't tell you anything about him.' She glanced at her brief. 'I realised I wouldn't be believed, you see.'

Mr Millan took some papers from his briefcase. 'I have a statement here naming Patrick Kelly as the distributor.'

Kate stared at the little man in his cheap suit and shook her head in complete and utter disbelief.

Jenny turned her round forcibly and pushed her outside.

'I will be pressing charges, Miss Burrows, you can bank on that.'

Suzy's laughter followed Kate from the room.

Chapter Twenty-Eight

'You bloody fool, Kate!'

Ratchet's voice was loaded with anger and sheer embarrassment.

'You should never have raised a hand to her. You have done exactly what she wanted.'

Kate was aware of that herself; she didn't need this buffoon to point it out to her.

'What on earth possessed you? I've been put in an impossible position now. She's not only pressing charges but insinuating that you had to have known about everything. I have no other option than to suspend you pending further enquiries. I have never been in such an embarrassing situation in my life.'

'Let's worry about you then, shall we, sir? Is that what the real problem is? You and how this affects your life? Only you are part and parcel of Patrick Kelly and his legal businesses, aren't you?' Kate turned from him scornfully and left the room.

Jenny was waiting in her office.

'I can't believe this, Jen, can you?'

She shook her head sadly. 'I know this isn't what you want to hear, Kate, but could Kelly have been a part of it?'

Kate looked into her face. A depression covered her now, like a cloak.

'I will never believe that, never. Whatever else he might be guilty of, there is no way he could ever be a part of anything like that.'

Jenny couldn't look her in the face and Kate felt a great sadness wash over her.

'Listen, Jen, I would lay my life on what I just said. Patrick has his faults, and they are legion. No one knows that better than me. But he would never, *never*, be involved in anything like this.'

Jenny still couldn't look at her.

'You don't really know what he was involved in, do you?' she said quietly. 'Be honest. He had the lap-dancing club – you knew nothing about that, remember?'

'With respect, Jenny, a lap-dancing club is legal in this country, so I don't think having an interest in one of those automatically makes him a child pornographer, do you? Or maybe you think I am a mug, and that he *is* the distributor for paedophile literature and videos. Look, he knew I was investigating those same films and the mothers who were allowing their kiddies to take part. It's a wonder he didn't tip them all off, isn't it? Christ, Jen, I can't believe that you honestly think he is actually a part of it all, knowing what a slippery bitch Suzy is, knowing that she's already in with Ratchet's mob. We were warned off her, remember? Think about it, Jen, doesn't all this strike you as odd at all?'

Jenny didn't answer her and her silence told Kate everything she wanted to know.

Picking up her bag, Kate walked from the office and left the building. In her car she felt the sting of tears, but they were tears of anger. Anger and disappointment. It seemed her association with Patrick was leading her into more trouble than she could ever have guessed at before.

Her mobile rang and it was Golding.

'I have a copy of her statement, ma'am. It's there whenever you want it.'

Kate smiled gently. Her relief at having a friend overwhelmed her.

'Bring it to the hospital and we'll see what Patrick has to say, eh?' She turned off the phone.

Help came from the strangest places. She had disliked Golding so much, yet Jenny who lived at her home and had become a friend had doubted her. She had believed that she was trying to cover up for her man. Life kicked you in the teeth and you never knew who the final blow was going to come from.

Well, she would get to the bottom of it all. Whatever she found out, she would at least know the truth. Once and for all.

She wheelspinned out of the station, the screeching of her tyres giving her a sense of satisfaction, and drove straight to the hospital.

'Leave it out, Kate. There has got to be someone here who can see what a shower of shite all this is.'

Kate sat on the bed gripping his hand.

'She must have something, Patrick, to go this far. She has to have something concrete; she wouldn't dare otherwise. The worst thing is, she was laughing at me. This was calculated.'

She took a deep breath. '*Have* you ever been in on any kind of distributing? If you have been in on any porn film-making or have financed it, I need to know now, Patrick.'

He wiped a hand across his face. He had half expected this question and knew that he had to give her an honest answer.

'I have fingers in so many pies, Kate, I couldn't swear at this moment in time that someone ain't doing something with money I might unknowingly have provided. I am sorry, darlin', I can't tell you what you want to hear because I honestly don't know. Through the club I could be down on paper for all manner of things I actually have no knowledge of.'

It was what Kate had expected to hear, but it didn't make it any easier. At least he was being upfront and honest. For that much she was grateful.

'Golding has her statement. She must have given up a few bodies to make it believable. Once he gets here we can see if you know anyone by name.'

He nodded. 'I'm sorry to the heart for this, Kate. Do you think they are going to arrest me?'

She shrugged. 'Get your doctor to say you are too ill to be questioned and leave it to me. I'll see what I can do.'

He half smiled. 'It makes a change, eh, us two working together?'

'I could do without all this, Pat, to be honest.'

He said craftily, 'Did you smack her one hard enough to make her remember it? I hope so, Kate. She sounds like a good slap has been on the cards for years.'

Kate sighed. 'I can't laugh, Patrick. After patting myself on the back these last days I now have to fight my way out of yet another dirty big hole. I was on top of everything. I had Suzy even though Ratchet had told me to ease off her because she has friends in very high places. She's actually on video with those kids, showing them what she wants them to do. Christ knows how Robert got hold of them. I can't even talk to him now because I have in effect ruled myself out of the enquiry by losing my temper with Suzy.'

Patrick felt bad. Once more he was the cause of Kate's being investigated. It was high time for him to pull himself together and start hauling them both out of the shit before his dreams of retirement and marriage to Kate went straight down the pan.

Willy ambled into the hospital room eating a bag of crisps.

'All right, Pat?' He lowered himself carefully into a chair.

'Still in pain?'

Willy nodded, screwing up his face. 'It's me nuts, Pat. They did take a hammering, boy.'

Patrick couldn't help grinning and Willy laughed as well.

'You've been a good mate, Willy Gabney. The best.'

Willy was embarrassed. 'Stop being a tart, Patrick, and tell me what's going down?'

He explained about Suzy Harrington and what had happened to Kate.

Willy was amazed. 'How can you be involved in all that?'

Patrick shrugged. 'No idea, and I don't recognise any of the names in the statement she gave either. Someone is up to a large piece of skulduggery and my name is at the top of the list of suspects. I got Tarbuck to give them the sob story. I am not only a suspect, I am going to get me fucking collar felt and all. But they won't come in here with a warrant.'

Willy frowned. 'It has got to be Duggan, Pat. He was into everything. Weren't there no addresses – nothing?'

Patrick shook his head. 'Her statement basically says that she gave the films to a third party, who she didn't know, who then allegedly gave them to me to distribute. I was protected because I had a bird who was a filth. The usual old fanny, but that's the general drift.'

Willy finished his crisps.

'It can only be Duggan,' he grunted. 'I mean, if you're involved without knowing it – and I reckon you could be, given what we know now – that means Boris must have some knowledge, don't it? He's in the driving seat now. Which brings me to what I came here for. I went to the club and had a chat with Pascal.'

He shook his head once more in consternation.

'That Boris is a right saucy fucker, Pat. He is still letting the club's fucking bills be settled in your name while he is skimming off the cream. He needs a serious sorting out and I am just the fucking man to do it. I have a few numbers and addresses from Pascal. I think I may have to waste that Russian cunt, Patrick. Just for the piss-take, like. And it ain't like I ain't got reason, is it? I respected him as a businessman, but this last lot is too much. He needs the hard word.'

Patrick agreed with what Willy was saying but wasn't so sure he wanted his old friend in on it all.

'Listen, mate, I am going to sort him out so stop worrying. Get the addresses and numbers checked out by Billy Baines. He is trustworthy. We'll work from there, OK?'

Patrick picked up the phone and called Ratchet's private line.

'I have just had a thought, Willy. I think I will pull in a favour.'

Robert Bateman looked at Kate in disbelief.

'I was under the impression you were not involved any more.'

She could tell he knew what had occurred and wondered who had enlightened him: the police or his brief.

'Is this a *legal* interview?' Kate didn't answer and he grinned. 'Oh, I see.'

He sipped at a glass of apple juice. 'It's all I can drink these days. Now then, what do you want to know?'

She sat opposite him and lit a cigarette. 'How did you get your hands on those videos – the ones with Suzy in them?' She saw his cunning grin and held her breath.

'I told you, I have keys to a great many homes. Including Suzy Harrington's.'

'Where are those keys?'

'Oh, you are in a hurry, aren't you?'

'I certainly am, Robert. And I'm not feeling very patient at the moment as you have probably guessed.'

He pushed back his hair in the feminine gesture Kate had come to know so well.

'Temper, temper, Katie.'

She had had enough.

'Robert, you were mad to do what you did but not so mad you can't remember it. Now then, how can I put this? If you keep fucking me about I am going to come round that table and kick your head in! This is no idle threat. Ask Suzy what I'm capable of when I'm upset. So tell me what I want to know and I'll leave you in peace.'

Robert seemed to be enjoying himself. 'What exactly do you want to know, dear?'

'Who distributed the films?'

His soft-eyed expression was replaced immediately by a look of disdain. 'Are you really telling me you don't know?'

Kate closed her eyes and murmured a prayer that he was not going to try and lay it at Patrick's door. If he and Suzy had shared a brief then Kate was finished and she knew it. It had been a long shot anyway and

Ratchet had put his arse on the line allowing this interview in the first place. Not that that bothered her, but to come all this way and then find out that Robert was in collusion with Suzy would be the final straw.

'The distributor was a recent recruit. Suzy went to her old friend and mentor Lucas Browning, of course. I'd already guessed she would use him.'

'How do I know any of this is true?'

Robert straightened his shoulders and said gently, 'You don't. I am telling you this because you asked, dear. I liked you, Kate. Liked you a lot. You can take it from me it's true – Suzy told me. You see, I had already let her know I was on to it all. She thought I was part of it. I would drop hints about kids I thought might be ripe for her kind of offer. Mothers who were hard up, in debt or just basically pieces of shit.'

Kate couldn't believe this fresh twist. 'So you actually gave her some of the kids you say you were protecting?'

He nodded. 'Terrible, aren't I? You see, sometimes I think one way, really loving kids and wanting to help them, and then another time I think something completely different. So I would tell her and then watch from the sidelines. I am ashamed to say I enjoyed it.'

He looked suitably contrite: 'Barker had been to see her. I waited for him to come out of her flat before approaching him. He had also been to see Sharon Pallister. I killed her shortly after his visit. Trevor told me all I needed to know. I toyed with making it look like Barker had killed her but in the end I couldn't be bothered. By then I was just taking everyone out as and when the fancy took me.'

He sighed then said gravely, 'You know the worst thing of all, Kate? Once you kill, it gets easier and easier. Strange that, isn't it? Someone should write a paper on it. I enjoyed it so much that I needed the buzz again and again and again. I would kill now if I got the chance but don't quote me on that one, dear. And I felt I was making a difference, was ridding the world of scum, so I had righteousness on my side into the bargain.'

He chuckled and shook his head. 'I always wanted to be a do-gooder.'

He had lost it again. Kate watched as his mouth opened wide and he literally roared with laughter.

'Were you in on all this, Robert, really?'

He stopped laughing and was quiet again. It was as if someone had turned a switch and shut him down.

'Who knows, Katie?' he said quietly. 'Who *really* knows anything?'

Then he was off again and she left him shortly after, his laughter echoing in her ears and his fanatical eyes burned into her memory. It seemed that now he was caught, now he was locked up, he didn't have to keep the threads together any more. He was insane, she already knew that much, and he liked playing games, which was why she couldn't really believe what he had had to say until she had investigated it fully for herself.

As she passed Golding he ignored her and she was pleased. He was learning to play the game. Once he had finished he was going to be a good officer, she was sure of that.

She held her head up as she left the station, but it took all the strength she had to do it.

Evelyn had gone to the hospital and Kate was glad to have the house to herself. She went upstairs to shower and change and without thinking walked into Jenny's room and looked around.

All her stuff was gone. Clothes, smellies, everything.

Kate felt bitterly disappointed. She could understand Jenny's not wanting to be implicated by staying with her now but Kate had at least expected her to say she would be leaving to her face. She felt sick from the letdown.

While she was showering she heard the front door open and, assuming her mother was home, she wrapped a towel around herself and walked down the stairs.

Two men were standing in the hallway. She recognised Boris as soon as he opened his mouth.

'Miss Burrows, so pleased to meet you at last.'

He looked her up and down and Kate stood like a statue, one hand on the stair rail, her eyes wide with anger and fear.

'How did you get in here?' Thank God her voice didn't waver, she was pleased about that. She needed to keep herself together.

He smiled easily. It was an oily smile that made him seem less handsome.

'Please don't insult my intelligence by asking me

something so mundane. I can get in anywhere, Miss Burrows. Or may I call you Kate?'

'You can call me what you want but I have to inform you that you have entered my premises without permission and you are now being asked to leave.'

Sergei decided he liked her. She was obviously nervous. The fact that she was near naked gave them an added psychological advantage over her. Fully dressed people are much more inclined to be brave; it was one of the first things he had learned from Boris. Strip your enemy. It takes away their confidence and with it, their power to reason.

He smiled gently. He couldn't see Kate covering herself in her own shit in an effort to even things up. That was what the men usually did when stripped and humiliated. It was the only thing they could do to defend themselves. No one wanted to touch someone else's shit, it was human nature.

Kate stared at the two men. Her heart was beating so loudly it was like a drumbeat in her head. She was frightened and she knew it was imperative that she didn't let it show. For the first time ever she wished she still had Benjamin Boarder as her minder.

'What do you want?' Her voice was quivering and she knew that both the men had picked up on that.

'I just want to talk to you. That is all.' Boris held up his hands to make himself seem less of a threat. 'Please, get dressed and we will talk.'

Kate stood uncertainly at the bottom of the stairs. Her legs were weak with fear and she wasn't sure she could move.

'I want you out of my home now, Mr Stravinski. You *and* your ape.' She glared at Sergei as she spoke, then wondered if her hard woman act had perhaps gone a little too far.

Boris chuckled. 'Get dressed, and we will make ourselves a drink.' He took the phone off the hook and gave it to Sergei. 'I will trust you not to use your mobile upstairs. But hurry, I don't have much time.'

Kate made her way back to the bathroom and pulled on a thick candlewick dressing gown belonging to her mother. She was back down the stairs in seconds.

'Please, sit down,' Boris told her.

'I really don't need you to offer me a seat in my own home. Now state your business and then leave.'

'I need your help, Miss Burrows. I want you to do for me what you do for Mr Kelly.'

Kate screwed up her eyes. 'I beg your pardon?'

Sergei liked her more by the second. She was brave, he had to admit that. He knew men who would have been gibbering wrecks just to find Boris in their home.

'Are you trying to insinuate that I am doing something illegal for Mr Kelly? Only if so I will have to disabuse you of that notion here and now. He and I are partners in the personal sense, but not in business. I'm sorry, you have been misinformed and I resent your even making that statement without any proof.'

Boris shook his head as if at a recalcitrant child.

'Let me rephrase that, Miss Burrows. You *are* going to work for me as and when I require you to. Do you understand what I'm saying to you?' His voice was harsh now, his accent stronger with anger.

Kate stared into his eyes. He really was an extraordinarily good-looking man. She guessed this was usually used to his advantage.

'I understand, Mr Stravinski, but I am afraid I have to decline your offer. Now, if you don't mind, I am very busy.' Her voice was still strong though her body was shaking.

'You don't seem able to understand me, Miss Burrows. This is not an offer. I am telling you that you are now working for me.'

Kate knew by his voice that she was in no position to refuse what he asked. He was at the end of his patience and she already knew what he was capable of. Swallowing her pride, she said with as much dignity as she could muster while wearing her mother's dressing gown, 'I understand you perfectly, Mr Stravinski. If you would be kind enough to leave me now, I will think over what you have said. But as from today I am under suspension from my job. I am sure you can verify that if you need to. I attacked a prisoner in my care.'

Boris looked at her with a mixture of surprise and respect.

'So I don't think I shall be of any use to either you or Mr Kelly in the future.' Kate was quaking in her boots. 'Once again, if you gentlemen will excuse me, I have rather a lot to do.'

Boris smirked. 'Miss Burrows, you are now working for me. I'll be in touch.'

Kate didn't answer him and he left the house with Sergei in tow. She slumped down on the sofa, her heart still in her mouth and her legs weak with fright. It never rained but it poured was an expression of her mother's that had irritated her over the years. The last few days, though, had made her realise that clichés could also be true.

She was dressed and out of the house in five minutes flat.

Patrick listened to what Kate had to say without interrupting her once.

'He seems to think that I am bent. That I have been bent for you. Patrick, he threatened me without actually using the words.'

He nodded his understanding. He had done the same thing to people himself many times.

'Leave it with me, Kate. I'll get it sorted.'

'What are you going to do then, threaten him back?' Her voice was low, scared.

''Course not, you silly mare,' he laughed. 'I will simply let him know that you aren't up for it and leave it at that, love. He'll understand what I'm telling him.'

Kate looked into his tired blue eyes and felt a moment's sorrow for adding to the burden she knew he was already carrying.

'I am so sorry, Pat. I should never have told you, should I?'

'Yes, you should. He's a right saucy bastard as Willy has already pointed out today. I have to give him the hard word, Kate. Have to. If I don't, that sod will walk right over me and mine. Now you sort out your own problems and let me sort out mine, eh?'

She tried to smile.

'I spoke to that ponce Ratchet and all,' he continued. 'Told him what I think of him, and what he has to do now. There's a bent filth in the Home Office can sort this for you, darling, so stop worrying. But I think you should know that I'm going to retire after this lot and maybe you should too.'

'Are you really going to give it all up?'

He could hear the incredulity in her voice.

'I know I've said it before but I mean it this time, Kate. I ain't got the heart for all this any more.' He waved his arm at the room. 'Look where I am, stuck in here, on the verge of getting me fucking collar felt and hiding behind a moody doctor. I'm worth much more than that, love.'

He was sweating and Kate knew he was tired and still not well enough even to get himself out of bed. She also knew that he might well think all this while he was down, but once he picked up he would be singing a different song.

Wisely, she kept her thoughts to herself.

'I'd love to give up work now, Patrick. I realised today that there's something wrong with this country and the people it classes as criminals. Robert Bateman will never get to trial. He'll be judged as mentally unfit even though he's playing games. Oh, I don't dispute that he is mad, but it's a calculated madness that he uses when it suits him. Yet it will also get him into a nice mental hospital with a softer regime and access to most things that people outside enjoy, from computers to takeaways. He is a senior social worker so he'll know his rights. Yet here am I – I work my arse off and get suspended because I'm expected to sit and take the shit that people like Suzy dish out without a word of protest. She deliberately goaded me, Patrick, used the one thing she knew would make me lose my rag. And I fell for it. I destroyed my career and my credibility with one rash action.'

Her voice was so sad that Patrick, in his weakened state, felt an urge to cry with her.

'We'll sort it all out, Kate. Now stop worrying, for fuck's sake,' he said gruffly.

She could hear how exhausted he was. She kissed him gently on the lips and hugged his body to her own tightly.

'I love you, Patrick Kelly.'

'I love you too, girl, you know that. One thing that's come out of all this, mate – at least we both know who we can trust, eh?'

'Hurry up and get better, Patrick, please.'

'I'm getting better by the day, love.' He sounded much more confident than he felt. He needed to sort out the Russian then he could get back on his feet. He needed to make himself known once more as Patrick Kelly, hard man and serial rogue. He needed to make sure that he was back in the number one spot so he could breathe easy, finally stop this worrying.

But he didn't tell Kate that. He knew she was worried enough as it was.

His sisters turned up then and Patrick was grateful to see them. He wasn't sure he could keep himself together if he talked much longer to Kate. He had inadvertently put her in the shit and he had to get her out of it as soon as possible.

Boris Stravinski had taken the ultimate piss out of him now. He had encroached on Patrick's woman. For that alone he was going to pay, and pay dearly.

Chapter Twenty-Nine

Golding and Kate were sitting in a parked car in East London. It was after one in the morning and the streets were noisy, full of young people. The air smelled of onions, grease and exhaust fumes. Kate watched as a teenage girl was chased half-naked by three young men. Her screams were ear-splitting but not a single curtain twitched.

Golding sipped some coffee and swore under his breath.

'She can't be more than thirteen and look at her. All tits and legs and giving anything in trousers the come-on. I mean, what would you do with a daughter like that?' His voice was disgusted. 'What gets up my nose is that when the little mare goes missing or gets raped her parents will expect us lot to sort it all out. But look at *it*, ma'am. She's an accident waiting to happen. Little slag!'

Kate didn't answer. She knew what it was like to have a girl that age who carried on in exactly that way. She noticed how the other girls egged her on. She would give them something to talk about and would keep the reputation she was giving herself all her life. The worst of it all was, she was probably not as bad as the others. She just didn't have the savvy to keep what she did to herself.

Her parents would think she was tucked up in bed at a friend's house. She had thought the same thing enough times herself. The girl was probably as good a liar as Lizzy was. She had believed her daughter was at friends' houses, or wherever Lizzy had said she was; she had had no reason to doubt her. It was what happened to parents. You *wanted* to believe your children so you did.

'We'll go in soon. I want to get him on the hop,' she told Golding.

The young constable nodded. In the half-light he looked quite handsome and Kate wondered if he had a significant other. He wasn't the type of person you could ask personal questions. Or maybe she felt like that because it had never occurred to her before that he might actually have a life outside his job.

'Would you like children?' she asked suddenly.

He glanced at her and laughed. 'I already have two, ma'am. Three and one, boys. Pair of sods they are.'

He grinned and Kate felt ashamed that she didn't know about them.

'I didn't even know you were married.'

He wiped his mouth and grinned. 'I'm not married. I live with a bird.'

Kate didn't answer.

'I don't know if I want to commit meself, see? She

wants to get married, but I ain't sure.'

Kate turned in her seat and said honestly, 'You have two children with this *bird*, but you don't want to commit yourself. Well, I'm sorry but it doesn't get more committed than having children together, does it? I mean, financially she has you by the balls for the rest of your days.'

Golding thought about what she said and after a few beats he said quietly, 'That's one way of looking at it, I suppose.'

Kate opened the window to let in some cool air. 'Take no notice of me, I'm not in the best of moods.'

'Well, that's understandable really, ma'am. But personally I think that the way they treated you is out of order. You brought in Bateman and you sussed out Harrington. The least they could have done is given you a break of some kind.'

Kate felt elated at his sheer loyalty. It was unexpected and all the more important because of that.

'I think that Patrick Kelly is all right meself. I mean, he ain't exactly illegal, is he? He is a businessman after all. At the end of the day, I know filth who duck and dive. Look at Maretta over at Harcourt. He's a thief, he buys off lags and he drinks with bank robbers. Thinks he's the dog's gonads. But I sussed him out years ago. According to him it's ten grand now for a guaranteed five years for a biggie. He *brags* about his criminal connections. He thinks it makes him someone.'

'Maybe it feels like that to him,' Kate commented. 'I see Patrick as a person. I try and forget about what he does. Christ knows, everyone takes great delight in reminding me!'

Golding laughed.

'Ratchet is shitting himself,' he told her. 'I heard through the grapevine that he's being investigated by CIB.'

Kate didn't answer for a while. 'I've been there myself,' she said eventually. 'I don't envy him.'

Golding laughed again, this time louder.

'The thing with him is, though – what bodies will he give up to protect his own arse?'

Kate took the warning on board and filed it away for future reference.

'How come you hear so much and get so much information?'

'Because, ma'am, like most Old Bill I am batting away from home. I've been seeing a little bird called Rochelle for about two years. She works in CIB now. Only a secretary but she can find out anything. She's a computer whizz.'

'Does your partner know about her?'

He shrugged and said nonchalantly, 'What do you think? My Diane's a good kid and a great mother, but we were never the love of a lifetime types. I think she guesses. That's why we ended up with my second son. He wasn't exactly planned.'

Kate didn't answer, just felt desperately sorry for a woman she didn't know, trying to hang on to a man she would never own. She knew the feeling. Golding was Dan all over again except he had the work ethic.

'Don't hurt Diane if you can help it.'

'She hurts herself. She knows me and she knows what I'm like. She also knows I will never change. Like tonight, I *really* am working – albeit not for your actual police, of course. This is a favour, because I think you were badly treated and I am loyal in that respect at least. Loyal not faithful – there's a difference. But I bullshit her I'm doing overnight surveillance and she can't know if I'm telling her the truth or not, can she? I don't hurt her intentionally.'

Kate couldn't find an answer to such honesty. And he *was* loyal, he had proved as much to her.

'Jenny left the case today,' he went on. 'Did you know?'

She shook her head.

'Off to another place, another case. She couldn't get out of Grantley quick enough. Mud sticks is her attitude. And, let's face it, with her sexual preferences she knows she can't be embroiled in any shit whatsoever.'

'She was only covering her own arse.' But even as Kate spoke she was still hurt by her so-called friend's actions. Jenny hadn't even bothered to phone or leave a note for Kate or Evelyn. Nothing.

They were quiet for a while watching the young kids bait one another.

'What's the time?'

Golding squinted to look at his watch in the half-light. 'Just on two.'

'Let's go and see what we can find out.'

Lucas was in a bad mood. The young girl with him

was getting on his nerves. Her name was Janine and she was fifteen years old. She had worked for him for the last eighteen months but it had taken its toll on her though she wasn't as yet aware of that. She talked and he looked her over. She was quite tall and big-boned. Her skin had the greyish pallor associated with being up all night and sleeping all day. She also had the usual bruises and scratches that seemed endemic to prostitutes.

He knew she was doing it in cars; there was a certain type of injury, small, not painful but highly visible, that came from working the motor trade. Bruised shins from getting in and out of different vehicles, and around the neck from being squeezed up against men in the close confines of car seats. He recognised these things and wondered how the girls didn't realise it for themselves.

Janine also had the bitten nails and rough hands of the streetwalker. Basically he wanted shot. Once they looked sixteen or over he had no time for them; the big money was gone and he only kept on the girls he felt were easy to control. Others he sold on to a network of pimps he had around London and the South East. Very occasionally a Northern girl would be placed nearer home if she requested it, but only when her big earning days were over.

Janine loved being a prostitute. Brought up on a diet of soap operas and trash TV, she thought it was glamorous. Thought that sleeping with men for money gave her an edge over the law-abiding population. She wasn't alone; many young girls thought this. In fact, as

Suzy pointed out, if they hadn't been paid whores they'd have stayed as the class bike, shagging friends' boyfriends and neighbours' husbands after babysitting. They were a type, and they were the ones who made the real money.

Now Janine was sitting here, boring the arse off him and trying to convince him she was still able to kick it in the little-girl stakes.

No way.

'Janine, listen to me. You look awful.'

Lucas was wheezing and coughing, bringing up phlegm and spitting it into a soiled handkerchief. His enormous bulk quivered with each hawk of his throat.

'Jesus, Lucas, you are gross!'

Her voice did not endear her to him further and nor did the words she used. His fat hand shot out and slapped her round the face. It was a noisy slap and Janine sat back in her chair, more amazed than hurt.

'You fat bastard, I don't have to take that no more.'

But her voice was lower; she was scared. And she had every reason to be scared, she knew that. Lucas could make you disappear if he wanted to and she always kept that fact in the forefront of her mind.

Her voice a whine now, she said petulantly, 'I just want to carry on as I have been . . .'

She stressed the last word and it made him shudder. She had the whore's whine off pat and that told him all he needed to know.

'You are out, OK? Now I know you're on the prowl because I can tell. You were warned about the street and yet you went on it. Suppose you were picked up, put in a children's home, locked away? What would you do then? Because it can happen, you know, and I wouldn't help you. You're a liability, just too bloody obvious. Look at your dress, your voice.'

He waved his fat hands in annoyance.

'You *look* like a teenage whore, dear. You look what you are. The eyes are already dead, you take drugs and your skin is greasy and gone to pot. Basically, love, I couldn't give you away nowadays. Not for real money anyway. You'll be doing blow jobs for a tenner within months.'

Janine was already doing blow jobs, but she charged fifteen quid – she still had some pride. She wasn't going to admit it to him.

'I'd look all right in a school uniform, like when I done them photos.'

Lucas raised his eyes to the ceiling and said through gritted teeth, 'You are annoying me. You made your bed, love, you can lie in it all day now if you want. But our little partnership is finished.'

She knelt down before him.

'Let me give you a good time, show you that I'm still the best at it. Still got the nous.'

He looked at her face. It was still smooth-skinned, but ageing daily. She had a greyness about her; her teeth looked off-colour from vomiting and speed, her heavy body coarse and unwelcoming.

Three more years and she would either be dead or dosed. That much was a fact.

'Are you using condoms?'

She hesitated before answering and it told him all he needed to know.

'You've learned nothing from me, have you?'

She licked her dry cracked lips and he saw the white ooze in the corners that told him she was speeding out of her head.

'Please, Lucas, I don't want to be alone.'

Her voice really did sound young now but it didn't sway him. She was street fodder, he didn't want her. But he might be able to make a few more quid out of her.

'I know a pimp, a black bloke called Marcel, but I warn you – he's a hard taskmaster. One side look and he'll chiv you without a second's thought.'

He saw her eyes light up and sighed inwardly. She was street all right. She wanted a protector, someone to work for. Someone to give her hard-earned cash to. Someone new to abuse her. And if he was hard then she could kid herself she'd had no choice in the matter, when all she had ever wanted to do was self-destruct.

It was laughable really.

But Marcel would like her well enough. He would see potential where Lucas only saw a disgusting piece of dirt.

Each to their own. And these two would be a match made in hell. Marcel liked roughing up the women, and Janine liked the fear associated with men like himself and Marcel. She thought it gave her an identity of some kind.

'Give me the phone.'

Janine smiled happily and passed him his mobile. Lucas rang Marcel and did the deal.

'He'll pick you up in about an hour.'

Lucas pulled open his legs and grinned. 'You can practise on me. Marcel is going to want a freebie and you'd better be at your fucking best, girl, or he won't have you.'

She stared down at his flaccid member.

'You'd better do a good job, love. I couldn't raise a smile at the moment.'

'Shall I get me tits out?'

He pulled her towards him by her hair.

'Oh, no! It's bad enough looking at your ugly fucking face.'

Golding and Kate stopped outside Lucas's flat. Kate tried the door. It didn't budge. Golding swung back his foot and kicked it in. The lock broke and the door hit the wall with a mighty crash.

They were down the hall and inside the lounge in seconds. What they saw there made them both stop in their tracks.

Golding's voice was disgusted as he muttered, 'For fuck's sake!'

Janine looked at them from her position on the floor and Lucas was trying to cover his grotesque body with his dressing gown.

'Who the fuck are you?'

He still had an air of command in his voice although he was visibly rattled. They looked like filth, especially the woman. She was staring at the girl as if she had never seen a tom before.

'Who am I? I am your worst enemy, Mr Browning, that's who I am,' said Kate. 'What I want to know is the name of this obviously underage young person we saw giving you a blow job as we arrived on the scene.'

Janine could smell trouble. Serious trouble. She looked to Lucas for protection and saw that his face had gone a pale and sickly grey colour.

Somewhere, deep inside her, this fact pleased her no end.

'Just get me up and help me get dressed.'

Patrick's voice was loaded with menace but Willy stood his ground.

'Will I fuck get you up! You are ill, mate, and you are going to rest. Boris ain't going nowhere, he'll keep.'

Patrick was half up from the bed already, and pain was visible on his face.

'Look at you, like a fucking baby. Now get yourself back down and let me plump your pillows.'

'I am warning you, Willy. I want up and I mean to get up.' Even as he spoke he was lying back down. His head felt as if a steel band was crushing it. His whole body was drenched in sweat.

'Don't you understand what I'm telling you? That Russian ponce has been round Kate's house. Let himself in and as good as threatened her. He wants her on board with him, the saucy cunt!'

Patrick's voice was menacing once more and Willy knew he had to do something.

'Get your arse back in that bed, Patrick Kelly, or I swear I will chin you – and I mean it.'

Patrick heard the concern in his old friend's voice and sighed once more.

'I have to sort this out once and for all, Willy. I can't have him taking the piss like this. It was bad enough when the bastard shot me. *Me* – Patrick Kelly. Fucking lunatic he is. Well, I might have swallowed me knob on that one for a while but I can't let this go. No way can I let this go. If I swallow this, the next thing I know he'll be pushing me over so he can get in me bed and have a kip. I have to give him the hard word.'

'And you will, Patrick. But not until you are able. You've had a big shock to the noggin and you ain't capable of crushing a grape at the moment, let alone taking him on and all that entails. In a few days you might be able to get up and scout around, but until then you are staying put.'

Patrick knew his friend was right, but he also knew that something had to be done and fast. He knew exactly what Boris was after and that Kate would have to give in if she wanted to carry on living. Boris Stravinski was a bully boy for all his good looks and educated patter. He might dress like a male model, he might look like a male model, but he was street through and through and that was what was scaring Patrick.

Kate wouldn't have any option but to do what Stravinski wanted. No option whatsoever. But he knew that she wouldn't see it like that. She would think she could refuse – and then she would find out what the Russian was capable of.

Kate knew Boris had had him shot, but she was still naive enough to think that her very femaleness would stop the Russian from doing anything to her. Also, she was essentially a good person and wouldn't misuse her knowledge for anyone. Even Patrick had received short shrift when he had asked her to look on the police computer for him.

No, Patrick knew he had to take that Russian fucker out, and he had to do it soon.

Willy seemed to read his mind and said gently, 'You can't help anyone in the state you're in. Even you have to admit that much. Leave it for a while, a few days at least, then we can sort it out once and for all. Kate is OK. I know that for a fact. Ben's mate Everton who was here at the hospital is watching her.'

What Willy didn't say was that he had a feeling Everton had been sabotaged by the Russians. That would be too much information at the moment.

He saw Patrick's gratification and grinned.

'You got a lot of mates, Pat. More than you seem to realise. Benny himself was tailing her for a while so stop worrying. He helped her with Joey and Jacky and he's a good bloke as you know.'

'I owe him a hefty fucking drink by the sounds of it, Willy.'

'All in good time, Patrick. You get a bit of Sooty. If you don't take care you could end up a raspberry ripple and that's the last thing you want.'

Patrick realised that what Willy was saying was true.

But it was still hard to know that he had placed Kate in so much danger. Without him she would never have come to the notice of the Russian. If anything happened to her he would never forgive himself.

'Kate's a sensible girl, Pat. Bear that in mind. This will keep for a few days. Get some sleep and get your fucking head together, for Christ's sakes.' Willy looked at his watch. 'I have to go, Maureen will have my balls if I don't get me arse in gear.'

Patrick grinned. 'It must be love.'

Willy shrugged, his huge bulk looking out of place in the dainty hospital room. 'It is, I reckon. Gonna marry it, Pat. I've made up me mind.'

Patrick was amazed and it showed on his face.

Willy smiled in embarrassment. His large moonlike face was tinged pink. Even his neck was flushed.

'She's a good one, Patrick, and you don't meet many of them at our age. She's been round the turf a few times but she's all the better for that, mate. I never wanted a wilting virgin, know what I'm saying? Her youngest boy could do with a firm hand and all. Got a lot of potential, Duane has. Going to buy her a nice drum, the whole kit and caboodle really.'

Patrick grasped his friend's hand and squeezed it. 'I'm pleased for you, Willy, I really am.'

He was red again, but smiling, showing crooked white teeth.

'She makes me laugh, Pat, makes me feel good about meself. I like the feel of her lying beside me. She makes me feel special. She's a good cook and all, I can't deny that's part of the attraction. But after all these years, Pat, I need someone for meself. I realised that when the Russian had me. I knew she'd be worried out of her mind and it was nice, if that makes sense.'

Patrick nodded. 'I know what you mean, mate.'

''Course you do. I shared Mandy and Renée with you for years, didn't I? And you was a good mate to let me do that, Patrick. The best. You are family to me, mate. Fucking real family.'

Patrick, in his weakened state, felt a strong urge to cry at the big man's loyalty and friendship. He was feeling emotional a lot lately. But Willy had tears in his eyes, too, and that made Patrick feel better.

'Right pair of fucking tarts we're turning into in our old age, Pat. I reckon it's time to retire, don't you, and live off the fruits of our rather dodgy labours?'

'That's if I don't get me collar felt, of course.'

Willy shook his head. 'We've got out of worse than this, boy. You'll be OK. I have that feeling.'

They looked at one another, the friendship of years acknowledged, their total trust in and care of one another evident.

'You have been a good mate, Willy. The best.'

He shrugged. 'You ain't been too bad yourself.'

They were laughing again. Patrick knew that theirs was the perfect friendship. At this moment in time that was important to him. More important than he had ever realised.

'I took a few flowers over to Mandy's grave today, Patrick. Pink roses for her cheeks. She was a good-looking girl. Maureen scrubbed the stone and give it a polish, like. I told her Mandy was the nearest thing to a daughter I'd ever had. She understood that. She *understands* me. She's a good woman, Pat. The best.'

But Patrick couldn't answer him. The tears were choking him.

Golding was smoking a cigarette and Lucas watched him warily.

'What do you want?' he growled.

'We want the truth, mate,' Kate told him. 'We want to know who the distributor of your videos really is. You see, I am Patrick Kelly's better half – emphasis on the "better" there – and you have given me a right royal fucking off, you and Suzy Harrington. So I thought a personal visit was called for.'

She laughed nastily. 'Basically, it's a case of you tell me what I want to hear or you'll be in serious trouble. Am I making myself clear?'

Golding was grinning, listening to Kate's talk. She had it off pat and he was impressed despite himself.

Lucas wiped a furry tongue over yellowing teeth. 'As crystal. But what can I tell you?'

Kate was as surprised as Lucas and Janine when Golding's foot shot out and connected heavily with Browning's face. The fat man's head rocked back and hit the seat he was sitting in, hard. His nose split and his teeth were hanging in his mouth by threads. He looked like something from a horror film.

Janine screamed out in fear.

Golding leaned forward and said with deadly emphasis, 'You are already winding me up. Now if you want games I can play games, you fat piece of crap. I'll have you screaming with no one to help you, because we are the Old Bill and we are also very pissed off. So you can see our quandary, can't you?'

Lucas was in mortal fear now. A bully, he was terrified of any pain he wasn't inflicting.

Kate suppressed her own shock and tried to look nonchalant. She knew that Golding was only doing what Patrick would have done but this knowledge didn't make her feel any better. Instead she knelt down and started looking through the pile of videos on the floor. She placed one in the machine and turned it on.

A young girl of about thirteen was smiling nervously at the camera. She was underdeveloped, her narrow ribcage evident, and the painted face looked garish and frightening on her.

A man came into focus. He was in his fifties, big-bellied and naked with a leer on his ugly unshaven face.

'Friends of yours, are they?' Golding's voice was low and his face was set like stone.

Lucas was trying to talk through the broken teeth in his mouth.

'Please, I beg of you, I'll tell you what you want to know. But calm down, I can't function when I'm nervous.'

Janine watched him begging and felt a thrill of satisfaction. Kate pushed her from the room.

'Go away and don't come back unless you want me to nick you, little lady.'

Janine didn't need to be told twice. She ran out of the flat fast.

Golding grabbed Lucas's hair and dragged him out of his seat. It was a brave effort and he was gasping for air by the time he had finished. Lucas was kneeling on the floor now, his dressing gown wide open and his fleshy body in full view.

Golding kicked him a few times, hard body blows that sounded muffled against the mass of sagging skin.

'*Who is the distributor?*' he spat.

'I am! I am doing it! That's why the films are all in here. I have the masters. Now please – will you let me get up? Let me get up . . .'

Golding looked at Kate. 'What do you think, ma'am?'

'I think he is lying,' Kate said coldly. 'He is too fat and too stupid to do this alone. And, what's more, the word is he never leaves this flat. So, I am asking you one more time, Browning. Who is the distributor?'

Golding pulled back his foot and Lucas realised that he was about to get even more badly beaten.

He put up his arms and cried out. 'I can't tell you! Please, they are too dangerous . . .'

Kate sighed heavily. 'I really am getting fed up with you. Now you better tell me what I want to know.'

He looked at her imploringly; his mouth was bleeding profusely and his broken teeth were extremely painful. Kate slapped him hard across the face.

'I want to know and I want to know now, or so

help me God I will let my colleague go to town on you – and believe me when I say he is aching to take you out of the ball game.'

'I AM HURTING!'

His voice was a loud scream and Kate laughed. 'Only you can stop the hurt.'

Golding punched him hard, knocking him backwards so that he was half lying against his chair. Blood was pouring from the big man's mouth and nose and he was groaning loudly. The extreme pain was making him faint.

As Golding prodded him gently with his foot, warning him of the beating to come, he screamed out: 'It's the Russians! I am working with the Russians! They have the edge with all this. They have the contacts and they have the technology.'

Kate stared at him in abject disbelief. 'What Russians?'

He was crying now, snot and blood running down his face.

'Boris Stravinski. He works out of Soho. I met him through Barker ages ago. When this opportunity came up I thought of him. He was up for it, the money is phenomenal.'

Kate's head was reeling at what he was saying.

She put in another film. This time it was full of little children she didn't know.

'You have quite a network of children, Mr Browning. Tell me this: is Suzy Harrington involved with them as well?' Her voice was dead-sounding now; she was on auto-pilot.

He nodded.

Golding looked at the screen and sighed.

Then the kicking really started.

Willy was in the middle of a field and he was sweating. Taking off his jacket, he placed it carefully on the grass verge and began digging again. He was over in East Hanningfield, Essex, in a field owned by one of his old mates – only the man didn't know he was visiting.

After a few minutes more he uncovered an oilskin. Kneeling down, he dragged a heavy bundle from the hole. He cleared off the worst of the dirt and opened the oilskin. Inside was a small arsenal of weapons.

Willy removed a pump-action shotgun and cradled it gently in his hands. It was a favoured weapon, a Winchester – he had cut it down a few years previously. At short range it would take out three people at a time.

He wrapped up the other guns and replaced them in the ground. As he filled in their shallow grave he was humming to himself. Patrick needed help and he needed it soon. Boris had pissed them all off too much. Now Willy was going to do what Patrick would have done in his place.

He was going to take them all out in one fell swoop.

Willy carefully rewrapped the Winchester and walked back to his car. Placing his jacket on the passenger seat, he tidied himself up as best he could and made his way to Maureen's house.

He was looking forward to his job. Seeing Patrick lying in the bed unable to move properly had set off something in his brain. Patrick couldn't do the deed, but there was nothing to stop him doing it.

He had thought it through carefully, because if he got a capture, he was putting Maureen on the line. He would be looking at hard time – seriously hard time.

But Patrick would do the same for him. He knew that as well as he knew his own name. They were real mates. And real mates didn't come along very often.

That Boris needed to be taken out once and for all. Willy Gabney had decided that he was the man to do just that.

This was personal, as well as business. He was sure Boris would understand the logic of that.

He was still humming as he drove along the A13 back to Maureen, Duane and the good life.

Chapter Thirty

M arcel Jackson was handsome in a skinny, sharp-faced way. He kept his Jamaican ancestry evident, his dreadlocks and ever-present joint making him feel like he was a Brutha. In fact, his accent was forced and he had had a respectable upbringing by religious and hard-working parents.

Marcel had gone to university, studied Economics and Sociology, come out and trained as an accountant, then had decided there was more money to be made without the hag of actually working. He had started dope dealing and soon gravitated to pimping. Nowadays he drove a top-of-the-range car, smoked only the best weed and had a very high sexual drive. All in all he was a natural-born pimp. His mother still thought he was an accountant.

Marcel wasn't a great believer in work as such; he had no respect for the women he dealt with and liked to spend the money they brought in as and when he got his hands on it. Consequently he was weighed down with gold, even replacing some teeth with ones made of gold. He slept only infrequently after indulging in high-class pharmaceuticals.

He had sex as often as possible with as many different women as possible, and had fathered six children to his knowledge. He lived part-time with a white girl called Leona, who was a graduate and worked in advertising. They had a young son called Marcus and the kind of relationship most men dreamed of. She asked for nothing, neither his money nor his time. She too lived her own life. He supplied her with a bit of puff and a few Es for her weekend outings.

All in all, life was good.

As he tripped up the stairs to Lucas's flat Marcel was humming. Relighting his joint, he strolled through the open door – then stood still in amazement as he entered the lounge and saw the battered body of Lucas on the floor, and a good-looking woman and a younger man going through his video collection.

Kate smiled a welcome. 'And what can we do for you?'

Lucas moaned softly. Through the bloody pulp of his face, his eyes were beseeching Marcel to help him. But Marcel, being the type who covered his own arse and no one else's, turned around and walked straight back out of the door.

As he started his car up, he was shaking his head in wonderment. Lucas had been an accident waiting to happen for years. Marcel had told him over and over the kids were wrong. Older girls already on the game were one thing, but even Marcel balked at the use of kids. It was a bone of contention between them.

In a way he was glad that Lucas had had his capture. Whoever those two people were they were serious about what they were doing. He wondered briefly if they were Old Bill. After all, a kicking like that for a known pimp wasn't exactly unheard of from the police. He'd keep his eye out in case they decided on a repeat performance with him.

As he drove by the end of the road he saw a young girl sitting on a wall. Instinct told him she was ripe and might be willing. Stopping his Jaguar, he smiled at her.

She looked at him with spaced-out eyes and said nonchalantly, 'Marcel?'

He nodded and she jumped into the car happily. Marcel drove away, thankful that his journey had not been fruitless after all.

The girl was chattering about Lucas, a beating and being frightened. Marcel listened with half an ear, wondering whether she was worth the hag.

A blow job and a joint later, he decided she was.

Boris and Sergei went into Girlie Girls at just after 2 a.m. It was still buzzing. The air was ripe with music, sweat and alcohol. It was Stag Night and the place was full of drunken men and their wallets.

Girls danced on tables, their bodies moving suggestively to the raucous music, their faces devoid of any real expression. It was late, they were knackered and they wanted to go home.

Boris watched the scene with interest. A pretty girl

with large hips and surgically enhanced breasts was arguing with another girl who had apparently muscled in on her punters. The men, a crowd of City boys with loosened ties and red alcohol-laden faces, thought it was hilarious.

The second girl, a stacked blonde with a sequined G-string, was the real aggressor.

'Fuck off! Ask them who they want dancing for them.' She moved one hand down her body. 'This is all mine, darling, which is more than you can say.'

The brunette brought back a meaty forearm, the punch landed a nano-second later and then the bouncers were between the women, trying their hardest to separate two semi-naked hellcats.

False nails and stilettos flew everywhere, the bouncers taking a hammering from the screaming girls. Eventually, they picked them up bodily and half dragged, half carried them off the small stage. Their sweaty bodies were practically impossible to keep a grip on and the girls kept escaping and running back, bent on killing each other.

Cocaine-induced paranoia was the real problem between them.

It was always the same at the end of the night. If one didn't make as much money as she expected, or another girl seemed more popular, it caused fights. Tomorrow they would be bosom pals, or at worst respectful rivals.

Boris sighed. But this place was a useful front and once he had overhauled it and changed it to what he really wanted it would be a good earner. Plus, it laundered money for them. In fact, that was its primary function at the moment.

He followed the two bouncers through to the dressing area. The girls were on the floor still fighting, and even Boris understood the men's reluctance to stop the fray. Other dancers milled around, shouting encouragement and laughing at their counterparts who were in a state of drug-crazed anger. The smell of sweat was overpowering, and he curled his lip at the sight of the women and girls avidly watching the fight.

They were like animals. They hunted in packs and felt safer in a crowd. But ultimately they were all out for number one.

The blonde girl had the edge. Now she was kneeling on the brunette and punching her face over and over. He nodded at Sergei who took the blonde by her hair and dragged her over to the exit. She was slung out naked into the cold night air.

One of the bouncers, a large black man called Curtis, was nursing a deep scratch on his face. The other man, also black, was laughing at the girls' antics. But Sergei's intervention and Boris's presence made the onlookers nervous and they were gradually growing quieter.

Finally everyone fell silent as Boris said loudly, 'Those two girls are out. They will have to find alternative employment. And if I ever see a scene like this again, you'll all be sorry.'

He snapped his fingers at the bouncers. 'You two, collect your pay and fuck off. I am not paying you to be entertained.'

The two men were shamefaced, the women subdued. It was how Boris affected people.

Back in the club, business had died down. They were gradually wrapping up for the night. He nodded for the main bar to close and walked over to get himself a drink. There were still a few drunken revellers about but Boris ignored them. Some girls were still working, dancing for the last few quid. Their body make-up was running and one girl clearly showed flea bites from her cats around her ankles. Boris curled his lips once more. He himself had never understood the male need to make a show of their masculinity in public. As he watched a young man on his knees trying to lick one of the girls' buttocks he felt his stomach revolt.

Sergei joined him at the bar and they ordered Remy Martins. They sipped them and chatted as the club gradually cleared. By 2.45 there were only a few stragglers and the usual handful of girls waiting it out for the last couple of tenners. The cabfare girls, as they were known. They didn't come into their own until the men were too drunk to be over-critical of their bodies.

It was as they watched a girl remove her G-string and scratch at her ample buttocks that Sergei noticed Willy Gabney enter the club. He put his hand on Boris's arm to alert him. Distracted by a quarrel between two late revellers and the barman, he did not immediately notice. When Willy removed the Winchester from under his coat, Sergei felt his bowels loosen and pulled hard on Boris's Armani jacket.

He finally looked at Willy but it was too late.

Even the late-night drinkers took on board the large ugly man with the pump-action shotgun.

Willy nodded pleasantly, then began blasting.

Boris's face was a study in shocked incomprehension. His body moved as if to make a run for it as the impact of the first shot lifted him off his feet and he careered into Sergei, who was still standing rooted to the spot.

The second shot sprayed their upper bodies, taking away bone and skin, sending muscle and hair flying in all directions. Any resemblance the two men bore to human beings was gone.

The third shot was unnecessary, but guaranteed Willy Gabney peace and quiet until he had made his escape. The last few shots were what were known as the warning shots. They told people to keep away and not attempt to be a hero – and warned others in the business that this was serious, and any attempt at retribution would be met with the same.

When Willy had finished the club was deathly quiet. Even the music had stopped. The two sacked bouncers watched everything impassively. The girls were all white-faced and terrified.

Willy lowered the gun, nodded his head as if taking leave of a business acquaintance and walked out of the club in a nonchalant manner, the same way he had entered it.

Passing the stunned doorman, he smiled. 'Nice night for it anyway,' he said politely.

Then he disappeared into the darkness.

Ratchet arrived at Lucas's flat at 3.45 a.m. What he saw astounded him, and made him more aware than ever that Kate Burrows was not only a good policewoman but also the sort not to take anything from anyone without coming back.

Half of him admired her for that, the other half hated her with a vengeance. He saw Golding's smirk as they presented the evidence to him and he had to stand in the flat of a filthy paedophile and take it.

Kate picked up her bag. Nudging the grotesque man still lying bleeding on the floor with one well-shod foot, she said, 'I will leave all this in your capable hands. And I'll tell you now, I am not going to be the fall guy for you or anyone else. Do you understand what I'm saying? Because if push comes to shove, Mr Ratchet, I will open my mouth so loud the Home Secretary won't need a phone call to inform him of what I'm saying, he'll hear me all the way from here to Whitehall.'

'You get yourself home, ma'am. I'll finish up here,' Golding offered.

She nodded her thanks, then added to Ratchet: 'You'll find films here that contain images of the children I was investigating, besides other children and young adults of whom I have no knowledge. Mr Browning has agreed to make a statement concerning allegations against Mr Kelly that I think you will find removes any suspicion you might have had about your Masonic friend and business partner.

'In the light of that,' she went on, 'I expect to be back in my job on Monday morning as usual. I also expect to receive credit for all the work I have done in bringing these paedophiles to court, and also for bringing in Robert Bateman who I think can safely be classed as a serial killer. I also insist on being the one to arrest and formally charge Suzy Harrington.'

She breathed out a long sigh. 'Now I will go home and get some rest. I trust you will sort out this little mess with the minimum of publicity and the maximum of respect, sir.'

As Kate marched out of the flat and down the stairs, her eyes were burning with rage and fatigue. Her whole body was rebelling against all the shocks it had received over the last few weeks.

In short, Kate was terminally exhausted.

As she went over to Golding's car which she was going to borrow, she saw Benny Boarder out of the corner of her eye. He was leaning against a BMW, smiling.

'Am I glad to see you!' Kate told him.

He grinned. 'Oh yeah? Same here. Get in. I just spoke to Patrick. I need to take you to the hospital.'

She got into the car, not even asking him what he was doing so close to her. At this moment nothing could faze her and there'd be plenty of time for questions in the days and weeks ahead. For now all she wanted was to put her arms around Patrick Kelly and find peace at last.

Maureen knew that something wasn't quite right with Willy. He had come in earlier in the evening, changed his clothes and then gone straight out again. He had

not offered her any explanation and she had not asked
for one. She knew how to play the game, but she
would bet her last ten quid that skulduggery was
afoot. All she hoped was that he didn't get his collar
felt and that she didn't have to look forward to years
of visiting him in prison.

Though she would, if that was the upshot.

When he came home he made a call on his mobile,
out of earshot, and then placed a small folder in her
lap. Duane had gone to bed and they were alone.

'What's this then?' Maureen's voice was shaking.

'Look inside and decide which one you like the
most and I'll buy it for you. It's a cash buy, and no
matter what happens, darlin', it will be yours, OK?'

She opened the plain buff folder. Inside were estate
agents' details for large detached houses in the Manor
Park area. Her eyes misted with tears. She looked at
him in wonderment.

'Is this a joke?'

He shook his head. 'Look, Maureen, I had to do a
last bit of work tonight and it might come on top. If it
does I'm looking at a serious lump, but I had no
choice. Either way, you'll own this house outright,
whether I am there or not, OK? If I get a touch, we
can get married, and hopefully live there happily ever
after.'

'Oh, Willy. What did I do to deserve you?' She was
nearly in tears and her face, already puffy, was in
danger of further damage from violent crying.

He put one meaty arm around her shoulders. 'I am
the lucky one, girl. I know that better than anyone.

You're me bird, ain't you? I have to take good care of you, mate.'

'I don't need houses, Willy, you know that.'

He nodded gently. 'Yes, I know that. But I want you to have it. I want me, you and Duane to have a proper life. In a nice area with nice things.'

Maureen stared down at the pictures of the beautiful properties and then looked around her own council flat.

'There is only one stipulation.'

She looked into his eyes. 'What's that?'

'No disrespect, love, but you'll have to let me sort out the decorating. I can't live with pink like this for the rest of me natural.'

She smiled through her tears. 'You can do what you like, Willy Gabney, you know that. I am just glad to be a part of it all.'

He pulled her into his arms. She was all right, was his Maureen. He felt he was a very lucky man. A man who had finally found out what life was all about.

He only hoped it wasn't too late to enjoy it.

Detective Inspector Martin Haskiss looked at the carnage in the club and sighed heavily.

'Any idea who these two were?'

No one seemed to know. A search of the remains gave up no identification whatsoever.

Pascal had already cleaned them of everything, from mobile phones to wallets. He knew the score and was glad that Willy Gabney had sorted it all out. He had also cleared the club of most of the witnesses, only leaving the people he thought were intelligent enough to give believable statements. The men who had been visiting the place were too stoned or pissed to know what had gone down and the dancers had all had it away on their toes.

All in all, not a bad night's work.

He took the wallets and phones directly to a contact and booked himself on an early-morning flight to Ibiza. A couple of weeks of sun and the opportunity to look over a club he had a share in there was suddenly too good a chance to resist. The offices had been cleaned of anything pertaining to Patrick Kelly and all seemed above board and legal. Let the filth wonder what they liked, Patrick was banged up in hospital and was never in the place anyway, according to witnesses.

Pascal spoke to Patrick briefly on a clean mobile, registered to a woman who worked in the law courts, then settled himself down for a few hours' kip before his flight. He was humming as he left his house for the airport.

Evelyn heard the news about the club as she made herself a cup of tea. She was scandalised, as were most of the population. Public shootings always caused a stir, but in Soho at least they were well away from the more law-abiding section of the population. The fact that this had occurred in a lap-dancing club only confirmed that. But still it was a scandal.

Evelyn, however, knew that this club was owned in part by Patrick Kelly, so she kept an open mind. Time had taught her to do that much.

She put a drop of her Holy Water in her morning tea as she still felt a bit shaken up from the previous few weeks' exertions. She was looking forward to seeing Patrick and Kate, who had not come home again.

As she looked round the little kitchen Evelyn smiled. And if that eejit of a daughter of hers tried any more of her hysterics about living at Pat's, Evelyn was going to put her in her place as soon as possible.

Please or offend, she was determined to get everything back to normal as soon as possible. Patrick Kelly was going to need looking after – and wasn't she just the one to do it? She was determined to get her family back on track, in every way. Jesus Himself knew she was even willing to put up with that Grace, if and when she had to. So if she could make a sacrifice, she was bloody well sure the rest of them could.

Kate awoke to find herself wrapped in a pair of strong arms that felt suspiciously like Patrick's. She looked contentedly at his sleeping face. He looked older, he looked ill, but he was still a good-looking man.

She felt the overstarched sheets clinging to her body, hospital sheets. The door handle was being rattled and she realised that was what had woken her up.

She started to giggle. She couldn't believe she was lying in a hospital bed after a night of rather energetic sex. Patrick seemed not to have been affected in that department at all, though she had a feeling that it was the reason he was looking so pale and tired this morning.

As the door handle was abandoned she relaxed back against him, wondering what the day was going to bring. She just hoped they could all get back to normal. It occurred to her that since knowing Patrick she had hit the heights of happiness and the lowest pits of depression. But she wouldn't have her life any other way, not really.

Patrick had explained that Boris had died in his club. He did not mention Willy Gabney's involvement and Kate had not asked any questions.

She had learned so much since she had known him and the main thing was not to judge a person unless you had the full facts. She had also learned that the criminal world and her own world were not that far apart. It was one of the first things she had been taught by Patrick. Now, though, she wanted those worlds separated.

Patrick had been a fool to keep his finger in so many pies, but even he admitted he too had learned a valuable lesson: when living with a policewoman, expect to get a capture.

Now he stirred beside her and opened his eyes. 'You look good enough to eat, girl.'

But as much as he meant what he said, she knew it wasn't going to happen. He was wiped out, he was ill and he was hers. She squeezed him to her tightly.

'There's plenty of time for all that, Patrick Kelly, when you're back on your feet.'

He closed his eyes and yawned. 'I was hoping you'd say that, Kate. You took advantage of a very sick man last night.'

They laughed together.

'Dream on, Kelly.'

He relaxed back against the pillows. 'The sooner we get home and back in our own bed the better, eh, girl?'

His voice sounded strained. He was much weaker than he tried to make out. She understood that; it was part and parcel of being him, of being Patrick Kelly. He had to be the eternal hard man. He could never be seen to be ill, worried or in any danger whatsoever.

Normally it drove her to distraction. At this moment in time it made her love him more than ever.

'What do you think will happen now, Pat?' Her voice was serious.

'I think that if Ratchet has half a brain, and I'll credit him with that at least, we should be high and dry by lunchtime.'

She knew it was taking a lot for him to sound so confident. He gripped her hand tightly.

'Whatever happens, my love, I will make sure you are well out of it all, OK?'

She kissed him gently on his brow but she didn't answer him. She didn't know what to say.

It was 2.30 in the afternoon and Suzy Harrington had just showered and changed. Her cases were packed and in the hallway and she was sitting on her bed counting out piles of money.

She made sure her jewellery box was empty for the tenth time and sipped at her coffee. She was waiting for a cab to pick her up and take her to London. A while back, she had bought herself a little pied à terre in Barnes in case of emergencies. No one knew she owned it – it was her hideaway. For the umpteenth time she looked in her bag and checked that both her false passports were inside. She was definitely taking no chances. She looked around the small flat one last time to make sure that she had not forgotten anything.

When the phone rang, she let the machine pick up any message. She was going to disappear off the face of the earth then start up again at some point in the future.

There was a knock at the door and she answered it quickly. It was the cab driver. She gave him the cases and, picking up her handbag, she locked the flat up carefully. She wanted to put a few miles between her and this place as quickly as possible so she could feel like she had walked away from everything.

Robert Bateman and Harry Barker had made her life difficult for a while and she knew that she was still a prime suspect. But knowing all she did about the police, she didn't really believe they were going to come after her for a conviction. They wouldn't dare.

She was far too protected. Had been far too clever. In fact, she was so sure of herself that she was ready to use the same contacts at the Home Office that she had already used.

Walking carefully down the stairs because of her impossibly high heels she made her way out to the white Ford Granada that was to take her away from this dump once and for all. The cab driver was smiling at her and she got into the car gracefully, her flirtatious side to the fore today. After all, the driver was very good-looking.

They drove away and she looked back at the flat, feeling nothing except relief and a twinge of regret at leaving her good furniture. She wondered if she would ever be in a position to come back and get it.

Essex Radio was on and they were playing Michael Bolton. His haunting voice was lifting the air around her. She had always liked him. As he sang a song about losing his love and finding her again, Suzy realised that the cab was going in the wrong direction.

'Excuse me, mate. You've made a wrong turn,' she said.

The driver was grinning at her and she felt the first stirrings of apprehension.

'Stop the fucking car – now!' Her voice was high with fear and suspicion.

'When I'm ready.'

He turned up the radio and Michael Bolton's voice drowned her out. He was driving at speed and she knew it would be foolish to do anything now. She tried the door, so as to be ready. Baby locks were in place.

Five minutes later they stopped outside Grantley Police Station and she saw a grinning Kate Burrows waiting for her.

The car door was opened.

'We intercepted your calls and decided you might

be better off coming here as opposed to Barnes.'
Kate's voice was quietly confident. 'I take it you know
about Lucas and his statement?'

'You fucking bitch!'

Kate was smiling again.

'Between him and Bateman, I think we have you
bang to rights.'

Suzy lay back in her seat, her face white and drawn.

'I've been looking forward to seeing you again, Ms
Harrington. I love it when I can complete a job and
know that it was well done. A bit like yourself there,
eh?'

Suzy didn't answer her. She was frantically trying to
think who the fuck she could call to get her out of the
gigantic mess she found herself in.

Kate walked into the station a new woman.

'I have so many videos for you to watch and lots of
people for you to tell me about. I think it's going to
be a long day, don't you, Suzy?'

In a small holding cell twenty minutes later Suzy
was on the verge of tears as Kate came in alone. The
two women looked at one another for long moments
before Kate gave Suzy a stinging slap across her face.

'That, miss, is just for starters. I'll make sure that
for every child you corrupted, you get a life sentence.
For every crime you committed, I'll see you squirm,
and for every flash statement out of your mouth I am
going to make sure you do hard time. Do you finally
understand where I'm coming from now?'

Suzy didn't answer. She was fucked and she knew it.

Kate felt lighter than she had in years and it

showed. Her life was suddenly 100 per cent better. Patrick was safe and now all he had to do was recover. Boris was dead and taking all the flak meant for Patrick. Kate herself was back on track and waiting to charge this woman and take credit for the biggest paedophile ring broken in the South East, ever. Plus the added kudos of catching another serial killer into the bargain.

She was already being offered whatever she wanted, and already taking congratulatory calls from all and sundry.

It was a good day, and finally taking Suzy Harrington had made it a great one. Kate wanted to see Suzy and all the others pay for the tiny lives they had broken without a second's thought.

It was rough justice.

It was what Kate Burrows was best at.

Epilogue

'You look nice, ma'am.'

Golding's voice was full of admiration and Kate was gratified that the spending of nearly two thousand pounds on an outfit was justified. She looked fabulous and she knew it.

'I thought you was off today for a few weeks?'

She smiled. 'I am. I'm going to a wedding. But first I have to see someone.'

Golding grinned. 'Looking at you, can I ask you something, ma'am?'

'Of course.'

'Is it your own wedding, by any chance?'

Kate shook her head. 'No. Not mine.'

Her phone rang and she picked it up.

'My guest has arrived,' she told Golding. 'Will you bring her through, please, and organise some coffee?'

He nodded and said in a voice filled with feeling, 'You look great, ma'am. Really great.'

She knew he was impressed and it gave her a good feeling.

'I scrub up OK,' she said.

He laughed. 'I'll bring your guest through, ma'am. And if I don't see you again, have a good holiday.'

Kate checked herself in the small hand mirror from her bag. She felt good and looked better.

Five minutes later Julie Carmichael came into the office. She was obviously bowled over by the star treatment and, seeing Miss Burrows, thought she looked like something from a magazine.

'You look wonderful!'

Kate grinned. 'Sit down. I've organised some coffee – or would you prefer tea?'

'No, thank you, coffee would be fine.'

They made small talk until Golding brought in the coffee. Kate saw that he had even organised a milk jug and sugar bowl. She was impressed.

When he left the room, Julie Carmichael stood up and walked to the window. She stood looking out over the car park and Kate let her be as she knew the other woman was getting ready to talk to her.

'I just want to thank you for finally getting justice for my daughter,' she said at last. 'I know it won't bring her back but at least I can rest easy now, knowing that it is finally over. I haven't slept a full night since she died. I would just lie there wondering if Barker was still up to his tricks, and whether I could have stopped her going out that day. I'll never forgive him for what he did to our girl, but at least I can finally lay Lesley to rest.'

She turned and Kate saw that her face was less lined; her whole demeanour seemed changed, and she was grateful for being able to help in some small way.

'When I read about Robert Bateman, how he had murdered Barker, I couldn't feel anything. As bad as Bateman is with his murders and everything else, in killing Barker he finally put my mind at rest. I know that bastard can't harm anyone else now. None of them can. But most of all I want to thank you for caring, when I thought no one in the world but me was bothered about what had happened to my daughter.'

Kate stood up and hugged her gently. 'It's all over, Julie. Finally it's all over.'

They drank the coffee and talked about nothing very much. Everything that needed to be said between them had been said.

As Kate left to go to Maureen's house and then make her way to the small church in Essex, she passed her new Chief's office. The woman came out and said with genuine pleasure, 'Christ, you look fantastic.'

Kate blushed. 'Thank you, ma'am.'

'You have a good holiday, love, and when you come back I want us to have a long lunch and catch up properly, OK?'

Kate nodded.

'There's a bit of news,' the Chief went on. 'We've had five requests this week alone – offers to take you on different teams around the country. I hope I can refuse them for you in your absence?'

Kate nodded. 'I want the promotion, ma'am,' she said. 'I reckon I've earned it.

'I think we can safely say that is in the bag,' Lynda

Chisley beamed. 'I am glad – I thought we were going to lose you.'

'It had crossed my mind. Life hasn't been exactly easy here, you know.'

'I know,' Lynda grinned. 'But I'm here now.'

Kate liked her and after Ratchet that alone was a good feeling.

'Anyway, get yourself off and relax,' the woman went on. 'I have a feeling you need a break. By the way, this came for you.'

She gave Kate a letter. It was in a prison envelope, unsealed. She recognised Robert Bateman's writing.

'He took quite a fancy to you, didn't he?'

Kate nodded but didn't answer. She just slipped the envelope into her bag.

'By the way, did you hear that Ratchet is running as the local Conservative candidate?' Lynda asked her.

'I heard.'

They burst out laughing together and then Kate made her excuses and went on her way. Ratchet had actually had the cheek to ask Patrick to put up some money for his election costs! But that was Ratchet: always after the main chance and always at pains to establish that he didn't bear grudges.

Kate knew that if ever she'd genuinely disliked someone, it was her old boss. Now she was back in charge of Patrick's house she would make sure he didn't get the opportunity to cross the threshold for any reason whatsoever.

Evelyn was at the house putting the finishing touches

to the wedding feast. It looked wonderful. As she fiddled one last time with the cake she turned at the sound of her grand-daughter's voice.

'Do you think this might be a bit too much of a shock for me mum, like?'

'Jasus, Lizzy, haven't you been giving that poor woman shocks for years? What's one more!'

Her grand-daughter's face was a picture of sadness and Evelyn was sorry she had spoken so frankly.

'Oh, sure, Lizzy, I don't mean the half of it, child! She'll be OK. You know what she's like – and a new life can only be a cause for celebration.'

Lizzy smiled in relief and lowered her huge bulk into a kitchen chair. The pregnancy had changed her beyond recognition. The boy was standing by her, though, so that at least was something. She had flown in from Australia the night before and stayed at a friend's house in Grantley. It was her granny's decision to surprise her mother like this. Evelyn hoped it would make things easier for Kate, this being Willy Gabney's wedding day.

'Go away into the drawing room and settle yourself, child. They'll be here soon enough.'

As she saw Lizzy walk away Evelyn sighed. A new life inside her and she with the brain capacity of a peanut! Jesus help and save them all! Still, Evelyn had no doubt that Kate was best surprised with it among a houseful of guests. This way, she would have to keep quiet until she'd had time to get used to the fact she was going to be a grandmother.

Evelyn hoped that Patrick left the Glamorous

Granny jokes until the news had sunk in a bit. But she didn't hold out much hope.

She was smiling as she fiddled with the food once more. She was back home and she was going to be a great-granny! Her life was full again and she was loving every minute of it. Every last bloody second.

No more talk of fecking Russians, paedophiles or murderers. Just weddings, houses and children. At last they were sounding like a normal family.

Maureen looked fabulous. Kate had gone shopping with her to pick an outfit and she looked and felt stunning. It was six months since their world had gone mad and now they were all finally getting back to normal.

Maureen had dropped two stone and the transformation was complete. She was glamorous in a cream satin suit worn with a wide-brimmed hat. Her accessories were in pale blue, which emphasised her enormous eyes. Her make-up was subtle, her hair professionally cut and tinted. She looked and felt like a different person.

As she arrived at the church with Kate, who was dressed in a pale green designer suit with matching hat, shoes and bag, they were eye-popping. Neither Willy nor Patrick had seen the finished ensembles and the women were looking forward to making an impression. Especially Maureen, who wanted Willy to be proud of her.

Kate had no doubt he would be.

In the church the small band of invited guests were

quiet and patient. Benny Boarder was there with his wife and brood of children, as was Pascal. All Maureen's children were there, well turned out, amazed and pleased that their mother had so obviously landed on her dainty little feet.

Patrick looked fit and well in his tails and Willy . . . Willy looked like Willy in a dress suit. He knew his looks did him no favours in any way but he was confident that his Maureen would love him whatever.

As the two men stood in front of the altar Patrick was smirking.

'I can't believe I'm here, Willy, and it's your first wedding!'

The big man shrugged. 'Tell me about it. I hope to fuck it will be me last!'

'Stop swearing.' Patrick's voice was full of laughter.

'I can't help it, me nerves are shot.'

'It will all be over soon.'

He was interrupted by the Wedding March. They turned to see Maureen and Kate, both carrying small bouquets, coming down the aisle.

'They look handsome, Pat, don't you think? Old Maureen looks the dog's . . .'

'Willy! Not here, not now.'

Maureen did look good but Patrick had eyes only for Kate. As she walked down the aisle he was looking forward to the day she would be walking towards him for their wedding instead of Willy's.

But Kate being Kate wouldn't settle on a date. She wanted him 100 per cent fit first, and her daughter over from Australia into the bargain. But it would happen, he was sure of that. After all they had been through together, it was only right and fitting that they should finally have a happy ending.

She was also waiting until he had sold everything he owned that was even remotely dodgy – and that included businesses where he was a sleeping partner. He was glad about it, though he pretended he wasn't. Inside he had had enough of ducking and diving. At least, that's what he told himself, anyway.

The service was short and over quickly. Outside they had the photos taken in record time and were all on their way back to Patrick's and the reception that had been planned for weeks.

In the back of the Rolls he kissed Kate full on the lips.

'I've lost me best mate.'

She grinned. 'No, you haven't. You've gained a new one.'

'You like old Maureen, don't you?' he said fondly.

'What's not to like? She's fun, she's intelligent, and she's making Willy the happiest man on earth.'

'When are you going to make *me* the happiest man on earth?'

Kate chuckled throatily. 'I thought I'd already done that – last night and twice this morning.'

Patrick scratched his chin as if deep in thought. 'Well, let's just say that once I'm fully better we can get back to normal, eh?'

Kate closed her eyes and groaned. 'You have to be the vainest man on earth.'

'No, I can think of a few who are vainer than me.

But it's hard for other men. I have good reason to be vain, don't I?'

'Oh, really. Is that so?'

'I am good-looking, rich, have a wonderful personality and the best body this side of the Watford Gap. I mean, what more could a man want?'

Kate was grinning. 'I don't know, what on earth could any man want who had all that?'

He kissed her on the mouth. 'A nice little bird to keep the crows at bay, of course. And that's where you come in!'

She smashed him over the head with her handbag. 'You are one flash bastard, Kelly.'

'That's another thing. You're going to have to stop this swearing when we get married . . .'

She hit him again with her handbag, harder this time.

The new driver, who was to take over from Willy, was observing them in the mirror. He was a thirty-five-year-old who had served time for murder. Patrick had always taken an interest in him. As he watched the verbal sparring in the back quickly become physical he smiled to himself. He had a feeling he was going to like this job. He had certainly never experienced anything like the last few weeks with these two. She might be a filth but she was all right.

As for Patrick Kelly, he would never change all the time he had a hole in his arse.

He had heard Patrick was unloading all his businesses, but would believe that when he saw it.

He couldn't see Patrick Kelly becoming too legal.

Not for long anyway. It wasn't his nature.

They were kissing in the back now and the driver could see a long expanse of shapely leg. He grinned again.

Yes, he had a feeling he was really going to enjoy this job.